A Reunion *of* Ghosts

ALSO BY JUDITH CLAIRE MITCHELL

The Last Day of the War

A
Reunion
of
Ghosts

Judith Claire Mitchell

HARPER

An Imprint of HarperCollins*Publishers*

A REUNION OF GHOSTS. Copyright © 2015 by Judith Claire Mitchell. All rights reserved. Printed in the United States of America. No part of this book may be used or reproduced in any manner whatsoever without written permission except in the case of brief quotations embodied in critical articles and reviews. For information, address HarperCollins Publishers, 195 Broadway, New York, NY 10007

HarperCollins books may be purchased for educational, business, or sales promotional use. For information, please e-mail the Special Markets Department at SPsales@harpercollins.com.

FIRST EDITION

Designed by Jo Anne Metsch

Library of Congress Cataloging-in-Publication Data has been applied for.

ISBN: 978-0-06-235588-1

14 15 16 17 18   OV/RRD   10 9 8 7 6 5 4 3 2 1

For my parents,

Leo and Claire Mitchell

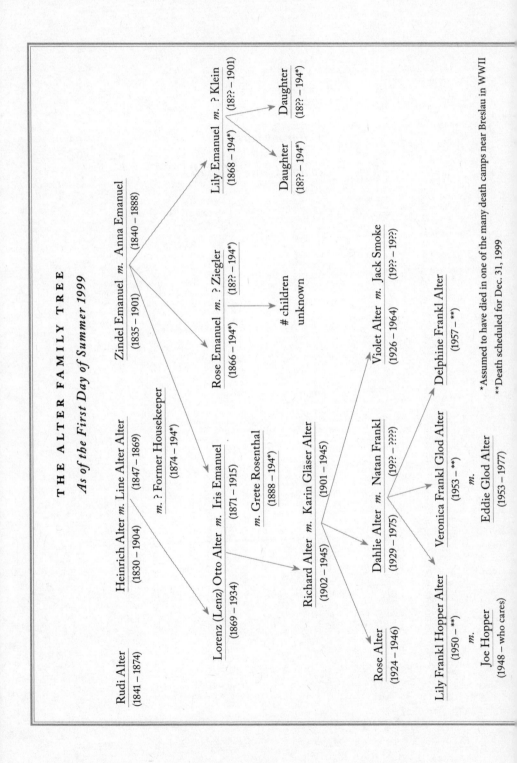

THE ALTER FAMILY TREE

As of the First Day of Summer 1999

Zindel Emanuel *m.* Anna Emanuel
(1835 – 1901)   (1840 – 1888)

Lily Emanuel *m.* ? Klein
(1868 – 194*)   (18?? – 1901)

Daughter   Daughter
(18?? – 194*) (18?? – 194*)

Rose Emanuel *m.* ? Ziegler
(1866 – 194*)   (18?? – 194*)

→ # children unknown

Rudi Alter
(1841 – 1874)

Heinrich Alter *m.* Line Alter Alter
(1830 – 1904)   (1847 – 1869)

m. ? Former Housekeeper
(1874 – 194*)

Lorenz (Lenz) Otto Alter *m.* Iris Emanuel
(1869 – 1934)   (1871 – 1915)

m. Grete Rosenthal
(1888 – 194*)

Richard Alter *m.* Karin Gläser Alter
(1902 – 1945)   (1901 – 1945)

Dahlie Alter *m.* Natan Frankl
(1929 – 1975)   (19?? – ????)

Violet Alter *m.* Jack Smoke
(1926 – 1964)   (19?? – 19??)

Delphine Frankl Alter
(1957 – **)

Veronica Frankl Glod Alter
(1953 – **)

m.

Eddie Glod Alter
(1953 – 1977)

Rose Alter
(1924 – 1946)

Lily Frankl Hopper Alter
(1950 – **)

m.

Joe Hopper
(1948 – who cares)

* Assumed to have died in one of the many death camps near Breslau in WWII

** Death scheduled for Dec. 31, 1999

. . . And Some of the People in Their Lives

In Breslau, Prussia and Breslau, Germany

Frau Geist, a dance instructor
Richard Lehrer, a professor of chemistry
Marthe Lehrer, Lehrer's wife

In Berlin, Germany

Theo Meyer, a lab assistant
Dr. Moritz, a lab assistant
Prinz Alter, a Labrador Retriever
Albert Einstein, a physicist
Mileva Einstein, Einstein's first wife
Hans Einstein, Einstein's oldest son
Eduard Einstein, Einstein's youngest son

In New York City

A dentist in Riverdale
Beef, a golden retriever

Joshua Gottleib, a bike messenger
A hardware store owner
Gurley, a tattoo artist
A man with a gun
A widower with a child
Nim, a chimpanzee
Delph's boss
Jan, an oncology nurse

On Long Island

Freddie, a bartender
Danny, a bar singer

In Chicago

A retired professor of chemistry

NAMES OF PERSONS MENTIONED IN
A REUNION OF GHOSTS

Names of verifiable historical or public figures **bold.**

Alter, Delphine (Delph)

Alter, Eddie Glod

Alter, Heinrich Lorenz

Alter, Iris Emanuel

Alter, Karin Gläser

Alter, Line Alter

Alter, Rudi

Alter, Lily Frankl Hopper
(Lady)

Alter, Lorenz Otto (Lenz)

Alter, Richard

Alter, Rose

Alter, Veronica Frankl Glod
(Vee)

Barry, orgy participant

Beame, Abe

Beef, the dentist's dog

Bismarck, Otto von

Boggs, Bill

Boleyn, Anne

Brownmiller, Susan

Bunsen, Robert

Carson, Johnny

Costello, Abbott P.

Curie, Pierre and Marie

Dodsworth, Alan

Douglas, Mike

Einstein, Albert

Einstein, Eduard

Einstein, Elsa

Einstein, Hans

Einstein, Mileva

Emanuel, Anna

Emanuel, Zindel

Frankl, Dahlie
Frankl, Natan
Fillmore, Millard
Franz Ferdinand (Archduke)
Freddie, bar owner

Geist, Frau
Ginsberg, Allen
Gottlieb, Joshua
Gurley, a tattoo artist

Hahn, Otto
Hari, Mata
Hepburn, Katharine
Hitler, Adolf
Hogan, Hulk
Hollander, Xaviera (the Happy Hooker)
Howdy Doody

Jan, an oncology nurse
Jones, John Paul
Joplin, Janis

Kazootie, Rooty
Kennedy, Bobby
Kennedy, John F.
Kennedy, John-John
Kennedy, Joseph
Kirk, Grayson
Kram, Arthur

Lehrer, Richard
Lehrer, Marthe
Little, Rich

Matthau, Walter
Meitner, Lise
Meyer, Theo
Millet, Kate
Mommsen, Theodor
Moritz, Emil

Nevelson, Louise
Nim Chimpsky
Norman, orgy participant

O'Keeffe, Georgia
Oyl, Olive

Patty, dentist's wife
Planck, Max
Popeye
Prinz, Lenz and Iris's dog

Rosenthal, Grete, Lenz's mistress
Ruffin, Jimmy

Sainte-Marie, Buffy
The Shine brothers
Shore, Dinah
Smoke, Danny
Smoke, Jack

Smoke, Margo
Smoke, Sharon
Smoke, Violet Alter
Son of Sam
Snyder, Tom

Taylor, Opie
Thiessen, Vern
Treitschke, Heinrich von

Unnamed bus passenger
Unnamed bosses (Delph's and
  Lily's)
Unnamed clerk at City Hall
Unnamed dental hygienist
Unnamed dentist
Unnamed female orgy
  participant
Unnamed ghosts at Karin's
  deathbed
Unnamed housekeeper
  (Heinrich's second wife)
Unnamed information clerk at
  Penn Sta.

Unnamed nursing home
  supervisor
Unnamed oncologist
Unnamed paralegal friends
  of Vee
Unnamed radiologist
Unnamed super of Riverside Dr.
  bldg.
Unnamed tattoo artists (2)
Unnamed therapist (Delph's)
Unnamed widower

Wayne, John
Weizmann, Chaim
Whitman, Walt
Wilhelm I (Kaiser)
Wilhelm II (Kaiser)
Williams, Tennessee

Younger, Cole

Zappa, Frank
Ziegler, Rose Emanuel

The only reason for time is so that everything doesn't happen at once.

—ALBERT EINSTEIN

2nd epigraph TK

—ATTRIBUTION TK

PART ONE

The Ghosts

CHAPTER 1

From a distance the tattoo wrapped around Delph's calf looks like a serpentine chain, but stand closer and it's actually sixty-seven tiny letters and symbols that form a sentence—a curse:

the sins of the fathers are visited upon the children to the 3rd
& 4th generations

We are that fourth generation: Lady, Vee, and Delph Alter, three sisters who share the same Riverside Drive apartment in which they were raised; three women of a certain age, those ages being, on this first day of summer 1999, forty-nine, forty-six, and forty-two. We're also seven fewer Jews than a minyan make, a trio of fierce believers in all sorts of mysterious forces that we don't understand, and a triumvirate of feminists who nevertheless describe ourselves in relation to relationships: we're a partnerless, childless, even petless sorority consisting of one divorcee (Lady), one perpetually grieving widow (Vee), and one spinster—that would be Delph.

When we were young women, with our big bosoms and butts, our black-rimmed glasses low on the bridges of our broad beaky noses, our dark hair corkscrew curly, we resembled a small flock of intellectual geese in fright wigs, and people struggled to tell us apart. These days it's less difficult.

Lady is the oldest, and now that she's one year shy of fifty, she's begun to look it, soft at the jaw, bruised and creped beneath her eyes. She's the one who wears nothing but black, not in a chic New York way, but in the way of someone who finds making an effort exhausting. Every day: sweatshirt, jeans, sneakers, all black. "I work in a bookstore," she says, "and then I come home and stay home. Who do I have to dress up for?" She wears no bra, hasn't since the 1960s, and these days her breasts sag to her belly, making her seem even rounder than she is. "Who cares?" she says. "It's not like I'm trying to meet someone." Her hair, which she wears in a long queue held with a leather and stick barrette, is freighted with gray.

Vee is the tallest (though we are all short), and the thinnest (though none of us is thin). Her face is unlined as if she's never had any cares, which (she says with good reason) is a laugh. She doesn't like black, prefers cobalts and purples and emeralds, royal colors that make her look alive even as she's dying. "Isn't that what fashion is?" she says. "A nonverbal means of lying about the sad, naked truth?" She wears no bra either, but in her case it's because she has no breasts. She has no hair either. Chemo-induced alopecia, they call it. No hair, no eyebrows, no eyelashes. Her underarms, her legs—they're little-girl smooth. As is the rest of her. Little-girl smooth.

Delph is still the baby. Even now, two years into her forties, she looks much younger than the other two. She's the smallest, barely five foot one, and the chubbiest, and she still wears girlish clothes: white peasant blouses with embroidery and drawstrings; long floral skirts that sometimes skim the ground, the hems frayed from sidewalks. As for her hair, it's always been the longest, the wildest, the curliest, those curls bouffanting into the air, rippling down her back, tendriling around her big hoop earrings, falling into her mouth, spiraling down into her eyes. She says there's nothing to be done about it; it's just the way her hair wants to be. "There's plenty to be done about it," Vee has said more than once. "Just get me a pair of hedge clippers, and I'll show you."

So: black-clad, gray-haired, saggy, baggy Lady. Pale-skinned, bald-headed, flat-chested Vee. And little Delph. Three easily distinguishable women. And yet people still mix us up. The aged super who has known us since we were children. Our neighbors, old and new. We don't resent it. Even our mother used to get jumbled up and call us by the wrong names. Sometimes we do it ourselves.

"I'm Delph," Delph will say to Lady, who has just called her Vee for the third time in an evening. Most of the time, though, we let it go.

And sometimes one of us, sleepy or tipsy, catches a glimpse of herself in a mirror, and for a moment even she mistakes herself for one of the others.

Also, sometimes we confuse things by wearing each other's clothes.

Like many of the Alter women in the generations before ours, we were named for flowers—but Lady is how Lily pronounced her name as a toddler, and it stuck; Vee is as much of Veronica as anyone has ever bothered to utter, and Delph is short for Delphine, which our mother thought was the name of the vivid blue perennial, but actually means "like a dolphin." We don't mind the nicknames. You might even say we've cultivated them. The flower names our mother picked never thrilled us. The funereal lily. The purple veronica, known for its ability to withstand neglect. Delph's name that isn't quite what it was supposed to be. "Neither the gods of flora nor the gods of fauna knew who had jurisdiction over me," Delph likes to declaim. "No wonder I fell through the cracks."

The truth is, we all fell through the cracks, and that's where we've stayed. Our father left when Lady was seven, Vee four, Delph swaddled. Our mother . . . well, that's another sad story. But life between the cracks isn't so bad when you've got sisters. It can be cozy and warm, when that's what you want. It can be filled with in-jokes and conversational shorthand and foolishness, if that's what's needed. Or it can be silent and still, which we tend to appreciate these days, given that, in addition to everything else, we've grown ever more introverted, even a touch agoraphobic.

All of which makes us well suited to the project we embark upon tonight, namely writing this whatever-it-is—this memoir, this family history, this quasi-confessional.

Our subject is the last four generations of Alters, up through and including our own. We plan to record all the sorrows and stumbles as well as all the accomplishments and contributions. We're sorry to say there've been many of the former, far fewer of the latter. This is especially true when it comes to our own generation. We're the entirety of the fourth generation; we're the last of the Alter line; we're that's all there is, there ain't no more; and we've brought the family name no glory.

On the other hand, we've brought it no shame either, which is more than certain preceding generations can say. That first generation, for instance, which starred our infamous great-grandfather, Lorenz Otto Alter, World War I hero, World War I criminal. Genius and monster. He was the sinner who doomed us all.

Still, he accomplished things. Good things, bad things, Nobel Prize–winning things. Not so the three of us. We've accomplished nothing, contributed even less, and we fear for the poor sap who'll someday be saddled with our eulogies. What will this hapless orator say? Delph Alter, the youngest sister, never left a filing cabinet less organized than she found it. Vee Alter, the benighted monkey in the middle, spent her entire adult life as a paralegal at a law firm where she drafted wills and settled estates—a deadly occupation. Lady Alter, the eldest, stood behind a cash register, ringing up purchases of paperbacks and magazines, saying little all day besides thank you and do you need a bag for that and romance is the third aisle on your left.

Clearly all three died of excruciating boredom.

Yit'kadal v'yit'kadash. Requiescat in pace. Th-th-that's all, folks.

We've been thinking about our eulogies lately because this is not only our memoir; it's also our suicide note. It's true: we've set the date at last. Midnight, December 31, 1999. New Year's Eve.

We've always known we'd die by our own hands sooner or later. Sooner has now come a-knocking.

"Six months to a year." That's what Vee's doctor said.

We talked it over at dinner. We slept on it that night. The next morning we made a pact. All for one and one for all. If one of us goes, all of us go. Everybody out of the pool.

We have a joke. Well, not a joke. A riddle:

Q: How do three sisters write a single suicide note?
A: The same way a porcupine makes love: carefully.

Also, tenderly and slowly and by pressing on even when it hurts.

We also have a chart. A week or so after our mother died, Delph, who was then eighteen, drew it up. She made it pretty and tacked it onto the back of her bedroom door, where some girls hang pictures of teen idols. There it remains, our great-grandfather, the curse's catalyst, at the top, and our mother, the hapless Dahlie, down at the bottom, bearing his weight and the weight of all the others who went before her.

Who	When	Age	How	Where
Great Grandfather Lenz	1934	65	Suicide: morphine	A hotel in Basel
Great Grandmother Iris	1915	43	Suicide: gunshot	Her garden
Grandfather Richard	1945	43	Suicide: auto-defenestration	The bedroom down the hall
Aunt Rose	1946	21	Suicide: cyanide	A men's bathroom in Chicago
Aunt Violet	1966	40	Suicide: suffocation	Her lovely home on Long Island
Our Mother Dahlie	1975	46	Suicide: drowning	The Hudson

We like the chart. We like the tidiness of the rows and columns. We like the repetitions and subtle variations. We're fascinated by the emergent narrative.

It's said that descendants of suicides view life as forever chaotic, but when we look at this chart, we see the opposite of chaos. We see order and routine. We see soothing predictability and reassuring inevitability.

Without the rows and columns, all you'd have is a crazy game of Clue. Great-Grandma Iris in the garden with a gun. Aunt Violet in the bedroom with a plastic bag. Mom in the river with rocks in her socks.

But with the rows and columns, you have our family tree. Every family's got one. This one is ours.

CHAPTER 2

While all three of us have previously contemplated suicide, only Lady has given it a serious go. Several serious goes, as a matter of fact, and the first one took place almost twenty-three years ago, the long Fourth of July weekend of 1976.

Times were fraught. Over the past twelve months New York City had been through stagflation and gas lines and "Ford to City: Drop Dead," while we'd been through Vee's first bout of cancer, plus our mother's swan dive into the Hudson, plus Lady's swan song for her five-year marriage to the egregious Joe Hopper, an ill-conceived enterprise that had not only caused her unhappiness but also forced her to go by the name Lady Hopper, which, she maintained, sounded like something you'd call a cartoon frog wearing pearls and a diadem. It didn't help to use her given name, either. Lily Hopper was even worse: same frog, less jewelry.

We tried to look on the bright side. No more Joe Hopper, for one. No more Richard Nixon, for two. Vee had been cured. (That's what her doctor had said. That's the word he used. *Cured*.) And now it was the Bicentennial, a three-day weekend when incensed New Yorkers took time out from their calls for Ford's impeachment to cheer the whistling comets and fiery chrysanthemums bursting above the World Trade Center.

Oh, that summer. Delph, nineteen, had a scholarship to Barnard, the women's college just a few blocks uptown that all three of us attended, though only Vee and Delph graduated. Vee and her husband, the faultless Eddie Glod, were living in Vee's bedroom. They were both twenty-three. Eddie worked several part-time, dead-end jobs while trying to figure out what to do with the rest of his life. Vee had begun her job as a paralegal. She'd bought two used business suits at a thrift shop, along with one clunky pair of broken-in, broken-down heels. Only her several pairs of pantyhose were new, packaged for reasons we will never understand inside large plastic eggs.

She enjoyed her job. Each will she prepared was like an allegory, where this everyman called Testator gives away his house and his furniture, his cars and his cash until there's nothing left but his kids. He takes a deep breath and gives them away, too, hands them over to some guardian who will never love them like he does. Now bereft of all he's ever held dear, he signs his name and admits it at last: he's going to die. Vee found the whole process romantic and literary. Also, there was medical and dental and a fully vested retirement plan.

As for Lady, in 1976, she was twenty-six and living alone on Amsterdam Avenue in the slummy fifth-floor walk-up she'd once shared with Joe. The weekend she decided to kill herself, she was nearing the end of a ten-day vacation that had been neither her idea nor her desire. It was the dentist she worked for who'd suddenly decided to take some time off and shut the place down. "Spontaneity is the word of the day," the dentist had said, a line he'd clearly rehearsed.

The hygienist had been thrilled, but not Lady. She was the one who had to call the patients, reschedule appointments. "Something's come up," she had to say. "An emergency," she'd add if a patient got testy. Or, if a patient grew concerned, "A less-than-dire emergency."

The patients weren't really the problem, though. The problem was that she didn't know what to do with a vacation. Ten days. New York in late June, early July. It wasn't as though she had a little place in the Hamptons.

"Remind me again why we're doing this?" she asked the dentist after the hygienist had left for the day. She'd been working for him for four years by then, ever since she dropped out of school to marry Joe. It had been a wretched idea—the marriage, not the job. The job she liked. Office manager slash receptionist was not the sort of occupation Barnard wished for its girls, which, bewilderingly, was how that self-proclaimed bastion of second-wave feminism referred to its students, but Lady was as aspirational when it came to career as she'd been when it came to finding a life partner—that is, not very. She'd married Joe because he'd trusted her with his deepest darkest secret, a secret that had caused him such shame he'd bitten his lower lip as he revealed it, until a few discreet drops of blood dribbled into his Frank Zappa–esque lip beard. He wasn't aware that he'd nibbled himself bloody, that's how wrapped up he'd been in confessing this secret—and stoned, he'd also been extremely stoned—but Lady had seen the self-inflicted cut in his trembling lip, and it had touched her heart. Such a vulnerable boy behind the layers of sarcasm and arrogance, and of all the women he knew, he'd unburdened himself to her. How could she resist? She didn't even mind that he was unemployed. He had a higher calling: he was working away on his master's, after which he'd be getting a

PhD in literature. Then a professorship somewhere Ivy Leaguish. His area of specialty was Victorian female poets. How could Lady not support this? He was a feminist! He wanted women artists to take their rightful place in the academy! They'd tied the knot in Central Park, and she'd willingly left school and taken the first job that allowed her to cover the rent on the apartment they were already sharing.

Joe Hopper, lanky and hairy, with a penchant for fringed suede vests over bare skin. He disliked Lady's job, found it personally humiliating. Dentistry. It was so bougie, he said, so middle-class. Even a minimum-wage job would have been better. The store on 112th that sold cheap sundresses and paper parasols was hiring. Ta-Kome always needed someone to make sandwiches. Or, if it was all about money, then what about waitressing at some Midtown dance club where lawyers and bankers tipped beaucoup? She said that she preferred the receptionist job—she liked getting to sit down all day—and reminded him about the benefits and free fillings. Their dental was even better than Vee's, she said. Why didn't he just lie to his friends about what she did, if he was so embarrassed by it? She wouldn't care if he made up a story. "Tell them I man the ovens at Ray's Pizza," she said. "Tell them I drive a cab in the Bronx." She'd go along with it, she assured him. She'd lie too.

"I'm not as comfortable with lying as you seem to be," he said.

She didn't take offense. How could she, when he wasn't wrong? And he didn't know the half of it, had no idea how much of her life was a lie—although she wasn't lying when she said she liked the receptionist job. She did; she was content—fulfilled, even—to help the dentist build his practice. She was the woman behind the throne, which in her case, was a dentist's chair. That was her joke.

It was true, too, that she liked the dentist himself. He'd been just out of dental school when she joined him. He'd talk to her about his hopes for the business as well as his worries. He told her about his love for his slimy work in painstaking and mildly disgusting detail. He gave her generous Christmas bonuses that, in those first years, she knew he couldn't afford, the amounts of which she had to swear never to reveal to the hygienist, an older woman with a belly slack from four pregnancies and a tight gray bun pierced with the extra chopsticks the delivery boys from Nos Gusta La Comidas China included in their lunch orders.

Lady loved that they shared a work ethic, the dentist and she. His involved never taking more than a long weekend off. Hers involved never taking even that much. What would have been the point? If she stayed home, Joe Hopper would be there, working on his thesis at the coffee table. The title of his thesis was "'Lips—That Like Bruised Pomegranates Blush': Victorian Woman Poets and the Sapphic Gaze."

"His field is vaginas," Vee finally explained to Lady, who'd been misinterpreting the reference to lips. "Vaginas and lesbian sex, and not in a political way. If I come by and you're not home yet, he insists on reading from it to me. He stands really, really close." She made a face. "It's pretty porny."

Lady'd told Vee to stop flattering herself, but she'd also gone home and reread the thesis, and she had to admit Vee's point. She tried to look on the bright side. Joe loved what he was doing. He was always engrossed in his research when she returned home. He'd gesture at her, a sweep of his hand. It meant be quiet, take off your shoes, keep your greetings, footsteps, breathing, basal metabolism rate, to a minimum. Or he'd be waiting for her, wanting to take her to bed as soon as she came through the door, some poem he'd been explicating having turned him on.

"It was my wife's idea," the dentist said of the vacation. He momentarily averted his eyes; at least he had the decency to do that. "She put her foot down. She goes, 'All work and no play.' " He shrugged as if he hadn't an idea in the world what that meant. Then he grinned, something he was good at. "You know what you should do?" he said. "You should go to one of those Club Med places. Guadalupe! Spontaneity! You could run around naked. No one's in the city now anyway."

"Then why not run around naked here?" said Lady.

The dentist's face was wide and boyish. He looked like Rootie Kazootie, like Howdy Doody, like Opie Taylor—all those red-headed, apple-cheeked, freckle-faced goyishe icons of our youth. But now the face grew stern. It was as if he thought Lady was making a suggestion, offering him an alternative.

Which she supposed she was. That's where her being a liar came in. Lady and the dentist had been screwing around on his raspy office carpet after the hygienist went home pretty much since she'd been hired. Oh, maybe for the first six months or so, flattered but loyal to Joe, Lady had gently discouraged the dentist's advances. But when her marriage had quickly begun going south, so, with the dentist, had she.

His own recent marriage hadn't changed anything. The woman he'd married had a name—it was Patty—but he never spoke it in Lady's presence. He used the generic term instead. The wife's coming in for a cleaning. If the wife calls, tell her I'm doing a root canal and can't be disturbed. Yeah, the wife bought me this jacket; it's not my taste, but what are you gonna do?

Lady never mentioned or even hinted at her relationship with the dentist to anyone, not to the hygienist over shared egg foo yung, not to Vee or Delph during her frequent visits home. Not even to the dentist himself. He and she had agreed upon conducting an utterly wordless affair. Their very agreement had been wordless.

Once, only once, had Lady tried to talk to him about what it was they were doing. This was soon after he'd announced his engagement, although *announced* wasn't quite right; it had been more like an aside at the end of a busy day. She hadn't even known he'd been seeing anyone. She felt knocked for a loop, stunned and disbelieving, like those women you sometimes hear about who go to the doctor with a stomachache and learn they're not only pregnant, they're in the end stages of labor. Still, she hadn't said a thing other than the pleasantries anyone would utter in response to such wonderful news—the same pleasantries the hygienist had just offered.

But a few days after he'd confessed to the engagement, the two of them in his office, Lady straightening her skirt, the dentist hanging up his white tunic, Lady thought it would be nice to reassure him, to let him know she would not be falling apart or making a scene, which, while sobbing in the shower that morning, she'd decided would have to be the case. Her reassurance, she thought now, would be a type of engagement present. What else could she do? She'd long known she had no rights. She'd always known what she'd signed up for. She wanted to tell him that. "You know," she said, pulling her sweater back over her head, "the thing about our relationship is—"

He was zipping his trousers. "We don't have a relationship," he said.

She made the mistake of plowing on. "Well, of course we do," she said, "and the thing about it is—"

"We don't have a relationship."

Now she was considering making a scene. Although, having never made one before, she wasn't sure how to go about it. "I agree we don't have a *relationship*," she said, "but we have a relationship."

He put on the jacket he allegedly hated, tawny suede, expensive, indisputably gorgeous, and popped the collar.

"What I mean," Lady said, "is that we may not have a romantic relationship with any kind of future. I get that. But we do have a relationship. I'm your receptionist. I'm your co-worker. Any two people who know each other have a relationship. It's what the word means. The kid I buy snow peas from at the Korean market—I don't know his name, but we have a relationship."

"Maybe you and snow pea boy have a relationship," he said, "but you and I don't."

By then she couldn't remember what she'd wanted to say in the first place. She'd forgotten what the thing about their relationship was. She said, "You know what? I'll see you tomorrow," and went home. She was exasperated, but only because he'd refused to admit she was right. Even at the time, even in the middle of whatever it was you'd call what they had, what they were doing, what they were to each other, she knew she didn't love him, not really. She certainly didn't count on him, not ever. She never initiated anything with him, although sometimes she dropped hints.

Just as she told nobody she was screwing the dentist—even after her divorce, she'd told no one—so she told no one about her mandatory vacation. Day after stifling day she remained indoors with the shades pulled, a futile attempt to stay cool. Even now she remembers the oily sweat between and under her breasts, how she'd pull up her T-shirt, baring her chest, the T-shirt absorbing the sweat on her forehead and cooling her nape and covering her hair like the veil of a topless nun.

She also remembers the small rabbit-eared TV in her bedroom—her entire divorce settlement, the retention of that little TV—that she watched almost nonstop during those interminable days. One afternoon she tuned into *Bill Boggs* to find an impressively drunk Tennessee Williams slouched on the couch while Rich Little did impressions of Johnny Carson and John Wayne. Right after *Boggs*, Walter Matthau appeared on *Dinah Shore*, and, right after *Dinah Shore*, Walter Matthau showed up again, this time on *Mike Douglas*. Lady had nothing against Walter Matthau—who didn't like Walter Matthau?—but his reappearance, his repeated gags, the same clip from *The Bad News Bears*, made her feel unhinged. Then night fell with its soothing reruns of *Rhoda*, *Phyllis*, and *Maude*, and later an appearance by the Happy Hooker on *Tom Snyder*. Lady was beginning to understand how this could become your life, how it could make you feel like you had companions with whom you'd chatted and done things that day. Rhoda, Phyllis, Maude, Xaviera, Tennessee. Girlfriends.

Each day she told herself that she'd do something productive, that she'd watch no more TV, but each day she'd stay in bed, dozing on and off until midafternoon. Then she'd break, she'd crack, she'd turn on the set. Also she'd drink. And sometimes there might be some eating, might be some showering, might be some teeth brushing with the Oral-B extra-firm and sample-size Crest she got free from the office. But most often there was none of the above, just TV and cocktails and her T-shirt pulled over her head like a snood.

Not a day went by that she didn't order herself to call Vee or Delph or even Eddie—maybe just Eddie, the most compassionate of the lot—to say that perhaps she hadn't mentioned it, but she was on vacation, and she seemed unable to get out of bed, and could they please come over and yank her to her feet and make her get dressed. Maybe bringing some food would also be a good idea. A pizza. A turkey sandwich. An entire pound cake.

But she didn't call, she couldn't, because that was the week her fear of talking on the phone materialized as suddenly and surprisingly as a paper bouquet from a magician's sleeve. All at once: *poof*, you're telephobic.

The unanticipated phobia was accompanied by nausea and nerves and stomach adventures, and it escalated rapidly. At the beginning of the vacation she just ignored the ringing phone, a taupe standard Ma Bell table unit that could, if properly wielded, kill someone. By the end she was skittering across the hall, hiding in the bathroom, where she kept an extra a bottle of vodka so she could calm herself until the jangling stopped. She would drink directly from the bottle, one glug, then two, call it a dry martini—which it was, sans olives—or an extra-dry Gibson—which it was, sans cocktail onions. Also sans ice bucket and stemware. She was a self-proclaimed hippie; she didn't much care about elegance or ritual, which was good, given that she kept the crystal clear bottle of Popov on the sweating top of the toilet tank, alongside the green container of pHisoHex and blue jar of Noxzema and brown vial of Miltown, the latter prescribed by the dentist.

It wasn't until the final Saturday of the vacation—the third of July—that Lady emerged from her apartment. She hadn't left before then, not for companionship, not for exercise, not for fresh air or groceries, not for snow peas, not for nothing. But then something came up, or rather something came down. A switch plate in the bedroom had lost its top screw several weeks before. It now hung upside down from its bottom screw, exposing the electrical box and the unpainted wall behind it.

Joe Hopper had taken all the tools when he'd moved out— that had been *his* divorce settlement—so she tried to stick it back

into place with Scotch tape. When that didn't work, she tried ignoring it. That didn't work either, and the switch plate had come
to remind her of someone hanging from a ledge, holding on to
its lip with the fingertips of one hand. It was driving her crazy.
She needed to get to a hardware store and buy a screwdriver.

The dentist's office was—maybe still is—in shabby downtown
Riverdale by the elevated train station. On weekdays Lady
reverse-commuted there. Daily she clattered down the metal
staircase, and, at its landing, propelled herself over a puddle that
she swore never evaporated. The weather might be hot and dry;
the mayor (little Abe Beame) might have banned residents of all
five boroughs from watering their houseplants and flushing their
toilets. It didn't matter. The puddle remained, shrunken perhaps, sometimes a mere muddy outline, but there nonetheless,
dead leaves on its surface. In 1976 the puddle lay directly across
the street from a dive called the Terminal Bar, a fairly ominous
name if you thought about it, and given Lady's proclivity for
both suicide and puns, she did. Accordingly, Lady had named it
the Puddle Styx.

On one side of the Terminal Bar was a four-story office building. The dentist's office was on its second floor. On the other side
of the bar was a hardware store owned and run by a pair of aging
brothers, two irritable men, short and ovate, with glaring black
eyes, bulbous thread-veined noses, and patchy pubic beards. Despite the countless hardware stores on the Upper West Side, it
was this hardware store—half an hour from her apartment if
there were no delays, but of course there were always delays—
that Lady decided to patronize.

She had a reason for traveling that distance when she didn't
really have to: she wasn't at ease inside hardware stores, and at

least she'd been in this one before. Not often, but sometimes the dentist sent her there to pick up some Windex or a three-way plug adaptor or an extension cord. She would feel less unnerved in the somewhat familiar surroundings.

On this summer morning no one in the store paid her any attention or asked if they could help her or gave any indication that they'd seen her before, or, for that matter, were seeing her now. She didn't care. In stores, as in most places and situations, she preferred to be left to herself. This was particularly true now, consumed as she was with the switch-plate crisis.

Before leaving home, she'd unscrewed the plate completely, using her fingers to turn the bottom screw, which was also on the brink of falling out. She'd put the plate and the screw inside a baggie and put the baggie in her purse, which turned out to be smart. In an aisle filled with, surely, over a hundred bins of over a million screws, she was able to find the one she needed.

Buoyed, she continued to the next aisle with its multiple bins of screwdrivers, but here she was at a loss. She wasn't sure how to choose among screwdrivers, didn't know which characteristics of a screwdriver were determinant. She decided to go by color.

She considered one with a rubbery blue handle, rejected it, picked up another, cherry red, put it back. She walked up and down the aisle, then snatched up a model with a handle of trans-lucent plastic, acid green, a hue she'd once experimented with, borrowing an Indian tunic in that shade from Delph. "It makes you look dead," Joe Hopper said, and she returned it unworn.

So—fuck you, Joe Hopper—she took the acid-green screw-driver by the shaft and made her way to the register. She imag-ined him watching all this, frustrated by his inability to criticize a thing she'd done. She fantasized Walter Matthau sidling up to her, asking for local restaurant advice. The two of them would chat a bit, amusing each other, hitting it off; then they'd go to the Terminal Bar for a couple of vodka tonics, some chicken parm and spaghetti, and, after a couple of self-deprecating jokes about expanding waistlines, a shared slice of pie. What Walter Matthau would be doing in a Riverdale hardware store, she'd work out another time.

After she left the store, she put the bag with the screwdriver in her purse. She thought about her dungeon of an apartment. She decided to take a walk. Van Cortlandt Park was right across the street, summer green and lush. She stood on the corner, waiting for the Walk signal.

But as she waited, the idea of crossing the street became overwhelming. It was such a vast street, this section of Broadway, and the thought of traversing it, of sprinting from cement island to cement island as cars and taxis whipped by, discouraged her, depressed her, filled her with a fear that, she immediately registered, would not serve a New Yorker well. But what could she do? The new fear was upon her, and she changed her mind and decided to admit defeat and just go home.

Instead she pivoted and went into the building where she worked. She climbed the two flights of stairs. She tried to peer through the opaque window set in the office door, the dentist's name painted on that glass in an arc like a rainbow. She saw nothing, just the wires threaded through the safety glass.

She rummaged through her purse for her keys. She unlocked the door. Inside, she turned off the alarm, turned on the lights.

Everything in the reception area was as she left it. The magazines and brochures were undisturbed, the gray dustcover over her Selectric untouched. Something was off, though, and she figured out what it was when she poked a finger into the soil of the leggy philodendron on the windowsill. Someone had been here and watered the plant—someone had done her job for her.

The door to the dentist's private office was shut. She crossed the room, put her hand on the round knob. She didn't turn it, just held it. She put her ear to the hollow wood. Although she heard nothing but the loud ticking of his desk clock, she felt uneasy. She found herself picturing the dentist on the other side of that door, splayed on the floor where she and he had their trysts, his wife standing over him just a little ashamed of herself, holding a bloody Huber probe. It was a premonition, she later realized, not of an actual murder but of something gone terribly wrong in there. Or maybe it was a wish.

She held her breath as she turned the knob, but she didn't take the next step of pushing open the door. She was annoyed by how jittery she felt. Her reaction was inexplicable, really. Stupid, if she were being honest. She went in and out of that office all the time. True, the door was almost never shut as it was today, but still . . . Fear of picking up a ringing telephone's receiver was bad enough. Then there'd been the anxiety over crossing the street. Was her fear generalizing; was she now going to become unable to open doors as well?

But no, she thought. Her hesitancy wasn't a sign of neuroses—or not only that. She was hesitating because she was not supposed to be there that day. She was feeling like a trespasser, like a vandal. She had to give herself a stern talking-to. Entering that office was allowed. It was part of her job; it was something she did all the time. The dentist went out for lunch, and Lady went in to do the filing or find an invoice or sit in his comfortable chair and work the crossword. She didn't need to ask permission. "Mi office es su office," he'd say, and why not? He was lucky to have someone like her, a self-starter, diligent and devoted.

An example of that diligence: she would do the filing right

now. She'd straighten up some of the mess that had been left on his desk when they closed in late June. It would be good to get that work done, good to get a jump on things before the office reopened on Tuesday.

Yet even as she opened the door, she couldn't shake her apprehension. Now she imagined finding not a body on the carpet— still life with slit throat—but two bodies, much alive, naked, sparkling with perspiration. Giddy husband and naughty wife. If this were a TV show, a movie, isn't that exactly what would happen next? Music swelling, the receptionist gasping, then rushing to the street below, pressing her hand to her heart, the tears welling, as she cries out his name—

Or no. Because the receptionist would be the villain in the movie, wouldn't she? She'd be the housebreaker, the slut, the brunette. The camera wouldn't think to follow her once she left. It would be the dentist's wife the camera would care about, the dentist's wife who'd be the heroine. That would be the name of the movie, in fact. *The Dentist's Wife*.

The door was slightly ajar now, but Lady still didn't peek inside. She only listened again, listened harder. All she could hear were the clicks of the passing seconds. She took one more of those seconds to inform herself that she was an idiot. Then she pushed the door fully open and flicked on the light.

No swelling music, but she couldn't help herself—she gasped anyway. It wasn't just that the soil of the ficus tree inside the dentist's office had also been watered. It was that the walls, for the past five years the same grayed white as the plaster of paris dentition molds in the prostheses closet, has been painted a feminine mauve. It was that an ornately framed O'Keeffe had been hung by his desk. The flower in the poster was meant, of course, to evoke a receptive vagina, pink and clitoral—Joe's work and O'Keeffe's had that in common—but Lady suspected it had been viewed instead as the pink gums and beckoning uvula of the wide-open mouth of the dentist's dreams.

His desk had been cleared too. Gone, the stack of unfiled insurance forms, the stack of unfiled patient info, even the stack of pink While You Were Out messages, those little notes from her to him. "Mr. Bonfiglio's temp fell off," followed by two exclamation points with a caret underneath:

!!

^

Sad bunny, she called it. (It's true. She invented the whole emoticon thing.)

She also had a happy bunny and a confused bunny, and then there was the one he'd made up, the one he'd draw on the back of one of those While You Were Out slips and leave on her chair on afternoons he hoped she'd stay late: Playboy bunny, the two exclamation points plus a wiggly come-hither grin.

As she gawked at the pristine desk, the absence of clutter felt like a rebuke. Other than the noisy brass clock, every item on its surface was new: a leather blotter, a set of unimaginative but shiny Cross pens, a deluxe version of Galileo's Pendulum, blond wood and steel balls.

And there was more. On the wall above his credenza, the diplomas documenting his unadventurous education—NYU undergrad, NYU College of Dentistry—had been framed and hung. On a nearby shelf, photographs, once propped against books, their edges curling, had also been framed and arranged in ascending height order, like a Rockettes kick line.

The smallest of these photos was of the dentist and his golden retriever Beef, a sweet aging dog that Lady had, at various times, taken to the vet's or groomer's. Next there was a slightly larger shot of Beef alone, a professional portrait in which Beef's mouth was open and his pink tongue lolling, so he looked as though he were smiling, although he was probably just panting from the heat of the photographer's lights.

Next, larger still: the dentist and his wife under a chuppah. Beef was in this one too, sitting alongside one of the chuppah bearers, both the bearer and Beef in paisley vests and bow ties. Then there were two new additions, each one Beef-free. There was an eight-by-ten, just dentist and wife squinting into the sun on their honeymoon. There was a nine-by-twelve, dentist and wife aboard a sailboat that Lady hadn't known he owned but could see was named *The Tooth Ferry*.

And on the credenza itself, a small piece of white card stock tented over like a place card at a dinner party. Surprise!! it said. Lady opened it. Happy Anniversary!! it said. Love!! Patty, it said. And along with the exclamation points—not deliberately silly and facetious exclamation points like Lady's bunny ears and wide bunny eyes, but conventionally employed and rather hysterical exclamation points—were Patty's hearts and *x*'s and *o*'s.

Lady returned the card to the credenza. She took the professional photo of Beef, the one with the tongue. She held the frame with both hands, looked into the dog's brown eyes. She dropped it, frame and all, into her purse.

Leaving, she made sure to close the door to the dentist's office, to punch in the alarm code, to secure the outside locks—to do everything methodically and correctly so nothing would let on she'd been here. Once outside, she hurried past the Terminal Bar, pliéd over the Puddle Styx, trundled up the metal staircase, and caught the Broadway local, which was shimmying on the platform, waiting to take her home.

The blade of the acid-green screwdriver didn't come close to fitting into the grooves of the screw. Lady looked at the tip of the blade and realized the thing she'd purchased wasn't a screwdriver at all. Oh, sure, it looked like a screwdriver, but it was something else, a screwdriver's stepbrother, a bastard screwdriver, the tip shaped like a crucifix.

She was so disappointed in herself, felt so inept, so useless, she couldn't help it; she, who never cried, began to weep. She had to give herself another little lecture, tell herself that it wasn't a big deal, that she'd simply return to the store and exchange the screwdriver-like tool for an actual screwdriver. How hard would that be? She knew she could alternatively stick the impostor screwdriver into a drawer, then go out and buy a replacement within blocks of her apartment. It wasn't as if the aggregate cost of the almost-screwdriver and a genuine screwdriver both was going to break her. But if she did that, then she would have to live with a screwdriver-like device that made her feel stupid. She might as well have invited Joe Hopper back.

She wiped her eyes with a nearby dish towel and got a grip. The truth was, she needed to go back to Riverdale anyway. She not only had to return the goddamn screwdriver, she had to return the photo of Beef. How stupid to give in to the impulse to swipe it. How baffling the impulse itself. Had she imagined that the dentist, when he surveyed his new and improved office, wouldn't notice its absence?

Of course he'd notice its absence. A professional portrait, scheduled, paid for. He'd ask the wife if she had deaccessioned the photo; the wife would say no. Then one of two things would occur. He'd accuse the wife of lying. He'd tell her he'd always known she didn't love Beef. He'd say that this, her stealthy elimination of his dog's portrait, was the first step in removing

Beef from his life. He'd add that mauve was no color for a man's office. A fight, then a divorce, would ensue. He'd tell Lady he'd been a fool.

Or he'd figure out at once that it was Lady who took the picture in what, he'd conclude, was some sort of statement, some sort of expression of Lady's attachment to him, of her never expressed but clearly out-of-control desire for him, of her persistent if wrongheaded conviction that they had a relationship. Or maybe he'd think it was some kind of threat—admit we have a relationship or you'll never see your dog again—when all it was, really, was an irresistible urge to screw with the wife's prissy and predictable sense of interior design, to violate the rigid order of the photographs.

But he'd never get it, would never see the verve, the art, the sly humor in what she'd done, and so, when she went back to the hardware store later that same day to return the acid-green piece of useless crap she'd bought, the photograph was still in her purse so she could return it too.

She should have realized the hardware store would close early on the Saturday of a long Fourth of July weekend, but she hadn't, which is why, at two o'clock, she found herself standing on the street looking at the half-lowered security gate sprayed with graffiti: gang symbols, swastikas, the names of lovers in hearts.

One of the brothers who owned the place came outside, crouching to avoid hitting his head on the gate. He was wearing dark blue work pants and a malodorous short-sleeved dress shirt. On his head he'd plopped, of all things on this sultry afternoon, a felt homburg. The hat appeared to possess gravity-defying properties, remaining atop his head even as he exited the store in this half-bent position, as if he were dancing the limbo upside down.

He was sweating oceans, of course. Each of the large pores of his purple fleshy nose was ringed with gray moisture. He stood, looked briefly at Lady, then turned his back on her.

This was what courage looked like for Lady: she didn't immediately retreat. Instead she pulled the screwdriver from her purse, explained her problem, told him the whole sad saga.

"Forget it, lady," he said when she was done. He still hadn't turned to face her. "I ain't taking that back."

She looked around, as if for support, as if there might be some neutral observer stepping up to assist her. But it was the Saturday of the long Fourth of July weekend. It was New York. The street was empty.

She tried explaining again. Right screw, wrong blade.

He spun around. For a moment she thought he might hit her, that's how angry he seemed. She thought his anger might have something to do with his heavy accent. Perhaps he didn't understand English all that well, perhaps he'd misunderstood her, thought she'd said something rude or belittling. But it turned out she was the one who didn't get it.

"It's a Phillips head, lady," he said with disgust.

Over the course of her twenty-six years on this earth, Lady had become extremely adroit at distinguishing the proper from the common noun. Still, his repeating her name, even unwittingly, was disquieting.

"But it didn't work," she said. "And I only bought it this morning." She could hear her voice, the high pitch, the way it fluttered with nerves. "And I have the receipt. Look. It says right here your return policy is seven days."

"We have a no returns policy for people who don't know their asses from their elbows," he said, and then he was back to struggling with the gate. It had gone off its tracks, was the problem.

He shook it back and forth, jiggled it, jostled it. She saw that her presence was distracting him, exacerbating his struggle. She took a step back.

He mumbled something, but she didn't try to make sense of it. She was still caught on what he'd said just before, his verbal addenda to the store's return policy. She wondered if she'd possibly misheard him. His accent was so thick, after all, that she'd had to stare at his lips to make out his words. She'd stared even though his mouth repelled her, surrounded by that beard, all that short wiry hair. Her perverse mind suddenly compelled her to imagine kissing him, his tongue and facial hairs inside her mouth.

Something she tried never to think about came to her then. It was something that happened about a year earlier, on a warm spring night a few days after Vee and Eddie celebrated their first anniversary. This thing, it had been completely the fault of Joe Hopper. He'd whined and sulked for so long that night, she'd finally given in and agreed to have sex with a small group of their friends: three guys, including Joe, and one other woman.

One of the guys had just acquired a new waterbed. He'd right that minute finished filling it, he told Joe over the phone, and could think of no better way to break it in than with an orgy. Not that any of them had ever participated in an orgy or knew anyone who had. And not that Lady had any interest in an orgy. She couldn't even abide the word, the way it sounded like some sort of obnoxious diminutive. Pudgy. Budgie. Orgy. But *Time* and *Newsweek* and *Life* and *Look* all reported that young people like Lady and Joe and their friends were constantly having group sex, and then there was *Bob and Carol and Ted and Alice* and also John Updike, and now Joe and some of the others had come to feel ripped off.

As they walked to the waterbed owner's apartment, Lady was silent. It was more, she realized, than her not being interested. She was actively opposed. And even if she had been into it in theory, the specifics disturbed her. She didn't like the 3:2 male/female ratio in general or the males and other female involved in particular.

On the other hand, she was always trying to prove that she was the opposite of your typical bourgeois dental receptionist, that, unlike all those women the Beats of the Upper West Side had married—women Lady sometimes recognized pushing carts in Gristedes—she was not the kind of wife whose conventionality could destroy an entire literary movement or even a single evening out. So okay, fine, she decided as she trudged alongside her husband. She would go along. When group sex is inevitable, she told herself, one should just lie back and enjoy it . . . and enjoy it . . . and enjoy it. Still, the phrase *ad nauseam* came to mind.

But in the end all her worried ruminating had turned out to be unnecessary. A bottle of Jack and several joints later, the only one of the three boys who could sustain an erection was the satyrical Joe Hopper, and Lady had consequently wound up having sex with no one besides her own husband. Later, while Joe fucked the other woman, the waterbed's owner asked Lady to help him out by using her mouth, and when she demurred, he said well, what about her hand, and in the interest of not being a complete wet blanket she said okay, fine. "Obviously I'm not attracted to you," he said pensively as she worked away with no discernible results. He was speaking more to himself than to Lady. "I always thought I was, but"—and here he looked down at the final arbiter—"you can't argue with The Bone Dog."

"Or with the absence of The Bone Dog," the third guy said.

He'd given up almost immediately, had taken himself and his own sad puppy to a mildewed easy chair where, still naked, he was reading a yellowed *Columbia Spectator* from 1968. The riots. The takeover of Grayson Kirk's office. The good old days.

"Maybe if you pretend you don't want it," the waterbed owner suggested, and Lady said, "To be honest, Barry, I don't." She considered this a pretty clever response. She was telling the truth, yet Barry and The Bone Dog were free to interpret what she'd said as the pretense requested. But as it turned out, both were wise to her, and her words hurt their feelings. The Bone Dog turned the color of the sky before a thunderstorm and scuttled into itself. It had been small and retreating before; now it looked inside out.

Lady got up off the bed and put on her underpants. She turned her attention to selecting and stacking records on the turntable—the good hostess, even when it wasn't her party— while Joe Hopper and the other woman went at it for a second time, moaning and grunting far more than was necessary while the unheated and underfilled waterbed gurgled and sloshed.

On the walk home Joe Hopper blamed the other guys' failures on her. "You never act like you want it," he said. "You radiate not wanting it. It's so clear you don't want it, you rendered a roomful of men at their sexual peak impotent."

He kicked a trashcan. She found it horrifying: she'd married a man who kicked trashcans. "Well, first of all, the room wasn't full of men. It was just Barry and Norman. And second of all, Barry asked me to radiate not wanting it."

Joe Hopper was neither mollified nor distracted. "Sometimes," he said, "I feel like you tricked me into marrying you by pretending you liked sex."

"No," she said. "I tricked you into marrying me by pretending I liked you."

"I want a divorce," he said.

Outside the hardware store, this memory, in the way of memories, came and went in an instant. The hardware store owner was still wrestling with the gate. What struck her as she stood there holding the Phillips head was that as offensive as he was to her, it was plain she was equally offensive to him. She was, in his eyes, an ignorant woman, a fool who had gotten this far in life without learning the first thing about screws and screwdrivers, professionalism and dilettantism, asses and elbows.

She stepped forward, tried to place herself in the line of his peripheral vision. She was looking at his profile now. He would not turn his head even ninety degrees to look at her. All he did was shake the gate angrily and ineffectually. He reached up, trying to push it back, trying to start all over. As he did, his sleeves fell back, and—his age, his accent; it was no surprise, really—she saw the numbers.

She could never deny she saw them, and she could never deny she knew what they were. Our father, Natan Frankl, had come to the States from a displaced person camp too. Though most of Lady's recollections of him were faded or shadowed, some remained vivid.

But her own arm was already in motion. And maybe she didn't care. Maybe the fact of those numbers didn't make a damned bit of difference to her. Surely, along with the good and the innocent, plenty of assholes had been carted off to those camps: men who would someday abandon their daughters or insult their well-meaning customers or blithely do unto others as they wish hadn't been done unto them. She had a theory. About 95 percent of all people populating this sad planet are assholes, she believed, regardless of race, religion, or creed. Accordingly, whenever you meet any member of any demographic, you have a 95 percent chance of meeting an asshole. Which, if you don't know enough other members of the group, leads you to extrapolate your negative impression to the whole lot of them. This was why Lady believed in integration, mixed marriages, busing, anything that would increase the chances of people encountering and huddling together with the non-assholian 5 percent of humanity.

At this moment, though, she wasn't reviewing her asshole theory. She was too busy feeling attacked and dismissed, abused and ignored. She was feeling, feeling, feeling, and so, unattended and ungoverned, her arm did what it wanted to do, and what her arm wanted to do was throw the acid-green screwdriver at the hardware store owner's head.

She never had much upper body strength, she never played sports of any kind—back in sixth grade, when she'd been forced to participate in the Presidential Physical Fitness Test, she'd scored in the lowest percentile for throwing—and so she hadn't expected the screwdriver to go very far. She'd imagined it would fall and hit the sidewalk before it reached the head her arm had been aiming for. Instead the screwdriver did an elegant somersault, and as if assisted by an indiscernible breeze, its cruciform blade struck the man on the side of his cratered nose. He cried out—more in surprise than in pain, Lady felt certain—and covered his nose with both hands.

Now he was looking at her. Now he'd taken note. And now she was ignoring him. She squatted and darted under the half-closed gate. She knew exactly where to go what to do. She didn't run, just walked purposefully, to the aisle she wanted, to the right bin, and she took the one thing she was entitled to. Then she strode back to the door and upside-down-limbo'd into the slash of sunlight beyond it, where the stunned store owner stood, Phillips head at his feet, hands at his nose, blood seeping between his fingers.

She held up the screwdriver she'd taken, the rubbery blue. A couple of dollars less than the acid green; he was making money on the exchange. He didn't care, though. "Oy, mein shnoyts," he bleated from behind his hands. He dropped his arms, showed her the damage. It was nothing. A lot of blood, yes, but just from a single cut on the side of his left nostril. Nothing deep, nothing dangerous, although it did seem a fragile nose, all that excess purple flesh. It seemed as though it might hurt were someone even to touch it gently. Certainly it had made her wince to look at it.

The only way to avoid looking at it now was to leave. He was yelling about calling a policeman. There was something ridiculous in that—not a cop, not the police, but a *policeman*, like a small child with great faith in all public servants.

"Go ahead," she said. "We'll see whose side he takes," and she turned and flounced off. She did—she *flounced*. Entitled and superior. A mean, spoiled brat. She who was none of those things, not ever.

Over the Puddle Styx, up the stairs, onto the train. Even now she wants to say that this was when she first began to grasp the enormity of what she'd done, but that would be a lie. She'd known what she was doing as she was doing it. Stop it, she'd thought as she raised her arm. Walk away, she'd thought as she threw the green tool. What the fuck are you doing? she inquired of herself as she slithered under the gate.

She hadn't stopped, though. Hadn't walked away. Thoughts versus feelings, and the winner had been feelings. A huge upset. No one would have predicted it.

But as the euphoria of her fury wore off, Lady became aware of a terrible pain inside her, sharp and systemic, as if she'd swallowed the millions of screws in the store and they were now scraping her organs as they tumbled through her bloodstream. She knew the reason for the pain. The entire encounter had been a test, and she'd failed, and she was hurting inside over that failure—because no matter what that man had done, no matter how badly he'd behaved, no matter how much of an asshole he'd been, she should have been kind. She'd seen the numbers. She'd known his life. Our family had played a part in that life, that living death.

And what had she done? She'd thrown the screwdriver.

To this day, whenever Lady thinks of the hardware store owner—and she thinks of him more often than you'd imagine—she feels the same shame, the same painful scraping of threaded metal through her body. She has to stop what she's doing. She closes her eyes. She focuses on her breath. She inhales. She exhales. She tries to envision the store owner, wherever he is—dead, she supposes, given that the store is long gone, and he was an old man even in 1976—and when she has conjured him, she does her best to bathe him in love or as close to love as a sinner like Lady can manage.

But back then, as the train carrying Lady home tunneled underground, she felt no love for anyone. She felt only the pain. She was mortified, and she didn't use the word casually. You didn't have to be a Latin scholar to figure out its derivation. She wanted right then and there to *mort*.

CHAPTER 3

1868

The American Civil War is three years over. Abraham Lincoln is three years dead. Jesse and Frank James have just joined the Cole Younger gang. And in the city of Breslau, in the Kingdom of Prussia, a pair of first cousins have fallen in love and eloped.

When the cousins return home and announce what they've done, the groom's father and bride's uncle declare the union unnatural. The bride's father and groom's uncle pour themselves stiff drinks. The mother-aunts embrace and sob.

"What kind of child do you think a marriage like this will produce?" the fathers and mothers, the aunts and uncles, demand.

We think it's sad that the bride never gets to say, "Oh, I don't know, maybe a Nobel Prize–winning kind of child." She never gets to say it because she dies nine months later while giving birth to the future laureate. From the first, his head is exceedingly large.

1871

The Franco-Prussian Wars have ended. The unification of the German Empire is complete. The Second Reich has begun, though of course the real power remains with Prussia. The former Prussian king, Wilhelm I, is emperor. The former Prussian prime minister, Otto von Bismarck, is chancellor.

When affairs of the empire bring Bismarck to Breslau, the widower Heinrich Lorenz Alter leaves his dye factory to stand among the throngs waiting to see the champion of iron and blood emerge from his carriage, chest out, shoulders squared, head held high as if he's a figure in a portrait by an artist enamored of the golden mean. As Bismarck passes, the crowd heaves like an unfettered bosom in a bodice ripper. Much of the attraction in coming to see Bismarck is being a part of this impassioned heaving, this surging forward—this element of danger, the possibility that one may be caught in a lustful stampede, may be knocked to the ground and literally perish from love of king and country.

The first time he brings his motherless son with him, Heinrich hoists the boy onto his shoulders. The child perches there stolidly, expertly. He's a sober two-year-old who's been left to the care of redoubtable nurses with quick tempers and paddles and switches. He's well trained in the art of keeping still. Even when Bismarck arrives and a roar takes over the square as the crowd buffets Heinrich, the boy makes no sound. Heinrich has to twist his neck, look up at his son to make sure the boy isn't frightened. When he does, he sees tears, but they are tears of joy; Heinrich's certain of that. "Two years old," Heinrich writes to his youngest brother Rudi, the only member of the family he still speaks to. "Two years old, and such depth of feeling for his country."

"You're raising him well," Rudi replies dutifully, "and under such difficult circumstances."

Heinrich revels in Rudi's praise. It's true, he thinks. He has raised the boy well. There's a small photograph of the dead mother, Line Alter Alter, in an oval frame on the boy's bedroom dresser; the child is tasked with kissing it each night before getting beneath the blankets. But what dominates the nursery is the portrait of Bismarck that hangs on the wall facing the bed. It's the same portrait that currently hangs over the toilet in our Riverside Drive apartment. The generations before ours hung it in the foyer, the centerpiece of an arrangement of old photographs and paintings. As soon as we could, we moved it.

The tragedy of unrequited love for the blond beast, Einstein will someday call the love that Jews like Heinrich Alter (and later, Lenz Alter too) harbored for Germany, but Heinrich Alter calls it patriotism. He calls it *Heimat*. Being Jewish is his culture, but being German is his faith. He's determined that his child will embrace this faith too. Even the boy's name is meant to play its part. Heinrich Lorenz Alter chose the name himself, no female sensibility involved, although he believes Line would have approved. The boy is called Lenz, but his full name is Lorenz Otto Alter. Lorenz to remind him of Heinrich. Otto to remind him of Bismarck. Alter—it implies age and wisdom, and who, Heinrich argues, is older and wiser than God?

No mother, but three fathers. This is what Heinrich tells the baby long before words have any meaning to it. Leaning over the cradle, his palm cupping the crown of the small head, Heinrich croons manifestos in lieu of lullabies. "Three fathers," Heinrich says. "Me, Bismarck, God." Lenz's job is to disappoint none of them.

Meanwhile, across town, Zindel Emanuel is also teaching his children about Bismarck. When military parades pass by, he takes his two oldest girls, the five-year-old and the three-year-old, out onto the second-floor balcony. "You remember all the speeches about iron and blood?" he asks Rose and Lily, who stand on their toes and peer over the balustrade. "Well, those rifles the soldiers are holding—that's what Bismarck meant when he said iron. And you see that sleeve pinned to that soldier's shoulder—or there, the patch over that guy's eye? That was the blood. You'll notice, though, that while the iron's still held high, the blood's been washed away."

He lifts them, one at a time, so they can more easily take note of the weapons and prettified gore.

"They love talking about blood," Zindel Emanuel says. "It stirs the passions of the sheep. But they'll never let the sheep see the blood. Sheep love talk of blood, but they faint dead away at the sight of it."

"Baaa," Lily calls to the soldiers below. The ones directly beneath the balcony look up, laugh, wave to her.

Emanuel's wife joins them, new baby in her arms. "Lily," she says. "Don't make barnyard noises at the infantry." She gives her husband a look that's both reproving and affectionate. "Maybe we should try one more time to get you a son. You're training these girls to behave like little boys. Yelling at people in the streets. Thinking all the time about politics."

Emanuel takes the infant from its mother. Iris Emanuel is overwrapped in linen and lace; she looks like nothing more than a small, smiling doll's head. "This was supposed to be my boy," he says.

Iris beams at him, at the clouds, at the soldiers, at whatever her eyes land on. When she grows up, her father thinks, she will look like the goddess Isis: dark hair, fair skin, blue eyes. This doesn't please him. He has no intention of raising an Isis, a goddess of domesticity, of weaving, of the moon. And he's concerned about those blue eyes, so unusually pale. A curse in some cultures, the least sensitive of his acquaintances say. "They'll darken," his wife says defensively—though time will prove her wrong—but that's not what bothers Zindel Emanuel. He's unfazed by curses, he's not superstitious. He doesn't believe in mythology, not the myths of Egypt though he knows them all, not the myths of his own people—the Jews. Not even the myths of the Prussians. He enjoys pointing out that despite the infantry uniform the chancellor wears, Otto von Bismarck was merely a reservist. He never served a day in the active military. He neither carried iron into battle nor shed a drop of blood—or at least not a drop of his own blood.

No, what Zindel Emanuel dislikes about the toddler's pale blue eyes is the attention they're already commanding. He doesn't want this girl to be admired for her appearance. He has high hopes for Iris, a disappointment by virtue of her sex, true, but a child who, he has already determined, will disappoint him in no other way. There's something about her—how alert she is, how lively, her arms and legs churning even in her sleep as if she's climbing or building something—that has convinced him she'll be the person he's already imagined.

"No more babies," he assures his wife. "I'm going to work with the materials you've given me." He lifts the little girl so she too can see the parade. He busses her on her cheek, his wife on the forehead, and, Iris still in his arms, leaves the balcony for the warmth of the house. The two older girls follow him: his acolytes, his ducklings.

Alone now, his wife looks down at the victorious soldiers parading by. They fall into two categories: the hobbled and maimed, and the unscathed and ashamed. Such a relief, she thinks, not to have sons.

1874

Heinrich Lorenz Alter's dye factory is the most successful in western Europe. The dark blue of the Prussian infantry's uniforms? The forest green worn by the Jaegers? The Prussian blue of Bismarck's own tunic? The dyes for the cloth come from the Alter Dye Works. And if Heinrich has made the military's uniforms rich, the military has returned the favor.

When Heinrich speaks of his exquisite dyes, it's with tenderness, with genuine love. Mention his spring green, that precise shade of lettuce upon its first fragile leafing, and Heinrich's suddenly as effusive as Keats encountering an old vase. Ask about his scarlet, and he'll tell you it's more vibrant than a cardinal's feathered belly. Bring up Alter indigo, and he'll describe it the way other men might their mistresses, praising her unparalleled beauty to people who smile and nod and glance at the nearest clock.

Because Heinrich wants Lenz, his son and sole heir, to begin working at the factory as soon as he completes his basic education, Lenz's training begins early. "Never too young to start developing an eye for color," Heinrich writes Rudi, "especially with a boy who seems already to have a natural aptitude for nothing."

This has been a revelation: the number of things that Lenz, now five, is bad at. He's clumsy with balls and bats, he's slow at his letters, he still needs assistance in tying his shoelaces, and though he's eager to spend time with other children, he seems to put them off. The once silent little boy has become a blabbermouth. He stands too close, tells long, tedious stories about war, his favorite subject. He's fascinated by war. He corners little girls at birthday parties and expounds upon the campaigns of Napoleon.

"I'm going to be a general," he tells his father.

A Jewish general. Heinrich winces. He pats the boy's shoulder. He says, "You'll be the general of Alter Dye Works. You'll dress the generals in the military. You'll give them the pride they need to win wars for Germany."

Lenz may be socially awkward and dull and only five, but he knows when he's being patronized. He also knows how he feels about the factory. All his biographers agree: from a very young age he dismissed the idea of taking it over. Still, that particular battle between father and son is more than a decade in the future. Now, his father not yet realizing it's a waste of time, Lenz's training takes place on the streets of Breslau. Every evening before dinner Heinrich insists that Lenz accompany him on a constitutional, and every evening Lenz, knowing what's coming, sulks and grumbles, but ultimately obeys.

We have a photograph of him at that age. He's the most mournful little boy we've ever seen, his tremendous noggin home to large dark eyes and lips that are pursed as if he had been about to cry when someone—Heinrich, probably, although maybe it was the photographer—ordered him not to move a muscle. And so he stands miserably and rigidly next to the ornate wooden chair that these days lives in our foyer (where it's laden, sometimes to the point of tipping over, with our handbags and jackets and winter scarves and, back in the day when Vee still wore a wig, that luxuriant prosthesis slung on one of the uprights). In the photograph, though, only a boy's beribboned boater lies on the chair's seat.

The boy himself wears a child's version of an infantry uniform, the brass buttons oversize, the collar flat, the trousers cuffed over knee-high boots. His hair is severely parted close to his right ear. He holds a rifle as if it's a walking stick, its butt on the ground, its muzzle pointed at the ceiling.

And here's another photograph of the young Lenz Alter, this one with his uncle, Rudi. According to the fat biography of Lenz Alter on our living room bookshelf (*Lenz Alter: Deutsch, Jude, Heilige, Sünder*), Rudi Alter was a homosexual, malarial dwarf—that's a quote—with delicate features and charm to spare, and we have to admit the description is supported by the photo, where Rudi, not much taller than Lenz, is matinee-idol handsome with kohl-rimmed eyes and the ornate and waxed facial hair of the times—the handlebar mustache, the scalloped muttonchops—not quite concealing a sweet smile. He also possesses a pair of sculpted, fine eyebrows.

This photograph must have been taken during one of Rudi's brief visits home, because his work as a trade consulate keeps him mostly in Asia. In 1874 he's Germany's trade representative to Japan. This means that Rudi is either so competent and charming that he's overcome what we assume must have been his government's reluctance to have a quote unquote homosexual malarial dwarf represent it, or it means that the German government in the late nineteenth century was far less uptight than our own is today. We suspect the former is the truth, that Rudi's charm overcame prejudice, but that could be because we have a collective crush on him. We love that in this photograph, he and his small nephew are both dressed in identical kimonos. We love that Rudi's kimono is accessorized with several long strand of pearls.

Rudi is the person responsible for the dye factory's indigo. He's the one who negotiates the exclusive deals between Heinrich and the best *ai* farmers in Japan, the one who has arranged for hundreds of cases of sake to accompany the *ai* leaves as they're transported from Hokkaido Province to Breslau in the damp holds of ships. That's the heart of the recipe for Alter indigo: imported *ai* leaves and imported sake with some imported wheat bran tossed in. Heinrich also throws in some domestic lye because he doesn't have it in him to turn his back on western techniques entirely. The mixture is then stirred for several days by the factory's workers, those immigrants and day workers from Poland wielding wooden rakes also imported from Japan until the dye bath is the color of a fresh bruise and its fumes turn the sclerae of the workers' eyes crimson.

That there's nothing like Alter indigo anywhere else on the continent is one of the dominant themes accompanying the father and son's constitutionals. "Look," Heinrich says, loud, rudely pointing. "Do you see that worker's uniform? That indigo is close to ours, but not as complex."

Or, "Look at the eye of that peacock feather in that woman's hat. That's close to our indigo but not as rich."

Or look at the blueberries on that vine or the violas in that field or the arc in that rainbow. Close but not as pure, not as perfect, not as poignant.

Every night, not only their neighbors' clothes but nature herself are judged and found lacking.

Lenz is found lacking, too. His mind wanders. He's more interested in the dyeing process than the colors the process produces. He likes to imagine the moment when roots and petals and the carapaces of insects magically turn into cerulean or chartreuse or the vermilion that Uncle Rudi mixes with beeswax and daubs on his cheeks just above his muttonchops, brushes onto his lips just below his mustache. This—the process, not the cosmetics—holds a degree of fascination for the little boy. But his father's lectures are those of an artist, not a manufacturer.

His father carries on about aesthetics, about the general populace's inability to distinguish muddy colors from crisp colors, their failure to appreciate natural colors, with their variations, their own personalities, from the monotony of the new chemically made dyes. Even at eight Lenz knows he's part of that general populace. He's inferior. He's undiscerning.

Then—it's still 1874—comes the afternoon in early May when Rudi Alter—he's still in Japan—decides to take a walk through a park that, like the park across the street from our apartment, runs along the river of a port city. We imagine the Japanese park filled with bamboo fountains and cherry trees and miniature red maples, the latter pretty much the same height as Rudi. In our imagination he's wearing native dress, but his own native dress. A suit, a straw hat.

He's climbing a hill when he feels a poke in the back. He turns, smiling, expecting to see a colleague playfully jabbing at him with the tip of an umbrella. Instead he finds himself grinning foolishly at a young Japanese nationalist brandishing an antique Samurai sword.

From the autopsy report:

Wound 1: scalp entirely pierced through
Wound 7: carotid artery completely severed
Wound 11: entire elbow joint completely severed

It goes on. Twenty-two wounds in all. Twenty-two fully pierced or completely severed pieces of Rudi Alter.

The nationalist says that the gods came to him in a dream. They sent him to the park to kill the first foreigner he ran into. That turned out to be Rudi. The nationalist saw him from behind, took in the European garb, perhaps the scant height as well, and the gods said yes, go ahead. They said what are you waiting for? The young assassin has composed a poem about the whole thing, which he recites from memory at the police station. He recites it again at his trial. He's declared insane. They behead him anyway.

At the foot of the path where Rudi died—a young man of thirty-three—the port city erects a granite monument shaped like a giant headstone. On its base the words "Our Brother" are engraved in German. *Our* is misspelled.

On the day that Rudi Alter dies in Japan, the temperature drops dramatically in Breslau. People stop strangers in the streets to comment on it. "This is the kind of weather that causes influenza," they inform one another. They say, "This morning I had to take off my jacket, I was so hot, and now I'm wearing it buttoned to my chin and I'm still chilled to the bone."

By the time Heinrich and Lenz leave the house for their mandatory evening stroll, the sky over Breslau is the sleek gray of an iced-over lake and the streets are shadowed in wintry violets. Because it's so cold, Lenz is less amazed than he should be when several snowflakes waft down and alight on his father's outstretched palm.

"Look closely," says Heinrich. "Each one different," but by the time Lenz looks, the snowflakes have melted. Heinrich wipes his wet hand on his trousers. He cranes his neck, searching for more drifting flakes. There aren't any. It's May, after all.

What there is, though, is an inky slash along the horizon that makes Heinrich's heart lurch. He points to the slash with such energy he feels the gesture in his shoulder socket.

"Look!" he cries. "Look. Lenz, do you see that? There! Now, that—that's ours!"

The color of the slash between earth and sky is rich and complex, pure and poignant. It's the precise shade Newton observed on the day he understood that the spectrum contained not six colors, as everyone believed, but seven, and this color, this purple-blue, the one too long overlooked.

In a moment Lenz will also see the ribbon of indigo, but for now he completely misunderstands. He thinks his father is pointing to the entire sky. "That's ours," his father has declared, and Lenz believes his father means the whole canopy, the boundless firmament, every square inch of the heavens. For a fleeting, confusing, yet immensely gratifying and possibly life-changing instant, Lenz Alter believes his father has declared himself heaven's landlord.

And here is Lenz, son and sole heir.

Death in childbirth. Evisceration among the cherry trees. Typos on your tombstone. These were the stories our mother told us. Bedtime stories, we called them, though we were talking her bedtime, not ours. The three of us tended to stay up long after she went to sleep. But though she turned in shortly after dinner, she slept in fits and starts, as we often do now, and she'd wake up throughout the night and sometimes she'd shout our names, and we'd leave our beds or, more likely, whatever late-night movie we were watching in the living room and troop in. By then she'd be sitting up, cigarette already lit. We'd take our positions at the end of her mattress, Lady in the middle, the younger ones on either side of her, Vee a smaller version of Lady, Delph a smaller version of Vee. "The nesting dolls," our mother called us, and we could tell she found this off-putting rather than cute.

Even we found it a little unnerving to look at each other. So that's what I looked like when I lost my front teeth. So that's what I'll look like when I've entered adolescence. And yet this resemblance was also the only reliable and reassuring thing in our lives. There was the sense that we would always have each other. There was, to be honest, a never-articulated belief that we actually *were* each other, just at different stages of a single life. When our mother called us for bedtime stories and we arranged ourselves at her blanketed feet, each of us heavy-lidded, Vee and Delph lolling their heads against Lady's arms, we must have looked on the outside as we felt on the inside: a single creature, strange and many-limbed, and in desperate need of a good night's rest.

Of all the stories our mother told us when we were girls, the story about Lenz and the snowflakes and the sky was our favorite. We were children ourselves; we empathized with a little boy's failure to understand an adult's message. We got why his misapprehension was cute and silly, but we also got why it was wonderful, why his was a glorious way to see the world: not reduced to one of its component colors, but broad and encompassing and mystical, and the whole thing revolving around little old you.

As time went on, though, when we requested this story our mother began adding new details. When Heinrich and Lenz left home, they were led through the city streets by an eerie light that was an iridescent silver like mother-of-pearl. When Heinrich looked up, it was because a clap of thunder or shooting star or roaring voice had called his attention to the horizon.

In these new versions, on the day Heinrich caught the snowflakes in his palm, he understood at once that they weren't snowflakes. (Snowflakes in May, our mother said. Did you actually believe that?) He knew immediately that they were Rudi Alter's essence, fragments of Rudi's very soul making their way to his brother on that day: Rudi's deathday. Heinrich Alter had no way of knowing his brother was dead at the time he saw that indigo slash. But, said our mother, Heinrich Alter *knew*.

Eventually even the punch line was no longer a punch line, Lenz's conclusion no longer the funny misunderstanding of a little boy but a genuine revelation. In these new versions, when Heinrich pointed upward and proclaimed, "That's ours!" he *did* mean the entire sky, he *did* mean everything the human eye could see. He meant everything the human eye couldn't see, too.

Soon, when our mother told us the story, she was no longer looking at us, her purported audience, but gazing upward with confusion and wonder just as her great-grandfather and her little-boy grandfather had done all those years ago. Perhaps she was addressing the faces that we too could see in the swirls of ceiling plaster when we softened our vision. Perhaps she was talking to someone only she could discern. Maybe it was the ghost of one of her gone-by relatives: her mother Karin, her father Richard, her great-uncle Rudi. Or maybe it was Lenz, who she'd known briefly when she was a very young girl, her grandfather Lenz who told her some of these bedtime stories before Hitler came and the family fled. Or maybe she thought she was talking to Der Alter, that is, to the God she'd always told us did not exist.

"What does it mean?" our mother asked the ceiling or the ghost or God. "If my great-grandfather owned heaven and my grandfather inherited it from him, what does that mean for me now? Shouldn't it be mine? Isn't that the law?"

At first we tried to persuade ourselves that she was clowning, trying to amuse us. She wasn't, though. Wasn't clowning. Wasn't amusing.

Sometimes it seemed as if the ceiling was responding to her. For us it was like listening to one side of a phone call. "Yes," she'd say, and then a long pause. "Well, yes," and another silence. Finally, "I understand your argument, but I think some of your basic premises are incorrect."

Sometimes she remembered that we were sitting there, and she frowned as if we'd interrupted or voiced disapproval when we hadn't said anything at all. "Don't worry," she'd say with exhaustion. "When I die, it will all pass to you. No one's going to deny you your potage."

She never said this with passion or conviction or joy. She said it as if she were recalling one more tiresome chore on her life's to-do list. She managed the jewelry and cosmetics department at Woolworth's, and if we never were well off, we always had rent money and food and a substantial supply of lipsticks and plastic clip-on earrings. She took care of us as best she could. If she said she'd get us our potage, we believed her. Of course, we thought potage meant porridge, and we wanted no part of it. We made faces. She chafed at our lack of gratitude. "Don't look so stricken," she'd say. "This is the good news. It's the only good news anyone unlucky enough to be part of this family's going to get."

Other times she said nothing, just smiled wearily. This was worse than her conversations with the ceiling. We dreaded her smiles. They were time machines that carried her away, transported her to the distant past or the faraway future, left us with only her body, a hand with a cigarette dangling off her bed, hot ashes wafting down to the carpet fibers like snowflakes in Breslau, like cherry blossoms in a Japanese park. One night she came back from one of those trips and said, "If God owns heaven and I own heaven and there's only one owner of heaven, what does that force you to conclude?"

It took us a moment to realize she was talking to us.

"That you're God?" Vee said.

Our mother nodded as she considered that answer—hers had been a genuine, not a rhetorical, question—but Vee, upon reflection, glowered. "I thought we were atheists," she said.

"I thought we were *humans*," Delph said.

"We *are* atheists," Lady said. "Which means, if (a) there's no God and (b) Mom's God, then (c) Mom's nothing. That's called the transitive property."

Our mother looked at us as if we were all very wise, and being wise was a terrible burden she wished she could have spared us. Her eyes filled with tears. She drew on her cigarette, blew the smoke up toward the faces in the ceiling. She tried to be careful about us and her smoke.

"They're right," she said to the ceiling, tears dribbling down her face. "I'm God and I'm just some old bag of bones and I'm nothing, all three at once."

God, bones, and nothing. Lady calls this the Alter version of the holy trinity. Delph says it's the best definition of mortal man she's ever heard. We are, at all times, all three.

Vee thinks that from God to bones to nothing is also a pretty good description of life. It's sad, she thinks. It's the opposite of the way she wishes life worked. From nothing to bones to God—that's what she longs for, that's what she wishes for—the fantasy, the fairy tale, the capacity for faith. But Vee can't go there. None of us can.

CHAPTER 4

When she got home from Riverdale, Lady dropped the blue screwdriver on the kitchen counter—because, as bad as she felt about everything, she hadn't relinquished it, she'd held on to it, clutching it the whole train ride home as if it were a wand or scepter; she has it even now, today, in a drawer in her bedroom—and not bothering with the switch plate, she headed straight to the bathroom for a drink. For many drinks. She sat on the tiled floor and she pulled her T-shirt up over her head, and she thought about how unhappy she was and how unloved and unlovable and how strange and, now, how violent, and she drank from the bottle, one glug, then two, and she called it drinking from the bottle. From time to time the phone rang, and she had another drink or she turned on the faucet to drown out the sound. She stared up at the peeling paint of the ceiling. And when the ringing stopped, she had another drink.

She toyed with the idea of a note. The fact that none of our family suicides had left one had always struck her as a dereliction of duty, or, if that was too strong, at least a missed opportunity.

She had always imagined that when the time came, she would leave an explanation behind. Just a few years before, an actor had killed himself (pills) and left a courteous note she'd admired: "Dear World," he'd written, "I am leaving because I'm bored." Ever since, Lady'd imagined leaving behind an equally pithy and frank declaration, a sentence unassailable and plucky and concise enough to fit inside a Hallmark card. But now, as she thought about it, she realized that if she were being honest, her note would have to say, "Dear World, I am leaving because Shine's Hardware at B'Way and 242nd refused to honor its returns policy," and so by the time she passed out, banging her head on the side of the tub in the process, doing more visible damage to herself than she'd done to that sad entrepreneur in Riverdale, she'd already ditched the note concept.

She woke up several hours later, headachy and parched. She chewed a handful of aspirins and drank the taste away with several glasses of fuzzy tap water. She washed her face.

In the tradition of Jews in the hours before the Cossacks arrive, she spent the rest of the day cleaning her apartment and packing her things. She filled a cardboard box with volumes of literature from her truncated college career, *Reader, I married him* crammed next to *I can't go on; I'll go on.* She put the box out by the staircase. Her hope was that one of the building's families, immigrants all of them, would take the books for their children and perhaps think well of her.

The day latened, and she stopped to take in the sunset, that purple, magenta, and orange offspring of innocent nature and despoiling industry. It was beautiful, the sunset, in the way poisons sometimes are—the berries of the belladonna plant, shiny black as patent leather; the apple of the wicked stepmother, blood red and irresistible. An unnatural natural phenomenon, those dangerous and gorgeous colors, and she looked at them longer than she meant to. She had to shake her head, turn away from the window, before she could continue with her chores: fetching, bending, placing material things in boxes. It was as active as she'd been in weeks. The muscles along her spine, shocked at what was suddenly asked of them, twinged and chided.

She dragged a second box out into the hall, this one filled with cartons of Irish oatmeal and bags of brown rice and a dozen or so dented mini cans of soup. FREE TO A GOOD HOME, she'd printed on its side.

Her dented Campbell's Soup for One Chicken with Stars. Her dented Campbell's Soup for One Split Pea with Ham. "I would rather dump a gallon of soup gone bad," Vee had said only a few weeks before, holding up one of those little cans, she and Delph laughing at Lady's expense, "than buy something that informs the whole world, or even just the checkout girl, of my desperately lonely existence."

Lady hadn't minded the teasing, and it still made her smile to recall that evening. Eddie Glod was at his night job, mopping floors at Union Theological, so it had been just the three of us on Lady's futon, wooden plates balanced on knees. She and Joe Hopper had bought the plates at Azuma, figuring that, wood being unbreakable, the set would last them forever. And certainly none of the plates had broken or chipped. Still, there was something about eating off wood that was like nails on a chalkboard, and there was a slightly rancid smell due to the vegetable oil Lady used to keep up their color, and eventually you had to watch out for splinters.

Lady hadn't made soup that evening. Vee had come across the soup-for-one cans while searching Lady's cabinets for the vodka. ("In the bathroom," Lady had been required to say.) Lady'd made only spaghetti, pouring Kraft blue cheese dressing over it, a favorite meal of ours, one she'd been preparing for Vee and Delph since our childhoods.

"I don't care what supermarket checkout girls think about me," Lady told Vee, although this wasn't true; she cared what everyone in the world thought about her, including impotent college boys and irritable hardware store owners. "But," she added, "you know what those cans of soup make me think of? Men. All the men I meet, all the men I know. Not Eddie. We all love Eddie. I'm talking about Joe and his friends and the men who come into the office, all flirting and puffed up with themselves as if I don't know about their tartar and bad breath and gangrenous wisdom teeth. Even the guy I work for. There's something wrong with all of them, I swear it. An entire gender of dented soup cans, all damaged and marked down, and you have to wonder, is the dent just because it fell on the floor and you're getting a bargain, or is it caused by something like botulism and it's going to kill you? My feeling is, Why take the risk? What's the best that can happen? A bowl of cheap soup? Better to go soupless, that's what I think."

"You're twenty-six," Vee said. "It's too soon to give up on soup."

Delph disagreed. "Who says? I'm only nineteen, and I have no interest in soup whatsoever."

"Yes, honey," Vee said, "and no offense, but that's not normal. I'm not saying you have to run out and lap up the first bowl of soup you stumble across. You should wait for a variety you like. But you should at least be wanting soup. In fact, you should be craving soup. You should be dreaming about slurping it from bowls and drinking it from mugs and ladling it from the pot straight into your mouth."

"I'll have the salad," Delph said.

It took Lady the rest of Saturday evening and all of Sunday, the actual Fourth of July, to finish packing. She owned so little; she was surprised it took as long as it did. But it was all the trips to the liquor store to mooch cardboard boxes. It was her sudden compulsion to fold the clothes she normally just stuffed into drawers, every black T-shirt, every black sweater, every pair of black jeans folded as if by a saleswoman in a luxury boutique. It was her decision, after she'd filled those boxes, to pile them neatly, geometrically, a waist-high room divider that was somehow both sturdy and flimsy.

When she was done, she took off her black t-shirt and jeans and changed into a black sundress she'd laid out on the sofa. She stepped into flip-flops and went to the kitchen and took her will from the otherwise empty junk drawer, where she kept it with the take-out menus and magnets from banks and broccoli rubber bands. A will at her age: it was a perk of having a paralegal for a sister. All the estate planning you could ever want. Who cared that you had no property to speak of? "Yes, but what if you get hit by a bus?" Vee had argued when Lady and Joe were newly separated, "and your executor sues the city for millions and wins? Don't you want a say in who those millions go to? Or who they *don't* go to?"

"You don't have a will, though," Lady pointed out.

"Because if you die intestate without kids, the law gives everything to your spouse," Vee said, "which I don't mind. But you should."

The truth was that Lady didn't care one way or the other. Let Joe inherit her rabbit-eared TV. Hell, let him inherit the fortune reaped by her estate after her imaginary collision with a bus. But Vee wasn't having it. "Over my dead body," she said, and she came by the next night with the document, ten legal-size pages although only two sentences in the entire thing mattered. The first of these sentences said, "I give and bequeath the rest, residue, and remainder of my property in equal shares to my surviving sisters." The second one said, "It is my intention that this will shall not be revoked by my forthcoming divorce from Joseph Hopper." All the rest was archaic gobbledygook.

Lady hadn't looked at the document since she'd signed it. But now, given that it was soon to take effect—to *mature*, as Vee would have said—now, before folding it into thirds and slipping it inside her purse, Lady stopped to skim it. She wished she could blot out the reference to Joe. The divorce was no longer forthcoming. It was done, it was history. Why did he still have to be a part of her story?

She wished, too, she could cross out "the rest, residue, and remainder," and replace it with a phrase that sounded like something she'd actually say. Something like "I give all my shit to Vee and Delph, although why they'd want any of it, I have no idea ."

"The rest, residue, and remainder," she'd said the evening Vee had presented her with the document, Vee proud of herself the way a kid is when bestowing a handmade Mother's Day card upon the kind of mom who gets off on such things. "Doesn't that sound like what's left after you kick? Ash residue? Skeletal remains? Eternal rest?"

Vee had been annoyed. "It's just legalese." She'd expected gratitude and admiration, not a bad review.

"Why can't it just be English?" Lady asked.

"Jesus, Lady," Vee said. "None of our clients who actually pay an arm and a leg for these things stop to read them. Why do you have to? Just sign whatever your name is these days."

Her name then, as now, was Lily Alter. No longer Frankl, our father's name. No longer Hopper, her husband's name. The new name was such a recent acquisition it still felt like an alias. As she wrote it, she felt as though she were committing fraud.

"Okay, you can die now," Vee said when Lady put down her pen.

The witnesses, a Korean mother and her adult daughters who lived in the apartment next door, had scowled. They understood more English than they spoke. They didn't like Vee's sense of humor. Smiling comfortingly at Lady, they sang out a Korean word that sounded like "muenster," as in the cheese.

"Man-se," the mother said, enunciating. "Means may you live ten thousand more year."

The final thing Lady did before leaving the apartment that Sunday was gather the diaries she'd kept on and off through the years. She took those small spiral notebooks filled with her dull day-to-day and threw them into a black trash bag.

She knew that the most recent of the notebooks contained a recap of the soup conversation, and she considered stopping what she was doing to find it and read it over, see if she was remembering it correctly, but she forced herself to resist succumbing to nostalgia and fondness or anything else that might interfere with what she was planning to do later that night. Instead she slung the trash bag over one shoulder and left the apartment.

It was a little past midnight. She trudged west, pushing through the thick heat of the night, the black plastic sack sticking to her back. Standing on the broken concrete and exposed rebar that was the bank of the Hudson, she hurled the bag as far as she could. Not very far, but far enough. She watched as slowly it sank.

It was a relief to be rid of the weight of the journals. The literal weight, she meant. The contents of the notebooks weren't weighty at all; she never wrote anything revealing. She rarely wrote anything that was true. She didn't lie, per se. She just committed literary sins of omission. Sleeping with a married dentist? Who's sleeping with a married dentist? She was drowning those notebooks not to prevent people from learning the discouraging facts of her life, but to prevent them from laughing at all she'd left out.

She reflected, too—how could she not?—on our mother's leap into this river the year before. Vee had called her. Lady was answering phones then.

"Mom's not here," Vee said. "She hasn't left the house in weeks, and now suddenly she's not here."

"Enjoy the time off," Lady said.

"We thought she might be with you."

"With me? When has she ever walked the four blocks to see me?"

Later in the day Vee called her again.

It was not Lady's choice to die the same way our mother had. The method Lady preferred had come to her almost immediately. She would hang herself in the basement laundry room of the Riverside Drive building. She might have done it in her own building, where there was no chance that her sisters would be the ones to discover her, but she was being a little selfish: she didn't want to die among roaches and rats. The basement in our building was cleaner.

But although she debated over which building to die in, she never wavered when it came to the method. She was actually good with ropes and knots; she'd made a number of intricate wall hangings and plant hangers from rope over the years: the macramé craze.

Walking away from the river, she saw few people. The professional pyrotechnics of the holiday were over and done with. All she heard now were the occasional explosions of cherry bombs in nearby Spanish Harlem. Tomorrow, the last day of the long weekend, the last day of this wretched vacation, there would be newspaper articles about the accidental mutilations of reckless boys by reckless boys, about the deliberate mutilations of cats. She was glad she wouldn't have to read any of it.

It was already tomorrow—the early hours of Monday—when she reached our building. She let herself in with the key she'd had since always, and boarded the waiting elevator. Without thinking—a muscle memory—she pressed the button to our floor. It was only when the doors opened and she heard music seeping out from under our apartment door—Buffy Sainte-Marie, all that vibrato, and the volume much too loud considering the hour—that she realized she'd gone up when she'd meant to go down.

For a brief moment she stood in the elevator, annoyed and uncertain. When the doors started to close, though, instead of letting them, instead of pressing B as she should have done in the first place, she extended her hand, and the doors reopened.

She stepped into the hallway and stood on the welcome mat, a little rag rug that had lain before the door for three generations, the fibers frayed, the colors rubbed away. She was unsure what to do next. Then she made a decision: she reached into her purse, retrieved her keys again, and let herself in. Leaving the door ajar, she stood inside the foyer, just stood there, as if she had no idea how she'd come to be where she was.

Vee and Delph, on the other hand, reacted as if they'd been expecting her. They were both awake despite the hour, and in the kitchen, Vee in a ruby-red Gap T-shirt and cutoffs, Delph in a calico granny dress, both in bare feet.

"Hey," Vee said. "There you are."

Delph was leaning against the fridge, eating a peanut-butter-on-pumpernickel sandwich. "Want some?" she said, advancing toward Lady, holding the sandwich out. "I'm eating it, but I'm not even hungry."

"No thanks, and don't get peanut butter in my hair."

That this is what came out of her mouth surprised Lady as much as any of the other surprising things she'd done that weekend. Concern for her hair, her terrible wiry hair. Although the truth was that Lady had made a bit of an effort with her hair that night. She was hoping to look halfway decent when she was discovered. There'd be the broken neck, the Basenji-blue tongue, the bulging eyeballs, maybe (she was sorry to say) a horrid mess on the floor beneath her, but at least she'd be wearing a nice dress and her hair would look attended to, restrained with one of her leather barrettes, her turquoise earrings gently undulating back and forth.

By way of apology she said to Delph, "That is one very brown sandwich."

Delph smiled. "It's really dry, too." She took another bite as she closed the front door with her ass.

Lady dropped her purse on the hall chair. She stepped into the living room. "Is that my album you're playing?" she asked.

"You're the one who left it behind," Vee said. "That old saw about possession being nine-tenths of the law? It turns out to be true."

"I don't want it back," Lady said. "That's not what I'm saying. I'm happy you like it. Mi shit es su shit." She looked around. "Where's Eddie?"

"Exhausted. Asleep."

"I'm going to make you a sandwich of your own," Delph said. "With jelly. I think you've lost weight. You look terrible."

"Especially the way she has her hair pulled back," Vee said. "So tight. She looks like Olive Oyl."

"Well, she's not that skinny," Delph said.

We ate in the living room, Delph transporting two sandwiches, two glasses, and a bottle of Southern Comfort, managing everything at once, though this meant she had to carry her sandwich in her teeth, wedge the bottle under her armpit.

"Since when Southern Comfort?" Lady said.

Vee shrugged. "We're listening to Buffy and drinking like Janis." And when we were situated, the sandwich-eaters on the couch, Vee on the floor, she said, "Delph's right, Lady. You do look like crap."

"I got it. I didn't think the Olive Oyl comparison was a compliment."

"Look at your eyes. It's like you've been crying."

"When have you known me to cry?"

"Well, you don't cook, so I know you weren't peeling onions."

"I cook," Lady said.

"Spaghetti's not cooking."

"I cook things requiring peeled onions all the time."

"So you were peeling onions?"

"No." The record had ended. We listened to the sound of the needle lifting, returning to the first track, same side. "They're painting the halls outside my apartment," Lady said when the music began again, the song about the sexy woman who was pursued by every man in town. The three of us used to sing it together in Lady's room, wiggling our hips, using roll-on deodorant bottles as microphones. "What's hoochy koochy mean?" Delph would ask. "What's oversexed?"

"Really?" Vee said. "The slumlord's painting the halls?"

"The fumes are killing me. My eyes keep watering."

"So stay the night here," Vee said.

"Maybe I will."

"Stay two nights. Stay forever. Come home. Nobody understands why you don't."

Lady looked down the hall to the master bedroom's ever-
shut door. We've long called that bedroom the Dead and Dying
Room. Our grandmother Karin died in it after many years suffering with an unnamed illness we assume was cancer—cancer
back in the day when no one said the word out loud. And a
couple of weeks after she died there, our grandfather Richard
died there too—although technically speaking he didn't die *in*
there, but *from* there: he'd opened the window, hoisted himself
up on the sill, wobbled for a moment, then propelled himself
forward. Our mother had been in her bedroom across the hall
doing math homework when she heard the screams from neighbors as his body passed each floor.

Like her father, our mother hadn't literally died inside the
Dead and Dying Room, but it had been her bedroom when she
drowned herself across the street.

"I don't know," Lady said. "Sometimes I do think about
moving back. But it's a little haunted house-ish here."

Delph nodded. "Tell me about it," she said.

As botched as Lady's attempt ended up, that's how promising
it had seemed at roughly four in the morning when she left her
old bed where she'd been lying in her dress. She stepped into her
flip-flops, patted her hair back in place, and headed to the front
door. She stopped before she opened it, took a moment to look
into the living room, where her half-eaten peanut butter sandwich remained on the coffee table, where the empty bottle of
Southern Comfort lay on its side on the carpet. She could hear
Vee and Eddie and Delph snuffle and snort in their sleep. She

gazed out the window and saw the park and the Hudson and, when she looked uptown, the George Washington Bridge, its necklace lights ablaze for the holiday after two years of energy-saving darkness

But once she was downstairs in the laundry room, she didn't dawdle. She headed straight to the rusted shelving units where tenants kept cardboard boxes of detergent with their apart- · ment numbers marked on the sides and where the super kept old wooden soda boxes filled with hammers and nails, electrical cords and rags, things like that. A few Phillips-head screwdrivers. Lady recognized them now.

The box that interested her was the one containing a few old clotheslines. She chose a waxy white rope that seemed cleaner and stronger and less likely to burn her fingers or abrade her neck than the ones of brown hemp. She was also drawn to the obsessive tidiness with which it, of all the clotheslines, had been stored. It had been curled around and around itself until it lay in a flattened circle, a pretty coiling pattern like a sisal placemat.

Her head began singing. *A pretty coil is like a melody.* She questioned the lyric. Was *melody* right? Or was it *memory*? *A pretty girl is like a memory?* She was feeling a memory coming at her now, she was recalling Joe Hopper during their happier years, which had lasted from her freshman year of college right up to her weak-kneed decision to marry him spring semester of her junior year. She was remembering the way he used to cheese down the docking line of the small sailboats they'd sometimes rent on City Island. Cheese down. It meant to coil the tail of the line to give a neat appearance. He'd taught her the phrase, couldn't believe she knew so little about sailing. "New Yorkers think they're so sophisticated," he'd said, "but the truth is, you're all rubes in your own way."

She thought he hadn't minded that she was an unsophisticated New Yorker. She knew he liked educating her. "You're probably wondering why I'm going to all this trouble," he said the first time he wound the line so it lay on the sunny pier like a hairy snake nuzzling its own tail.

She hadn't been wondering. She'd been gazing out at the bleached horizon, trying to distinguish the migrating strips of white that were clouds from the subdued circle of white that was the sun from the broad canvas of white that was the sky. But she listened as he explained. She knew that was her job. She didn't mind it. She liked learning new things.

"It's a seaman's tradition," he'd said of the whorled rope. "A gesture of courtesy for the next sailor."

He said this as if he'd come from a long line of seamen rather than a long line of life insurance agents. He said it as if taking out an eight-foot dinghy once or twice a summer made him John Paul Jones or Popeye. When he'd been fifteen, his parents had made him transfer from his local public school to an all-male prep school in New England, the kind with mandatory chapel and a dress code involving navy blue blazers and rep ties and an impressive record of sending its students on to the Ivies. This was where he'd learned to sail. But, as he later told Lady, he'd also found himself having sex with his roommate, which had freaked him out, and he returned the next year to the coed high school in his hometown in Connecticut, a comfortable suburb on the outskirts of a moribund mill city.

This had been the shameful secret he'd told her that night, the secret that had been so hard for him to utter that he'd bitten through his lip trying to get it out. The sex with his roommate. She and Joe had been getting high on the roof of Lehman Hall on the small Barnard campus when he'd told her. He'd taken a hit off the joint, inhaled, exhaled, posed. Then he'd come out

with it. He'd never told anyone else about it, he said. He teared
up a little as he told her, not only because he was ashamed, but
because he was relieved. And as he confessed, his front teeth tore
into his lip and the blood dribbled into his lip beard, turning a
few strands a deep, sticky mahogany. She blamed those mingy
tears—the tears of saline, the tears of hemoglobin—for her accepting his proposal that night.

He had draped his arm over her shoulders. He had begged
her to keep his secret. "Promise me you won't tell anyone," he
said.

"Of course not," she said. "Who would I tell?"

He cut her a look. They both knew perfectly well who'd she
tell.

"My sisters wouldn't care. Don't lots of boys experiment that
way?"

"I wasn't experimenting," he muttered. "I was doing what I
had to do." He looked grim and resolute, as if recalling a march
into battle. "It wasn't homo sex," he said. "It was prison sex."

Lady took the white clothesline to the long table where tenants folded warm clothes fresh out of the dryers. Sitting on the
metal folding chair that she planned to stand on in a few minutes, she began to coil the rope, this time not a flat coil but a
three-dimensional coil, a cobra-rising-from-a-basket coil, and
not merely a pretty coil, but a coil with a purpose, a function, a
goal.

When she was done, she looked at her creation and was
pleased. At the same time she couldn't squelch the thought: no
noose is good news.

Our father, the aforementioned Natan Frankl, was born in
Munich to a family of scholars. Like the rest of them, he was
an excessively educated man, fluent in numerous languages. He

loved language the way other little boys love dogs or yo-yos. He liked to play with language, he liked to make it do amusing tricks. English, he told Lady, was the best language to play with. Next came French. Italian was good, too, especially for poetry, since all the words rhymed. The worst was his native German. In fact, he told Lady, he could no longer stand the sound of it. He blanched even when he heard someone say gesundheit.

Our point is this: we know no one likes the puns and word-play. We're sorry about them. But we can't help it. They're Natan Frankl's fault.

He'd been a chemist too, our father. That's how he'd known the Alters. But while our mother's family left Germany early, our father's remained until there was no getting out. He'd been a scientist unable to interpret the data all around him—there was a lot of that going around—and he ended up in one of the camps. We don't even know which one. That's how little any of this was discussed.

We do know that after liberation he was moved to a displaced persons center, and that when he subsequently managed to get to America—not easy; America didn't want any of the displaced persons—he looked up his old friend Richard Alter, i.e., our grandfather. But, given that our grandfather had already killed himself—that window in the Dead and Dying Room—he met only our mother.

That's their meet-cute story.

In New York the only work he could find was among the other Jews on Seventh Avenue. He sold clothing fasteners to the trade: buttons and snaps, hooks and eyes, frogs and kilt pins. He used to bring discontinued samples home for Lady to play with. She turned them into little families. Brass pea coat buttons embossed with anchors were the fathers. Silk-covered buttons were the mothers. The tiny white buttons you find on collars were the babies, unnecessary and largely decorative, but cute.

He'd been an observant Jew before the camps; he was a cynical atheist after. On Saturday mornings he took Lady and Vee to the Central Park Zoo. Vee doesn't remember this at all—she was still in her carriage—but Lady does, though vaguely. Lady is Vee and Delph's sole conduit to our paterfamilias. She's the one who remembers what he looked like: fair and blue-eyed and nothing like us. She's the keeper of his puns. She used to do an impression of his impression of the Central Park polar bear, our father and the bear lolling their big heads this way and that. "It's as if he's swaying to secret bear music," our father would say. "He can bear-ly restrain himself." She told us how hard the two of them laughed at that. Bear-ly restrain himself. They'd thought it was the funniest thing.

In one of her dresser drawers—the same one in which she keeps the rubbery blue screwdriver—she has an old business card of his, soft and cottony from handling, and at the bottom, beneath his useless contact information, it says:

The fastener invented after the button

was a snap

So when Lady says our father gave her plenty a closure, but never any closure, she can't be scorned. When Vee says the reason Natan Frankl left us may have been his palindromic first name ("Coming or going, it was all the same to him") or maybe his German surname ("He probably left to find the missing *e*") or that maybe the reason had nothing to do with his name at all, that maybe the reason he left was all those months he spent in that relocation camp before coming to New

York ("Looks like relocating became his thing") she must not be judged harshly.

And when each of us—Vee upon her marriage, and Lady after her separation, and Delph as soon as she came of age—ditched his surname to go by our matronymic, and Delph repeatedly described the name change as no big deal, just a slight Alter-ation, you can't punish her for being punnish. You can't roll your eyes when we're speaking Frankly. It's all that the man who left us left us. In no other way did he provide for us or, apparently, care about us. In fact, you might say that Frankl, our dad, didn't give a damn.

All right, all right; we'll stop. That's our entire repertoire anyway. We have nothing more to say about him, no idea where he went. A business trip, our mother told Lady, the others too young to ask, but after a while, because even kids know that business trips end and the businessman comes home, often with presents, our mother had to admit the unsatisfying truth, or at least what she maintained was the truth: she hadn't a clue where he'd gone. One day he never came home from work, and the next day, the same thing happened, then etcetera, etcetera, until she stopped expecting him. She called the cops—a good citizen, she did that much, or so she said—and they nosed around a bit and reported that nothing untoward had befallen him, that wherever he was, it was where he, a grown man, wished to be, and it was no longer their, or, we supposed, our, business.

Even so, over the years Lady continued to press. Soon Vee and Delph joined in. Then our mother would offer up possibilities. Maybe he sailed back to Germany. Maybe he was still living in New York, but with a different wife, tidier daughters who didn't have to be nagged to make their beds. He might be dead, you never knew, the cops could have been wrong. It's not like cops weren't wrong all the time. Or he could be alive somewhere and—again, who knew?—he might decide to come home someday. When we least expected it, he might walk right back through that door.

"Which would you prefer?" she asked, as if his fate could be determined by popular vote.

We won't deny that we grew up father-hungry. But over the years we've come out the other side. No one has had more therapy than the three of us, that ineffectual if gratifying institution—me! for fifty whole minutes let's talk about me!—but really, we didn't need therapy when it came to our father. At a certain point when we were still children, each of us cycled through the kiddie version of the five stages of grief, namely, denial, anger, bargaining, depression, and crazy-ass conspiracy theories.

Leaving his office one evening, he'd fallen down the stairs and now had amnesia!

Because he spoke German, he'd been recruited as a spy for the CIA and was now skulking heroically behind the Berlin Wall!

Suffering from some terrible and highly contagious disease, he'd had no choice but to remove himself from our presence. Now he rented a room in the apartment across the side street that both our mother's and Lady's bedroom windows faced. Every night, through powerful infrared binoculars, he watched over us all as we slept, our mother in her bed and the three of us sardined in Lady's.

But of all our theories, our favorite, or at least the one we kept coming back to, was that our mother had killed him. Vee had proposed this possibility one night with a wicked smile, and we all liked it. We enjoyed speculating how our mother, that little woman, that lonely and abandoned waif, would have ac-

complished it, and what she'd have done with the body. We eyed
the hallway incinerator with suspicion and a newfound respect.

Let us be clear. Our mother did not murder our father. Even
as we entertained the notion, we knew we were doing just that:
entertaining ourselves. There was something cathartic in imagining our father dead and our mother a powerful killer. It was far
more satisfying than the fantasy of him watching us sleep, which,
to be honest, had begun to feel creepy and sometimes gave Delph
bad dreams. But the idea of a woman like our mother—another
short, bosomy, and luckless ugly gosling—dragging a man to the
incinerator late one night was rather invigorating. Therapeutic,
one might say.

One final thing about Natan Frankl, and then we won't mention him again. It really doesn't matter whether he went back
to Germany or found himself a second, superior family or was
chopped into his component parts and fed to the incinerator. All
that's relevant now is that he was years older than our mother,
closer to her father's age than her own, and if he didn't die back
then, he's surely dead now.

So no matter which version of the Father Stories you or we
like best, the ending's the same. We may not know the details,
but we promise he won't be showing up at any point in our story.
We urge you to forget all about him. We assure you, as we were
assured, it's all for the best.

So back to the basement, back to no noose is good news. Back
to Lady standing on that folding chair, Lady smiling a self-
consciously wry smile as if she were onstage and wished to signal
her state of mind to the audience. She imagined that audience to
consist of both our parents. She saw them smiling back at her,
but warmly, encouraging her. She'd often thought about—had
dreams about—how willingly and quietly each had left her. Now

she found herself thinking about how willingly and quietly she was leaving Vee and Delph. Although the difference was, Vee and Delph didn't need her. Vee had Eddie. Delph had Vee and Eddie.

Perhaps each of our parents had thought the same thing. The girls don't need me. They have each other. Or perhaps—a new thought was coming to Lady—they hadn't meant to leave us at all. Perhaps they'd meant for us to follow them. As Lady was doing now. Perhaps she hadn't been abandoned after all; she'd just gotten lost for a while.

DNA as a trail of bread crumbs. Suicide as salvation. She felt awash with sorrow for herself, and it was this self-pity, that most delicious of emotions, that made the tears come.

To chase away these emotions, she distracted herself by reviewing her reasons again. She was alone. She was lonely. This was her daily dilemma: she wanted no one in her life; she couldn't bear to live life alone. Also, she was tangled up with a dentist who seemed not to like her, and she was engaging in behavior that would cause the dentist's wife pain—Patty, the woman's name was Patty—were she to find out about it. To punish herself for hurting Patty—that was reason enough to do what she was about to do.

Not to mention the fact that she'd bloodied a Holocaust survivor's nose with a screwdriver.

And then there was the rest of it. She was fundamentally incapable of taking care of herself or even, it seemed, of answering a phone or crossing a busy intersection or buying a simple hand tool. Her apartment had roaches and a switch plate as suicidal as she was. Also, it was definitely possible that she was an alcoholic, which would mean she should give up drinking, and why would she want to live like that?

But though the reasons were endless, the reasons were also

meaningless. She was back to that again. There was something else driving her, something unsayable, just a feeling, just an urge, but a something that was so very strong. It was a something that Joe and the dentist and the dentist's wife and the hardware store owner hadn't a thing to do with.

She regretted this. She wished it were grief or guilt propelling her. She wished she were about to commit an act of heartfelt atonement. But that wasn't what she was doing, not really. It was something else.

We've all struggled with this: how to explain the desire to do something most people find pathological at best, selfish at worst, incomprehensible always. We sometimes describe it as a chit we were each handed at birth, a card to get out of jail free, if one thinks of her life as jail.

Or we talk about the horizontal light, which is how we refer to the light that sometimes replaces sunlight, the light we see for a brief moment virtually every day, the light that isn't golden, but is as silver as the nacre inside a seashell, and comes not down from the heavens but from beyond the skyline, oozing and seeping until it lies over the day like an opalescent blanket inviting us to slide beneath it. There's no telling when we'll see the horizontal light; it appears at a different time every day, and most days we overlook it—it tends to come and go in an instant—and on other days we see it and it lingers, but we manage to ignore it, or at least, after a while, to look away from it.

But then there are the days we can't look away. "Man, the horizontal light was really strong today," one of us will say, and the other two will say, "But you resisted," and the first one will say, "Yeah, well, today I resisted. Who knows about tomorrow?" and we all say, "Who ever knows about tomorrow?" and we refresh our drinks.

Lady kicked off her flip-flops, stood on the chair. She looped one end of the rope around a ceiling pipe the way you'd loop an identification tag around your bag's handle before a trip. She looped the other end around her neck. Her legs were shaking, but she was doing well. True, she was still crying, but she wasn't sobbing; the only reason she knew she was crying was by the feel of her tears, silky yet itchy. No noose is good noose would be her last pun, and this would be her final pleasurable experience: the warmth of big fat tears sliding down her cheeks, tippling off her chin.

Her feet were bare and sweating. She knew that by now they must be stuck to the chair's metal seat and that it would require some effort to break the suction when she stepped forward. She would have to add this to her calculation when she made her move.

This must be the way an Olympic diver felt. Observing the conditions of board, of pool, of body. Perfectly poised, needing only to achieve the perfect mindset, the Zen focus, the courage of one's convictions. And then, the ability to say one-two-three-now.

She stood for what seemed like hours, sometimes getting to the one, sometimes getting to the two, but never getting to the three, never getting to the now. All she was getting was dizzy, so dizzy she began to worry she'd die of something else, something heart-related—a stroke or an aneurism. She didn't want to die like that. She wanted her place on the chart.

It was that thought—fierce pride, family loyalty—that got her to the three, to the now, that got her to inch her feet off the chair, first just her right foot, then the left. When her toes felt nothing but air beneath them, her heel kicked the chair away.

This was when she remembered Beef.

She'd meant to return the framed photograph of the dog to the dentist's office. She'd forgotten entirely. It was still in her purse, and her purse was upstairs in our foyer.

In the fascinating slowing of time that occurred as the chair skittered away, right before her second heel felt nothing beneath it, she realized she needed to stop what she was doing. She needed to deal with that photo, put it back on the shelf. Posthumous humiliation was not what she was after. The dentist going through life citing the purloined photo as incontrovertible proof that she'd died for want of him—this was not her goal.

She reached out, trying to grab hold of something to prevent her body from dropping any farther, but there was nothing to grab, no solid surface to stand on. There was nothing for her to do, no way out, no means of saving herself. She was going to die. And in that briefest, yet longest moment of her life, before she began to flail and kick, she understood she'd been wrong, that this wasn't her time after all, but it was a realization that made no difference whatsoever. She dropped completely, the rope taut and intransigent.

She hadn't counted on the building management's years of neglect. She hadn't realized that the pipe to which she tied the rope was hardly a pipe, was pretty much nothing but rust in the shape of a pipe. It snapped in two as soon as it felt her full weight. She fell hard, not to her death but to the concrete floor, where she landed awkwardly, heard the snap of a bone in her left calf, screamed from the shock and the physical pain. At the same time a downpour of cold water fell onto her from the broken ends of the so-called pipe, a continuous brutal waterfall.

To get to the elevator she had to drag herself through what was quickly becoming a shallow but numbingly icy lake populated not with fish but with clumps of multicolored dryer lint and sodden stray socks. In the elevator she had to reach up, grab the rail, and exert all of what little upper arm strength she possessed to pull herself to one foot and push the button to our floor.

When Delph, half asleep, responded to the pounding on the door, she found Lady prone on the old welcome mat, drenched, shivering, writhing, large flakes of rust in her sopping hair and a noose encircling her neck, its white tail running along the floor like some sort of soggy leash. Delph felt herself begin to shake. She was as unnerved as she'd ever been, though less unnerved than she would be in a few hours, five in the morning, when she took a taxi to Riverdale and, consulting the scrap of paper on which Lady had written an address and alarm code, broke into a dentist's office to return a photograph of a dog. Delph trembled uncontrollably during the decommissioning of her sister's crime, certain the dentist, wanting an early start to the day following his first-ever vacation, would suddenly show up. But he hadn't, and she'd gotten away with it. She got back into the waiting cab, directed the driver to St. Luke's Hospital.

"I did it," she told Lady, who lay on a gurney in a hallway while waiting for a room to free up. Vee and Eddie sat on the floor by the gurney's wheels, Vee's head on Eddie's shoulder, the two of them snoozing.

Woozy from painkillers, her neck chafed red, her leg in a cast, Lady looked up at Delph. She managed despite everything to speak.

"Someday this will be funny," she said.

CHAPTER 5

1878

It's in Frau Geist's dance class where the boy who will become our great-grandfather first places his hand on the waist of the girl who'll become our great grandmother. Naturally, they're paired: nine-year-old Lenz Alter is the smallest boy in the class, seven-year-old Iris Emanuel is the smallest girl. Even so, when they converse, he has to look up. And conversing is mandatory. Conversing while dancing—preferably in French—is as important as knowing the steps. It's part of doing it well.

Also, the boy must begin the conversation. Lenz has his opening line at the ready. "Bonjour," he says. "I hate this stupid dance."

The girls are encouraged to ask the boys questions. "Quelle danse do you prefer?" Iris asks.

"I hate them all."

"Even the polka?"

"Maybe not the polka."

"All the boys like the polka. And the mazurka."

"En français," Frau Geist sings out.

"It's all boring," Lenz says. He turns her, turns her again. "Ennui," he says.

"I pretend we're Earth," Iris says. "I'm the western hemisphere, and you're the east. We revolve in a circle as we rotate around the room."

Lenz glances to the center of the circle. "That makes Frau Geist the sun," he says. This is very funny if you've ever seen Frau Geist, and they snicker through a few more turns.

Before the dance ends, Lenz has made two requests: one, that the next time they're partnered, he get to be the western hemisphere, and two, that Iris marry him. All the other boys are doing it—proposing—although what one does after one becomes engaged, he's not entirely sure.

Iris seems not to know this game at all. "I'm too young," she says, frowning, perplexed.

He rolls his eyes, though he, too, is perplexed. Improvising, he says, "Not now, Later."

"When?"

He does some calculations. "Eighteen eighty-six," he says. He'll be seventeen, done with gymnasia.

"But what about university?"

"I'm not going. I'm going into my father's business."

She says, "I meant moi. What if I want to go?"

None too gently, he apprises her of the fact that girls can't go to university. She shakes her head. She knows all that, she says, but her father says the rules will change by the time she's sixteen, and if they don't, her father says, well, then, by God, the two of them will change them.

"All right," Lenz says. "We won't get married until after you finish university."

"Ça va," she says.

The music stops. They're back to the spot on the floor where they began. He bows. She curtsies. Frau Geist applauds. Lenz leans over to the couple nearest them, the second shortest boy, the second shortest girl. "Iris and I are engaged," he confides.

"Good show," says the boy.

When Iris returns home, she announces her betrothal at dinner. "That's it," her father says. "No more dancing for you."

1879–1881

From the essay "A Word about Our Jews" by Heinrich von Treitschke, professor, historian, deputy to the Reichstag, and archconservative:

> Year after year, out of the inexhaustible Polish cradle there streams over our eastern border a host of hustling, pants peddling youths, whose children and children's children will someday command Germany's stock exchanges and newspapers. . . . What we have to demand of our Israelite fellow citizens is simple: they should become Germans. They should feel themselves, modestly and properly, German.

From the pamphlet "Another Word about Our Jews" by Theodor Mommsen, professor, classical scholar, Nobel laureate, and ultraliberal:

> Remaining outside the boundaries of Christendom and at the same time belonging to the German nation is possible, but difficult and risky. . . . He whose conscience does not permit him to renounce his Judaism and accept Christianity will act accordingly, but he should be prepared to bear the consequences.

. . . The admission to a large nation has its price. It is the Jews'
duty to do away with their particularities. . . . They must make
up their minds and tear down all barriers between themselves
and their German compatriots.

From the mind of Lenz Alter, age twelve: Where's the problem? Everyone's taking sides, von Trietschke versus Mommsen,
but it seems to Lenz the two men are in agreement. Yes, it's
true that von Trietschke hates the Jews, while Mommsen only
suspects them, but they both advocate the same solution: hatred
and/or suspicion will vanish if the Jews become truly, completely
German. What's there to debate, then? Where's the disagree-
ment? Where's the conflict?

And given that both of these men, respected and learned
men, German patriots, agree that what the Jew must do to
become truly German is simply give up Judaism—well, Lenz
doesn't understand why it hasn't already been done. En masse, as
a celebration, a festival. Has a less onerous task ever been asked
of a people? It's not as if he or his father or his uncles or any of
the Jews he knows use their Judaism for anything.

Heinrich and Lenz sit at the polished walnut table in the
dining room, draperies drawn, observing their usual prandial
silence. The new housekeeper sashays in, seventeen if a day, her
soup tureen held low by her hip as if she's a milkmaid coming
in from the cow barn. Heinrich observes the excessively long
and somewhat perilous arc of her ladle as it carries the hot broth
from tureen to bowl. He's wondering if he should correct her
form when Lenz unexpectedly speaks.

"I have a question of philosophy and conduct," he says.

"Do you?" says Heinrich.

"Oh, my," says the housekeeper.

"I've been wondering, given the general consensus that two of my three fathers cannot happily coexist, which of those two should I please: Chancellor Bismarck or God?"

"I thought Bismarck *was* God," the housekeeper says. Heinrich, who likes his housekeepers quiet and reverent especially vis-à-vis Bismarck, decides he will fire this one later that evening. As it turns out, though, after dinner he'll become distracted rereading his Mommsen and will forget all about her. Then one thing will lead to another, and within a year he and the housekeeper will be married, and Lenz will have a stepmother a mere five years older than himself, which will require extensive revision to the fantasies he'd been enjoying since she arrived.

"It's not a matter of either/or," Heinrich says. "In this house we stick to our own flag. You're a Prussian Jew who does what I say. And thus do your fathers coexist."

It's not until the next evening that Heinrich suddenly puts down his knife and fork and says, as if no time has passed since Lenz brought it up, "I'll say only this and I'll say it only once. Convert, and you no longer have this father." He picks up the utensils again, attacks his dinner, the only violence life allows him.

The man who practices nothing of his faith clings to it nonetheless. It makes no sense to Lenz; it never will. For now, though, he backs down. "I didn't say I was going to convert," he mutters. What he wants to say, but can't, not yet, is that if he converts, yes, he may lose Heinrich. And of course this Yahweh he's heard so much about but has never really been introduced to—he would also go by the boards. But Lenz wouldn't be completely orphaned. He'd still have the best of the lot.

Sometimes we picture it carved into the bark of a tree: Otto von B. + Lenz A. = true luv 4-ever.

1890

From the article "Appropriate Dress for Dancing the New Knickerbocker" by Alan Dodsworth, Dancemaster:

> Many ladies are wearing the instep skirt for the evening dance, while others still cling to the long sinewy train. But those who wear the train for round dancing are advised to hold it up . . . for to drag a train around the ballroom endangers the life of the gown, not to mention the lives of the other dancers.

Death by ball gown. Iris Emanuel wants no part of it. Anyway, you just have to look at her to know she's an instep skirt kind of girl. The abbreviated hemline, the show of her boot. It makes her look a little taller, a little bit slimmer. Not that she cares about that sort of thing. What she cares about is that the short skirts allow her to peek at her feet while she's trying to master a new step at Frau Geist's. She also enjoys the new fashion's ability to offend the type of woman who clings to the train—Frau Geist, for instance.

"Charmingly! Delicately!" Frau Geist, elderly now and fatter than ever, still wears her garish yellows. She bangs the floor with a cane. "Daintily, daintily! And here comes the glide!"

"And here comes the groom," whispers Iris's dance partner, her sister Lily.

Iris looks to the door. There stands Lenz Alter in his Prussian blue reservist uniform, chest out, shoulders squared, head held high. Iris lets go of Lily's waist so she can wave to him. She hasn't seen him since he left for university three years before. After completing gymnasium, he'd gone to work in the dye factory, just as he'd told her when they were children, where he'd implemented some sort of clever innovation that caused some sort of unmitigated disaster that resulted in the loss of a full day's production of synthetic crystal violet. His father had fired him and sent him to Berlin, which was where he'd wanted to go in the first place. There he studied chemistry, but only for a single semester. Next he'd gone to Heidelberg, where he lasted a mere summer. Now he's finally making something of a go of it at the Technical College of Charlottenburg.

Even before he left Breslau, Iris had run into him only rarely. At parties or concerts they flirted in the parlors of mutual acquaintances or in the lobbies of theaters, leaning against walls softened with velvet damask. They discussed politics and the sciences. He liked to talk Goethe—she had outgrown Goethe long before—but she'd been happy to listen, to ask the occasional question. Eventually, though, he would bow (exaggeratedly, facetiously), kiss her hand, and return to whomever he'd come with, a different girl every time, but always a girl prettier than Iris and simmering with jealousy in a corner.

He's here on his own now, and only Lily's simmering. Lily holds on to Iris firmly, twirling her overenthusiastically. Focusing on keeping her balance prevents Iris from breaking away and heading to Lenz at once. When the music stops, Lily takes Iris's arm and escorts her to him, an attempt to control her sister's pace. But there's only so much Lily can do. "Unteroffizier Alter," Lily says, nodding at him, setting an example, but Iris cries, "Lenz!" and that's it for propriety and restraint.

He beams at her. He kisses her cheeks. He's taller than she remembers, though he remains a short man. Still, she's now the one who raises her chin to meet his eyes, which are deep brown with golden spokes, pretty enough to help her overlook his less felicitous features: the light brown hair already thinning and receding, but what's left of it so densely curly it grows upward like a shrub; the bridge of the nose so broad, so prominent, so *Jewish*, that his pince-nez seem a size too small, ready any second to lose their grip and spring into the air.

She doesn't mind his plain looks, though. She's charmed by his enthusiasm, by how glad he is to see her. "This is the last place I thought I'd run into you," he says. "I thought you were banned from dancing years ago. Just like a Catholic on Good Friday."

"It wasn't dancing our father minded," Lily says. "He just didn't like her coming home talking of marriage at the age of six."

"I was seven," Iris says before turning to Lenz. "*You* didn't expect to see *me* here?" she says. "Imagine how I feel. I thought you were at Charlottenburg."

Yes, he says, turning from Lily, focusing on Iris. Yes, his studies. He's finding Charlottenburg quite stimulating, both intellectually and socially. Of course his earlier work at Heidelberg with Bunsen was even more exhilarating. Thrilling to work with the old man himself. And now he's taken a year off from school to complete his military service. The same reserve unit Bismarck once belonged to, as a matter of fact. It's been a wonderful experience, the reserves. Travel, opera, the theater. An amazing country, Germany. No other like it.

"Quelle chance," Lily says, "that we all happened to be born in it."

He's in Breslau for a few weeks now, he says. He thought he'd come to Geist's, pick up the latest steps, bring them back to Berlin.

"Really?" Iris says. "You think this is where all the new dances originate?" He smiles. She blushes. "Oh. You're teasing."

"Well, in any event," he says, "here we both are again."

"Quelle coincidence," Lily says. She turns away, takes a seat along the wall, folds her arms across her chest, does the unthinkable because she's not really thinking: she crosses her legs.

"Don't mind her," Iris says. "She was hoping to learn the New Knickerbocker, but she knows I'd rather dance with you."

"Are you sure?" he says. "I don't even know the old Knickerbocker."

This turns out to be untrue.

Lenz Alter, age twenty-one, puts his hand on the waist of nineteen-year-old Iris Emanuel. For the rest of the evening they revolve and rotate around the aged and bloated sun that is Frau Geist, occasionally glimpsing the cold distant planet that is Lily, her petulance increasing their pleasure by making them feel as if they're misbehaving.

Older now, Lenz has learned patience. This time he waits a week to propose.

Tears and torment! She's in love with him, she tells Lily. He's so charming, so funny. They have so much in common. Two nearsighted, secular and, of course, intellectual Jews from Breslau with a passion for the sciences and a sum total of four left feet. But the timing's all wrong.

"Bien sûr," says Lily. "You've known him for only seven days."

"I've known him all my life."

"You've glimpsed him on the street all your life. Every now and then you've spoken to him for ten minutes or so, at which point he returned to a girl he preferred. But you don't know him at all. And now he's come back, showing off about Bunsen. If he's so intimate with Bunsen, why did he leave Heidelberg? Because he's not as smart as he'd have you believe. Also, did you notice he's already losing his hair? Take my advice. A girl like you should marry a brilliant man with a full head of hair."

She does turn him down, but not because of anything Lily has said. "You've still got another year before you earn your doctorate," she says as they walk along the river. "You shouldn't marry until you have it in hand. And certainly I'm not going to marry anyone until I have mine. I couldn't live with myself."

"Given that women can't attend university at all," he says, "am I to assume this is your polite way of saying you won't marry me unless hell freezes over?" As if by way of illustration, the Oder itself is concealed under a thick layer of scarred ice.

She shakes her head. She declares herself an optimist and a reformer. "The hell that's the current university system is going to freeze and crack any day now. You'll see." He looks skeptical. She frowns. "Aren't you still liberal on this matter?"

"I never really was," he says, "but I *am* still German, and as such I'm sufficiently confident in my own worth to have no fear of educated women." Without a moment's hesitation he stops walking and recites, "Ladies heed this pithy sermon / Ne'er will you best a manly German," and she asks if he's just made that up on the spot, and he admits that indeed he has, right that moment off the top of his head, that it's a little hobby of his, the extemporaneous heroic couplet, and she laughs and has to bite the inside of her cheek until the urge to throw herself at him, to press herself against him, to insist he take her somewhere for immediate, immoral, impassioned gratification, subsides.

She's embarrassed to admit it, but the truth is that even when it comes to sex and the amount of time she spends thinking about it, wanting it, needing it, she's more like a boy than a girl.

The Gay Nineties

A year later Lenz Alter completes his dissertation. Of it he writes to a friend, "It was a pitiful effort, but they'd had enough of me by then, so we all sat around a large table drinking champagne and pretending I'd done a superb job."

He's awarded the PhD in chemistry. It's May 1891. He's twenty-two.

Iris, meanwhile, mopishly attends, and two years later disgustedly accepts her degree from the local teachers' seminary. It's May 1894; she's twenty-three.

Friends stop her in the streets. "Have you heard the latest about your Doktor Alter?" they say. She says she hasn't and doesn't care to. They tell her anyway.

He's in Berlin, unable to find a university position: a shame. He's back in Breslau, unemployed after being fired again from his father's dye factory: an incompetent. Now back in Berlin, where he's been turned away from officer training school: a Jew. Now in a mountain sanatorium: a complete nervous wreck.

"You ought to visit him," they say. Even Lily says this. Even Lily pities him.

Iris takes long walks by herself in the cold. She drinks her father's liquor. She picks up an old volume of Goethe. Somehow he has begun speaking to her again, so much so that when she combines these activities—the liquor and Goethe—she sobs a great deal. She has regressed: she's undone anew every time young Werther kills himself. She thinks about becoming an authoress, of committing a few literary murders herself. But she writes nothing, not even a letter to Lenz. She's afraid he may take any word from her as encouragement to propose again. She doesn't want to risk breaking anyone's heart yet again. Not his. Not her own. I'm a stoic, she thinks, and develops a habit of clenching her teeth, which leads to a habit of migraines.

Finally Lily brings home news. Lenz has converted to Christianity and—*quelle coincidence!*—the next thing you know he was hired by the University of Karlsruhe. Oh—and he met someone there. He's engaged.

"Quel soulagement!" Iris says.

She sleeps for a week, then reads *Die Leiden des jungen Werthers* for the fifth or sixth time—an experiment that results, this time, in no tears at all. "Quel soulagement," she says again, this time to her bedroom walls. "I'm finally over romanticism," she tells the wall nearest her dressing table. "From here on, it's nothing but the life of the mind." The life of the mind, clenched teeth, headaches, and grim self-pleasure. She's a modern woman.

A few weeks later—talk of coincidences—Breslau University begins accepting women.

Is there a catch? Of course there's a catch. Women may attend classes only as nonmatriculating auditors. But that's better than nothing, and Iris immediately takes and passes the rigorous admission exam designed for the women alone. She proceeds to audit classes year after year. It's 1896, '97, '98. She's twenty-five, she's twenty-six, she's twenty-seven . . .

It's 1898, and she's twenty-seven and still a virgin . She has a teaching diploma, but no interest in teaching. She has a job as a governess, but doesn't like her young charges. She attends classes at the University of Breslau, but has to sit in the back of the room. "If you could please speak a little less frequently," the professors say. "If you could please defer to the actual students."

In the attic room her employers have barely decorated for her—as is appropriate for a stoic, she writes Lily, she lives like a Spartan—she drinks in bed. She's learning the tricks of watering down their scotch, of concealing their English gin in her morning coffee.

She tries never to utter his name out loud. Sometimes she slips. "What have you heard from our friend Alter?" she asks a mutual acquaintance one spring day. Is he married yet? Does he have children?

"Who, Lenz?" the friend says. "You haven't heard? His engagement ended some time ago."

When getting ready to seduce a man, some women buy new dresses or change their hair. Iris Emanuel converts to Christianity. She was going to have to get around to it eventually anyway. Now she has reason to write Lenz.

He writes back, singing the praises of Jews who commit one hundred percent to Germany and telling her all about his newest fiancée.

"A whirlwind romance," he writes, "which, as you know, is my style. I see what I want. I think, Why should I wait? You'll like her, I'm sure."

Before she can throw herself in the Oder—that, or cut off her hair, don a suit, change her name to Heinz, and try to gain admission to university as a man—she learns that ice-skating in hell has commenced: Breslau has decided to permit women to take the new and even more brutal entrance exam designed for female applicants only. Mere auditors no more, they can pursue degrees. Iris is the first woman to take the exam, the first woman to pass it, the first woman to matriculate into the doctoral program in chemistry. There's an article in the paper about this accomplishment, and with it a photograph: Iris looking down at her feet as if she's at Frau Geist's, while Zindel Emanuel looks straight at the camera and grins. Zindel cuts out the article, frames the photograph. He places it, gray and grainy, on the mantel between Rose and Lily's respective wedding portraits.

"Father and Son," Lily calls it.

Her mother is ten years dead by now, so Iris, like Lenz, is motherless. Also like Lenz, she has more than just a biological father to please. Not Bismarck in her case, and certainly not God. Her other father is, aptly, her *Doktorvater*, the valence theorist Richard Lehrer.

Lehrer is nothing like Bismarck. If Bismarck's the Iron Chancellor, then Lehrer's the Silken Professor. Sweet and smooth. You accede to his will not because he's powerful, but because he makes you think you're exercising your own.

He's a handsome man, too, Richard Lehrer, tall and lean, a Jew who appears so Aryan he hasn't bothered to convert. He wears his fair hair close-cropped and his mustache thick and waxed and curled up at the ends. He has a pink dueling scar from his left earlobe to the place where his mustache stops and his lips part. He's only a year and a half older than she is, yet he's so many years ahead of her in every way. Career, reputation, published books, spouse, babies.

At their first meeting he takes both her hands and says, "Promise me you'll never marry."

She's taken aback. She has, until this moment, assumed that of course she'll marry. First the doctorate, then the prestigious position at Berlin or Charlottenburg or even here under Lehrer. Then, at last: the spouse, the family, the complete life—just like his. Although only one child. She'll have work to do outside the house, after all.

But now, her hands in his, she blushes at her own limited vision, at the conventionality she never realized till now she's succumbed to. Also, the act of his taking her hands, looking into her eyes, making a heartfelt request for a lifetime commitment— it's like a marriage proposal itself.

"I won't," she swears. "I've waited my whole life to come here. I want to be a scientist more than anything else."

She's sincere, and yet he doesn't believe her. "Or," he continues as if she hasn't said a word, "if someday you feel absolutely compelled to marry, then promise me you won't make it worse by marrying a scientist less talented than yourself."

"That's easy to promise," she says. "I would never find such a man interesting."

He smiles. Her hands remain clasped in his. "You and I have an acquaintance in common," he says. "Lenz Alter was briefly my classmate in Berlin."

She feels herself redden again. "Lenz Alter," she says. "Now there was a catastrophe avoided."

Only then does he let her go. He invites her to his home for dinner. She becomes friends with his wife. She isn't jealous of Marthe. She has no plans to seduce Richard Lehrer. All she wants is to be his favorite student, his indispensible lab assistant, his adored colleague, the coauthor of his papers, his occasional drinking companion, and the person he talks to late into the night about valence theory and her own fascination: soluble salts.

And, yes, there's a part of her that wouldn't mind if fate arranged things so that she wound up becoming his second wife—and she's very aware which part of her that is—but how can she ethically wish for that? First, she promised him she wouldn't marry. Second, it's tantamount to wishing Marthe dead, because before she can allow herself to imagine his lips on hers, his hands beneath her honeymoon nightgown, she has to first fantasize Marthe dying. It isn't any good otherwise; she can't enjoy the fantasy if she has to imagine him unfaithful or divorced or never married to Marthe in the first place.

No, if she wants to fantasize about Richard Lehrer—and nightly, it seems she does—she first has to imagine a tragic but efficient illness that ends things for Marthe rapidly and without too much suffering. Only then, after Marthe's tragic but painless passing, can Iris go on and imagine, first, Lehrer's proposal—

"When I asked you never to marry that day, it was only because I knew from the moment I laid eyes on you I wanted you all for myself"—and, next, their year of decorous waiting, and finally their lovely wedding and finally finally—the sex.

In short, she has to lie in bed planning an elaborate funeral and imagining Richard mourning for a full year so that no one, not even any of the characters populating her private fantasies, will fault her for too quickly marrying Marthe's husband. Sometimes getting to the place where they're at last married and embarked on their wedding trip takes so long that she falls asleep before she boards the imaginary train to Italy or Spain. The next morning she wakes up disgusted with herself. What kind of freethinker is she, this woman who's a virgin not only in life but in her sexual fantasies too?

December 1900

In the final month of what is technically the last year of the nineteenth century, but is generally considered the first year of the twentieth century, Iris Emanuel is awarded the PhD in chemistry. She's the first woman to receive the degree from her university. She graduates with honors. There's another article about her in the local paper. In the accompanying photograph, she and Richard Lehrer shake hands.

"Father and Daughter," Lily calls it.

Iris can't help demurring. "Lehrer and I have the same degree now. We work in the same field and on the same matters. We're close in age. I don't think of him as a father. He doesn't think of me as a daughter."

"Of course you don't," Lily says. "And of course he does.".

Her sister Rose has less to say. "Fräulein Doktor?" She shakes her head. "Let me know when I can call you Frau."

1901

The following summer she boards a train that will take her to the electrochemistry conference in Freiberg. She's interested in the lectures, but more so in one of the lecturers. She's tried the usual ways to nab a university position. Now she's resorting to sex.

"How happy I am to hear that," Lily said at the Breslau station.

"I didn't think you were so easily shocked."

"I'm not shocked," Lily said. "But you'd better not let Papa or Rose find out."

Iris smiled. She'd turned thirty-one a few days before. "If they do," she says, "just tell them to think of it as a modern job interview."

On the train Iris writes multiple letters to Richard Lehrer. "It's no secret why I accepted Alter's invitation," she says, "and it's not because I plan to break my promise to you. It's just that I'm so tired of lecturing about the chemical properties of household cleansers to ladies' clubs. Here I am with my doctorate, and I'm still sipping tea and nibbling cakes in their suffocating parlors."

What she wants to add, but can't: "And that's why I'm going to prostitute myself in exchange for a lectureship at Karlsruhe."

Tea cakes and ladies' clubs and her persistent virginity. She wants to be done with it all. And so her fine flyaway hair, usually piled on her head in a careless bun, has been braided and pinned just so. She's bought a new dress. With the skill acquired from her frequent purloining of bottles of liquor from other people's cabinets, she's appropriated a vial of Lily's White Heliotrope. Not that Lily wouldn't have gladly given her the perfume had she asked. It's just that Iris was too embarrassed to ask. She reels between defiance and shame.

She mails the letters to Lehrer at the stations along the route. Standing on these platforms, she takes in the passengers on the trains going the other way, back toward where she began. But when the whistle blows, she returns to her car. She dabs on a bit more perfume.

As soon as she enters the hotel lobby, tired and bedraggled but redolent at every pulse point, she spots Lenz. He's sitting on a midnight-blue button-backed velvet sofa, his legs crossed. He's pretending to be absorbed in a newspaper, pretending he hasn't observed her arrival. Only when she raps her fingers against the back of the paper does he lower it and look up, feigning surprise. Only then does he rise and embrace her, kissing her on each flushed cheek. He recites what she is meant to take as a spontaneously composed. heroic couplet.

Later, the two of them in his bed, Iris trying to figure out how to initiate a conversation about career possibilities, Lenz proposes for the third time. She wasn't expecting it. Really—she wasn't. He hadn't let on at all. He seemed startled and mildly flustered when she said she wanted to see his room, babbling some inanities about the view provided a conference speaker.

Now, her head against his bare chest, he asks for her hand and she hears herself laugh. "There's no need to buy the cow at this late date," she says. "I come bearing free milk."

"Iris—" he says, wounded on her behalf.

"It's fine. I'm not one of those girls you used to take to parties," she says.

"I understand. You're not a girl at a party. I understand that."

"I'm not even a girl."

What she doesn't say is that she can't possibly marry him. She's pledged her troth to another. No husband. No lesser scientists.

"It's just that I don't think I believe in marriage," she says. "Though I'm not opposed to"—she fishes for a word—"alliances," is what she comes up with.

It surprises her to see how hurt and humiliated he is. His color rises, his cheeks turn scarlet, his eyes begin to fill. Tears and torment! He has to turn away, collect himself. But when he faces her again, he's smiling, not broadly, not gaily, but a sweet smile, as if the whole afternoon has been nothing more than one of their dances around the sun. "Why is it," he says, "that whenever I look up, there you are?"

He confuses her, this mediocre chemist with his multiple fiancées, his many nervous breakdowns. "But you invited me here," she says.

He nods as if she's missed the point—she *has* missed the point—and he changes the subject. "Shall we dress and go down for dinner?"

She claims exhaustion. "Trains," she sighs.

"I know."

"It's the coal soot. So irritating. My eyes."

"The fumes can make you dizzy for hours."

They agree they'll each rest this evening. Apart. They'll meet again tomorrow for coffee and cake before the morning's first lecture.

"Goodnight, Fräulein Doktor," he says.

And so she descends several floors to her own room, much smaller, much darker. She locks the door and with a washcloth sponges the journey off her face, the perfume off her wrists, Lenz off her thighs. What just happened? she wonders. And what's her next move?

The carpetbag she borrowed from Lily has been left on a chair by some bellman. Iris unpacks it. She sits on her mattress.

She drinks the ounce of complimentary eau de vie in the crystal decanter on the bedside table. Carrying the decanter and pretty little cordial glass to the sink by the gray marble-topped bureau, she rinses both out, replaces them on the bedside table. She calls down for a *salade de truite fumée* and a bottle of Riesling. When a boy in a uniform gaudier than Bismarck's on parade days delivers her tray, she points to the decanter.

"It was empty when I arrived," she says. "The last time I stayed here, it contained just a dab of some lovely eau de vie."

She's worried the boy will inform her that he knows perfectly well she's never been a guest of the hotel before, but of course he doesn't. What he does is abase himself for the staff's lapse. He leaves with the decanter, and when he returns, it's filled to the halfway mark.

"With our compliments and profound apologies," he says.

"Oh, that's really too generous," she says. "I'll have to share it with colleagues. I'm here only two nights. I just wanted a small sip before dinner."

She gives him an excessive gratuity. It wasn't frugality that prevented her from simply ordering a bottle.

The next day she wakes at noon. The wine bottle is empty, the eau de vie nearly gone. Her temples and occipital lobes throb. Her tongue is furred. There's a note slipped under her door, Lenz noting that she failed to appear not only for coffee but also for any of the morning's lectures. He hopes she's well. He asks if she would like to meet for the afternoon's luncheon. She bathes and dresses, and now she's missed luncheon too. At the desk in her room, gray marble-topped like the bureau, she writes her own note.

"Dear Richard," she begins. And ends, "Accordingly, I approach marriage as I would any scientific experiment. I plan to study the institution from within, to analyze it objectively, rationally, and with no preconceived expectations. I plan to be both subject and dispassionate observer, both lab rat and scientist. I plan to take copious notes and eventually publish the same."

There's no mention of love in the letter, which currently lives in a box beneath our mother's bed in the Dead and Dying Room, along with other letters from Iris to Lehrer. We believe there was a time when Iris truly loved Lenz, but by the time they got engaged, she loved him no more. Still, her mother had often advised her daughters to put more stock in a man's intellect than in love. "Love and passion fade over time," her mother had said before going off and dying young, "but a good man who enjoys sharing his ideas will sustain you forever."

Iris can see the wisdom in her mother's advice. She can see how a collaboration with Lenz could be a happy one for a woman like herself. She will be his indispensible lab assistant, his adored colleague, the coauthor of his papers, his occasional drinking companion, and the person he talks to late into the night about his fascination with nitrogen fixation, and her own ideas about soluble salts.

And so—here's what looks like their happy ending or promising beginning—they find each other at the evening's banquet and she says yes and he says, Do you mean it? and she says yes, and he takes a spoon to the rim of his wineglass, and forty male chemists grow silent. Then cheers, then toasts, more rounds of wine than anyone can count, and now forty drunken chemists know her name.

"Frau Doktor," her sister Rose will call her at last.

At the end of the conference, after she kisses Lenz good-bye, waves at his receding carriage, returns to her room, packs Lily's bag, and runs out of reasons to linger any longer in her room, she regards the now empty decanter. She takes Lily's perfume from her traveling bag, pours its golden contents into the crystal carafe. "There," she says out loud. "One ounce." She tucks the empty vial in the bag. Moments later she's heading for the train station.

One year later the only child of the Alter-Emanuel marriage is born. Richard Otto Alter. He's named for their respective true loves.

CHAPTER 6

"Someday this will be funny," said Lady from her hospital gurney, but it's been twenty-four years since the flood in the laundry room ("Thank God nobody was down there at that hour, or someone might've been hurt," said the neighbors), and mostly it still isn't.

Nor were Lady's two additional attempts funny. The second effort, razor to wrists shortly after Eddie Glod died, did little damage to Lady, but made an astonishing mess of the bathroom. Vee and Delph spent days cleaning it, and yet for months afterward they kept finding additional splotches and splashes of blood behind the toilet, between the silver coils of the cast-iron radiator, on Otto von Bismarck's frame. It was as if the blood were being replenished every night while we slept. It was like cleaning the bathroom of Lady Macbeth.

The final effort took place in the shitty expanse of time known as the 1980s and involved one bottle, each, of Valium and vodka. Lady had tried to be more considerate that time, to choose a method that would spare Vee and Delph any cleanup, and in that she succeeded.

She also succeeded in another way: she died. Not permanently, perhaps, which we admit is generally a critical component of dying, but for a harrowing thirty seconds. When the
doctors shared that bit of news, it left Vee and Delph quivering.
In fact, Delph felt her legs give out; she wound up on her knees
in the hospital corridor. She hadn't realized until then the melodramatic things her body was capable of.

But it had been after that first effort, the mismanaged hanging when Delph decided she wanted to do something special for
Lady. The idea of the tattoo came to her right away, even though
it was 1976, when women with tattoos tended to work in circus
sideshows or belong to motorcycle gangs or perhaps had once
spent time in Hitler's death camps and now never went sleeve-
less. Still, Delph felt the idea was inspired. The tattoo would
be a message of sympathy and a gesture of solidarity, indelible
and heartfelt, a proclamation that Delph, too, was an Alter, that
Delph, too, saw the horizontal light every day of her life, that
Delph's day would also come.

And it wasn't as if there were other alternatives available to
her. What was she supposed to do? Mail a get-well card? Send a
balloon bouquet?

The first time we heard the curse spoken was in 1963, the
weekend of the Kennedy assassination. Along with our mother—
along with the entire country—we spent those November days
watching TV. There was no work, no school. Our mother set
up the ironing board in the living room, directly in front of the
blond console. She was wearing a quilted bathrobe the color of
canned salmon. She had a Lucky between her lips and a can of
Tab that was 50 percent vodka on the wide end of the board. A
kerchief of pink netting covered her hair except for her bangs,
which were bobby-pinned around a black wire roller. Her exposed calves were skinny, and her veins were varicosed. This

wasn't an aberrant or slovenly look. It was what tired mothers looked like, at least during the daytime, in 1963.

That assassination weekend was when the 1950s turned into the '60s. We were watching something we'd never before seen. We don't mean the assassination itself, though there was that too. We mean the fact that the coverage of the assassination was twenty-four/seven and uninterrupted by commercials. We mean the way the reporters were shoving their gargantuan microphones in the faces of anyone and everyone, the famous and ordinary alike. Eisenhower said something ponderous and canned about praying, and that was as expected, we were used to that sort of thing. But immediately after, live from Rockefeller Center—only four miles from where we sat, folding sheets—a teenager in an open coat, a girl with braids whose black face was brightened with tears, said, "I don't know where to go. I don't know what to do," and this startled us.

Those two sentences: they seemed meaningless, and then they seemed heartbreaking and profound, and then it seemed as if the God we didn't believe in might have put those sentences into her mouth, that they might have been the sentences God would have uttered if someone had pushed a mike in his face. Or maybe the girl *was* God.

It seemed impossible that anyone would dare say another word after that girl had uttered those sentences. It struck us that maybe no one would ever say another word ever again.

That's when our mother spoke up. She raised the iron, hot water dribbling and sizzling down the sole plate cover and onto a pillowcase. "The sins of the fathers are visited on the sons to the third and fourth generations."

How were we to know it came from the Bible? We thought she'd made it up on the spot. We thought she was being poetic.

So poetic, in fact, we didn't understand what she was talking about. Whose father? Our father? Which sons? Who had sons? She had to give us a primer on Joseph P. Kennedy. "You just wait," she said. "Over the years all those children will go down like dominoes thanks to that father of theirs. Already three of them are gone. And watch, it's going to get the grandchildren too. That'll be the third generation. Then there'll be one more to go."

We thought about this a few days later when John-John up and saluted. We were incredulous. "Why?" we asked. "What do the grandchildren have to do with anything?"

Our mother shrugged. "What do I know?"

Nothing, it seemed. She knew nothing. For instance, she seemed oblivious to the curse's applicability to us. Of course, back then we were oblivious too. It was Delph who first realized, so many years later, sitting by Lady's hospital bed, that in this single and unenviable way we were in the same boat as the Kennedys.

Delph got the name of the tattoo parlor from her best friend, a gay bike messenger named Joshua Gottlieb. Every day Joshua came by the small office where Delph worked that summer. The office consisted of a single room filled with gray metal. Her boss's big gray metal desk was pushed against the wall near the windows that looked out on Broadway and Gray's Papaya. There was a gray metal air-conditioning unit in one of those windows, unplugged and bearing a handwritten sign that read, "Broken! If you touch this you will die!"

Delph's small gray metal desk was pushed against the opposite wall. There were fist-size holes punched into that wall, and the linoleum throughout the room appeared to have been attacked with the claw of a hammer. The name of the business was Elite Information Exchange.

Elite Information Exchange sold subscriptions to dozens of daily newsletters, each newsletter devoted to one unique investment opportunity—gold, real estate, oil, cattle futures, cocoa, pork. Her boss dictated the content for each of the newsletters onto little cassettes at night, and Delph typed them up the next day, then walked to a copy shop to have them reproduced and collated and stapled, then returned to the office to address them by hand, then walked to the post office to have them mailed to the eager and gullible, the literally poor fools who believed that each newsletter had been researched and written by a different economist or investment guru, every one an expert in his particular field. The experts' names were all long and Waspy and male—Hamilton M. Carlisle had been one, and Vee had asked, "Why not Chatsworth Osborne Jr.? Why not J. L. Gotrocks? Why not Carlisle M. Hamilton?"—while the subscribers had names that caused Delph to make assumptions she wasn't proud of. Not quite Jed Clampett, she said, but close to, and their addresses seemed to be disproportionately in places like Mississippi and West Virginia and Oklahoma and North Dakota, places where, she knew, plenty of intelligent and educated people lived—William Faulkner! Booker T. Washington!—but still, she suspected that those intelligent and educated people did not reside at the specific addresses within those states to which she was sending those letters.

In short, the hours she spent in the Elite Information Exchange office that summer were guilt-ridden and lonely and boring. They were also criminal: soon after Delph returned to school, the boss was arrested for mail fraud and sent to Danbury for a couple of months.

On the other hand, Joshua Gottlieb was also a part of that summer. That was its saving grace.

We're all of us shy, but Delph is the shyest. You only have to look at her to know it. She slouches when she walks, slumps when she sits. She keeps her head down, letting her hair fall across her face. That hair. When we were young, the three of us in the same tub, Lady would shampoo it, massaging the green glob of Prell until it coated and straightened every strand with thick white suds and she could style the foamy concoction atop Delph's head—here's how you'd look with a slicked-back pony-tail; here's how you'd look with a French twist—in an effort to convince Delph it would look better, even *be* better for her, if she did something about the way she presented herself, if she tried to look more like everyone else. But Delph wasn't inter-ested in looking more like everyone else. She still tells stories about the magical properties of her hair, about how, in school, she would sit at her desk bowing her head as if in prayer and her hair would flop forward and conceal her face, and she would be rendered invisible. Teachers who might have otherwise asked her to stand and recite a geometric proof or conjugate a verb in a language not her own would suddenly forget her name and harass someone else. Kids who normally tormented her could no longer detect her presence. She still likes her cloak of invisibility. She likes keeping a distance between herself and others. People are her third favorite species, she says. First cats. Then dogs. Or, no, wait—fourth favorite species. The Central Park horses are number three. Those enormous sad eyes, those heartbreakingly silly hats.

Crowds of people, she says—that she doesn't mind. You'd think she would, but she doesn't. Hustle and bustle, New York City, that's all right with her. It's actual encounters with one of the individuals who constitute those mobs that she dislikes. She doesn't mean Lady, she doesn't mean Vee, she never meant Eddie. It's outsiders she means. Literally—the people outside our apartment, with all their gossip and clever bon mots at the expense of others. Imperfect beings who spend their lives judging other imperfect beings. Frauds and liars. Scolds and snobs. She's afflicted, Delph says, with the ability to read the thought bubbles over other peoples' heads. Those other people, they never—not ever—have anything nice to say about anyone.

"Such meanness," she says.

But there are exceptions to every rule, and now and then she has run into a person with whom she feels comfortable. These people—all of them men—have been so few she can count them off on one hand.

There was her eighth-grade English teacher, whose love of England up through the Elizabethans touched her for reasons she could never explain. For almost all of eighth grade he'd buy a couple of BLTs from the teachers' cafeteria, and they'd eat in his classroom, Delph safe from meanness and thought bubbles for a full forty-five minutes, as he told her stories about British kings and queens and she recited passages she'd memorized from Shakespeare because she wanted to give him gifts but didn't know what a man his age would want. The Shakespeare, it turned out, was just the thing. He would beam. He would say, "Who can say more than this rich praise, that you alone are you." How she mourned when June and promotion to high school came along. It was like a death for her.

Later, at a time when our mother's craziness was peaking, Delph found herself able to talk to a therapist at the nearby free clinic. This was a young man with jutting cheekbones and protuberant eyeballs and a habit of sitting quite literally at the edge of his seat, so that every part of him seemed to be leaning toward her, eager to hear the next thing she had to say. His manner, however, was tentative, almost shy. He'd only just begun to meet with clients, he confided, and she'd feigned surprise, though she was confident she'd have figured that out on her own, given his tendency to talk about himself at length and his habit of alternating long periods of silence with blurted interpretations that were always wrong and sometimes inappropriate. "Sheesh," he said, interrupting Delph as she came to the fourth family suicide during their initial session. "Is this your life story or the plot of *The Guiding Light*?"

"Really?" Vee said. "He honestly said that? A therapist?"

Delph's initial reaction was also shock, but the more she thought about it, the more she thought his response had been fair. Who could deny that our family history was a little soap-opera-ish? "I think he was nervous," she said in his defense. Unlike Vee, Delph didn't hold it against him, the fact that he was not the world's greatest therapist. He was working at a free clinic where the fees were determined by a sliding scale. She was being charged five dollars per session. If he was mediocre—well, you get what you pay for, don't you? She believed he was doing the best that he could, and she was pleased, even proud, as he improved over time. He interrupted less frequently. He generated fewer cynical thought balloons. Finally, he changed her life when he told her that he didn't care what his supervisor or anyone said, he would not put her on the autism spectrum, he would put her on the introversion spectrum—at the low end of that spectrum, perhaps only a scooch away from the high end of the autism spectrum—but on the introversion spectrum nevertheless.

"But did you ever think you were autistic?" Vee said when Delph reported the good news.

"Not until he told me I wasn't. But then I started thinking.

You know, he's not very good at this therapy stuff. So what if he's wrong and I am autistic? High-end autistic? Super-high-end-autistic? Then I'd be doing great just to be getting up and going out into the world every day. If I were autistic, it would do wonders for my self-esteem."

As was the case with her erudite English teacher, she loved the incompetent therapist dearly—and by this time she knew what transference was (she'd taken out every book in the Barnard library on clinical therapy to learn how to avoid doing or saying anything that might make her less than a perfect patient), so she just let herself enjoy her adoration of him. Not that she ever discussed that adoration with him. Why should she? she thought. She'd also learned what countertransference was, and she didn't notice him talking about his adoration of her. "By now you must have developed sexual feelings for me," he once said—they talked a lot about her lack of interest in sex—"because it's only normal, just part of the process." And you for me, she thought as she hid behind her hair and said nothing. He said nothing too, waiting. They sat like that, in silence for the rest of the session. What a job, she thought on the walk home. You sit there staring and nodding, while people sit across from you all day long, falling in love with you and wanting to screw you..

Then—long before she was ready—the therapy terminated. She still becomes enveloped in misery when she remembers the day the therapist told her he was moving back home, Brattleboro, Vermont, and opening a small practice there. He'd had enough of the city. Also, he didn't like working at the clinic. Some of his patients were kind of disturbing, he told her. "I've started carrying a knife," he said.

"How long have you known you were leaving?" she asked.

"It's been in the works for a while now," he said.

"What does that mean, 'a while'?"

He pursed his lips. "Now, you know we're not here to talk about me."

Since when? she thought, but what she said was, "I'm just thinking about my abandonment issues."

"I think I've mentioned before," he said, "that what goes on in here is a reflection of what goes on out there. If my leaving triggers old fears or traumas, that will be very useful when you begin work with someone else."

"My therapist is moving to Vermont," she told Eddie and Vee that evening. "Doesn't that sound like a line from a Woody Allen movie?" Then she'd gone into her bedroom and sobbed for the rest of the night. She continued sobbing at night throughout the next week, the next month, long after he was gone. She sobbed in her room, in Vee and Eddie's room, in dark movie theaters, everywhere but in her therapist's office, where she gritted her teeth and got through it and when the time came shook his hand and wished him luck. And although it wasn't the first time she'd contemplated suicide, her suicidal ideation, as the therapist enjoyed calling it, had never before been quite so detailed, quite so step-by-step planned. She'd have told him all about it if he'd still been a few blocks away.

Even now, at her current job, where she runs the file room for a company that administers tests to life insurance agents, tests that determine the strings of letters that come after the agents' names, she finds herself able to talk to one of the partners, an old guy who is loud and comical and comes into work wearing cowboy boots and a Stetson and a belt with the buckle oversize and rhinestoned. Once, the two of them alone on the elevator, she got up the nerve to say, "I know you're from the West Side, but this is maybe too much." Her head was down when she said it, her face largely concealed as she whispered her joke, but she'd known her audience, and though it took him a beat to get it, he guffawed and gave her a hug that literally lifted her off her feet, and that she thought about for a long time after.

Sometimes the partner comes down to the basement, where the file room takes up the entire floor. He sits in the chair next to her desk and tells her that technology is soon going to render the firm's services, and certainly her position, completely and forever obsolete. He says, "I'm an old man. I'll just retire or die. But what about my people? What about you? You're too young to quit and too old to learn new tricks. What's your future going to look like?"

These are the men who have been the men in Delph's life.

And then there was Joshua Gottlieb. On her first day at Elite Information Exchange, as Delph sat by herself on a shiny leatherette secretary's chair with slashes in the fabric, trying to make sense of what she was hearing through the Dictaphone's headset, Joshua had barged in, dressed in his messenger duds. Nothing sleek, nothing Spandex. He wore red high-tops and fringed denim cutoffs and a ripe purple Sticky Fingers T-shirt with an actual zipper.

"Hey Elite Information Exchange," he shouted. "Package for the boss."

He didn't wait for her to respond, didn't seem to notice that she'd said nothing at all. He put the package on the big metal desk. He jerked his thumb toward the sign on the air conditioner and rolled his eyes. He stuck the dangling plug into the socket, stood in front of it as it blasted cold air onto his sweaty T-shirt. When he was cooled to his satisfaction, he crossed the room and perched on her little metal desk. She lowered her head, let her hair fall forward. She pretended to be concentrating on the pork predictions for August.

"So, hey," he said, shouting as if he were talking to her from New Jersey, "I've got some elite information I'd like to exchange: Millard Fillmore was the thirteenth president of the United States. What'll you give me for that? How about some elite info about, oh, I dunno, two-letter words in Scrabble?"

While she tried to figure out what to do about him, he kept talking.

"And don't think you can have Fillmore in exchange for some shit-ass two letter word like *to* or *as* or *it*. I want some kick-ass two-letter Scrabble words if I'm giving you Fillmore—"

Her initial reaction was panic with a jigger of regret for not locking the door. He didn't seem normal to her, and given her own mode of navigating this world, she had a generous definition of normal. Part of it was that he was not easy to look at, a startlingly unattractive young man with an acne-purple forehead and overlapping front teeth that, under the fluorescents, seemed the palest green. He was flat-nosed and scrawny with stark white bleached hair emanating from his head like a child's drawing of the sun's rays. Yet there he was, sitting on her desk, grinning at her as if she were the luckiest girl on earth because she was getting to spend time with him.

Here was the thing: she did feel lucky, so much so that she pushed her hair out of her face. She hoped he couldn't read her thought bubbles, although her thought bubbles weren't completely negative. He was as garrulous as she was taciturn. This was good because it meant she didn't have to worry about holding up her end of the conversation. And he was giving her plenty of time to come up with a snappy rejoinder to his silliness. She liked that too.

She even liked that he was deafening, which, rather than feeling like a gale wind blowing her out of her seat and onto her butt, felt like a warm, bright spotlight.

She swiveled in her chair so she was looking directly at him. Maybe it was his pale green grin. Maybe it was that she wanted to be professional and helpful and, just for once, friendly and personable on this, her first day at work at her first ever job. Maybe it was because he was obviously weirder than she was. Whatever it was, Delph felt as though the gods who'd abandoned her as pretty much everyone else had—father off to wherever, mother off to the murky river, therapist off to a less disturbing clientele in Brattleboro, even her English teacher off to the next eighth-grade geek—it seemed those gods had for some reason, on this day, noticed her living down there between the cracks and decided to do something about it. Not that the gods had rescued her. Not that they'd reached in and pulled her out and up into the sunlight. But they'd sent Joshua Gottlieb spelunking down between the cracks too. They sent Joshua to keep her company.

"I'm sorry," she said, "but your information regarding President Fillmore is not sufficiently elite for an exchange of that nature."

"Shit," he bellowed happily. "Okay, what'll you give me for it? I'll take whatever you have."

"I could see my way to giving you *i* before *e* except after *c*."

Witty repartee, she thought. Try that, people on the autism spectrum.

He grinned madly. "Done," he shrieked and reached out to give her a hug. She managed to dodge it, wheeling her chair away as he lunged. She hadn't lost complete track of herself. But she'd lost track just a little, and that was a pleasure.

His being gay was just one of the many things that made

him perfect for her. Saturdays were his date nights with other homely boys like himself. None of the dates turned into long-term things. Just because he was ugly, Joshua said loudly and exuberantly, didn't mean he wanted to date ugly or commit to ugly or look at ugly in bed for the rest of his life.

"Don't be mean," she would say.

He'd say, "How am I being mean? I don't see anyone falling in love with me either."

"Maybe you should broaden your horizons," she'd suggest, but if he guessed what she meant, he wasn't saying.

Thursdays and sometimes Fridays and occasionally Wednesdays were the nights he went out to acquire the dates that never turned into anything. Those were also the nights Delph went out with him. He'd stop by Elite Information Exchange to fetch her.

"Pardon me," he'd roar, "but I was wondering what elite information I could get in exchange for Ethel Merman won the Tony for *Call Me Madam*."

She'd give him something—bulbs should be planted in the fall or Greenland isn't green—then lock up, and they'd go downtown or to Ninth Avenue. They'd enjoy the scene: the good, the bad, and then there was their crowd, the lovable ugly, the boys who required no conversation from her, but who taught her how to do the Hustle and her eyes, the latter requiring her to let them see her face, which for reasons she could never fathom they insisted on telling her was beautiful.

"I'm not beautiful," she whispered into Joshua's ear. "I have a man's face." And, screaming over the music and chaos, he said, "Ain't nothing wrong with that, kidlet."

She was only nineteen, and a young nineteen. She was often the only woman there, unless you counted the drag queens, which she didn't in those days, something she's sorry about now.

She was also the only one not doing drugs, unless you counted alcohol, which she didn't in those days and continues not to.

Still, those were her best days, her only days of belonging to something. She would get home at 3:00 a.m., later. She'd stumble and stagger and bump into furniture. Eddie would put his arm around her shoulders, lead her to the kitchen, require her to drink two quarts of water before Vee put her to bed. Delph would resist. She wanted to stay up. She wanted to talk about how at ease she felt in those clubs with those boys, the white boys from the city and Long Island and Jersey, the black boys from Harlem and Nigeria, the brown boys with Cuban accents and Brooklyn accents, the angry Asian boys who wore leather and the mellow Asian boy who wore kimonos and pearls just like our great-great-uncle Rudi, all the boys, every boy, but especially with Joshua, how happy she felt with Joshua by her side and the DJ playing "Love to Love You Baby" and five or six Harvey Wallbangers sloshing around her stomach. She wanted to tell Vee how Joshua would playfully hip-check her into one of his friends, who would hip-check her back to him as if they were pinball flippers and she a silver ball, a larger version of the one in the actual pinball machine in the corner, a smaller version of the one spinning on the ceiling. She wanted to list all of Joshua's nicknames for her. He called her Philadelphia and the Oracle of Delphi and Elf and Ellie Information and Kiddo and Kidlet, and then so would everyone else.

"I'm queer," she'd tell Vee and Eddie as they tried to persuade her to lie down, sleep. Vee and Eddie would smile supportively, waiting—hoping—for the other shoe to drop. "That would explain so much," Vee often whispered to Eddie. But Delph would laugh and sit up and say, "Oh, God, no no no. Not *queer* queer. Just regular queer. The dictionary kind of queer. The you don't fit in with the regular world, but it turns out you fit in with this other world and it's so much more fun kind of queer."

"Except it's also the men all pair off at the end of the night and you come home drunk and alone kind of queer," Vee would say, although by then nothing Vee said could faze Delph. "But I'm happy," she'd say. "Look at me. This is happiness," and Vee would say, "Short-term happiness," and Delph would cry, "Sold!"

Joshua Gottlieb had a tattoo, and not a cheap-looking tattoo, the kind that most people had back then, a faded scar the color of rotten banana peels, but a beautiful, brightly hued tattoo, and this was the tattoo that got Delph thinking about acquiring one of her own. He'd shown it to her on a hot night outside a disco that was once a church while they waited on line. He'd wriggled his shorts down—this may not have been for her exclusive benefit—and she saw the muscled merman lounging from one end of his rear pelvic girdle to the other.

"He's gorgeous," Joshua said. He twisted his head one way and his spine the other, an effort to glimpse and admire the little sprawled body on his own body. "Am I right?"

Now, Lady in the hospital, her neck slathered in goo, Delph called him from the lobby payphone. "I'll trade you the meaning of life for the name of the guy who did your merman," she said as soon as he picked up.

"The meaning of life, huh?"

"Hey," she said, "when I say I've got elite information to exchange, I don't mess around."

He didn't ask why she wanted the tattoo, not then anyway. He was too excited. "I'll go with you," he shouted. "You're gonna love the subgenre of men there."

She did. Cross a pirate with his parrot, and those men

were what you'd get, big and burly and bandannaed, with long braided beards and skin bright and tropical—turquoise, emerald, orange. They were comically courtly, the kind of men who were always saying fuck this or fuck that, then asking you to pardon their French. They drank warm bourbon from old jars— not Ball mason jars, but peanut butter jars or jelly jars or pickle jars, which you could tell from the shape and the just-barely-there smell of the former contents. One of the men, tall and potbellied and wearing a bowling shirt that read "Gurley" on the pocket, which, like his Born to be Wild and Mom-inside-a-heart tattoos, turned out not to be ironically intended—Gurley was his Christian name, and he belonged to a bowling league, as evidenced by several trophies behind the counter—poured her a hefty four fingers as she waited her turn. Bourbon with the faintest whiff of apricot jam—lovely, really—and she downed it as if it were a shot. Because he didn't know her, Gurley was impressed. He whistled and praised her and poured her some more.

Even so, the longer she waited, and even though Joshua was right there by her side, the more she realized she wasn't as comfortable with these tattoo artists as she was with the boys at the clubs. She could feel herself getting nervous, angsty, stomachachy, as she sat on the window bench waiting her turn. The storefront window was soaped instead of curtained, and there were green-headed flies dead in the corners. She flipped through a Zap Comix that was old and crunchy from too much sun. She read a panel about a cow-woman who was tied to a chair and the chair pushed over onto the floor and her legs forced open so men could lick her. "You guys must have all hated your mothers," the cow cried as she struggled to free herself.

Delph didn't understand why she had such terrible reactions to things like this, why she identified so closely with the cow. She knew why she reacted badly politically. She'd read her Millet, her Brownmiller. But why did she feel so *personally* attacked? No man had ever held her down, forced her to do anything. No man had hurt her in that way, or, when you got down to it, at all, unless you counted the shoving and public ridicule by adolescent classmates. ("I had a dream," a boy said, a total stranger of a boy, but a boy popular enough to command total silence in the cafeteria as he spoke. "There was this sign and it said, 'Delph Frankl Knows All There Is.' And then the words rearranged themselves, and it said, 'There is Delph Frankl, All Nose.'") But this was just a cartoon: a cartoon of a cow. Although—cows. The brown eyes, the sweet mooing. They were probably her fifth favorite species.

"You guys must have all hated your mothers," Gurley said, hanging over her shoulder, reading the dialogue out loud, thinking about it, then laughing like Heckle or Jeckle.

Joshua glanced at the magazine too. He saw what she was reading—not the specific panel, just the cover with Mr. Natural—and he waggled his finger, brayed "Keep on truckin'," and she nodded, but she also felt herself turn into Delph. She ducked her head, let her hair fall forward. She thought about that popular boy in the cafeteria. She thought about Lady in the hospital. She thought about the curse, remembered the first time she'd heard it, and that made her think about the teenage girl in Rockefeller Center all those years ago. Where had the girl gone that day, after the reporter moved on? What had she done?

Delph no longer felt up to talking. She wasn't sure what to do about it. "I'm falling between the cracks," she whispered to Joshua.

"Don't worry, Delft China, I'm on it," he said. He put an arm around her, and she leaned closer to him. ("We're perfect for each other," she would tell Vee on those late Saturday nights, "because neither of us wants to marry each other or have sex," and Vee would say, "Honey, he wants to have sex; just not with you," and Delph would say, "Vee, I know what homosexual means," and Vee would say, "Delph, I'm not sure you do.")

When her tattoo artist was ready—she was relieved it was someone other than Gurley—Joshua accompanied her into the back room. He recited the curse and traced his finger around the part of her calf where she wanted the ink placed. Delph's tattoo artist nodded, recited the curse back. He seemed to be the only one with any customers. The other guys were just hanging around, drinking and kibitzing.

"So what's the story?" Gurley asked. "Who's the sinning father? And what sins are we talking about here exactly?"

"The father's her great-grandfather," Joshua said. "Huge sinner. His sins poured down on the family like maple syrup."

"Sounds delicious," the tattoo artist said blandly.

"Yeah, well, it's not. Poor Delph here—she's the fourth generation, right?—she's taking the flak. She's drenched in his sins." He smiled at Gurley. He was flirting. "A big sticky mess."

The men looked at her for confirmation. She looked to Joshua.

"For example," Joshua continued, "the great-grandfather I mentioned? He was kind of a notorious loudmouth. A big shot. A look-at-me kind of guy. And now she has trouble talking in front of people she doesn't know. See how it works?"

"No," Gurley said.

"So that was his huge sin?" her tattoo artist asked. "Being a horse's ass?"

"Well, that and the fact he was an infamous and unrepentant murderer."

"Far out." The tattoo artist was interested at last. "So who did he kill?"

Joshua frowned. "Well, no one really." He thought about this. "Or, actually, everyone. It was World War One."

Then the men, even Gurley, understood that the deaths weren't lurid and scandalous, just statistical and sanctioned, and they stopped pressing for details. They focused on the curse itself, what it said, where it came from, what it guaranteed.

"I've known other families like that," one of the quieter men said. A wild duck was taking flight on his bicep. "Generation after generation," he said, his passion rising like that duck, "no one can catch a fucking break. They can't fucking win for fucking losing."

"The fucking Kennedys," said the tattoo artist, by way of example.

"Fucking exactly," Joshua said.

Delph nodded too. It was 1976. Bobby was long gone. Also: Chappaquiddick.

The tattoo's unveiling took place on the following Saturday morning. It was too soon, really, for its first public appearance, Delph's skin still pink and oozy in places, but she didn't like keeping secrets from Lady and Vee; it felt too much like lying. She didn't believe in lying. Lady didn't mind lying, and Vee could take it or leave it, but Delph disliked it intensely. Lying was one of the many things in this world that made her feel bad, which is why, that morning, she removed the Saran wrap she'd been admonished to keep around her calf and patted at her skin with the shirt she'd worn the day before.

Dressed in the oversize T-shirt she slept in, she padded into the kitchen and made herself a V8 and vodka, her usual breakfast. She carried the mug to the dinette table, which was covered with flyers and form letters and circulars and bills and a baggie of grass and, in the trough of Eddie's *Blonde on Blonde* double album, rows of sifted-out seeds. There were also textbooks and notebooks and a week's worth of *New York Times*, each one karate-chopped into thirds by Vee for better subway reading. There was a pile of unread issues of *Ms.* and *Rolling Stone* and the *Barnard Alumnae Magazine*—three copies of the latter, one for each of the graduates and one for Lady, the dropout. Also a pile of *Mamm: The Magazine for Breast Cancer Patients and Survivors* that, though Vee had twice written to cancel her subscription— her freakish diagnosis at twenty-two an entire year behind her now—continued to show up in our mailbox as if the circulation department knew something Vee didn't, which of course it did not, although a couple years later when Vee was diagnosed for the second time, it certainly would seem like it did.

Delph sipped her spiked juice. She picked up one of the *Barnard*s. She turned to the back and read the class notes for Vee's year and what would have been Lady's if Lady had graduated. Everyone who'd sent in news was doing great. Good jobs or grad school, and of course, the kind of doing great that resulted in the name your classmates knew you by being corralled between parentheses. Marsha (Margolis) French. Donna (Harpootian) Davidson. She could write in on Lady's behalf, Delph thought: "Lily (Frankl) (Hopper) Alter is doing very well. The psychiatric nurse said so just last night."

She was engrossed in her thoughts when Eddie emerged from his and Vee's room. She hadn't realized he was home and gave a small shriek—"You scared me," she said—even though he was one of the men she felt completely at ease with. Sometimes she wriggled between him and Vee on their mattress so the three of them could do the *Sunday Times* puzzle together. Warm and cozy. This was what she enjoyed, this was her idea of going to bed with a man.

He was wearing only his jeans and was still half asleep. He was a bony and rangy boy, not terribly good-looking by the world's standards. His eyes were small and would disappear when he laughed. The bridge of his nose was so flat that Vee once balanced a little silver saltshaker on it while he snored on the sofa. "Don't you just love him?" she'd said, her eyes glinting with tears.

And he had enormous ears and his cheeks and chest were sallow and hairless, though a thin line of dark hair emerged from his pants and trailed up toward his navel. Delph tried never to look at that line of hair; Delph was always looking at that line of hair. As for the hair on his head, it was usually braided into a long single plait that reached to the middle of his back. But now, because he'd just woken up, it hung crimped but loose, an ear sticking through on each side.

Delph tucked her tattooed leg beneath her as Eddie took a seat across the table and rolled, tongued shut, and lit up a joint. "Vee's already at the hospital," he said. "She says for you to come spell her, so she can get half a day in at work."

If Vee had been the one asking, Delph would have made a face and said she was going to get ready in a second; in the meantime could she please be allowed to finish her breakfast without the guilt trip. But it was Eddie, so Delph brushed back her hair to let him see she was smiling, and she nodded and put down the paper. Father-hunger in action. It looked a lot like man-pleasing, but it was something else.

"Vee's at the hospital," Eddie repeated. "Man, I never wanted to have to say that again. I used to pray for it. Never again, please and thank you very much, Vee in the hospital for any reason. Well, having a baby. But not for any shitty reason. But I forgot to say I never wanted Lady in the hospital either."

"You have to be careful with wishing," Delph said. "It's so

easy to screw it up. You make a wish to lose ten pounds and the next thing you know your leg's being amputated because you forgot to specify you wanted the pounds to come exclusively from the fat storage cells in your ass."

He shook his head. "Fucking patriarchy. Fat talk, even now? Even with all this?" He wasn't angry with Delph, though. He was angry for her. We like to think of ourselves as feminists, but Eddie had us all beat. And not in a porny Joe Hopper way. In a genuinely appalled Eddie Glod way.

He went to take a shower, and Delph topped off her drink and chugged it down. While he was toweling dry and dressing and doing his hair, she was returning to the kitchen and dusting a little baking powder on the tattoo, which was oozing again.

He stopped in the kitchen before leaving for the day, surprising her, scaring her all over again. She stood on one foot, hiding the decorated leg behind her body. She supposed she looked like she needed to pee.

"All right, sweetie," he said. "Off to Mr. Moon's." He walked up to her, patted her poufy hair. He found it irresistible, he always said. He said he sometimes could see his handprint before it poufed back up. "Don't forget Vee."

On Saturdays he delivered Mr. Moon's savory buns to restaurants in Chinatown. When it came to cash flow, he, Vee, and Delph were just getting by. Vee made the most money at her paralegal job, but it still wasn't much. Eddie's jobs, Delph's job at Elite Information Exchange—they all paid minimum wage. This meant that the three of them lived on white rice and soy sauce, on spaghetti and Kraft blue cheese dressing, on peanut butter and grape jelly, the jelly from the individual plastic packs Delph took by the fistful from the Barnard cafeteria. On weekends they lived on stolen savory buns.

In the bathroom Delph walked over the jeans and briefs and wet towels Eddie had dropped on the floor and took a shower with what little hot water remained. Drying off, certain now she was alone, she launched into a medley of dead teenager songs—"Teen Angel" and "Last Kiss" and the one about the ghost who shows up at a dance. This was another secret she kept, the only secret she didn't feel guilty about: she had a good voice. She had daydreams in which she was coaxed up to a microphone in one of the live music clubs, one of the performers singling her out. "You, the girl singing along to every song. Yeah, you. You see any other girls here? It's just me and you, sister. Come on up here, let's see what you got." People smirking, nudging each other, expecting her to make a fool of herself. But instead . . .

In her bedroom she chose an outfit that went with both a tattoo and a hot summer day. She stepped into a short denim skirt and a pair of flip-flops, and intending nothing symbolic or metaphorical, but winding up being symbolic and metaphorical nonetheless—there are days and even entire eras when it's hard to avoid—she put on her lavender T-shirt with the skull and rose logo from the Grateful Dead's second live album. She looked at herself in the mirror. "Keep on truckin'," she said, and waggled her finger at herself.

At St. Luke's, Delph rode up to Lady's room in a mammoth stainless steel elevator designed to accommodate gurneys being wheeled to surgery. Vee had lain on such a gurney a little more than a year ago, this upon the occasion of her first cancer diagnosis. "Lumpectomy," Eddie kept saying. "What kind of name is that for a serious medical procedure? It sounds like something you do to gravy."

He hadn't been joking, he'd been genuinely horrified and offended, but Vee had found it funny and laughed uproariously. She was already sedated and was babbling happily. There'd been a shower cap stretched to capacity over her thick pile of hair, and, sticking out of the sheet that was covering most of her torso, there was the end of the needle locator a nurse had earlier stabbed into her breast. "Doesn't it look like a meat thermometer sticking out of a pot roast?" Vee had asked, lifting her head and trying to look at her chest, which gave her the appearance of having a double chin. But it hadn't looked like a meat thermometer in the least. It had looked like a huge hypodermic needle stuck into Delph's sister's boob.

That day the elevator had held Lady and Delph and Eddie and Vee and an orderly. Vee had become enamored of the word *orderly*, prattling on about how it was an adjective that looked like an adverb being used as a noun. "It would be like calling a housekeeper a tidily or a hairdresser a prettily," she said. After they wheeled her away, Eddie had begun to cry. "What if those were her last words?" he'd said.

But that had been last year's trauma, last year's story arc in the soap opera. This time it was Lady, not Vee, in the hospital, and Delph had the cavernous elevator to herself. She bounced on her heels, excited and anxious because she was not going to the third floor, the floor for the out-of-control crazies who were being observed, although the staff used the term loosely due to a nursing shortage, and the floor where Lady had spent the past week, her wrists tied to the bed rail with soft flannel shackles that were less true restraints and more a plea from the nurses that she not complicate their day by doing something rash, *rash* being the term everyone, even the psychiatrists, used to describe what Lady had done. Instead Delph was headed to the fifth floor, where they kept recovering patients. Delph had initially gone to the third floor, but the desk nurse, recognizing her, called out, shouting that Lady had been moved, and Delph reboarded the elevator. It was odd, she thought, that the healthier you were, the higher up they moved you. It seemed the opposite should be the case, that the sickest people should be the farthest from the bustle of the lobby and the revolving door that led to the noisy street, but perhaps, she thought, it was like Bloomingdales, where the better clothes—the designer lines housed in mini-boutiques—were up on four and five, while the tarty junior wear was on two. Not that she could afford a goddamn thing sold at Bloomingdale's, but sometimes she walked through Cosmetics after work and returned home with fragrance spritzed on one wrist.

Even before she got to the hospital and learned that Lady had been promoted, Delph had been in a good mood. Part of that feeling was attributable to the two cocktails she'd enjoyed in the apartment, plus the third she'd gulped down at the West End on the walk over. It was so hot that July. The air was so thick it was nearly chewable. As Delph walked east, making eye contact with no one, reprising "Teen Angel" under her breath like a crazy person, she'd found it necessary to pull her hair off her face and neck. She held it up in the air to dry the perspiration on her forehead and nape, to keep her own sweat from soaking the roots. Her hair, so fibrous and thick, sticking straight up in the air: she was sure she looked like a troll doll. But a cool and curly-headed troll doll. A Hell's Angel troll doll, what with the short skirt and tattoo and drunken, dancelike stagger.

When she reached Broadway, she'd ducked into the bar for a brief air-conditioned moment. She let her hair fall, and almost all of it did. The West End was the only bar she felt comfortable entering alone, back in those days when unaccompanied women tended to frequent only the new fern bars. Unlike those bars, the West End maintained no brightly lit section for its female customers—the wives of the old Beats, mostly, but also Barnard students who were dating their professors—but it was so near our apartment that Delph felt about it as she felt about Mondel's, the elegant chocolatier a few doors down: it was her local candy store. Also, not once, not ever, had anyone tried to talk to her there. Even the bartenders only grunted when taking her order.

She took a seat at the bar and peered around as she always did, looking for Allen Ginsberg. As usual, he appeared not to be there, though it was impossible to say for sure. It was always dark in that bar. Anyone could be slumped down in one of the booths. She turned to the bartender and ordered a bloody mary. Fewer vitamins than her V8 concoctions, but better tasting and with an actual vegetable or whatever you wanted to call the limp stalk of celery so old it was white. She downed the drink quickly, and when she was finished she sat for a moment and ate the celery and let herself think about the tattoo and the tattooers.

Two nights ago, that other tattoo artist, the one named Gurley, having taken her phone number off her check, had called the apartment.

"Delph?" Vee said when she answered the phone. "I'm not sure. Let me check." Delph shook her head. "Sorry, no," Vee said. "I guess she's gone out."

He called twice more, once that same night, again the next day. Every time the phone rang Vee and Delph were sure it was the hospital calling to say Lady had taken a turn for the worse, but it was only this Gurley, this bowler, this pest.

Vee finally got fed up with both him and Delph. The third time he called, she'd changed her voice a little and said that, yes, this was Delph; what could she do for him? and Gurley had asked her on a date. That had caught Vee completely off guard.

Delph had been lying, saying she'd met this Gurley person at a club, and Vee had assumed he was calling for Joshua's number. That had made sense to Vee; each time the guy identified himself on the phone, Vee'd thought he was saying his name was Girlie.

She opened her eyes wide and gestured at Delph with such urgency that Delph had obeyed and come to the phone. They stood there, Vee and Delph, their temples touching, both of them listening to Gurley suggest that he and Delph meet up on the weekend, maybe bowl a few rounds, maybe smoke a few bowls, maybe go clubbing.

Delph let her jaw drop to demonstrate her utter surprise and substantial disgust. She, too, was surprised that Gurley wasn't gay. She'd assumed all the men in the tattoo parlor had been. How lucky she hadn't known that at least one of them was straight or bi or whatever Gurley was. She'd have been even more unnerved than she'd actually been had she realized he was sizing her up, looking at her leg in a different way from the others.

Vee gave Delph a look: yes or no? Delph shook her head vigorously.

"Sorry," Vee said in her Delph voice, which was beginning to acquire a slight Scarlett O'Hara tinge. "I'm busy next Saturday."

"What about Sunday?"

"I'm sorry. Look, the truth is, I don't date at all." Vee smiled at Delph reassuringly.

"Oh, bullshit," Gurley said. "Hey, what if I stand under your window and serenade you until you change your mind?"

An idea came to Vee then. "Look," she said. "The reason I don't date is because I'm married."

She thought that would stop him not only now but forever, but it hadn't helped at all "You're married?" Gurley repeated, as if this were the most preposterous thing he'd ever heard, and

Vee said, "Don't sound so shocked," and Gurley said, "Not to that little homunculus you were with the other day, you're not. I know you're not his type."

"Are you referring to Joshua?" Vee said. She scowled at Delph. The southern accent became a touch more pronounced. "No, I am certainly not married to Joshua."

"All right," Gurley said. "Then what's your old man's name, if you're so fucking married?"

Delph mouthed and Vee dutifully parroted, "Allen Ginsberg." They had to cover their mouths to keep from laughing, until Gurley said, "So where does this Ginsberg work? Because I'm going to go there and wait outside and beat him into hamburger and then you'll be available."

Vee found herself furious. "That's my husband you're talking about," she said. "I don't want anyone else." She raised her voice. "I love only him."

As Vee declared her love for Allen Ginsberg, Delph had, to her surprise, begun to weep. She made a helpless, frantic waving gesture with her hands and ran into Vee and Eddie's bedroom, empty given that Eddie was at his afternoon job handing out flyers to tourists in Times Square, trying to get them to head to a nearby menswear shop and purchase two suits for the price of one. Meanwhile Gurley was apologizing.

"Hey, calm down. It was just a joke, for fuck's sake—pardon my French."

"I pardon nothing," Vee said, and she hung up and went after Delph. Delph's head was beneath Eddie's pillow, so Vee sat on the edge of the mattress and patted her through the percale and foam rubber.

"I know you don't like to lie to people," Vee said, "but he was so persistent we had to do something."

"It's not that," Delph wailed, muffled and sniffling. She wasn't crying because Vee—and she—had lied to Gurley. Nor was she crying because it might have been the first time she'd been asked out on a date, albeit in a roundabout way. She was crying because she had never before participated in a lie that felt so much like the truth. "I don't want anyone else. I love only him," Vee had said in her role as Delph, and Delph, hearing Vee say this out loud, had been struck by how painfully true it was. She wanted no one else. She loved only him. And he—he did not love her and never would. He was gay, and she knew what gay meant. It just hadn't been Allen Ginsberg they were talking about.

The first person Delph saw in Lady's new room on the fifth floor of the hospital was Vee, who was sitting on a gray-green vinyl chair and looking up at a TV somehow affixed to the ceiling. Stepping farther into the room, she saw Lady, propped up in her bed, looking at the ceiling too, though not at the television.

"About fucking time," Vee said. "Pardon my French." She was wearing one of her paralegal uniforms, a cheap suit in royal purple from the sale rack of Dress Barn, pantyhose despite the evil temperature, sturdy Pappagallos that looked like men's cordovan wingtips, but with short, stacked heels. The leather briefcase she carried, a hand-me-down from the firm's only female lawyer, who'd recently purchased a swankier version, lay on the floor. Delph saw that Vee had also taken the time to do her hair that morning, not just letting it dry but going at it with a blow dryer and round brush. The weaponry hadn't worked, though. The wings framing Vee's face had already begun to frizz.

Delph walked past her, strode directly to Lady's bed. She kicked off a flip-flop and flung her leg up on the rail as if it were a barre. "Look," she said. "This is for you. Read it and weep."

There was no weeping, just Vee catapulting out of the chair, Vee yelling what the hell's wrong with you and are you crazy and who does such a thing. On and on, the self-assigned mother. And answering her own questions too: "You want to know who does such a thing? I'll tell you who does such a thing. Sailors and drunks and whores, that's who."

"Who you calling a sailor?" Delph said merrily, her leg still elevated.

Lady was having trouble finding her glasses. "What is that?" she said. "What does it say?"

"Nothing," Vee said. Then, reconsidering, she came out with it. "It says no matter what we do, our lives will be shit. It's very encouraging. It's the perfect thing to show someone who's just done something rash."

The rash thing was already a joke with us.

"It *is* a nice thing to do," Delph said. She lowered her leg. She was becoming weepy. "It *is* encouraging. The curse only goes to the fourth generation, which, yes, okay, is us, but we've always known there was a dark cloud over our heads. What was last year with the cancer and divorce and Mom if not proof of that? But the good news is, it all stops with us too. The fifth generation is exempt. Our children will be spared."

This was back when we all thought we'd have children.

"What are you two talking about?" Lady said.

"It's a goddamn tattoo," Vee said. "The sins of the father blah blah blah to the third and fourth generations." She ran her hand through her hair as she spoke. A mistake, always, to mess with curly hair that's been tortured straight. The strands kinked at the touch of her fingers. Spaghetti to rigatoni, she sometimes said, laughing, but not now. Now she was in no mood for self-deprecation. "Great," she said. "Now we all have ridiculous scarring."

Lady's hand went to the choker of shining raw skin at her throat.

Vee, of course, had it over both Delph and Lady when it came to scars, even then, before her double mastectomy. Although maybe if, as Albert Einstein used to say, the past, present, and future are all a delusion, and time is just a series of random moments played out in random order, and some of those moments feel like they happened after others, but only because those "later" moments contain the "earlier" moments—well, then, if we accept that this is true even though, given our limited mental capacities, we are incapable of truly understanding any of it, then maybe Vee had already had her double mastectomy and her chemotherapy etcetera, etcetera, and that was why she was so put out when Lady and Delph voluntarily mucked up their previously unmucked-up bodies.

But in the moment we believed we were living in, Vee still had both her breasts. On the other hand she also had a biopsy scar and a lumpectomy scar and, along the side of her rib cage, a faint but large circular scar where she'd ripped off a loose scab the size and color of a blueberry tartlet that had formed over her radiation burn. These disfigurements, as she thought of them, weren't nearly as visible or dramatic as Lady's and, now, Delph's, but they were more numerous and, because she had never asked for any of them, much sadder.

In fact, now that she thought about it, Vee even had a tattoo of her own. Like her scars, Vee's tattoo had been acquired during her first case of cancer; it consisted of four blue dots delineating the corners of what would have otherwise been an invisible square on her left breast. Every weekday for eight weeks after the lumpectomy she'd been required to show up at a clinic where poisonous rays were blasted into the heart of the square. Into her own heart as well, which, after all, beat right there beneath her flesh that was hardly too too solid, that was actually porous and useless when it came to deflecting death rays she was meant to think of as lifesaving.

By the sixth week the radiation had so badly burned the skin not just of her breast but also of her armpit—that innocent bystander—that she had to keep it free of all contact with fabric, razors, deodorant, even her own skin. She had to walk around with her arm extended off to the side or sometimes up in the air as if the universe had asked a question and she, by virtue of the wisdom she'd recently acquired, wished to be called on to answer. But she tolerated the burning, the blood rushing from her arm, the ensuing pins and needles, because it was going to be over in just a few weeks. Also what else could she do but tolerate it? She had to have the treatment. Eddie Glod had demanded she live.

Vee had tentatively broached the alternative with him. "You know," she said, lying in his arms after sex, "they say my aunt Rose, when she was pretty much my exact age, decided enough was enough and . . ." But Eddie, who knew all our stories by then, said, "Veezie, do not even say it," which, in truth, had relieved her. Really, she was only trying the idea on, seeing whether it fit, and it didn't, not then. She endured the surgery and the radiation, never looking back, never shedding a tear, in fact making jokes and laughing more than she imagined possible under the circumstances, and the only time she balked about what was being done to her was when she was told about the need for the tattoo. "Just four little blue dots," the radiologist said, "so we know where to aim. Not even noticeable to someone who's not looking for them."

"Why not something temporary?" she asked. "Maybe you could use some sort of laundry pen."

He smiled, reached for his needle, took her breast, and pulled it taut. It was still tender from the lumpectomy. She tried not to grimace.

"I'm Jewish," she said as he worked. His name and visage indicated he was, too. She said, "Jews aren't supposed to get tattoos."

"Tattoos not for fun God gives a pass to," he said. He was already done.

She slipped the shoulder of her johnny back on. She didn't bother to tie it shut. You lost all sense of modesty in a hospital.

"And you know this how?" she asked. "You're a part-time rabbi?"

"Even better," he said. "I'm a full-time doctor."

An old joke, but a good one. And it wasn't really a Jewish thing anyway, her squeamishness about the dots. It was an impurity thing. She'd started out perfect, flawless—ten fingers, ten toes, a full head of hair—and ever since, it had been all downhill. The chicken-pox scar over her eyebrow. The year of no front teeth followed by the years of silver fillings. The Stridex era. Trivial and universal though they might be, these were all signs of deterioration, of decay. Even back then she was consumed with it. Even before the more devastating operations, she was sharply aware of it. She was every day dying. Cavities. Cancer. Blue dots. It was all of a piece.

But she came back to this: hers were impurities she hadn't sought out. This could not be said of Lady's necklace or Delph's tattoo.

Lady, meanwhile, had located her glasses behind the box of off-brand facial tissues on her bedside table. She peered over, read the message on Delph's leg.

"Oh, Delph," she groaned. "Tell me that's not really permanent."

"Well, yeah, it's permanent," Delph said.

"It's not maybe a joke?"

"It's a joke in the sense of the joke's on us. But it's not a practical joke, if that's what you're asking. It's not a joke like fake dog shit on the carpet."

Lady ran her hand through her own wild hair. No more Olive Oyl; she'd lost her barrette at some point during her stay. It seemed symbolic, but in a discouraging way: in this healing place she felt dizzy and dazed and out of control. She couldn't wait to get home, and by home she didn't mean her apartment on Amsterdam, she meant the apartment on Riverside, she meant her old bedroom. She was tired. It was impossible to get any sleep in a hospital. The third floor had been noisy enough, but now she was on a floor for people who were not really sick, that is, she was near the maternity ward, where the patients' shrieks and obscenities were even worse than the lunatics'.

Still, she wasn't upset about Delph's tattoo the way Vee was. Yes, it was a stupid thing for Delph to have done, and Lady saw years of jeans and opaque tights in Delph's future, just as she saw a lifetime of turtlenecks in her own. But how, really, was it her business what Delph did with her own skin? It wasn't Lady's leg, after all. Lady's leg had its own problems. Right now, atop the hospital's pilly, inadequate blanket, it lay armored in a pristine white cast.

"Delph," Lady said, more fondly than aggrievedly, "you are my baby sister and I love you more than anything, but God, you can be such an idiot."

Vee bent down to retrieve her briefcase. She began toward the door. Delph took her seat. She smiled at Lady, also fondly. She gestured toward Lady's throat. She gestured toward the cast.

"Right," she said. "Right. I'm the idiot."

CHAPTER 7

1905

On a stage in Paris Mata Hari, self-conscious about her small breasts, removes all her clothes save for a jeweled bra. In a desert in America, the city of Las Vegas is founded. In a clerk's office in Switzerland, a young physicist friend of Lenz Alter comes up with this: $E=mc^2$.

And in Lenz Alter's lab there's his own scientific breakthrough. We'd like to describe it in detail, but we aren't chemists. We can't really explain what it is Lenz Alter did in his laboratory that auspicious year. All we know is he figured out a way to run nitrogen and hydrogen through a steel contraption to produce liquid ammonia. Then he performed some additional hocus-pocus with that ammonia, and wound up with—ta-da!—a big pile of shit.

Not natural shit, obviously. Faux shit. Designer shit. Scientists call this synthesis of his the manna process. Bread from the sky. Food from thin air.

We're more than willing to concede that the production of

man-made nitrogen fertilizer is not as thrilling, not nearly as sexy, as the theory of relativity. Nor is it as exciting as the scientific miracles of our own times. Decoding the human genome. Untangling string theory. Making a teeny-tiny telephone.

Nor does the age of fertilizer, which is what science-historians call this period of narrowly averted famine, have quite the same ring to it as the age of reason or the age of technology.

But for those folks who were alive in 1905, when the human race found itself on the brink of starvation because seagulls— poor exhausted creatures—could no longer provide guano at the ever-increasing rates mankind demanded, Lenz Alter's figuring out how to revive the earth's depleted arable soil was pretty damned exciting.

And yet we're products of our age, not his, and we sometimes struggle to regard our great-grandfather's Nobel Prize–winning work with the appropriate awe.

We have a joke. Well, not a joke. A skit. You have to picture the stage in an old vaudeville theater done up like a mad scientist's lab. There are two scientists on that stage, both in white coats, both with thick German accents, one bald as an egg, the other with wild, wiry hair. The bald one is our great-grandfather. The other is his friend.

ALTER Albert, Albert, *mach schnell*! I've just solved humanity's biggest problem.
EINSTEIN No shit!
ALTER Exactly!

Also in 1905: Iris Emanuel Alter fixes dinner. She's proud of her husband's achievements. She's certainly proud that her name appears on the dedication page of his first book. Still, the dedication page is not exactly where she dreamed of her name appearing.

She's neither Lenz's lab assistant nor his colleague, his co-author, or his drinking companion, nor the person he talks to about nitrogen and hydrogen and liquid ammonia and fertilizer, much less about her continuing interest in soluble salts. When he wishes to talk about his work, Lenz talks with Einstein, with Planck, with Bosch, with Willstätter. He talks with Lehrer when Lehrer and Marthe visit Karlsruhe. He talks with his students late into the night. He talks with his three-year-old son over breakfast while the boy bangs on the table with a spoon. Once she heard him talking about fertilizer with the dog. "How many times must I tell you, we are no longer in need of your assistance in this matter," he said as Prinz, the timid black Labrador, cocked his head to one side and smacked the lawn with his meaty tail.

Iris is only what Lenz asked her to be: his wife. And being his wife is all-consuming, leaves no time for independent research, which, since she has no lab privileges or team, would be impossible anyway. The housework is more demanding than she imagined, although she admits this is partially her fault. Politically, she's nonhierarchical, which means she doesn't believe in servants. She does her own cleaning, shopping, cooking, sewing, laundry. She prepares the elaborate dinners Lenz requests in the mornings and fails to come home for at nights. She's responsible for every aspect of their entertaining. Her husband enjoys parties, especially those held in his honor. He's been known to converse exclusively in those extemporaneous heroic couplets of his, perfect iambic pentameter from the arrival of the guests to their departure, from pancake soup to black walnut cake. The guests ooh and ahh and chuckle and guffaw and sometimes they even applaud, but she's fairly sure that they, like she, have come to find the relentless performing more annoying than clever.

Needless to say she also cares for her own son, her poor sickly son with the iffy heart and the propensity to pick up colds and fevers and the inability to put on weight. For Richard, there are no housekeepers, no day nurses, no malcontent governesses, no paddles, or switches. There are no trips, despite doctors' suggestions, to sanatoria in the Alps. There is only his mother doing every last thing herself.

One morning she even apprehends her own mugger, chasing him down and repeatedly banging him on the head with a burlap sack containing hard cheeses and a large turnip. "I think she'd have killed him if we hadn't pulled her off," the admiring grocer tells the local press. The article includes a photograph of Iris looking shy and sheepish and holding a wedge of Emmentaler. It's her third and final time in the papers.

"Oh, dear!" Iris says that evening to Richard. He's in his high chair, a pillow behind his back, a sash tying him to the chair just in case he figures out a way to slide down to the floor. He's thumping on his little tray with his wooden spoon. She's grated the Emmentaler, the weapon reduced to fluffy slivers that soon will be sprinkled on the sliced, sautéed turnip, which in turn will be baked and consumed at dinner. "You know that normally I wouldn't hurt a fly. I'm a pacifist through and through. It was just . . . well, it was my handbag."

To the other Richard, Richard Lehrer, she writes, "Anger overtook me and I became an unrecognizable monster capable of doing murder with a cheese. Sometimes these days I find myself wondering if I've taken leave of my senses. But that's the wonderful thing about the monograph I'm planning to write, isn't it? Everything is data. All is grist for my mill."

The reference in that letter—that was the last anyone heard of this monograph, this book.

Iris cuts the photograph from the paper and sends it to her sister Lily. "What clever caption do you have for this?" she writes.

Lily writes back: "The cheese stands alone."

1911

From the speech of Kaiser Wilhelm II, delivered at the inaugural ceremony of the Dahlem Institute for Physical Chemistry:

> Our Institute director, Lorenz Otto Alter, is ideally suited to his new position. His scientific achievements have already given great momentum to the German chemical industry, in which we are world leaders. His current work is also critical to maintaining Germany's stature in the world, though I have been told that I can say no more about this work at this time. It seems the only persons more enamored of secrets than statesmen are chemists.

Iris hates everything about Dahlem.

"Really?" Lily writes. "Hate? That's a childish word, don't you think?"

"Fine," Iris writes back. "I'm a child." Because she does, she foot-stomping, breath-holding, hair-tearing, fist-pounding hates the place. She hates its bourgeois tidiness, the prissy lawns, the fussily clipped border shrubs. She hates the long commute when she wishes to go into Berlin—and when doesn't she long to go into Berlin, with its theater, concerts, museums, all the things that don't exist in this suburb? She hates the hours she spends with the faculty wives. She hates the monstrous animal in the mansion next door, a wolf the owners insist is not a wolf, but a new breed. "How can you dislike a dog called a German shepherd?" Lenz asks her, and she bites her tongue as she so often does these days. All she says is, "He lunges at Prinz every chance he gets, and he never stops barking." Let Lenz figure out what she means, but isn't quite saying.

Nor did it take her long to pass this judgment on Dahlem. She began hating it the very first week they arrived. She hated the inaugural ceremonies, the parade down the rainy main thoroughfare. She has an aversion to all parades, but this one was especially off-putting, first the peacocking Kaiser, next the famous Christian theologian, and then, the scientists, which is to say, the Jews, bringing up the rear. Germany, God, and her son's father marching up the street. And she, Frau Doktor, relegated to the sidelines. The pecking order codified once and for all.

By then they'd already moved into the handsome white residence the Institute restored for them. Naturally it's the largest of the faculty homes, a three-storied honor, unless you happen to be nonhierarchical. Then, not only are you embarrassed by its size, but you have that much more housework and cooking to do. So much more hostessing.

Although lately she's realized she doesn't mind the housekeeping as much as one would think after hearing her complain. She notices that she's begun seeking out additional projects and chores. She's taken to sewing all her own clothing, although that's not really a choice on her part. She wears only *Reformkleider* now, those voluminous dresses of rough material designed to conceal a woman's body so she may be judged not on her figure but on the quality of her mind and her character. You can't find these dresses in stores.

Also, she's taken up gardening.

The garden (and Prinz's doghouse, so close to his enemy's territory) is situated in the yard directly behind the house. Directly behind the garden wall is the physical chemistry laboratory where Lenz and his assistants and his students work. The benefits of having one's husband's lab so close that you can look inside it from your kitchen window are frequently enumerated by the wives in the adjacent houses: it's a very short walk when it's time to bring him his lunch or the papers you've been editing and typing for him or anything else he's forgotten. He comes home energized from the day's work rather than weary from a long train or tram ride. Even if he works late into the evening and misses supper, he's usually home early enough to see the children before they're put to bed.

Iris has enumerated the drawbacks to no one but herself: every day you get to see the place you want to be but aren't. Also, if he doesn't come home at night you can easily tell by the darkened lab windows it's not because he's working late.

"I've been out with the donors," Lenz will say when he arrives home, midnight or later. Or "I've been at the club with Einstein." Or with Planck or with Moritz or with Meyer. Theo Meyer, Iris's old friend from university who wouldn't be here if not for her. "But if I *were* seeing other women," Lenz says, "whose fault would that be?"

Iris looks at him, her eyes devoid almost nearly of color, almost entirely of suspicion. "Did I say a word?" she asks.

She has not said a word because his point is not without merit. She left their marital bed when Richard was born, and she has never returned. The doctors urged her to move a cot into the nursery. She didn't hesitate. Is there a mother who would? The same doctors now assure her that Richard is sufficiently robust to forego this careful attention. She disagrees. Yes, Richard is healthier now, though still skinny as a broomstick and prone to sore throats and sniffles, but would he be as healthy if she weren't always by his side, monitoring his breathing, listening to his heart, ministering to the slightest rasp or rale before it can turn into something serious, something deadly?

And doesn't that make Lenz's philandering, which is of course what he's doing on those nights he claims to be with donors or Albert or Max or Emil or Theo—doesn't that make his infidelity and lies and efforts to transfer the blame to her astonishingly selfish, given that the reason she no longer shares his bed is that she's making certain their child doesn't die in his sleep?

It's more than that, though, and she knows it. It confounds her that she, such a lustful virgin, has lost all interest in marital relations. In fact, she's more than uninterested. If Lenz touches her in passing, just a hand on her shoulder, she becomes as enraged as if he's a stranger assaulting her. She tries to hide her rage from him, to take deep breaths or think of something soothing—her roses, the hummingbirds at the bee balm, the torte in the oven, anything really—but it's all she can do not to strike him. This is her reality, this inexplicable fury that overtakes her when her husband indicates that he would like her to provide him with marriage's physical comforts. And so if Lenz takes lovers, she supposes it's his right. She bristles and deflects, but in her heart she knows the blame does rest on her. She makes and abides by a decision: as long as he comes home before Richard wakes up in the morning, she'll say nothing. She sticks to this decision. Nothing is all Iris says.

And, as she lectures herself repeatedly, it's not all bad in Dahlem. Dahlem has its good points. Dahlem is clean. Dahlem is safe. The schools are up-to-date in their curricula and pedagogical methodology. The place is full of Jews like themselves, so there's none of the hostility, none of the sneers, no sense that there are places one isn't welcome. At the same time, the Jews here have all converted, so there's none of the shtetl, none of the beards and fur hats and fringes, none of the superiority that thinly disguises self-hatred or the self-deprecation that so loudly conveys superiority.

And Theo Meyer, her old friend from university, has joined them here; that's a pleasure. And he and all of her husband's students address her as Frau Doktor; that's a pleasure too, a bittersweet kindness. She likes the boys in the lab. She waves to them from the garden. She feeds them when they, with her husband, burst into her house at night, filled with ideas and excitement. They are nice young men who include Richard in their conversations and milder horseplay as if he's an equal. Sometimes she offers her own thoughts, an insight here or there, and they listen to her, thank her.

From time to time she dusts off her old lecture about the chemical properties of household cleansers and delivers it to one of the area's ladies' clubs. She no longer travels for these lectures; that's another benefit of being the director's wife. The lectures are now held in her own home, in the public parlor on the first floor of the mansion. She doesn't have the bother of hiring a car, of lugging around her notes and the bottles of ammonia and bleach and scouring powders she uses for purposes of demonstration. She can go upstairs as soon as the house is all hers once again and crawl into Richard's bed, a wet cloth over her eyes, a glass of wine on his little bedside table. On the other hand, now in addition to updating the lecture, she's the one who has to prepare the room and the cakes.

"If you want to know the truth," she tells Richard in the dark of their shared room, "I think I'll be giving up the lecturing business. Everyone always assumes your papa writes my talks anyway." She laughs. "No one ever assumes he also bakes the cakes."

Richard, her biggest fan, finds this a riot. His father baking tea cakes. That, he says, is a good one.

Spring 1914

Iris Emanuel Alter may hate Dahlem, but Dahlem is quite fond of Iris Emanuel Alter. In fact, Iris is very well liked wherever she lives, wherever she goes. People who know her invariably describe her as nice. It's true that sometimes they also compare her to rodents, but always to the least repellent of rodents. A bit of a mouse, someone might say, or shy as a rabbit. But they always come back to nice. So very nice. So unfailingly nice.

Mileva Einstein, for instance. When Iris dies a year from now, Mileva will say, "She was as nervous and high-strung as a squirrel. It makes sense it would be her heart that failed her. Although who among us is so good at love they don't die a failure in the heart department?" She'll sigh at her own mot. "But honestly," she'll add, "it's very tragic. She was the nicest person I've ever known."

But that's next spring. This spring, Mileva and her boys are living with the Alters while Albert endeavors to sort out his love life and Lenz acts as a go-between. Albert wants to leave Mileva for his cousin, Elsa. Lenz refuses to allow it. "What can I tell you?" Lenz says to Albert. "I'm modern in all respects except when it comes to divorce. Have an assignation, fine, but you can't actually move away from your children."

In Lenz's opinion, everything is now proceeding apace. "Has Albert agreed to stop seeing her?" Mileva asks when he returns from dinner and negotiations. "Well, no," Lenz says, "but he tells me he misses the boys. So that's an encouraging sign."

Mileva is weepy and maudlin, but extremely grateful to both Lenz and Iris. She expresses this gratitude incessantly. "It's so nice of you to take us in like this," she says multiple times a day. She calls the white mansion her beautiful asylum.

Being thanked excessively is just another chore, Iris has come to realize. Every day she has to stop what she's doing or put off what she'd like to begin doing to reassure Mileva that she's a welcome addition to Iris's daily life. "Please, don't mention it," Iris says, but Mileva mentions it again, then again.

Another reason to dread Mileva's expressions of gratitude is that too often they're followed by her own attempts to be gracious. "I want you to know," she says, lowering her voice, "that if you ever need a similar favor, our door will always be open to you." *Our* door. As if the future is certain, as if Mileva hasn't a doubt in the world that she and Albert will soon be reunited, at which point she can devote herself to spackling over the cracks in the Alters' own marriage.

The worst part about Mileva's invitation is that Iris can easily imagine having to take her up on it. She can see herself walking through Mileva's door after Lenz finally—inevitably—meets a woman for whom he overcomes his distaste for divorce. She sees herself carrying suitcases, hers and Richard's. She sees herself sending Richard upstairs to play with the Einstein boys, sees herself standing in the Einsteins' parlor, feeling lost or, even worse, crying.

"Our house is your house," they say. "Stay as long as you need to." The same things she's told Mileva.

Iris has been in the Einsteins' house many times. Like Albert, it's always disheveled. The settee in the parlor is always busy with toys and papers, a plate or two in need of washing, several lozenges of unwrapped sucking candy that have been partially sucked. In her grim fantasy it's Albert who clears a spot on that settee so Iris can sit, Albert who pats Iris's hand and mumbles words of comfort, while Mileva hurries to the kitchen to brew tea. Even in this imaginary scenario Iris is too embarrassed to ask for whisky.

She has to play it through her mind only once. She'd rather kill Lenz than move in with the Einsteins. Or kill herself. Or perhaps carry out one of those murder/suicides one is always reading about.

But no—she doesn't mean it. She won't harm Lenz. Not even when he tries to kiss her and her body shivers not with desire, but with the urge to claw at him with her fingernails. Even then all she does is make a plausible excuse—that torte in the oven, the bath she needs to run for Richard—and hurry away. She isn't violent. She wholly rejects violence. When she daydreams about killing Lenz, she's only being self-indulgent, melodramatic. She'll never let Lenz drive her to such clichéd behavior. She has too much pride, too much education, to play the role of vengeful wife. She doesn't want to go down in history as Frau Doktor Hell Hath No Fury.

She holds her head up. She behaves as if all is well. She throws his parties. She waves and cheers from reviewing stands. She's not the first woman in this world to find herself married to a famous man who's unfaithful. There are worse things in this life.

She's tried to explain all this to Mileva. If Albert refuses to accept conventional understanding of the laws pertaining to time and space, why would Mileva expect him to accept conventional understandings pertaining to domestic life?

She means for Mileva to smile ruefully—the rueful smile is Iris's specialty—but Mileva, still a Serbian peasant at heart, finds Iris's philosophy shocking. "Are you saying there's no such thing as a man who is both a genius and a decent human being?"

Is that what she's saying? Yes, she concludes, that's what she's saying. "Can you think of any?" she asks.

"What about your Lehrer?"

If Iris weren't such a nice person, she would get up and leave the room. Who is Mileva to mention Lehrer to her? But polite as always, she does nothing but answer the question. "It's true that Lehrer was devoted to Marthe," she says evenly, "and that Marthe was equally devoted to him. And, yes, he was unquestionably superb in his field. And, yes, so good to his students, Lord knows. But even I wouldn't say he was a genius. Not the way Albert and Lenz are."

"The problem," Mileva says, "is that I didn't know Albert was a genius when I married him. I thought he was brilliant, but brilliant I could keep up with. It was when he crossed into the land of genius that it all fell apart."

In addition to unfaithful geniuses for husbands, Iris and Mileva have one other thing in common: Mileva is a scientist too. That's where she met Albert, in school, in Zurich, the only woman in the class, although sadly, and unlike Iris, she never managed to pass her exams. But what difference does it make, that Iris has a diploma framed and hung on the wall of her writing room, while Mileva doesn't? Neither works in her field. Each tends house and raises children and entertains guests.

Iris has lately found herself making lists in her head. One of them she calls "Things Mileva and I Have in Common." On it go sons, science, and husbands. The other list is called "Things People Might Say I Have Over Mileva." That list includes Iris's German birth, her larger home, her superior housekeeping skills, her relative equanimity when it comes to Lenz's dalliances, and her framed degree, useless though the latter may be. Also, Iris, with her small, unassertive features, is prettier.

Although this last item is not much of an achievement. If the first word people use to describe Iris is nice, the first word they use to describe Mileva is ugly.

"Uncommonly ugly," Albert has said to Lenz.

Iris, engulfed in her *Reformkleid*, feels guilty about including physical appearance on the list. She feels guilty keeping the list at all. And yet daily she adds new items.

On her first night at the beautiful asylum, when she came across Iris's diploma hung on the wall of Iris's writing room, Mileva cried, "Ah! There it is in all its glory."

"Yes," Iris said. "There it is. A piece of paper under a piece of glass."

Mileva advanced, as if to take her by the shoulders. Iris took a step back. "You should be proud of it," Mileva said, without retreating. "You fought for it and you earned it." And when Iris said nothing, Mileva said, "I never got mine because I had no one wanting me to succeed. You had your extraordinary friendship with Lehrer, may he rest in peace." That was the first time Mileva wedged his name into a conversation.

Iris could see her houseguest's profile, the short nose, nostrils permanently flared, the high Slavic cheekbones and small angry eyes, the thin smear of mouth.

"Yes," Iris said. "Lehrer and I had a lovely professional friendship. Had. Past tense." This is a bad habit of hers. She says things to make people feel contrite; then, when it works, she feels worse than they do.

"I'm so sorry," Mileva said, though she didn't sound sorry, or at least not sufficiently sorry. "It was so very tragic. He was so young. I never used to think one's forties were young, but now that I'm thirty-eight . . . well. And to die that way, by fire." She shuddered, her shoulders by her ears like vulture wings. "I wouldn't wish it even on . . . No. I won't say her name."

This was Mileva's bad habit: she never quit while she was ahead. "And to die so stupidly," she continued. "That was the worst part of it. Such a waste. You ask yourself: How can a man so smart be so stupid?"

So here's one more thing Iris has over Mileva. Iris is not as provincial, not as conventional. She doesn't place long life above everything else. Better to live a daring but short life. Better to chase pleasure, have adventures, fight to make dreams come true. What is it, she wonders, that the world finds so charming about old age?

Over the course of Mileva's visit Iris has sometimes tried to populate a third list: "Things Mileva Has Over Me." It's been a noble but ultimately impossible endeavor.

There's Mileva's relative youth—Iris is about to turn forty-three—but that's just an accident of birth.

There's the fact that Mileva has two sons to Iris's one. But Iris's Richard is worth twice Hans Einstein when it comes to temperament, intelligence, character—of course Richard is two years older; it's only fair to take that into consideration when comparing the pair—and as for Eduard, you can't really judge him at this point. He's three-going-on-four, still too much a baby for anyone to guess who he'll someday be. Too much a miserable baby, a crier, a bad sleeper, a fussy eater. Always the runny nose and the penchant for half-eaten sticky candy.

There's another item that might go on the pro-Mileva list, and that's the fact that Albert turned out to be the more brilliant and famous of their husbands. The ne'er-do-well clerk from Zurich, the wounded bird Lenz took under his wing: it's still hard to believe he's the one flying higher. But, as Iris keeps trying to explain to Mileva, husbands like Albert and Lenz can be as much a curse as they are a blessing, which means that in some ways Iris is the better off in this category too. The greater the genius, the worse the marriage, and so, in the end, she declares this item a wash. She puts it on no list at all.

This means the list in Mileva's favor has no entries on it whatsoever. Whereas the pro-Iris list is getting so long that, when she tries to go through it in her head, she's always forgetting one of its many items. It was a full week, for example, before Iris recalled the baby Mileva and Albert had a couple of years before they married. Mileva, back in Serbia with her unsympathetic parents, birthed it alone, and when she returned to Zurich, she returned alone. Adoption? An institution? A shallow grave? It's never talked about, although Iris once asked Lenz what had happened to the child. "As is the case with so many things," Lenz said, "only God and Albert know."

A baby unaccounted for. Certainly this went on the list of things Iris had over Mileva. Of all her faults and sins, Iris had never misplaced a baby.

It's June now. In fact, it's Iris's birthday. She mentions this to no one. She's just gotten through two separate parties, one for Hans's tenth, one for Richard's twelfth. She doesn't want to be cajoled into baking yet another cake, cleaning up after three messy boys.

It's also, as they say, the calm before the storm. In less than a week the archduke will be assassinated, and the events that will lead to the first world war will be triggered. (Pun intended. Pun always intended.) But for now Lenz is in Berlin, sitting on a settee glazed with sugar from Eduard's discarded candies, drinking whisky from a teacup—the glasses are all in the sink—and talking science with Albert, while Iris and Mileva are an hour away, sitting in the upstairs parlor in the director's mansion, sipping brandy that has been decanted largely for decorative purposes from crystal snifters that came with the house. Brandy is not what Iris usually drinks. She doesn't want to be drinking it now. She wants to excuse herself. She wants to get in some gardening while the sun is low, but if she goes to the garden, Mileva will follow and stand over her, talking and weeping and offering gratitude and advice. She doesn't relish working in a Mileva-shaped shadow.

"You don't have to entertain her all day," Lenz has said. "Just live your life."

Iris says she doesn't see how she can go about her day as if Mileva isn't there when she is there. "What do you know about it?" she asks. "It's not as though she's trailing you wherever you go."

"Don't ask for my opinion if you're just going to ignore my advice," Lenz snaps, and Iris hisses, "You're the one who invited her here. You're the one who decided only you could negotiate the Great Einsteinian Reconciliation of 1914," and that sets off what would normally have been one of their screaming fights if Mileva weren't in the house, but given that she is and given her relative proximity and the porous nature of walls even in fine homes like theirs, they whisper and mutter instead, thereby, Iris notes, proving her point.

"A little more?" Iris says now, not waiting for an answer, automatically refilling Mileva's glass and her own. Midday, and once again nothing is getting accomplished. There's not only the garden. There's the marketing. There's the wash. There's her correspondence. There's tonight's dinner—the many courses Lenz has requested but will not come home for, as per usual. At least, she comforts herself, she doesn't have to bother with cake.

"Here's a story about Lehrer," Iris says. She knows that when she herself brings up his name, it only encourages Mileva to do so at other times, which irks Iris no end. And yet there are times when she needs to talk about him, finds relief in saying his name out loud.

"Another *Doktorvater* story," Mileva murmurs. "You have so many."

"This one you'll find instructive, I think."

"I only meant that you were lucky."

"I was," Iris says. "And then I wasn't." She takes a sip from her glass before she begins, coating her tongue so the words flow easier. "When I finally realized my situation with Lenz was not going to be what I'd hoped," she says, "that is, when I realized that when Lenz asked me to be his wife, he actually meant he wanted me to be his wife"—here Iris smiles ruefully, and Mileva laughs outright—"I wrote to Lehrer."

She omits the fact that this was hardly unusual, that she wrote to Lehrer every day after she left university, frequently twice a day, that she continues to write to him every day even now, two years after his death. She writes late at night and then, when the ink dries, she folds the ecru sheets of stationery, pressing them flat with a heavy crystal inkwell.

"My letter went something like this," Iris says. "Dear Herr Professor: It seems as though I've married Henry the Eighth. All Alter wants from me is a son and to serve as the hostess of his parties and to look the other way when he's with this or that woman."

"Why doesn't anyone warn you?" Mileva asks. Her small eyes shine like two black beans after soaking. "Why doesn't anyone tell you we all wind up married to Henry the Eighth?" She looks at Iris with those wet eyes. Her flared nostrils widen even farther with anger. "Although, what am I saying? Nobody warned me, it's true, but Lehrer did try to warn you, didn't he? He asked you not to marry, isn't that right? I suppose he might have been justified if he'd replied you had no one to blame but yourself."

Iris has thought the same thing, though that doesn't prevent her from resenting Mileva for saying it. All right—the truth is, she hardly minds Lenz's other women. In some ways they've been gifts. But the unexpected exclusion from the lab—that was the surprise, the slap in the face.

She was angry with Lenz, of course she was. But she reserved her greatest fury for herself. She should have kept her promise, should have said no when Lenz proposed marriage at the electrochemistry conference. In fact, she *had* said no, hadn't she? But then she'd changed her mind. Why? She still doesn't know. The hope that it would lead to a university position— that's what she'd told herself. Now she finds the younger version of herself suspect and shallow. What had her motives been really? Loneliness? Sexual privation? Drunkenness? Someday, when she wants the answer, she'll ask Lily. Lily knows everything. So says Lily

Mileva is also generous in that way. "You ought to consult Dr. Freud," she says. She isn't the first person to make this suggestion. "I was blinded by my love for Albert when I married," she says, "but you, I think, were blinded by something else."

"What? What was I blinded by?" Iris is being sincere; she genuinely wants to know. Everyone else avoids the subject of her thwarted career, but Mileva thinks that she and Iris are two of a kind, that if they just share their data, together they can figure out what went wrong, and so, how to fix it.

"That's just it," Mileva says. "Neither of us has the first idea. That's why I'm suggesting the talking cure. Someone ought to find out what goes on the brains of women like us."

When Lehrer responded to Iris's letter—the one in which she referenced Henry the Eighth—he'd been as comforting as one could be in a situation where there was no solution. "My dear Anne Boleyn," he wrote. "The only way a woman can avoid waking up next to Henry is to model herself after his daughter Elizabeth and sleep next to no one at all. Look at Meitner," he added, leaping centuries, switching countries. "All alone in life, but able to do her work because of it."

Mileva drains the last drop of her brandy. "So what did Lehrer write in return?" she asks. "Did he throw Meitner in your face?"

Iris smiles faintly. "Well, I wouldn't put it quite that way. But yes, he mentioned her."

"They're always throwing her at us. I like her, I do, but enough already."

"The virgin queen," Iris murmurs.

"Hardly. She's been sleeping with Hahn all this time, you know."

"Who doesn't know? Besides Hahn's wife, that is."

"So she has it over us on two counts. No husband. Illicit sex, which, if I recall, is the best kind."

I wouldn't know, Iris thinks. But says, "And a career. So three counts."

Forgetting that her glass is empty or perhaps hoping for a last drop to miraculously appear, Mileva lifts the snifter to her lips, tips it nearly upside down. Nothing. Naughty as a cat, she darts her tongue out, licks the inside of the rim.

"Goodness," Iris has to say. "Let's just have another."

Outside, the boisterous laughter of young men. Inside, the delicate clinking of crystal.

"Why don't they ever bring up Marie?" Mileva asks. "Just once I'd like one of them to bring up Marie."

"Richard did, actually." The brandy is sticky on Iris's lips, thick on her tongue. It tastes medicinal, it tastes like a grimace, and yet she's acquired a taste for it, she has to admit. "He went on to say it wasn't fair of him to mention Meitner, but leave out Curie. But then he added, 'However, if Lenz doesn't see the Curies as exemplars, then what good does the fact of them do you?'"

"You know it by heart." Mileva's black eyes glint with pity, leaving Iris no choice but to smile broadly.

"Someone writes you an elegy," she says, "it stays with you."

"To us." Mileva offers the rim of her glass once again. "To the women behind the men."

"Far behind them," Iris says. She forces another smile. She glances out the window to the weedy flower beds behind the house. She knows what's coming next.

"I'm as responsible for special relativity as Albert," Mileva says, her glass still aloft. "We are Germany's Curies, Albert and I. It's just that no one is allowed to know it."

"Only Albert and God," Iris says, though she knows the only way Mileva has ever assisted Einstein in his work has been by preparing dinner and running the household—and she didn't do even that well.

"And you and Lenz are Curies, too," Mileva says ardently. She returns the glass to the table where it wobbles. "You're as responsible for the manna process as he is."

This isn't true either. But it's at least truer. Iris understands every aspect of Lenz's work. When he was working on the process, she made suggestions, offered opinions. She not only edited and typed his manuscript, she rewrote parts of it. She saw where his research was heading, she steered him in prof-itable directions, she was of use. She had, after all, that piece of paper under that piece of glass. But she says none of this to Mileva. She says only, "Another thing you and I have in common, then."

"I don't see how you can be so blasé about it. Our own hus-bands. They took our careers. They stood in our light."

"Maybe we should start sleeping with Otto Hahn," Iris says. "Apparently that's the path to success."

Mileva laughs. "Shtupping Otto. Have we not suffered enough?"

The brandy throughout the day. That's the only thing keeping her sane, the only thing keeping her from screaming all morning, all afternoon, and then, at night, baying at the moon along with the wolf-dog next door. A headache is almost always erupting behind her brow. Her eyes throb. She glances out the window, where Richard is roughhousing with the Einstein boys. She clenches her fists. Her gentle son.

Sometimes Richard Alter wakes in the middle of the night to find his mother propped on her elbow, watching him from the cot alongside his bed. It's neither a shock nor an invasion. She's slept beside him his entire life.

He's heard the story many times, how sickly he was as a baby, how close she needed to be. She insists she still needs to be that close, and who is he to doubt her? It's never crossed his mind to question the arrangement.

Because she worries, he worries too. Not as much as she does; that would be impossible. "Take a sweater in case it gets cold," she tells him on warm spring days, "and a salt pill in case it gets hot."

Every now and then, he dares to ignore her. Sweaterless, he sneaks out of the house, feeling as guilty and giddy as he assumes he would if he had a flask of whisky in his pocket. The guilt persists long after the giddiness dissipates.

Still, the larger part of him takes her concerns seriously. He will remain sharply aware of any shifts in the external temperature for the rest of his life; he'll retain an abiding suspicion of perfect weather and a grave mistrust of inclemency and cold. In 1914, a boy on the fulcrum between childhood and adolescence, he frets over his health as if he were an old man. His weak and tentative heart. His limited lung capacity. Heart attacks come about quickly and unexpectedly, Iris reminds him. He's only twelve, and, yes, he looks so much younger, but he is not to let chronology or physiology fool him. Terrible things happen at every stage of one's life if one doesn't watch out, and discretion being the better part of achieving old age, he declines his father's occasional invitations to engage in strenuous outdoor activities—biking, hikes, the constitutional.

It's true that the doctors say he's better now, perfectly fine in fact, but as Iris says, who is one going to trust, a doctor with hundreds of patients or a mother with just one son?

"You do know, don't you," his father says at the breakfast table—they rarely see each other anywhere else—"that the only person who hasn't recovered from your childhood illnesses is your mother?"

It doesn't occur to Richard that his mother's hovering may be not merely unnecessary but also embarrassing until the Einsteins move in. "You're how old, and your mother still sleeps with you?" Hans says. "Does she still bathe you too? Does she change your diapers?"

The thing is, she *does* still bathe him. Richard puts an end to that immediately, though it isn't easy. His mother is grief-stricken. Richard has to agree to a compromise: Iris will still run the bath, lest he get caught up in daydreaming and wind up stepping into a tub of scalding water. The rest of it—Iris sitting alongside him, their meandering conversations amid the warm steam, the two of them sometimes singing together, his little zipfel bobbing on the surface, then Iris holding out the big towel, Iris tousling his hair dry—

All right, she says glumly, he can tend to it on his own from now on.

The shared room, though—she won't budge on that. That, she says, is a matter of life or death. And because he has never really objected to her in the cot next to him and because he doesn't know who to believe when it comes to his health, he doesn't argue. He has no interest in dying in his sleep just so Hans Einstein will deem him manly. In fact, when you think about it, it's Hans Einstein's fault that Richard isn't pushing his mother out the door, back into her own room. Now that Hans and his brother and mother are living with the Alters, the only time Richard can really talk to Iris is when he wakes up in the middle of the night to find her awake too, staring at him.

"Bad dream?" she asks. "You were tossing."

"No," he says.

"Things on your mind, then?"

He hesitates, then—the hell with Einstein—he initiates the night game he and his mother made up years ago.

"If you want to know the truth," he says, "Hans and Eduard threw rocks at the ducks on the pond yesterday. I had to run over and stop them."

The game has no name, but it has rules. You tell the truths one can only reveal in the dark.

Iris says, "If you want to know the truth, Hans and Eduard are very angry little boys. Their papa is having a dalliance with his own cousin. He's not even trying to hide it. The whole world knows."

"If you want to know the truth, even I know."

"If you want to know the truth, many men are like Hans and Eduard's father."

"If you want to know the truth, when Hans told me about Uncle Albert, I told him about Papa. So he wouldn't feel so alone."

"You know about Papa? Who in the world told you?"

"You didn't say if you want to know the truth."

"If you want to know the truth, I would like to know who told you."

"If you want to know the truth, you and Papa are not the most talented of whisperers."

"Oh, God in heaven. What terrible parents you have . . . if you want to know the truth. We should be protecting you from this sort of domestic mayhem."

"If you want to know the truth, I think it's good for me to know. I think it's helping to form my character. When I grow up, I'll never treat my wife so poorly."

"We have each other," his mother says. "That's the most important thing. The most important truth."

"If you want to know the truth, I feel sorry for Hans and Eduard. Their father is just like Papa, but their mother is nothing like you. That means they have no one."

This last truth is a paraphrasing of something she has told him more than once: that no mother cares about her child the way Iris cares about Richard, that other children are so much more alone in this world than he. It's not unusual for his truths to be recycled versions of hers. Other than his occasional failure to pack a sweater, other than the times he tosses his salt pills into the pond, he has no misdeeds, no youthful crimes to confess. Also, because he restricts his sporting life, which in turn restricts his social life, he has few opportunities to accumulate interesting secrets.

So he appropriates her secrets and her ideas. That, or he downright lies. It keeps the game going, and if Eduard Einstein is utterly bewildered when Iris takes him aside and gently lectures him about the importance of kindness to animals, what does it matter? Eduard doesn't know why she's telling him all this, but he vigorously agrees with her. Stoning ducklings is a horrible thing for a person to do.

August 4, 1914

On the first day of the Great War, the Alter family breakfasts together. Lenz looks appraisingly at Richard, still so boyish, with the towhead and peach fuzz, the knobby elbows and knees. His facial features are those of his mother. Both are fair and their noses narrow, their eyes that pale and eerie blue. At least one of Iris's ancestors must have been intimately acquainted with a gentile across the nearby Polish border.

"Did you know that blind men's eyes sometimes turn that same shade?" Lenz teases. He waves a hand in front of Richard's face. "Can you see me? How many fingers?"

"Stop it," Richard says, brushing the hand away. "I see you. Believe me, I see you."

None of this strikes Iris as funny or even harmless. "Don't curse his eyes," she says.

She's not superstitious except when she is. There's a limit to what science can accomplish or explain. As a scientist, she knows this better than anyone. She sometimes wishes she'd paid attention to her aunts' remedies for dispelling a careless curse. Is this when you throw salt over your shoulder? Is this when you spit on the floor? Maybe this is the time when you spit on your husband; maybe a divorce is what's called for, maybe a person should steel herself to what seems to be her fate, should open the door, invite that fate in.

Mileva is gone. A few weeks before the war began, the two couples, Lenz and Iris, Albert and Mileva, sat at the formal dining room table, as Mileva silently read a document Albert had prepared for her signature: the terms by which he would permit the marriage to continue. When she finished reading, she'd requested a pen. "Will you witness?" she asked the Alters.

Lenz had recoiled. "I'm sure that's not necessary," he said. "I'm sure if you live up to your end of things, so will Albert."

"I'll sign," Iris said.

They'd left that day, the four Einsteins, the boys subdued and, Iris thought, apprehensive. The wisdom of children: the marriage had ended the day before Germany declared war on Russia. In the Einstein's case, both sides had failed to uphold their end of their alliance.

"Quelle surprise," Iris said to Lenz, who glared at her. Unable to save the Einstein's marriage—a personal defeat—he was now working out the terms of their divorce. When Albert received the Nobel—he would, of course; no one doubted that—the prize money would go to Mileva. Even Elsa, the cousin, the mistress, still years from becoming Albert's second wife, agreed.

"I'm so grateful to Lenz," Mileva writes Iris from a boarding-house in Zurich. "When the Nobel money comes, the boys and I will be comfortable at last."

"She resides in a fantasy land," Iris writes the late Richard Lehrer. "Yes, it's a satisfactory arrangement in theory, that is, if the theory in question is Albert's theory regarding time, which argues that Mileva is living in comfort in what we perceive to be the future, but, given time's fluidity, is actually occurring now. Unfortunately, she's impoverished in what we perceive to be the present."

As Iris would be if she left Lenz. If Lenz left her.

EINSTEIN'S CONDITIONS (ABRIDGED)
   A. You will make sure:
      1. that my clothes and laundry are kept in good order;
      2. that my bedroom and study are kept neat.

B. You will forgo:
    1. my sitting at home with you;
    2. my going out or traveling with you.
C. You will obey the following points:
    1. you will not expect any intimacy from me;
    2. you will stop talking to me if I request it.

It's like a horror movie, isn't it? It makes our eyes go wide and our jaws drop. And yet, like a horror movie, there's something about it we find riveting, almost delicious. Maybe it's that it lets us feel that in one way—basic kindness—we are superior to Albert Einstein. But also—we can't help it—we love its strict adherence to the outline form. We love the perfect punctuation. We love the pleasing repetitions. We like reading the first word of each sentence out loud, as if it's a kind of a poem—one of those minimalist Japanese poems like haiku or tanka—but a poem not about nature or love, but about *the* nature of love, the nature of marriage and human relationships:

that that
my my
you you

Bicker bicker bicker. Mine all mine. I blame you you you.

Of course it isn't Japanese in its meaning. Orderly, formal, degrading, it's very much what the three of us, products of the twentieth century, descendants of refugees, have come to think of as German.

December 1914

Lenz Alter has stepped up his work in the lab. The windows remain lit until dawn. Whatever he's doing in there, it's all still a secret. No one is supposed to know a thing about it.

"I'm the opposite of a blind man," Richard says when his father teases him about his eye color, his vision. "I see everything. I see through walls. I see in the dark. I see under water. I see the past and the future. I see ghosts and goblins dancing in our reception rooms, and when I look up at the sky at night I see Martians. Of course that means I also see what you're up to in the lab. That secret project of yours? The one you think I know nothing about? I see it all."

Unlike her son, who is only teasing back, who is all cunning and bluster, Iris is a chemist, and she does know what Lenz is working on, the kind of potions he's concocting.

"I see what's in your mind," Richard says. "I see the formulae in your head. I jot them down in my secret notebooks. I analyze them all through the night. I have a few improvements to suggest."

"You're not so funny either," Iris tells him.

He spends much of his winter break from school in his room. From his window he can see Prinz asleep in the garden's weak sunlight. He can also see into the lab. Especially when he's down with a cold—now, for instance, a late afternoon, his eyes and nose runny and his heart, in his opinion, beating a little faster than normal, which he decides not to tell his mother about, at least not right away—he kneels on his bed for hours, watching the students inside the lab running around, sometimes indulging in a spate of back-patting and hand-shaking.

Such a difference, he feels, between being eleven and being twelve. Or maybe it was all the time spent with Hans. Iris's reticence when he asks legitimate questions is beginning to make him feel less protected, more vulnerable. He's not angry exactly—he's incapable of getting angry with her—but he's frustrated. He wants to know what his father is up to. He has a right to know, he tells both parents. He gets irritated when Lenz won't tell him, but he's flabbergasted when Iris won't, not even under the cover of darkness. A betrayal, he thinks. She's taking the wrong side. And who else does he have, really, but her?

On the day of the explosion Richard first blames the French. He opens his window, hangs out, looks for biplanes overhead. But only the paltry winter sun is visible in the clear sky.

And yet there's a cloud. It's black in color, cumulous in shape. It scuds along, fast, but along the ground. It's emerging from a crumpled wall of the laboratory.

A bomb. What else can Richard conclude? Mystery solved: his father is building a new kind of bomb for the army, and someone did something wrong and it's gone off. What else can it be? The thunderation was so unprecedented he not only heard it, he felt it in his bones and his teeth. His eardrums are still reverberating. He feels as though he's been broken to pieces by a jackhammer.

He continues to watch, riveted, as the cloud sails through the garden. It drops cinders on the flowers and lawn. Prinz barks and bites at it, his chain taut and choking. Young men in white coats or in suits run out of the lab as if chasing it, as if trying to encircle it and coax it back inside. Their faces are smudged black. They're coughing, crying, shouting for help. Richard yells down to one of them, and the student stops for a moment, looks up.

Herr Professor is unharmed, the student shouts. But an assistant's hand has been blown off, and Theo Meyer is dead.

Later Richard will learn that his mother was in the room at the other end of the lab, where they keep the animals. He won't be surprised. It's a new cause of hers. She's always been fond of animals. The ducks, the birds, their own cowardly Prinz. If he wishes to know the truth, she has said more than once in the dark, she can't bear to think about the kinds of deaths those animals in the lab endure. The only thing worse, she says, are the lives they endure until those deaths. There have been complaints about her, Richard knows. His parents scream about it over dinner as Richard sits at the end of the table, holding his chin up with the palm of one hand, stabbing his meat with his fork. He doesn't like sausage as much as his father does—his mother has told him all about sausage—but there's satisfaction in feeling the tines puncture first the resisting casing, then the meat itself. He makes his dinner spurt yellow juice as, over his head, his parents shout about white mice and cats.

It's unnerving, the staff has told Herr Professor Alter, to watch Frau Doktor Alter interact with the animals as if they were pets. It puts the staff in an uncomfortable position, to be made to witness one of the condemned cats standing on her lap, reaching up, touching her cheek with its paw, touching its pink nose to her nose. It's bad for morale. It creates an unprofessional environment. It's as if the farmer's wife were giving affectionate names to the lambs they'll soon be asked to slaughter.

Lenz can't abide the petty complaints of his workers. Farmers' children give names to lambs and calves all the time, he has told them, and yet they all manage to sit down for supper. But he has also ordered Frau Doktor to stop visiting the cages.

When Iris hears the blast at the other end of the hall, she drops the orange cat she was explaining things to and runs toward the explosion. In the damaged lab she finds her husband standing over Theo Meyer. Lenz is rigid, helpless, staring.

"I was in this room not sixty seconds ago," he mutters. "Moritz called me into the hallway. If he hadn't, I'd have been here when it happened."

She kneels beside Theo, loosens his necktie, listens to his stuttering breath. His eyes are closed, not even a flutter behind the lids. She presses her hand to his heart, feels nothing but the heat of blood warming her fingers. It doesn't revolt her or make her dizzy. She's dealt with blood before: she's a cook; she's a woman; she's a mother.

She looks up for a moment. Her husband is still gazing around. He says, "I was in this room not sixty seconds ago. Moritz called me into the hallway."

When she looks back down, Theo is dead. She feels tears on her cheeks. She strokes his hair, forgetting how bloody her hands are. The strands of his hair become red and wet. Or, really, redder and wetter; it isn't as if he was pristine when she arrived. She wipes her hand on her skirt. Someone says quite matter-of-factly, "First the cats, now this. She's a ghoul."

She looks up to see who has said it. It's the young man who lost his hand. He's sitting in a chair in a corner. At his wrist is a tourniquet made from someone's shirt. Not Lenz's. Lenz is still dressed and clean, his tie still knotted.

"He's in shock," she says of the man with the tourniquet. "Keep him warm."

His calling her a ghoul—she honestly isn't offended. He said it without judgment or rancor. He was just making an observation, as scientists do. By ghoul, she believes he simply meant that she's a human being who isn't deterred by death, a woman who doesn't avoid attachments to animals slated to die, a woman who doesn't cower or faint when confronted with the bloodied corpse of a friend. Does he know she also believes that all living things continue to be, even after so-called death? She's written as much to the late Richard Lehrer just the other day. "We are energy," she wrote, "and energy doesn't simply disappear."

And because she never said it herself, we have to say it for her. There she stood, among these men, these scientists who daily let loose fumes that strangled cats to death, tweaking and perfecting, cheering and backslapping when they got it right, and yet *she* was the ghoul.

Richard spends Christmas and New Year's Eve sneezing and sulking. His parents refuse to tell him what caused the explosion. Then it's 1915, and still no one will tell him. In fact, no one talks about the explosion anymore. It's wartime; prolonged grieving is indecorous. When a loved one is lost, one is meant to shed tears at the funeral, then grit one's teeth and gird one's loins and get on with it. Only in the dark can Richard say to his mother, "Do you miss Herr Meyer?"

"If you want to know the truth, I very much do," she says. Her voice is brandy-thick, brandy-lazy, a muddy river. "He was my classmate at university. He worked with Richard Lehrer. I helped get him his position here. He was one of my only friends."

He'd asked the same question when Richard Lehrer died. That time, in the same muddy-river voice, she said, "I miss him every time I take a breath. And yet—listen, this is important—I still go on. The worst happens, and people go on. It may hurt to breathe, but that's no excuse to stop breathing. No matter what, you inhale and exhale. Your heart keeps beating. It may also harden, but never mind that. Hard hearts can keep beating. Do you understand?"

He said that he did. He thought that he had. But as it turned out, he hadn't. He thought she was talking about *her* breath, *her* heart. Only later would he realize she was talking about his.

"Also," she'd said, "I feel Herr Professor Lehrer is not really gone."

"You mean you think he's in heaven?"

"No." She became a little crisp. "No," she said again, softening. "I don't mean that at all. Someday when you're not so tired, I'll explain your Uncle Albert's theories to you."

It was one of those times he'd become resentful. He wasn't all that tired, and he had a handle on relativity. He wished she would just come out and tell him things.

He feels the same way now. He longs for clear messages. Save the mice! Free the cats! Messages like that he can understand.

Although now, a full month after the explosion, he realizes he no longer agrees. This is another recent change in his relationship with her: he no longer admires the things she says, the beliefs she holds. Free the cats? Then what would you have? A town full of feral cats and a reputation for mawkishness instead of a secret weapon to win the war.

He tries to trick her into giving him details by feigning certitude. "Everyone," he says, "knows that Papa is working on something that will end the war quickly."

"Do they?" she says.

"Everyone says it's a new kind of bomb."

"Everyone has a lot to say. Maybe everyone should focus on his own problems."

"Well, everyone's just guessing. But I'm almost positive he's right."

"Are you?"

"I'm curious about it from a scientific point of view."

She laughs.

"I'm his son. Shouldn't I know the details?"

"The details won't make you happy."

"I'm not a baby. I can keep a secret."

"Oh, Richard," she says. "What do you want from me?"

He says, "If you want to know the truth, I want to know the truth."

There's a pause. She sighs. "Richard," she says, "if I knew, I'd tell you."

They have no mechanism for crying foul, for penalizing a player who out-and-out lies. Also, she never cried foul when, a year ago, he was a child making up lies about poor little Eduard Einstein and ducks. So he returns the favor. He doesn't challenge her either.

April 1915

Here's the thing about the manna process: a little tweak here, a little tweak there, and instead of food for the starving, you've got yourself the first truly effective chemical weapon.

Once upon a time, our mother used to tell us, there lived a great German patriot who invented a weapon so powerful and, yes, so terrible, he was sure it would bring the Great War to a swift and just conclusion.

A little bit of whitewashing there, but isn't that how family stories go? "Once upon a time," said our mother, propped up in her bed, the three of us sitting cross-legged by the footboard, and "Once upon a time" made whatever she said next—the truth, a lie, a wish—something to remember and repeat and pass on.

We listened avidly. Our mother rambled, occasionally stopping to sip her Tab, blow her smoke. She told us that at first the German military rejected the great patriot's new weapon. The German generals wanted to stick to the old ways of war. They cared more about the rules of conduct than they cared about winning. They were gentlemen.

And so the great patriot went to the kaiser directly.

That's how great and important the patriot was: the kaiser received him in private.

"Tell me," the patriot said with great and persuasive logic, "how is being dead different if it's caused by chlorine gas rather than by flying pieces of metal?"

"When you put it like that, we'd be foolish not to use it," the kaiser no doubt never said, though our mother asserted that he had. "And surely, once France sees what the *giftgas* can do, they will surrender at once. After experiencing a weapon like that a single time, no one will want to encounter it ever again. We may just end war forever thanks to you."

Even back then we were suspicious. After school, when she was still at work, we'd take one of the biographies from the living room bookshelf and skim the index.

Wilhelm II, discussion of chlorine gas with

Lady would find and read the passage out loud. It was like discovering the unexpurgated Brothers Grimm version of a fairy tale you'd known only as a Disney cartoon. You thought the wicked stepsister merely tried to squeeze her big fat feet into the delicate slipper? Oh no—not so. She'd actually cut off her toes to manage it.

Our mother told us the army used the gas to win the Second Battle of Ypres. She never told us that Lenz stood on a hill in Belgium alongside the reluctant generals—the gentlemen—and, at 5:00 p.m., personally tested the wind. We try to imagine it: our great-grandpa holding a wet finger skyward. Our great-grandpa personally releasing the yellow-gray fumes.

Other things our mother never mentioned: that he raised his binoculars and watched French and Algerian soldiers fall to their knees in the face of the advancing, visible wall of gas. That he watched the same soldiers eat handfuls of mud and tear off their shirts, stuffing the material down their throats in a futile effort to quell the unfathomable and theretofore unimaginable searing produced by something once likened to manna from heaven.

She did tell us that within minutes of the gas's release, all gunfire ceased. But only the books told us that when the guns fell silent, so did the German troops. Instead of cheering their victory, they held their positions and looked into one another's eyes as they silently listened to the howling enemy and to another ghastly moaning they couldn't identify until a farm boy mouthed, "Milk cows." Decades later a private who'd been there that day would say he didn't know why, but this was what he heard in his nightmares: not the agonized shrieking of dying men but the anguished lowing of dying cows.

April 22, 1915, 5:20 p.m.: French soldiers retch yellow sputum. Their alveoli rupture and their faces turn yellow-green and they die in the fields on their backs. Or if they don't die, if they're one of the few who manage to get to a medical tent, they writhe on the ground beneath the canvas. The yellow-green cast to their skin turns a deep violet red, save for their ears and fingernails, which turn blue, and the mucus they cough up is green and so is the blood they spit. They lie on the ground a day or two more, delirious and gasping. Then they die.

Of course our mother didn't omit what for her was the best part: on April 24 he's given the title of captain by the kaiser himself. It's a remarkable honor for a civilian and, above all, for a Jew. Although our great-grandfather quibbled with the latter. "You know I'm not a Jew," he said to the officers who'd been with him at Ypres. "I became a Lutheran years ago."

"Ah," teased a duke, "clever and cunning and baldly duplicitous . . . but no, not Jewish at all."

Lenz no doubt laughed at that. Maybe he came up with a

witty couplet. *Schooled and baptized, even christened/Still, once a Jew, you're never Christianed.* All right, that's us, not him. But he was known to be a good sport. He was in a good mood those days, and why not? There'd have been cigars and women and invitations to join certain clubs that had previously been un-available to him, and all because of his manna process. Our mother took one lesson from the story: we were all descended from greatness. We took another: plucking life from the sky or raining death from the sky—it was all the same thing to Lorenz Otto Alter.

May 1915

Ten days after the gas is deployed in Ypres, Iris, at Lenz's insis-tence, gives a dinner to celebrate his promotion. Lenz will be leaving for the Russian front soon, Captain Alter reporting for duty, Captain Alter here to personally teach the generals in the east how to measure air currents, determine exactly when they should let the gas fly toward the Cossacks and Tatars and Slavs. He wants the dinner to take place before he goes, wants his friends to see him with his new insignia: tassels, braids, pips.

Iris schedules the party for the night before the trip to Russia. The day of the party she wakes up sick. ("Or so she says," says our mother.) In any case, she wants to cancel. Lenz slams his fist down on the breakfast table. She jumps. Richard keeps his eyes on his skittering plate. No, not cancel, Iris says. Postpone. When he comes back from Russia, there will be time enough to celebrate his teaching yet another set of generals how to suffo-cate boys.

Lenz puts his foot down figuratively, throws his newspaper literally. He doesn't wish to hear her politics. He uses the word *treason.* He uses the word *cruel.* It's bad enough, the things men have to do for their countries during wartime, but for her to speak to him as if he enjoys it, as if he relishes what takes place on the field of battle . . .

Richard leaves the table without bothering to ask permission. Iris raises both hands, surrenders. During the day she prepares the meal, sets the table. She presses and lays out his uniform. She chooses the wines. When all is ready, they have half an hour before the guests arrive in which to resume screaming at each other.

The first couple to arrive on the front step can hear everything and will later say that they stood at the grand door to the villa and exchanged worried glances, that the husband, a young chemist in Lenz's lab, leaned over and whispered to his wife, "They haven't seen us yet; should we run?"

But when the couple brace themselves and ring the bell, Iris opens it, appearing relaxed and welcoming and looking pretty despite the woolen dress that seems to have swallowed all but her head. Many years later the husband will tell Richard Alter that his father had been a lion and his mother a mouse, that this was the trouble with their marriage, and the wife will say, "Yes, that's all true, but she was a very nice mouse; everyone liked her."

Despite the unpromising prologue, the party's a success. None of the other guests have any idea that the host and hostess despise each other. The host, these other guests will say, was as gregarious and charming as ever, the hostess as sweet and attentive. She gave the first toast, spoke of her husband's genius. Later they'll find out she wrote a letter to the Supreme War Command that same day, a letter that described her husband's work with words such as *perversion* and *barbarity*, but tonight she gives no indication that she doesn't find poison gas to be a fine addition to the world's smorgasbord of armaments.

Grete Rosenthal, a secretary at one of the men's clubs Lenz has recently joined and the woman Iris and several biographers believe to have been Lenz's mistress, attends with an escort, a loud man nobody knows or wishes to know.

"She heard about it and asked if she could come," Lenz says when he finds himself alone with Iris for a brief moment. "What was I to do?"

"Did I say anything?" she says.

He says, "She's a relentless, exhausting woman."

He means this sincerely; he will believe it still when a few years later he marries her; he will cite it endlessly when a few years after that he delegates Richard, now grown, to break the news to her that she's being divorced.

Iris smiles at him. "Poor man," she says. "The things you have to put up with."

After the meal and the toasts, after the dessert and the brandy and the singing of patriotic songs, after a final extemporaneous couplet from the witty host and the guests' more mundane farewells, the last to leave being the now-morose Grete and her talkative escort, Lenz takes his usual barbiturate with a fresh glass of brandy.

"Thank you," he says to his wife, "for a lovely evening."

Iris is drinking brandy too. "What did their faces look like?" she says.

"Well," he says, "you tell me. Admiring, wouldn't you say? Proud? My success is their success, after all."

No, she says. No, that's not who she means. She means the soldiers on the field in Ypres. Those children. When he watched them through his binoculars the week before this week. After they inhaled the gas. What did they look like?

He says, "Are you drunk?"

She says, "Despite my best efforts, no."

He repeats what he said to the kaiser. Why is being dead worse when caused by gas as opposed to bullets?

She says, "If you think about their faces, maybe you'd have your answer." (The phrase "She says" isn't really accurate here. Try "She shouts." Try "She shrieks.")

He says, "I love my country, and I'm going to bed." (Try "He bellows." Try "He rages.")

She follows him up the stairs. "Where's your service revolver?" she says. And maybe here she thunders. Or maybe here she whispers. It would be interesting to know. It's the last thing she will ever say to Lenz Alter.

"What did she expect?" our mother would say at this point in the story, yawning sleepily. "It was a different time. A woman with a PhD. What did she think? That the world would throw her a parade?"

The revolver is where it always is, inside the top drawer of his bedroom bureau. Lenz Alter retrieves it himself, carries it to her writing room, places it on her desk directly on top of a barely begun letter to the late Richard Lehrer. "My dearest Richard," she's written, and then some initial poetry about the spring weather.

Lenz knows she still writes to Lehrer. He's found and read more than one of her flowery missives. *Another day of missing you. Another day in a world where no one knows me. So what advice have you for me now, cherished friend?*

"Please tell me you aren't actually mailing those letters to Lehrer," he once said to her, not unkindly he felt, but she blushed and said in a strained voice, "You're spying on me now? You're crawling around my writing room, reading my private thoughts?"

His apology was sincere. The letters, he knew, were a release for her, a kind of journal. Too adult for Dear Diary, she was writing Dear Richard instead. And although she refused to accept Lenz's apology, chose to assume he was being mean and sarcastic, several days later, out of the blue, she said, "I burn them." It took him a moment to figure out what she was talking about. Poor Lehrer, he thought when he understood. Subjected to the pyre again and again.

And poor Iris. She'd been so much happier when she could visit with Richard and Marthe Lehrer every now and again. His timorous wife had even dared go up in Lehrer's beloved hot air balloon on a number of occasions. She'd come back home practically trilling. Oh, the trees like tiny vegetables waiting to be picked. Oh, the birds so close you could feel the air stirred by their beating wings. Oh, the heat of the fire and the cool of the breeze.

Once she, the most fearful of mothers, even allowed Lehrer to take her own Richard up. Lenz put a stop to that as soon as his enthusiastic son told him about it. Iris carried on—"And you say I baby him!"—but then came the flames, the plummet, the crash.

Lenz didn't say anything, but she accused him of wanting to say something. He'd never seen her sob like that. Not when her father died. Not even when Lily's husband died a few hours before the minister sanctified Lenz and Iris's marriage. The three sisters, Lily and Iris and the eldest, the rarely-seen Rose, had held each other, weeping, before Lily left and Iris gathered herself and positioned herself at Lenz's side.

But he'd never seen the sobbing he'd seen for Richard.

Although, he thinks, didn't he sob just that way at Theo Meyer's funeral?

He's drained and weary and grateful that his pill is beginning to work. He gestures toward the pistol atop the letter. "I promise it's loaded. I'll be sound asleep in a few minutes. If you come in I won't even hear you, much less have the ability to defend myself. This is a great opportunity for you."

She says nothing. She's done with ranting and railing. She

stands rigidly, arms at her side, gun in her peripheral vision, waiting for him to leave.

Richard, who is in bed but not asleep, Richard, who can of course hear everything, stays awake listening to his father's arrhythmic snores. As long as he hears them, he'll know everything's all right. He means to stay up until morning, a sentry using his ears instead of his eyes. But he's weak and exhausted and twelve and it's late and his eyes eventually fall shut.

Only Iris is able to remain awake all night, her husband's ugly snoring stoking her ire. She works on her letter. She drinks her brandy. It takes so many hours for her to say what she wants to say that when she's finished, daylight isn't far off.

She extinguishes the unnecessary lamp. The air in the room is gray as dirty dishwater. She folds the many pages, presses them as flat as she can with the crystal inkwell, inserts them into an envelope. She seals it and writes RICHARD on the face.

When she exits her writing room, she has the envelope in one hand, the gun in the other. The envelope she places on a table in the hall. This allows her to take the revolver in both her hands. In her woolen nightgown, in her bare feet, gun pointed straight ahead as if it were a lantern and Iris searching for the source of an unsettling noise, she walks quietly to her husband's bedroom door and stands before it, aiming.

Pause here for a moment. Pause to heighten suspense, to build tension. But, no. What are we saying? We've done this all wrong. There's no suspense. You've already seen the chart. Iris in the garden with a gun.

All right. Then pause here because that's what our mother did when she told us this story. Or, no, it has nothing to do with our mother. Pause here so we can meditate on what we all know is about to happen. Pause here because this is important. The curse is about to take its first victim.

Einstein says there's no past, present, or future, but there is something, isn't there, some force that prevents us from going back and stopping her. We don't know how to shuffle the individual, timeless moments of human existence the way we can a deck of cards. We can't rearrange all those moments, we can't step into that garden, yell, "No!" All we can do is sit here in 1999 and report what happened in a certain moment in 1915. Iris turning from the bedroom door, heading instead to her garden, the first tentative blossoms of spring trellising along the fencing. Richard running outside when he's woken by the shot. Iris limp and bleeding in her son's arms: a pietà inverted. Lenz finally shaking off his drugged sleep, finally coming outside. Lenz confused, then sickened.

Father and son carrying Iris inside.

Soon after: the cover-up that will lead to Mileva Einstein believing Iris died of heart failure.

But before the cover-up, which will begin after the sun rises and a black limousine with tiny German flags suctioned to the hood comes to take Captain Alter to the eastern front, Richard scours the house for the envelope with his name on it. RICHARD. He saw it on the little table outside his bedroom as he ran down the stairs and out to the garden. A long letter written just to him, and now it's gone.

"I didn't see any letter," his father says that morning, and repeats for the rest of his life. "And, hypothetically speaking, if an envelope in this house were addressed just to Richard, it wasn't necessarily intended for you. It could have been for Richard Lehrer."

This is what Richard Alter finds unforgivable. Not that his

father's leaving for the front. It's wartime. Lenz Alter's a captain in the army. What choice does he have? And not that he's leaving Richard alone with his mother's corpse and no other instructions but to call his aunt Lily. But the lie. That's what he'll never forgive—and not merely the lie. The absurdity of the lie. Richard Lehrer has been dead since 1912.

The hearse arrives only a few moments after the limousine drives away. Richard pictures the two black cars passing each other on the road. The men in the hearse, stone-faced and dour. The captain in the limo, not glancing up, engrossed in a letter meant for his son.

It's May 2, 1915. Lenz Alter is forty-six. Iris Alter was forty-four. In a month Richard Otto Alter will be thirteen: a man.

CHAPTER 8

*D*uck Soup and Dachau have opened. The worst year of the Great Depression and the last year of Prohibition are about to come to an end. And back in April, there was this: part 3 of Germany's new Law for the Restoration of the Professional Civil Service:

1. Civil servants of non-Aryan descent are to be retired.
2. Section 1 does not apply to civil servants who fought during the World War at the front for the German Reich.

Section 2 protects Lenz Alter from section 1. Still, after reading section 1, he doesn't want any part of section 2. His eyes are open at last.

"Dear Minister Rust," he writes, "According to the directives of the National Civil Service Law of 7 April 1933 . . . I have the right to remain in office, although I am descended from Jewish grandparents and parents. But I do not wish to make use of this dispensation."

There were those who fought for him and the institute that, rid of its Jews, would turn into a shell, echoing footsteps in near-empty rooms and halls. Here's this from Max Planck's essay "My Audience with Adolf Hitler":

> Following Hitler's seizure of power I had the responsibility of paying my respects to the Führer. I believed I should take this opportunity to put in a favorable word for my Jewish colleague . . . without whose invention of the process for producing ammonia from nitrogen in the air the previous war would have been lost from the start. . . . I commented that there are different types of Jews, both worthy and worthless ones to humanity. . . . [Hitler] replied, "That's not right. A Jew is a Jew, all Jews stick together like burrs." . . . He broke out in generalities and concluded by saying, "People say that I occasionally suffer from neurasthenia. This is slander. I have nerves of steel." He then slapped his knee hard, spoke at an increasingly faster rate and worked himself up into such a rage that there was nothing else for me to do but to remain silent.

Nothing to do but be silent. By the next summer all the Alters have left Germany. Lenz has moved to Cambridge. Richard and his family—our mother is four—have settled in Paris. As the weather grows colder, Lenz writes to Richard: His heart is giving him trouble. The nitroglycerin helps, but not the way it once did. Could Richard secure morphine? Lenz will understand if Richard is reluctant to do so. But perhaps, when Richard remembers how his poor mother died, he will agree it's only just that his father die the same way, by his own hands.

Richard gazes out one of the Paris apartment's oddly shaped windows. This one is somewhat oblong, but irregularly bordered, like a small country. It's always raining in Paris; when Richard thinks of this city after they've left it, he'll recall rain-darkened cobblestones and an odd silvery light that so often crept toward him from just beyond the walls of the church of Saint-Merri.

He turns away from the street. He reads his father's letter again. There's a difference, Richard thinks, between shooting oneself in the prime of one's life, driven to such a desperate and painfully slow end by a husband's betrayal to oneself and all of humanity, and slipping out painlessly moments before the grim reaper would have shown up anyway. Lenz, so brilliant in so many other ways, seems unaware of this difference. He apparently equates the two modes of leaving this world behind.

His father's willful blindness doesn't make Richard angry. There are too many other things to be angry about these days. He sometimes identifies with the pigeons in the damp street below, walking in circles, shrugging and shaking their heads.

He doesn't want to punish Lenz. He doesn't need Lenz to make amends for Iris. If he secures morphine, it would be because he wants to help. He can see how debilitating and painful his father's heart disease is. It's terrible to see Lenz these days, terrible even to think of him, traveling from city to city, writing articles in English that no one publishes, delivering lectures in French that no one attends. And then there are the British chemists who make a show in public of refusing to shake his hand.

Richard loves his father. He loves his mother. It's one of the unanticipated and bittersweet pleasures of parenthood: to observe your own imperfections, to witness the damage you're doing your own beloved children, and so to find it within your heart to forgive and fall back in love with your imperfect, blundering papa and mama.

FROM THE LAST WILL OF LENZ ALTER

I direct my son Richard Otto Alter to arrange for my cremation. I direct that my ashes be buried in Berlin alongside those of Iris Emanuel Alter, my first wife. If, however, German policy is such that my son wishes not to travel there, then I direct him to bury my ashes and those of my first wife in such cemetery as my son determines. The grave should be marked with the inscription of our names and dates. Perhaps there may be added, He served his country in war and peace as long as was granted him.

March 1934

When the tram stops in front of his hotel, the infirm chemist boards and rides to its final stop at the city's border. This is where the Orthodox Jews of Basel live.

The chemist himself lived here a long time ago, after the war, hiding from the Allies who sought to arrest him for committing murder on an unprecedented scale—as if they hadn't resorted to gas themselves. The chemist had to leave his second wife and his teenage son in Berlin. He had to rent a room with access to a bath down the hall, had to dress in the same costume the rest of them wore: black coat to the ground, broad-brimmed hat. He grew his beard, his sidelocks. He felt unkempt, dirty. And the worst thing about the getup was that so long as he wore it, he couldn't go to nonkosher restaurants—that is, he couldn't enjoy the best food in the city.

The Nobel came through while he was hiding here. That was another place he couldn't go: to Stockholm. He had to wait another six months, which was how long it took England and France—the Americans never cared about him—to become distracted by other problems. He'd shaved, changed his clothes, and returned to Germany where he gorged on pork and arranged to leave again to pick up the Nobel. In Sweden he gave a speech about fertilizer; the other uses of the manna process were mentioned by no one. Upon returning to Dahlem, he began the work that would lead to his gold-from-the-sea project, his attempt to distill gold dust from seawater. His plan was to repay Germany's war debts. He was still in love with her, still willing to make a fool of himself for *Heimat*. It was a failure, gold from the sea—as projects involving alchemy always are—and it made him a figure of ridicule, but at least he and his son, who was then eighteen, got to spend a year at sea together. Robust men doing the things robust men do.

Now he's climbing the steep hill to Basel's old Jewish cemetery, several acres of land that have been on his mind of late. When he lived here all those years ago, he would watch the burials from his apartment window. He liked the rituals, the mourners approaching the open grave one by one, shoveling dirt onto the casket but using the back of the shovel. He could never ask why—he was pretending to be pious, he was supposed to know why—and when he returned to Germany, he forgot all about it. Now he knows the reason: the back of the shovel symbolizes the difficulty in letting the dead go, even while you're helping them leave.

On this day there are no burials taking place. Though the gate to the cemetery is open, there's nobody there, not even the caretaker. The chemist sits on a stone bench in the sunlight, waiting for his no-good heart to stop spasming. When he can breathe again, he rises and walks among the graves. He starts with the oldest ones, the flat mossy stones muddy from the morning's

rain. He finishes with the newest, the marble tombstones standing upright, each with an array of small rocks on its shoulders.
He knows none of the people buried here, but he knows people
who have the same names. There are Alters, there are Emanuels.
There are Lehrers and Rosenthals and Meyers.

When the rows of graves end, there's a patch of grass waiting
for a few more souls, and then the wrought-iron fence. The chest
pain has returned, and the chemist looks at his winter shadow
and mumbles the Shema, the only Hebrew prayer he knows by
heart. His new friends in exile are chemists and Zionists both.
Chaim Weizmann. That crowd. They've explained the customs,
taught him the tricks. "Say the Shema at the moment of death,"
they say, "and you ascend straight to heaven, no questions asked."

"And you wonder," he tells them, "why intelligent men turn
their backs on religion."

His friends see his point, but dismiss it. "What could it hurt?"
they say. "If nothing else, at least it's something to do in those
last few seconds. It's good to keep busy."

Standing by the iron fence that is the border of both the cemetery and Switzerland, the chemist looks out at the unattended
French frontier, the tawny cattails and brown grasses stiff with
winter frost. He doubles over, holds onto the fence for support.
He rests his forehead on the cold iron. Reaching into his coat
pocket, he withdraws a nitroglycerin tablet, places it under his
tongue, waits as it dissolves. Damned by explosives. Saved by
explosives. He grips the fence harder, his hands turning white.
And then—there. The pain, not gone, but smaller.

When he returns to the hotel—strangers have assisted him
onto the tram, off the tram, through the hotel doors—his son is
in the lobby.

"You came," he says.

"I did," his son says.

In his room, he lets his son help him undress. In his bed, he relishes the warmth of the feather duvet.

"Where will you go next?" he asks his son. "What will you do?"

"Haiti." The son looks at his shoes. "No other option at the moment. So, yes, Haiti, and then we'll wait and pray that Uncle Albert persuades America to relent."

"Palestine isn't an option?"

His son shakes his head.

"You could use my tickets," says the chemist. He wishes his son would raise his head. He'd like to see the blue eyes.

"You'll use your tickets," the son says. "When you feel better, you'll use them."

Last intelligible words: "I would have like to spend my final days there. I'm a man who needs a country he can love."

The doctor the son summoned arrives then, but there's nothing he can do. The chemist mumbles words neither the doctor nor the son understand, a rhythmic sort of chanting. The son makes a confession to the doctor. The doctor absolves him. He says, "If it were my father, I'd have done the same."

As they're talking about physical suffering, the chemist dies.

So much for aliyah. So much for God's love for the prodigal.

1938

Karin Gläser is the family apostate. When Lenz Alter's name comes up at the dinner parties she throws for their circle of displaced Jews in this very apartment—and his name always comes up—she says, "I wish we'd smothered him with a pillow while he slept," and there are murmurs and titters and gasps.

No matter how many times she says this, her husband comes to his father's defense.

"It was wartime."

"I don't care what time it was. You don't leave a twelve-year-old alone to bury his mother."

Their guests tend not to weigh in. They're embarrassed when Karin flies furiously at Richard, like a bird attacking its own reflection, but they do enjoy the details and drama. They sit in the dinette, at the same table where the three of us still eat, and they wait, understanding that the price of hearing about the death in the garden is having to stay for the spat.

"He was critical to the war effort," Richard says of his father's trip to Russia. "I may have been young, but I understood completely." He hesitates, smiles ruefully. "My mother, on the other hand, would have been furious," he admits. "Never," he says, "would she have left me alone under such circumstances—or frankly, under any circumstances, even the most benign. I was a wreck of a rowboat, and she was a gigantic barnacle attached to my side, my poor mother."

Karin gets up from the table, makes busy work for herself, clearing the dishes while guests are still eating, crumbing the tablecloth while Richard makes his points.

"I must be losing my mind," she says as she scurries about. "Did you just say your mother never would have left you? What do you call what she did, then?"

Richard says, "Well, yes, but you know what I mean."

"You always say that, but I never do."

He wants to end the conversation, but he knows she won't allow it. He says to his friends, "It was the only way she could separate from me. I think she did it because she understood I needed to enter my adolescence without her so close."

Karin's smile is as sharp as a sliver of glass. "Ah," she says, "she shot herself beneath her sleeping child's window so he could thrive. To you a bullet to the chest is good mothering. Rose is about the same age you were when your mother died. Is it time for me to go outside and put a bullet between my ribs? Rose— Rose, come here. I need your opinion on something. Everyone, you know our daughter Rose. Rose, we have a question for you. Would you feel more loved if I shot myself, Rose?"

"Oh, for God's sake, Mother," says Rose.

"All right, all right," Richard says. "But you know perfectly well what I mean."

May 1945

. . . and they're still having the same fight. And not only Richard and Karin. Scientists. Historians. Germans. Jews. Was he good or evil? A patriot or a monster? A savior or a slayer?

Biographers, scholars, students ask the same questions to this day. Skim through the titles of the various articles and essays. "Lenz Alter's Experiments in Life and Death." "Lenz Alter: The Father of Chemical Warfare." "Lenz Alter: Evil Scientific Genius?" "Lenz Alter: The Damned Scientist." "Deciphering the Duality of Lenz Alter's Mind." "Lenz Alter: Ploughshares and Swords."

Here's a newish one: "How Do You Solve a Problem Like Lenz Alter?"

A good question, the latter, and nice, the musical allusion. *The Sound of Music.* Nazis. Get it? It's so hard to resist singing along. But what rhymes with nitrogen synthesis? What rhymes with chlorine gas? What rhymes with Ecstasy? Because he synthesized that too. (We know. You're welcome.)

And what rhymes with Zyklon? Because, yes, in addition to fertilizer, in addition to gas, in addition to MDMA, our grandfather gave that pesticide to the world.

Zyklon. What are we supposed to do with that tidbit? That's

what we can never figure out. Do we interrupt our project to meditate upon the sins of our ancestors? Do we abandon our project—our own monograph, this writing—completely because, really, how can we ever justify our existences? Do we open our windows and scream our apologies to the Upper West Side of New York? *We're sorry as hell, and we just can't take it anymore.* Or do we just shrug and say, Don't blame us, we barely passed eleventh-grade chemistry?

We don't know. We just don't know what to do with this fact of our lives, this aspect of who we are.

And we're not unaware that we may be overdramatizing or that we might be using his sins to justify something we want to do anyway, i.e., die. We're not unaware that we are looking for a reason to do something we have no reason to do. For us dying is just a need as basic and urgent as everyone else's need not to.

Also—the truth is, he developed only Zyklon's first iteration. Unlike the chlorine gas he foisted on the generals, he had no idea what Zyklon would be used for. As far as he was concerned, it was nothing more than a pesticide, a boon to German farmers, that he was formulating at the behest of the government. Before he could even finish his work, the government he was working for invited him to get the hell out of the country. He probably didn't think much more about Zyklon after that.

It was the Aryan remains of his team who came up with the next iteration, Zyklon B.

Still, those good souls couldn't have done it without him. They added no fillips, no improvements, no surprises. Theirs is the exact formulation Lenz Alter came up with before his exodus, except for one thing. They removed the odor designed to warn humans that they were in the presence of a virulent poison.

Zyklon B. If you don't know what it was used for, go look

it up. Or go visit any Holocaust museum, where sooner or later you'll come to a display of old canisters filled with the stuff, some of the canisters placed on their sides, the better for tourists to see the gray-blue crystals artfully pouring forth.

Or, after we die, enter our apartment and go into the largest bedroom, the Dead and Dying Room that nobody's slept in for years, and get down on your knees and pull out the cardboard boxes we've stored under the double bed that's long lain fallow, and open the one with RICHARD & KARIN Magic Markered on the side. Rummage through the photographs and letters and other Alter artifacts. Locate and take out the journals of our maternal grandmother Karin Gläser Alter. Scan the dates until you find the journal from May 1945. Take this journal—note the soft gray leather cover; our grandmother liked her journals to be pretty on the outside—and have a seat in our living room. We recommend the sofa; three generations of Alter asses have seen to it that it's nicely broken in. Although, before you sit, please—how rude of us—please, fix yourself a drink, help yourself to whatever you find. One word of caution, though: if there's a blender in the kitchen with the residue of a fruit juice concoction, you'll want to avoid that.

Now that you're comfortable, turn to Karin's final entry. Don't worry if you can't read German. Just note the handwriting, not merely the old-fashioned flourishes and curlicues, but the quavering quality, the severe downward tilt, as if she couldn't hold the book upright or the pen steady. Just note the columns, how she tries to keep them perfectly lined up, like prisoners summoned to the yard for roll call.

Mein Vater, Hermann Gläser.   Todesursache: Zyklon.
Meine Mutter, Ruth Baumgartner Gläser.   Todesursache: Zyklon.
Meine Schwester, Eva Gläser Hirsh.   Todesursache: Zyklon.

Meine Schwester, Anne Gläser Bierman.   Todesursache: Zyklon.
Mein Bruder, Bernhard Gläser.   Todesursache: Zyklon
Meine Nichte, Katherine Hirsh.   Todesursache: Zyklon
Meine Nichte, Ada Hirsch.   Todesursache: Zyklon

Feel free to start skimming, because, as you will see, it goes on for pages. Of course it does. Imagine how many pages it would take you to list the names of everyone you've ever loved, liked, tolerated, despised, or just been introduced to at some party; everyone you've ever worked with or gone to school with or just run into from time to time or chatted up once or twice at a coffee shop. Many more nieces. Many more nephews. The children of the nieces and nephews. The children of those children. Her cousins. Her cousin's children and her cousin's children's children. Her classmates. Her daughters' classmates. Her teachers. Her daughters' teachers. Her husband's aunts, Rose Emanuel Ziegler, who she never met, and the long-widowed Lily Emanuel Klein, who she adored. The children and grandchildren of her husband's aunts. And neighbors, grocers, butchers, bakers. Dye workers. Hardware store owners. Page after page, name after name. Cause of death: Zyklon. Cause of death: Zyklon.

Maybe someone else has a diary even more aged and yellowed, with columns of names and next to them: Cause of death: chlorine gas. Cause of death: chlorine gas. If Iris had lived, perhaps that diary would have been hers. But Karin, at least in her youth, never thought to object to the gas. Quite the opposite. She was proud to marry into the family of Lenz Alter, war hero. When she became Lenz's daughter, if only by marriage, his development and deployment of the *giftgas* had still been a triumph, still something to trumpet.

Karin and Richard and their three daughters, one of whom

was our mother, never considered the development of chlorine gas reprehensible because Lenz had done it for Germany—his country! his love! his life!—and because it had been wartime and because he'd been feted and celebrated and promoted to captain. What had he said when people—the generals themselves—recoiled at the horror of gas?

"Death is death," he said.

Our great-grandfather, the Gertrude Stein of chemical warfare.

But now—May 1945—a second war ending, Karin sees how mistaken she was. Now she recognizes his invention and promotion of chlorine gas not only as a crime, but also as the first sign of a pattern that led to this, his destroying her world.

Richard hasn't stopped weeping since learning about the Zyklon. He's been a drinker all his life and is a full-out drunk now, and a drunk of the worst kind: he's melodramatic, emotionally flabby. Every day, it seems, there's another article he wants Karin to read, another revelation, another reference to the horror, but also to the irony: the poison was developed by a Jew.

Talk about too smart for their own good, an editorialist writes.

Karin stands at the kitchen sink, the same one that will some-day hold the remains of our final cocktail. Wearing her American muumuu, her bony legs managing to keep her emaciated body upright so long as she leans against the counter, she washes the dinner dishes because if she doesn't, who will? The two older girls are at college, the youngest appears oblivious to the fact that her mother is sick, and Richard's sitting a couple of feet away in the attached dinette, crying. Her disease has progressed, there's no saving her now, but she still wants her home to be tidy. She's careful with the soapy plates, slippery glasses. A strange part of dying: she drops things. Not only stemware, but keys and magazines and the earrings she still tries to screw on slide from her hands and fall to the floor. It's as if her fingers have decided to be the first part of her to give up material things.

"Your mother should have killed him when she had the chance," she calls to Richard over the running water. "*You* should have killed him."

Richard has the *Times* open. He looks away from the article he's been reading out loud to her. He rests his eyes on the adjacent ad for lounging pajamas, on sale, Lord & Taylor's. Even today, as skeletons clad in striped pajamas are being led from death camps, here is this ad. Thank God for it, Richard thinks. Thank God for the human capacity to hold both kinds of pajamas in our heads at once. He says, "He was a scientist, Karin. He was doing what scientists do. Oppenheimer. All of them."

"Am I talking about Oppenheimer?" Karin says. "I'm talking about your father. Your daughters' grandfather. I'm talking about us, you and me. We should be lined up and shot for not stopping him."

Richard puts down the paper, covers his entire face with his hands. "He didn't know what they'd use it for. He was just trying to help save crops. Think about it for a minute. They'd have used it on him if they'd had the chance."

"And on us," Karin says. "And on this little girl. Dahlie, come over here. Papa, look at Dahlie. You see this face?" Karin has that face in her hand, fingers pressing into each cheek as if she's trying to dimple them. "They'd have used it on her."

And when our mother jerks away from Karin's wet rubbered fingers and asks what they're talking about and Karin says, "Go ahead, Papa, tell her," and Richard begins to sob, then Dahlie, who is sixteen, says, "Oh. That."

Karin has long known that Richard is a weak man, but this is too much. Day after day. The bawling! The moaning! She unburdens herself to Dahlie. He cried when they had to leave Germany, she says. He cried when they had to leave Paris. He cried throughout the five years in Haiti—does Dahlie remember those five sweltering years in Haiti, the sunburns, the infected bug bites, the horrible natives, so foreign, so dark?—and again when his so-called Uncle Albert finally got them their visas for New York. That time it was tears of happiness, but still—again with the tears, always with the tears.

Also, he let out a sob on the day her doctor said he was sorry but there was nothing more he could do, it was time for her to begin putting her affairs in order. Just that one sob on that day, and he swallowed it quickly, but it would have gone on and on if she hadn't cut him with a look.

She's not a hypocrite, she tells Dahlie. She wants tears for no one, not even for herself. "No funeral," she says. "Tell your sisters I said so. No funeral, no memorial, no nothing. Just get on with it."

"I'm going to get on with my homework right now," Dahlie says.

"My girl," says Karin.

Finishing up with the dishes, Karin gives Richard the same look she gave him in the doctor's office. She gives it to him frequently, this look, but it no longer does any good. He can't control himself, he cries anyway, and it's driving her out of her mind. Is her reaction to his tears unkind? Well, what if it is? She's in pain. She's enraged. It's springtime—warm days and pussy willows and Queen Anne's lace by the river, and in the park, forsythia is beginning to bloom—and she's a young woman, only in her early forties, and she's dying. And, come to find out, dying's a far more arduous process than she ever imagined. How do weak, elderly people manage it? She's serious, she tells Dahlie. She can't imagine doing this old and frail. It's taking all her energy as it is. It's draining, it's brutal. And still he wants comfort from her. Every night, comfort and understanding and supper.

The dishwashing tonight has worn her out. She wipes her hands on her dress, struggles her wedding band back over a swollen knuckle. She heads back to her bedroom, leaning against the walls of the long hallway as she inches along. The hallway divides the apartment the same way Berlin is now divided: to its east are the shabbier, utilitarian rooms (dinette opening to the kitchen, then bath, then master bedroom), and to the west are the nicer, brighter rooms, the rooms with windows and expansive views (living room, then our small bedrooms, all in a row).

As Karin continues, making her way back to her bed, she talks out loud, loud enough so that both Dahlie in her room and Richard back in the dinette can hear her.

"Oh, to be the kind of person who can just put a bullet through her own heart and be done with it," she says. "Oh, to be the kind of person who can abandon her children, who thinks only of herself, her own troubles. Tired of living? Then just stop living. Who cares about the child left behind? Oh, to be a genuine Alter, an Alter by blood. How easy life is for an Alter. Why wouldn't it be? To the Alters life's the same as death. Meaningless. Empty. Death is death. Death is life. Life is death. What a family."

She reaches the bed, struggles into it. Richard sleeps on the living room couch now. "Not the girls' rooms," Karin said, when, chased from his own bed, he looked to sleep in Rose's. "It's their personal place even when they're not home." So the girls' rooms stay empty, and he sleeps on the couch, lets Karin have the sheets and pillows of the double bed all to herself so she can thrash and groan and rail, which are her only remaining pleasures, her only remaining weapons too. She pulls the comforter to her chin, then over her face. When the pain knifes her, she bites the fabric near her mouth. She's put holes in it. When the pain ebbs, she lets the comforter go. She folds it back so she can see her surroundings.

What she hasn't told him, what she's confided only to that last journal, is that since that final visit to her doctor she's turned away from her lifelong atheism. If you'd asked her even a couple of months ago, she'd have assured you she'd remain a nonbeliever to the end, that unlike all the weaklings of the world, death was not going to drive her to the obvious security blanket that is religion. But there came a night when, as she lay on her death-bed, she saw her far bedroom wall rise up like stage scenery, and there, instead of the bathroom, were people whose names she'd written in her journal—Cause of death: Zyklon. Cause of death: Zyklon—all of them milling about like ticket holders prior to some sort of gala performance. When they saw her, they turned to face her. They waved and beckoned. When they realized she wasn't going to get up and come to them, they conferred among themselves, and several were chosen to go to her. These dele-gates pulled chairs she didn't know she owned up to her bedside and engaged her in small talk. They reminisced about attending the cinema with her in Berlin or sharing a meal. They laughed about a difficult exam in the history class they'd taken together in grade school, recalling and ridiculing the questions they'd missed. "Not once in my life," her best friend from those days said, "did I need to know the dates of the Crimean War." They came back, day after day, often bringing food she hadn't tasted in years: soft white pretzels, fried wild mushrooms. Sweet, brown beer the likes of which America had never seen. For weeks she'd had no appetite, but with them she ate and drank with relish. With them she was ravenous. When they left, she was stuffed.

She was willing to entertain the possibility that the beckoning figures standing where her toilet and tub should have been might be inventions of a failing mind. But the people at her bedside—they were demonstrably real. If she spoke to them, they responded appropriately. If she touched them, she felt them, their skin as warm as her own. They touched her too. They took her hand, clasped it. They brought it to their lips and kissed it. When her hands shook and she couldn't manage a spoon, they fed her as if she were a cherished baby. They smoothed her blankets. They made her lean forward so they could pummel her pillows, make them fat for her. When she tried to get up to carry the empty bowls to the kitchen, to ferry the bare greasy plates and the steins, each one with just a puddle of beer sloshing at the very bottom, they wouldn't allow it. They took the dishes from her, carried them beyond the scrim, where they must have had their own kitchen. They cleaned up after her.

It isn't fear of death, then, that has made her believe in God and in heaven. It's the fact that she isn't a mule, that she can't deny what she's seeing with her own eyes. When Karin dies less than a month after VE Day, her whimpering husband and dry-eyed youngest daughter at her bedside, God will also be with her, just one of the crowd, just another casualty of war, whooping and hollering and spilling beer on her blanket.

September 1945

Three months after Karin dies, our grandfather Richard asks our mother not to disturb him while he takes a nap.

Dahlie isn't surprised that her father wants to be left alone. It's not the first time he's asked for this particular favor. He's having trouble sleeping at night, he tells her, not that he has to spell this out for her. Her own sleep is often disturbed by the sound of his pacing through the long hallway of the apartment. Sometimes—many times—she hears him crying. It makes her cringe, that he's become such a crybaby. She herself is doing a heroic job of getting on despite her mother's passing. Her mother's death occurred on a Tuesday in June, her sisters arrived home on Thursday, the funeral her mother begged them not to hold was on Friday. By Monday, her sisters were back in Chicago and she was back in homeroom.

Now it's the start of the new school year, her final school year.

"You're so brave," her teachers keep telling her, and she supposes she is, although maybe not as much as everyone thinks. It's not that she's unfazed by the loss of her mother. It's more that the death was so long in coming, so drawn out, that Dahlie came to accept it a long time before it actually happened. Her mother was sick for years. The final decline seemed anticlimactic and—Dahlie hates to say this, but it's true—overdue. By which she only means that a kinder universe would have taken Karin sooner, and a kinder society would have let Karin decide when it was time to leave. Not that Karin showed any signs of wanting to go any sooner than she did. "I'm a fatalist," Karin used to say of herself. "My philosophy is, let nature take its course."

Dahlie, it's turned out, is a fatalist too. She agrees with her mother—let nature take its course. Also, don't fight city hall. Although sometimes Dahlie does wonder if maybe she's just a horrible human being incapable of caring about others. That's always a possibility.

Or maybe her lack of emotion is to be expected. A youthful heart can ache for only so long. She told herself that at the funeral. Then, to her surprise, she choked up—it was the words *heart* and *ache*, their applicability to herself.

Her father, on the other hand, is suffering because, unlike Dahlie, he held on to unrealistic hope throughout the whole ordeal. This is why he's so unraveled, why he's left the high school where he has long taught German and, especially during the war when no one wanted to take German, French. Now, the first day of school for him too, he calls in, sobbing. "I can't do it," he says. The principal says he understands. There's some kind of arrangement. Sick leave. Sick pay. "Thank God for unions," says Richard.

It's Dahlie who doesn't understand why he can't go to work. She wishes she could push him out the door, back into the world. She's worried about him, of course, but more than that, he's driving her crazy. Not only his refusal to keep busy, keep going. But his constant references to the optimism that seeded his current, miserable pessimism. Somehow, even though no one ever recovers from the illness Karin had, Richard believed she would. It was as if he thought his need for her would be enough to keep her alive, as if he thought some caring force would look out, if not for her, then for him. Despite every awful thing that's happened to him during his godforsaken life, he still thought he was special enough to warrant that kind of concern and protection. This baffles Dahlie, it really does. Because if you want to know the truth, no one has watched out for her father since he was a twelve-year-old boy. Dahlie's heard enough family stories to know this. And yet somehow he's only figuring it out now, and he's devastated. He seems boneless, unable to support his own weight.

"I know I should be nicer to him," Dahlie whispers to Rose over the phone, long-distance and pricey, "but I can't stand having to comfort him all the time as if I'm the parent. I have to pat his hand all day long. It gives me the heebie-jeebies."

It's a strain to be with him, and so she welcomes these naps of his. On this day, for instance, while he sleeps, Dahlie stretches across her bed in what today is Delph's room, no longer having to be the parent, getting to be just a bobbysoxer with the very faintest of German accents doing her math homework.

When a gas experiment gone wrong blew a hole in the laboratory wall outside Berlin, the young Richard Alter feared it was an attack by the French. When Dahlie hears the screams outside her building, what comes to her mind is Japan. Japan, she thinks, must have roused itself for one final attack on America, this time the East Coast. She imagines the screams are coming from neighbors who are hanging outside their windows, pointing skyward, frantic and agape as turkeys in the rain, as they helplessly watch the fabled kamikazes shriek and eddy down from the skies. She imagines that in another moment the planes will hit Broadway and explode into flames, the wreckage demolishing buses and taxis and pedestrians and luncheonettes. She runs to the window on her western wall and sees nothing, but that doesn't mean the planes can't be coming from a different direction. The screams have come from the south, she believes.

The apartment has only two southern windows, one in the room that most recently belonged to Rose and the other in her father's room, directly across the hall. It's Rose's room she runs to. She presses her face to Rose's window. Indeed, there's a crowd on the sidewalk below, housewives in spring colors with baby carriages, all frantic and pointing upward. The sky, though, is clear.

Something terribly wrong has occurred; she has no choice but to understand that. Still, as she barges into her father's room, she doesn't know what it is yet, and so it's a shock to find the bed empty and the window open, its curtains swinging in the fragrant breeze.

CHAPTER 9

Veronica Frankl and Eddie Glod were married on May 17, 1974, the day after they completed their junior years at Barnard and Columbia, respectively. They'd told no one a thing about it, just took the subway to City Hall with their license and the happy results of their Wasserman tests tucked inside Vee's olive-drab backpack, which was decorated with iron-on peace symbol patches.

After the ceremony, such as it was, they went to another room in the same building and petitioned to legally change their last names to Alter. This, they'd been informed by a despotic clerk prior to the marriage, was the order in which they had to do it. First Vee had to get married and change her name to Glod. Then Eddie needed to sign a form granting her permission to change her name from Glod to Alter. He, on the other hand, could change his name to anything he wanted whenever he wanted.

"Really?" Eddie said. "That's what the law says?"

The anger emanating from the clerk, a small, thin woman, was almost visible, as if she were a comic strip character surrounded by short, wavy lines. "That's what I say," she said, "and I'm the one who can accidentally lose the papers on their way to the judge."

"Wow," Eddie said. "Why would you perpetuate the patriarchal system like that? You're a woman. Whose side are you on?"

"Read your Bible," the clerk said. " 'For the husband is the head of the wife even as Christ is the head of the church.' " Her lipstick had come off, leaving only a ring of lip liner. Vee could see her coffee mug on her desk, a fire-engine-red kiss on its rim. "You want to live in a matriarchy, go join a tribe of Amazons," the clerk said.

They'd been speechless. They still thought of themselves as kids; they couldn't get over the fact that an adult—a professional, a representative of the government for Christ's sake—had said such a thing to them. They'd also been surprised that the woman, who'd they'd immediately written off as grandly uneducated, knew the word *matriarchy*.

"I guess I shouldn't have said anything," Eddie said, as they made their way to city's idea of an altar.

"Maybe we shouldn't start the revolution today," Vee agreed.

"Maybe I should apologize," Eddie said. But he didn't, which he regretted the next year, the two of them in the oncologist's office after Vee's first diagnosis. "Remember that clerk?" Eddie said. "That *farbissenah* at City Hall? What she said about Amazons? Do you think she maybe jinxed your breast?"

Vee said no. She said that while the clerk had been very powerful when it came to ferrying documents to a judge, she was probably less so when it came to doling out cancer. Still, she had to remind herself repeatedly that she didn't believe in jinxes or curses, just in meaningless coincidences and random happenstance, the most mysterious forces of all. Which was not to say that the dyspeptic clerk hadn't gotten to her, too. She had ruined their wedding day, that woman. After they'd become husband and wife and Glods, they'd had to go back to complete their name-change petitions, and the woman had offered the most anti-Semitic mazel tov" they'd ever heard. By the time they reached their next stop, a small courtroom a few doors down the hall, they were depressed and wary. It had been a relief when the judge's hooded eyes turned out to be a sign not of hostility but boredom. Vee explained she preferred to no longer bear the name of the parent who'd deserted her. Eddie explained that his last name was Glod. Both reasons made sense to the judge, who scribbled his own name on something and sent them to a cashier, where they forked over some dough, and it was done. Vee and Eddie Alter at last, though none of us have ever called Eddie "Eddie Alter." None of us, not even Vee, has ever thought of him that way. He's always been Eddie Glod to us, Lady and Delph often using both names as if he were a Billy Joe or a Bobby Lee.

After the legalities were attended to, Vee and Eddie, with their assorted documents, headed back uptown, where they bought a cheap king-size mattress at the Spanish department store that used to be on Broadway near 96th. Only then did they return to the apartment to break the news to our mother and Delph: marriage, name change, and their plan to leave almost all of Vee's bedroom furniture on the curb—how else to fit that mattress in Vee's small room? Vee's furniture had once belonged to our Aunt Violet, she of the plastic dry-cleaning bag, but Vee thought of it as her own. She felt no fondness for the fussy writing desk, the rickety bureau missing several knobs, and if our mother did, Vee stopped her from saying so. "Attachment, Mom," she said. "Materialism. You have to let go."

Our mother had been home that day. This was her blue period, when she began missing work, calling in sick, staying home to drink and smoke in bed: turning into the father she'd once disdained. She'd begun missing other things, too. One day Vee fished something out from between the sofa cushions. A cola-stained bicuspid molar. She put it into a baggie and showed it to Lady over coffee at the Hungarian Pastry Shop, which, by the way, was the only reason for anyone to go to Amsterdam Avenue in the 1970s.

"We should call someone," Vee said.

"And say what?" Lady said, and Vee saw her point.

Our mother had emerged from her bedroom when Vee and Eddie came home. She'd shrugged on her salmon robe, removed the black wire roller from her bangs so they lay like a tube on her forehead. She was touched by the name change, pleased by the marriage, hurt by the ditching of the furniture. Most of all, though, she was deeply wounded by the wedding.

"Me, I understand you don't invite," she said. "When do you ever think about me? But your sisters? You don't even invite your sisters?"

"Don't make a whole *tsimiss* out of it," Vee said.

"Don't use that kind of language," she said. "We're not Polish peasants." She remembered Eddie. "No offense," she said.

"None taken," he said. "I'm not a Polish peasant either. I'm from Verona, New Jersey."

She smiled as if some things in this world were too complicated to explain, then turned back to Vee. "So why couldn't your sisters be witnesses?" She *v*'d the *w*. Vitnesses. When she was very upset or very drunk or just wanted to remind us of how hard her life had been, her old accent would reassert itself.

"It's not a big deal," Vee said. "It was just something we felt like doing." Her vitnesses had been the Italian American couple who were marrying next and about whom Vee later would worry during the whole Son of Sam thing, so perfectly did they fit the killer's doomed demographic.

Vee's desire to be free of the family during the wedding didn't extend to the rest of her married life. There was no question that she and Eddie would live in the apartment, the newlyweds squished into Vee's bedroom. There was no talk of contributing to the rent, of paying anything for board.

"They don't have two dimes to rub together," our mother told Delph, as if Delph had objected.

Our mother even offered to switch rooms with them. "What do me, myself, and I need with the big bedroom?" she said, and was hurt all over again when Vee laughed.

"Are you kidding? Like I'd really conceive a child in the Dead and Dying Room."

"All you girls were conceived in that room," our mother protested.

"Yes, and look at us."

"What's wrong with you? You'd all be perfect if Delph would just push her hair out of her face."

"You *are* all perfect," Eddie said.

Our mother looked up at him from beneath her tubular bangs. "Even me?" she said.

"Dahlie," Eddie said, mispronouncing it, as he always did. She preferred the German pronunciation, Dah-LEE-ah, but Americans were always calling her Dahlia or Dolly. She tended to forgive Eddie Glod, though. She forgave him the Polish roots he failed to understand made him a lesser, she forgave him his forays into Yiddish, she forgave him his inability to say her name. She forgave him because he said things like this: "Dolly, you are the perfection from whence perfection sprung," joking but not joking. "The child she never had," we'd say of her feelings for him. During the year or so they shared the apartment, she'd flirt with him. "You're my favorite son-in-law," she'd tell him, and he'd say, "Really? You honestly like me better than Joe? That's like telling Loeb you like him better than Leopold." And we'd laugh, even our mother.

But our apartment was the place mirth went to die. Not long after Vee and Eddie lugged her bedroom furniture down to the curb, a couple of chain-smoking teenagers from the Spanish department store arrived to drag the cheap mattress up to Vee's room, and our mother got upset all over again.

"You're going to sleep on the floor like hobos?" she asked.

"Box springs and bed frames are capitalism run amok," Vee said, "like weed-free lawns and vinegar douche."

"But it hides the carpet."

The carpet was shagged and beige. "I know," Vee said. "That's called a bonus. A fringe benefit." Eddie smiled, but no one else did. "It's a joke," Vee said. "Fringe. Because rugs have fringe."

"But this rug doesn't," our mother said.

"Dolly," Eddie said. "It's a Japanese look."

"Did I ever tell you," she said, "how the Japanese killed my uncle?"

"Great-uncle," Vee said. "Someone you never knew."

There were times when even Eddie couldn't move our mother. This was one of them. She shook her head. She returned to the Dead and Dying Room. It was hard to tell if she'd meant to slam the door or if it had slammed on its own from the pull of the spring breeze through her open window. She was on a peppermint schnapps kick at the time. She had bottles in the closet, dirty, sticky glasses on her bedside table. She'd sometimes emerge from her room slurring and staggering but with minty fresh breath.

Delph said, "I only wish she'd close that window. I think we should nail it shut."

"We're getting out of here as soon as humanly possible," Vee assured Eddie. But Eddie said, "I'm fine with it here, Veezie. I'd worry about her even more if we left. And I do love this little Delph person."

Beneath the hair that veiled most of Delph's face, she blushed and grinned. It was a happy moment.

But then

Vee has stopped writing. All these months, while we've worked on this project, Vee's been the most reluctant, not to write, but to write about Vee. "Can't we just skip me?" she asks.

"You have to tell your story," Delph argues. "That's how these things work."

Vee scowls. "Who are you?" she says. "The Emily Post of suicide notes?"

Even this evening, when we started writing about Vee's marriage to Eddie, Vee sighed with great weariness. "All right," she said. "Fine. Let's just get through it fast."

But now she's stopped. "What's the matter?" Lady asks. "Don't you feel well?"

No, Vee says. It's not her health. It's what we wrote. It's the last thing we wrote, the phrase "but then."

" 'But then,' " Lady repeats.

"I know," Vee says. "It's ridiculous." The word 'then.' " But she's never really thought about it before, she says. And now she has. The word *then*. It's captured her attention.

Lady and Delph regard Vee with a sisterly blend of compassion and contempt. "You're not suddenly taken with the word *then*," Lady says. "You're just avoiding writing about what we were about to write about."

"No," Vee says. "Really, I'm serious. Think about it."

"Think about what?"

"Think about *then*."

"I would like to think about then," says Lady. "I would like to write about then. You're the one who won't think about it."

"I don't mean think about the time then. I mean think about the word *then*."

"I know what you mean," Lady says.

"Who's on first?" says Delph.

"Then," says Vee. When you think about it, she says, that four-letter word, that most quotidian of adverbs—it's kind of astounding.

Then as adverb: I married my husband *then*. *Then* as adjective: I married my *then* husband then. *Then* as noun: I married my *then* husband *then* and after *then*, I was happy.

"I can't believe I've never focused on this before," Vee says.

"No more gin for you," says Lady.

Vee is drunk, it's true. But so are we all. It's only Vee who's this animated, gushing, alive. *Then!* This amazing, enchanting little word. See the adverb *then* travel in two directions at once! Watch it spin around, encompass both the past and the future!

The past: I hadn't noticed you *then*.

In this example, *then* means long ago and far away, it means a few seconds before I did notice you, it means that fall semester of college, that English class at Columbia where the professor, forced to admit Barnard women for the first time, refused to call on said women, thus reasserting the masculine hegemony, or as we put it back then, his male chauvinist piggery. And this boy on the other side of the classroom, this funny-looking boy with long hair and big ears, he raises his hand, ostensibly to comment on the use of kenning in *Beowulf*, but instead—ambush!—he goes, "Professor, you just called on me now, the very moment my hand went up, but you haven't called on that woman over there who's had her hand raised for half the class. How come?"

The future: And *then* I fell in love with you.

Here *then* means "next," which, by definition, means in the future, means later, as in one breath later, the professor getting hot, growling, "I'll damn well call on whoever the hell I feel like calling on if and when I feel like calling on them," and the boy gathering his books, *then* walking out, and the girl who's been raising her hand feeling obligated to gather her books too—the sound track to all this: Revolution has come! Time to pick up a gun!" as sung by the perennial protesters outside Schermerhorn—and *then* the girl chases after the boy, into the hallway, where she says—awkward and stammering, a disgrace to second-wave feminism, or, as we called it at the time, women's lib—"Thanks, I guess."

Then the boy proclaims, in a voice that echoes through the empty hall, "The dick-swinging dog shall sleep the sleep of the sword," thereby doing a little kenning himself, and the two of them walk to their respective registrars' offices together, first his at Columbia *then* hers at Barnard, both the boy and girl dropping the English class and signing up instead for an introductory class in pre-Christian religion where they will learn that the Egyptians worshipped the scarab beetle because it laid its eggs in shit.

"From shit!" the professor will exclaim. "From shit came life! And then . . ."

Two phrases of note: *and then* and *but then*.

And then, Vee has decided, is positive. It implies something to look forward to: *and then* the girl went back to the boy's dorm, *and then* the girl lost her virginity to the boy in the top berth of his rickety bunk bed while side one of *Surrealistic Pillow* played repeatedly until the guy in the room next door shouted, I get it, Glod, you've got somebody to fucking love, *and then* the boy and girl blushed and looked into each other's eyes and made the same gargoylish grimaces of embarrassed horror, *and then* they began to laugh, eventually so hard they were crying and their faces turned red, *and then*, when the boy was capable of speech again, he raised himself up on one elbow and looked at the girl's crimson and blotchy face, *and then* he said, "Wow, I always thought falling in love took longer."

Whereas *but then* has the opposite effect. *But then* is the treacherous hairpin turn in the road. It terrifies you, and it ought to. You can't see around it, but neither can you avoid it. You can't come to a stop or make a U-turn or veer onto a different route. All you can do is hold your breath, steel yourself, step on the gas, and blast forward, even though you suspect that—no, you *know* that—nothing good lies around that corner.

But you have no choice. You have to lunge forward. You keep your foot on the gas. You have to. This is life. Einstein said that time does not move forward like an arrow, but how can that be true? This life, the one we perceive, which is the one that matters, does exactly that; it goes relentlessly forward in one direction only, taking you with it. You're twenty-two and you want to be carefree, *but then* your husband finds a lump in your right breast. You get some treatment and put cancer behind you, *but then* your mother jumps into the Hudson.

The good news is that with Eddie Glod there's an *and then* for every *but then*. *And then* he makes you a bowl of oatmeal. *And then* he holds you in bed. *And then* he's willing to put up with your kid sister, your bad jokes, your big sister, your awful moods. And then he says, So what do you think? Are we ready?

And then you say that yes, you think you are, yes. And when you try and you try, but nothing happens, you don't give in to the dark thoughts and silver, horizontal light that keep coming at you, because, after all, you're both young and now you're both healthy and so don't you have all the time in the world? And it seems to be true, so you keep going on as if there'll never be a *but then* again

But then

If Eddie Glod had not gone out for a sandwich in August of 1977, there would have been 1,918 murders in New York City that year. But he did, so there were 1,919. A madman bursting into the old Chock full o'Nuts at 114th Street. A madman mowing down everyone having lunch.

In a fit of Jewishness never demonstrated before or since, Vee decided to sit shiva for him, or at least to do something resembling shiva. She said she did it for his parents, but everyone could see that, aged socialists, they seemed more bemused than comforted. They were nice people, Vee always said, and mindful of their profound grief she tried to forgive them for buttonholing Eddie's mourners and blaming Eddie's death on her. She came from a family of drunks and suicides, they said. A family that had for generations also been purveyors of horrible and untimely deaths. "If they're not killing themselves," they whispered to Vee's visitors, several of whom found it necessary to subsequently whisper it to Vee, "then they're killing the rest of us. Used to be they had to go into a lab and make the poison. Now they are the poison."

"I don't know why I did it," Vee says now of the shiva. "Maybe I just didn't want to follow the Alter custom of burning and strewing. Or maybe I just wanted to keen and rent my garments in a quasi-public manner."

The shiva was held in our apartment. There was no rabbi, no Kaddish. There wasn't so much as a cold cuts platter. There was only half-assed ritual culled from a library book the title of which we immediately forgot, but which we ever-after referred to as *Everything You Ever Wanted to Know about Being a Jew But Were Afraid to Ask*: mirrors covered with bath towels, Vee shuffling about in her socks, a torn black ribbon pinned to the sleeve of her gray Barnard T-shirt.

The mourners who were related to Eddie arrived with bakery boxes containing black-and-white cookies, checkerboard cakes. They huddled in the dinette with the Glods. The mourners who were Eddie and Vee's friends brought green jugs of cheap wine and lids of grass. While Vee sat on an overturned wooden soda crate that Lady had carried up from the basement—later Vee would have to pull a dozen or so tiny splinters from the seat of her jeans—her friends crouched before her and reeled off every sorrowful event she'd endured up to and including that day, as if, without their assistance, she might forget one or two. Christ, Vee, they said, we thought it was lousy enough, your father leaving you when you were a kid, but then you get cancer, which is so ridiculous you figure nothing else bad could ever possibly happen, but then your mom goes and freaking offs herself, so by now you're thinking all right, these things come in threes, she's in the clear, it's all smooth sailing, but then this shit happens.

Cancer, her mother, and Eddie. Her friends had seen her through three *but then*s in a row. They were just kids in their early twenties, her friends. They couldn't handle all those *but then*s, and she couldn't handle her friends, their lives a series of *and then*s about to begin. The wedding announcements, birth announcements. She couldn't find it in her to be happy for them. In a few years she'd be in touch with none of them.

But at the shiva, they all did their best, and Vee, in her own way, was grateful for the effort, even as it made her cringe and fume.

Jesus fucking Christ, her friends said, the whole thing's like some fucking Shakespearean tragedy.

Jesus fucking Christ, Vee said after they'd left and the three of us passed around a shiva spliff. The friends' recapitulations of Vee's personal plagues, the buckets of gooey sympathy—all that was bad enough. Did they have to misuse the term *tragedy*, too?

"These are people who were in Eddie's fucking classes at Columbia, and they don't have a clue what a fucking Shakespearean tragedy is," she said. "If this were really a fucking Shakespearean tragedy, that would make Eddie the fucking tragic hero. So what was his fatal flaw? His fondness for Chock full o'Nuts cream cheese on fucking date-nut-bread sandwiches?"

"Maybe it's you they see as the fucking tragic hero," Lady gently suggested, but Vee said, "Oh, please. I'm clearly a fucking French farce."

"Theater of the fucking absurd," Delph countered, and nobody argued.

For a while Vee was active in the gun control community, but when she was diagnosed for the second time, she quit. She and her doctor opted for a bilateral mastectomy and a rugged course of chemo. (A lopectomy, she called the surgery, as in, "I'll have a lopectomy; make mine a double," but as per usual, nobody laughed.) She'd been looking for an excuse to leave, and no one could argue with sorry, but I seem to have come down with cancer . . . again.

It was true that the surgery and the chemo made it hard for her to march in the streets with the gun control crowd. She felt wretched about it, and self-involved, but she knew she was justified. The chemo had destroyed her immune system, making hanging out in crowds potentially perilous. But she'd come to understand that even at her healthiest, she had no patience for activism. She couldn't tolerate the endless political setbacks; she wasn't able to rev herself up again and again. She hated the futility of the movement, the humorlessness of the members, and the vitriol of their opponents. Because her name had appeared in the paper—the activist widow, the angry surviving spouse—letters kept arriving detailing what people were going to do to her with their guns. Few involved shooting her outright, although some did. Most were just amateur attempts at porn. "Really," she'd say of their favorite threat, "is that word ever spelled with a k?"

She had tried to write about it. It was her first attempt at memoir. She wanted to explain what the loss of this particular person meant not just to her, but to the world. The vacuum he'd left. The goodness now gone. But she couldn't get the words right. Everything she wrote sounded sappy. She was ashamed of that failure. The surviving spouses of the other victims all seemed able to get the words right. She heard them use the right words at the Chock full o'Nuts survivors' support group meetings she still attended for a while. The others stood up and spoke extemporaneously and, if not in heroic couplets, at least in complete, heartbreaking sentences.

He was a brilliant, compassionate physician.

She worked with disadvantaged youth.

You'd think a twenty-three-month-old child wouldn't remember, but she just stands in her crib crying: Where my mommy go? Where my mommy go?

Vee watched them get the words right on the evening news. On Channel 7 the widower of a secretary who'd been on her lunch break was taped holding their baby in his arms. This was the aforementioned twenty-three-month-old child with the long memory. The widower showed the little girl a framed photograph of her dead mother. The song "What Becomes of the Broken-Hearted" played in the background. The baby took the photo and gave it a kiss. Close-ups of oil paintings came into view. The music faded, the widower narrated: She was a secretary, yes, during the day, but she was really an artist . . . she was just starting to get interest from galleries . . . and she'd come home, and I'd hand off the baby and I'd go to work and she'd try to paint . . . and it was all so . . . perfect.

"It doesn't sound so perfect," Vee informed his image on the screen. "It sounds like you were never in the same room at the same time. When did the two of you ever have sex?"

Before the shooting, the widower told the Channel 7 reporter, he'd worked evenings for the animal language acquisition project at Columbia. Vee knew that, of course. He'd mentioned it at the meetings. You couldn't get him to shut up about it, in fact. But she'd never seen him talk about it with such emotionality. Both the reporter and he had tears in their eyes.

"I loved that job," the widower said as Jimmy Ruffin sang on, "but I've had to quit; I have to stay home with the baby."

Now they showed the widower on the grounds of the mansion in Riverdale where the famous Nim Chimpsky lived. The widower and Nim were walking away from the camera, man and chimp dressed in jeans rolled at the cuffs, both signing intensely to one another.

The network had phoned Vee, too. An intern had asked her all about Eddie. She could hear herself being inarticulate. They thanked her, told her how helpful she'd been, but now she understood it had not been an interview, it had been an audition, and a different devastated spouse—the superiorly grieving widower—had gotten the part. Vee could see why. Eddie and she were not nearly as good-looking as the secretary and the widower. Eddie had not been an artist. She and Eddie had no baby, much less a baby plus a monkey in jeans.

He saw me through cancer, she wished she'd thought to tell

the Channel 7 intern. Surely they'd have leaped at that. Surely a young widow's cancer trumped a young widower's talking ape.

It was watching the widower signing, watching him communicate with Nim without uttering words, that made Vee think of the blips. They'd been a habit, or maybe the right word is tic, that Delph had developed in about eighth grade. A few years later she stopped, just like that. But until then, each day when she returned home from school, she'd explode into the apartment as if enraged, throw her books and bags down on the chair by the door, then walk energetically up and down the length of the hallway—that is, up and down the length of the entire apartment—her fists clenched and all the while chanting "Blip, blip, blip, blip," as if she were an overcaffeinated robot. It became so routine, the blips, so expected, that Lady and Vee would go on with whatever it was they were doing as if Delph hadn't even come home yet. They never greeted her, barely glanced at her, until she was done. If our mother stuck her head out of the kitchen (or, more typically, if Lady stuck her head out of the kitchen) and said, "Vee, what does Delph want for supper?" Vee would say, "I'll ask when she's done with the blips," and that sounded reasonable and routine to everyone.

After the news segment about the secretary and the widower and the baby and the chimp aired, Vee gave the blips a try. Behind her closed door she lay on the side of the bed that still smelled like Eddie. She pulled her covers over her head. She closed her eyes, clenched her fists, and whispered "Blip, blip, blip, blip," so softly that even she couldn't hear herself. She felt like an idiot at first, but quickly she was struck by how effective, how distracting, how enormously calming the blips were. Like repeating a mantra. It *was* a mantra, wasn't it, a word repeated until your heart slowed and your fists uncurled and you stopped worrying about making the rest of the world understand things that had nothing to do with the rest of the world. Lady was doing Transcendental Meditation at the time, had paid what was for her a hefty sum so a young man with a stutter would whisper such a mantra in her ear. "You're a seeker," he told Lady, "so I'm giving you a seeker's mantra." It was the words beginning with *m* that caused him trouble, his lips pressed together until that first sound exploded forth, followed by prolongation. *Mmmmman-tra. Mmmmmeditation.* The mantra he whispered had sounded to Lady like a hushed version of a cartoon car horn: *aa-aa-oo-ga, aa-aa-oo-ga,* although, given her initiator's disfluency, she wondered if her mantra was actually just plain *aa-oo-ga.* Of course she was too polite to ask him, and she figured it didn't really matter anyway. Still, the thought that she might be replicating not merely her mantra but also somebody's speech disorder distracted her until she gave up TM altogether.

But *blip, blip, blip, blip,* Vee thought, was a wonderful mantra. You repeated it until you stopped feeling competitive with motherless babies. You said it until you were able to remember that life is short and everyone dies and although some deaths may be more dramatic or fascinating or ugly than others—some so much so that they become memorable headlines: "West Side Jumper Son of Death Camp Gas Inventor"; "Woman Pulled from Hudson Identified by Daughters"; "Chock full o'Nuts Massacre Kills Eleven"—that once you're dead, it's the same state of nothingness for everyone, unless you believe in an afterlife where the good are rewarded and the bad are punished and loving couples are reunited, which Vee did and does not.

Blip, blip, blip, blip until you also remembered this other important thing that you kept forgetting: that being shot in the back when you don't expect it and are completely immersed in your date nut bread sandwich and an article in the *Post* about the Yankees creaming the Mariners (which means you are very, very happy) is probably as swift and therefore as good a way to die as any death can be.

"I was in Korea," one of the cops on the scene was quoted as saying. "I've seen men killed, lots of men killed, shot, blown up, mutilated, but never have I seen carnage like this."

At first Vee wished the cop hadn't said this, but now she was trying to be thankful. Like sudden death, carnage was her friend. Brutal, merciless, but above all excessive. An excess of bullets meant no lingering, no suffering, not even any turning around and seeing your fate standing just inside the revolving door.

She was never able to turn all this into prose, though. At the time she tried, but she'd quickly give up. "What's there to say?" she'd ask Lady and Delph. She knew him, she loved him, he died. When the cancer came back in the last year of the 1970s, our decade horribilis—"Could it have been triggered by Eddie's murder?" she asked her doctor, who said it was unlikely, but then again, there was so much they didn't know about complicated grief, and it was the first time but hardly the last she'd heard *that* belittling term—she thought it would be the end of the story, the end of the romance. He dies, she dies of a broken heart among other, less romantic things. But the bi-lat and chemo had worked, at least for a good long while.

At the survivors' group meeting she'd attended after the segment on the news, the widower had made fun of himself. "They literally smeared honey on the glass of my wife's picture to get the baby to press her mouth to it," he said. "And, you know the footage of me and Nim? You know what Nim was saying? I was saying good-bye, Nim, and I love you, Nim, and he was saying,

Me eat eat eat. The minute the camera stopped rolling I had to take him to the kitchen. He didn't give a shit about me. He just wanted his raspberry yogurt."

Vee actually wound up dating the widower for a while. It hadn't worked out. Under his competent and outgoing facade, he was needy, sad, intense. "You know," Vee told Lady, making a face, "human."

"Ugh," Lady said agreeably. "I mean, who needs that in their life?"

What she really objected to, Vee said, was that the widower had smeared the emotional equivalent of honey all over Vee to convince himself he loved her, and he wound up falling for his own cheap trick. His little daughter had been less of a chump. Not much more lingual than Nim Chimpsky, but no dummy either, she resisted Vee mightily, howling whenever thrust into Vee's arms. The widower asked Vee to marry him anyway. "We understand each other," he said, "in a way no one else ever could."

"Do you even love me?" Vee asked, because that had never come up, and he grew abruptly irritated and formal and said, "Well, of course I have the requisite feelings."

Even then she'd considered saying yes. But ultimately she told him she was pretty sure they wanted different things. He wanted a caretaker for his daughter. She wanted to obsess about Eddie for an unhealthily long time, i.e., the rest of her life. He didn't take the rejection well. He cried copiously. She tried to cry, but couldn't manage it. She was pretty sure the reason he was crying was because, once again, he wasn't getting a proper good-bye. He was giving Vee the chance to utter the perfect farewell, the last line in the movie of their unromantic romance, but she couldn't come up with it. She could only think of other last lines—I think this is the start of a beautiful friendship;

If you talk about this, and you will, be kind; Tomorrow's another day. She looked at him—he was so much better looking than Eddie—and she couldn't help it, she got a little mean. She wanted out of his apartment so badly. But then he grabbed hold of her wrist, told her he loved her, that he honestly did, and the perfect last line came to her. She said, "Vee red milk me eat," and his tears dried up in an instant and he told her to go fuck herself and that was that.

Over the years we've received calls from biographers and journalists and pushy PhD students requesting information and interviews about our great-grandparents. For the longest time those calls have focused on Lenz. Recently, though, the callers have been asking about Iris. This is especially true of the students, Jewish women who rattle on about their interest in talmudic hermeneutics and their readings of the midrashim and the exegetical commentaries of Rabbeinu Tam vis-à-vis self-death.

"My thesis," Vee will say, mimicking their tight-jawed, nasal voices sprinkled with a touch of Brooklyn, "considers the degree to which Iris's suicide conformed with the aggadic laws regarding self-death and apostasy."

The grad students refer to our great-grandmother by her first name, as if they're old friends of hers. Speaking slowly, they explain to Vee that Iris was a proto-feminist who killed herself in protest against her husband's unconscionable promulgation of poisonous gas. With great feeling, they break the news that Lenz was a self-involved bastard who made sure Iris had no career. A bastard who then went off to the Russian front, abandoning his little boy with his mother's fresh corpse.

Vee never says much in reply. She doesn't point out that there was more than one abandoning parent in the Dahlem mansion that day. She doesn't remind them that Lise Meitner and Marie Curie each managed to make a go of their careers, that Mileva Einstein found a less showy way of coping with a difficult husband. She doesn't share her opinion that Iris was no feminist, no hero, just a mouse crippled by repressed anger and unrequited love for her doctoral adviser.

Above all, Vee doesn't ask what the hell hermeneutics means. To be honest, we don't want to know. We're afraid that if we understand the word, we'll begin using it, and we'll start sounding like these women or, even worse, thinking like them.

We don't want to become analytical or intellectual or nasal. We have no time to read up on which self-deaths this Rabbeinu Tam person considered A-OK and which he considered no-nos. Once you decide to kill yourself, once you make a pact and circle the date on your calendar, you just have to go ahead and do it. You can't conduct a little scholarly research first. You can't check in with rabbis or God or your dissertation advisor. Suicide is not for academics.

"I don't think I can help you," is what Vee typically says to the bubbly women. "We didn't know our great-grandmother. Who are we—really, who is anyone—to speculate on her motives?" After some concluding politesse, she hangs up and primal-screams. Feeling guilty for never taking a turn on the phone, Lady makes her a cocktail: a sloe gin fizz red as garnets or one of the new martinis made with one of the new vodkas, sugary and juicy and blue. Or orange. Or green. Martinis the colors of New York's perverted sunsets. We are, after all, the descendants of not only a mass murderer but also a dyemaker. We, too, like batches of liquid color.

"Just wait," Delph says. "Soon they'll want to write about us."

"I doubt that highly," says Lady.

But you never know, says Delph. It's seems evident that there
are at least a dozen female Jewish scholars born in Brooklyn,
studying at universities throughout New York and New Jersey,
who are working on dissertations about Iris. Why not a dissertation about us? What did she think, our mother used to say of
Iris, that the world owed her a parade? Well, maybe the world
did.

Vee hasn't accomplished a fraction of what Iris did, and yet
Vee sometimes thinks that even she's owed a parade. The simple
fact that she continued to live after Eddie Glod died—isn't that
parade-worthy? Of course, she's not imagining a Macy's Thanks-
giving Day parade. She has in mind a Roman triumph; she, the
conquering general, waving to the admiring throng as a slave
leans forward and whispers in her ear, "You are mortal, you are
mortal, you are going to die."

She is mortal, she is mortal. "Really?" she said upon getting
her latest prognosis. "Only six months?"

"To a year," her doctor said. "And I only provided a prognosis
because you pushed. Who can really say, Vee? Prognostication
is more art than science. It could be a month. It could be five
years."

"But what is it really?"

"Six months to a year."

They sat knees to knees in his office. He was drawing a bisec-
tion of the new problem area on the back of a prescription pad.

"Breast cancer without breasts," she said. "You've got to
admit, it's impressive."

"It's not unheard of," he said with great and, she supposed,
appropriate solemnity. "I've read about it in the journals."

"Huh," she said. "And here I thought I was special."

He showed her his illustration, but not being visual, she

shrugged helplessly. They'd known each other for almost twenty-five years, she and this doctor, ever since that first lumpectomy, and still they had trouble communicating. He said axilla, she said armpit. He said mediastinal nodes, she said let's try that again in English. Well, no, she didn't say that. She said, "I don't know what mediastinal means."

"It's . . ." He pressed his hand against his blue shirt.

"Heart?" she said. "I have cancer of the heart?"

He looked pained, shook his head. "Chest," he said. "Your chest wall. God, I need a vacation. I'm losing my words."

"Only the monosyllabics," she said. "You still have mediastinal."

As she said it, she thought: Well, look at me, having a conversation as if it were any other day. And she thought: Well, it is just any day. There's nothing unusual about a person being told they're going to die. I'm mortal; you're mortal; he, she, and it are mortal. Well, maybe not *it*. But definitely he and she. Definitely you and me. It's the most ordinary thing in the world.

"There are still things we can try," the doctor said. "There's an experimental protocol I heard about just the other day that we may be able to get you into." He launched into an explanation: "If, as research suggests, your tumors are a heterogeneous set of molecular subtypes rather than . . ."

She shook her head. "Don't go all hermeneutical on me. My body is not a text."

"It is, in a way."

"Three times," she said. "I've gotten it three times. What's to interpret? I surrender. Victory is its."

He argued, but not as wholeheartedly as she'd expected. She heard frustration and hopelessness. She shook her head again, and this time he nodded. He folded his hands together: here is the church, here is the steeple. There were tears in his eyes, but they never fell. She appreciated both—the tears and the no tears.

He said, "Our goal, then, will be to keep you as comfortable as we can."

He hugged her good-bye, a hard, tight hug that made her remember how long it had been since a man had held her. Embarrassed by the depth of gratitude she felt at his touch, she broke away. She made her way through the waiting room filled with the ashen and the florid, the hairless and the bewigged, the resigned and the royally pissed off, the old and the much-too-young, all of them engrossed in years-old copies of *People* and *Sports Illustrated*, all reading of scandals unhappily resolved, of play-offs already lost, of the princess dead in a tunnel.

Surprisingly, the plan to actually kill herself hadn't come immediately. Stepping off the elevator, then out of the lobby, squinting for a moment against the sunny June day, making her way to the bus stop, fishing inside her purse for her MetroCard, she'd first imagined she'd simply be passive. She'd wait until her body quit. She imagined herself as one of those witnesses to a violent mugging who never dials 911, who just watches it happen.

It wasn't until the contemplative state induced by a long, familiar ride on a public conveyance came upon her that she realized true power lay in taking action.

Action—i.e., suicide—was so obviously the right thing to do that the only shocking thing was that she hadn't thought of it right away. She, of all people. Perhaps it was because she had no symptoms yet. Certainly she had no pain. Cancer was such a strange adversary, the way it hung around, biding its time.

Now she decided that as soon as the symptoms began, at the very first twinge of pain, she would take what people liked to call the easy way out.

But, traveling up Madison, commerce going on that day just as it would go on after she died, she began finding fault with this solution. She found herself turning the prognosis into a math problem:

If x = six months to a year or maybe longer, then what day is x?

It was an equation impossible to solve. On the other hand, how simple to determine x if the problem were tweaked just a little.

If x = precisely six months from today, then x is what day?

The bus made an abrupt stop. Passengers in the aisle lurched, and some—tourists, she assumed—cried out. Vee ignored them. She was not a part of their community: the community of people standing in the aisle trying to keep their balance. She was too busy looking through her wallet for the five-year calendar from the bank. She was too busy solving for x.

It made so much sense. Even the *tut-tut*ters and *tsk-tsk*ers would have to agree. If she solved for x—if she determined the precise day on which she'd die—she could quit her job. Why would she need any more income? She could start spending down her savings. She could live off her 401(k) plan, the penalties for early withdrawal be damned. Limit her life to a six-month span, and suddenly even a paralegal is rich.

Nor would she have any need for the other benefits the firm provided, not even her Blue Cross. A person who knew she was going to die on a specific day—Vee'd already decided on New Year's Eve, a little more than six months hence, true, but she liked the idea of going out at the same time as the century, and it would be so much easier for Lady and Delph to file her final income tax return if she died on the last day of the taxable year—such a person didn't need health insurance. Such a person wouldn't have to see any more doctors, not ever.

She wasn't thinking just of her oncologist. She was thinking of her optometrist, with all his which is better, this or this, and her gynecologist, with the soft sad way she'd say, every goddamn year, "So, are we still not sexually active?" But mostly she was thinking of the dermatologists, the fleet of baffled men and women who, for the past ten years, had been staring at her scalp, trying to figure out why, the chemo long out of her system, her hair had never grown back. All the creams and goos and and pills and steroids, the application of thick, smelly tar and ultraviolet light, every intervention doing absolutely nothing.

"This stuff will put hair on your chest," the latest dermatologist had said, a little alopecia humor as he wrote a scrip, but the stuff had put hair nowhere.

Some sort of emotional trauma was the conclusion they all eventually came to. Unresolved grief, they'd say after they heard her life story. Each one had sent her on her way with the name of a shrink scribbled on a slip of paper and a lifetime prescription for Valium. They made her promise not to misuse the pills, and she promised and kept her promises. She'd never misused a single pill because she'd never taken any. She only stockpiled them.

As for her unresolved grief, for the past ten years she had concealed it with scarves. She wore them Hulk Hogan style, low on her forehead, knotted at her nape, the ends flowing. She tried to femme up the look with earrings, large gold hoops or long feathers dangling to her shoulders.

But this day on the bus, having solved for x and feeling a warm tickling mixture of fear and relief, she abruptly reached up and removed her scarf, which was chocolate brown to play up her eyes, lashless, browless, and as stark as Raisinettes.

The removal of the scarf, the exposure of the pate: it had been wholly unplanned yet completely deliberate. Appalled and excited, she tried to detect her reflection in the dirty bus window, but the filth and the angle of the sun thwarted her. Or maybe—a bald, middle-aged woman—she'd literally vanished. Certainly no one on the bus was paying any attention.

She knew what she looked like without the scarf, of course. She saw herself without the scarf at home every day. This is what she looked like without it: awful. She was not one of those people who could carry off hairless. Bald made her look like some woman just escaped from an institution. Or, more accurately, like some man just escaped.

She turned from the window. She balled the scarf in her fist. Ever since the second occurrence, the one allegedly cured by the bilateral mastectomy and the chemo, she'd been trying to reach a place of serene acceptance when it came to her appearance. Body as narrative. Face as biography. The semiotics of Vee's recalcitrant scalp. What are they *saying*, the scars on her chest, the deep nasolabial folds by her mouth? What's the narrative? The first time Vee noticed those lines, she had thought they were streaks of dirt and tried to scrub them away with a washcloth. Lady caught her at it and laughed. Even unattractive women, even women violently widowed and prone to cancer, feel waylaid and queasy upon seeing—or, more accurately, upon letting themselves finally see—the first, indelible signs of aging. "Congratulations," Lady said, "and welcome to the land of the invisible woman."

If her body is a book, it's a horror story. Chapter 1: I Am Born. Chapter 3: I Get Cancer. Chapter 6: I Acquire Jowls. Even so, it's her book, her story. So as not to interfere with the unfolding plotline, she's rejected even the smallest of palliative interventions over the years. No face powder to take off the shine, no contacts to eliminate the red divots on her nose, no padded bras to fill out a blouse. Certainly no implants. She gads about town greasy-faced, flat-chested, and four-eyed.

For a while she wore a wig, but when she continued to age poorly and it became too bright, too full, too Farrah, for her face, she'd thrown it away. "Don't put it in the trash," Lady had said. "Donate it to some cancer clinic, " but Vee had said, "No, the wig must die," and dropped it in with the garbage.

"The wig is dead," Lady had said then. "Long live the scarf." Now the scarf was dead, too, suffocated in Vee's fist.

She was on the M4, sailing along Cathedral Parkway. She had no recollection of transferring, that's how lost in thought she'd been. For a few minutes, for a few stops, she'd already left the world, and she hadn't even noticed. That, she thought, was probably what being dead was like.

As for the final six months of her life, she was determined they would be the six months of her dreams. Unemployed, she would stay home and read. She would go to movies. She would drink all day long, including first thing in the morning. Better yet, she'd never have to see the morning; she could sleep every day until noon and start to drink then. Or sleep until three. She could have six months of being a slob and a sloth, a potted plant with a buzz on. She would go to her final reward with the chest of an abused teenage boy and the hair pattern of an elderly man and her bone marrow sucked dry by her own turncoat cells, but she would be well-read and well-rested.

It was right about then, as she was making her list of fun things to do during her final months of life—Broadway! She could afford to see every damned play on Broadway!—that she took note of the man sitting beside her. She didn't exactly do a double take, but she realized at once that she'd seen him before on this very bus line, that he'd taken the empty seat next to her at least once before.

She found this surprising, but less shocking than the other shocks. She knew lots of people would find it full of meaning, running into the same stranger more than once on a bus in a city the size of New York. Delph, for instance. Delph would swear it was a sign. Perhaps a bad sign: the man was Vee's cancer personified. Perhaps a good sign: the man had been sent by Eros, a last chance at love, a Yogi Berra–ish kind of encouragement: it ain't over till it's over.

Vee didn't believe in that sort of thing. She didn't believe the angry clerk at city hall had given her cancer, and she didn't subscribe to the curse that encircled Delph's leg and supposedly lay on all three of our heads. For Vee, the meaning of life had always been that life had no meaning, and the moral of the story was that there was no moral of the story. Things that seemed significant weren't. While her philosophy of life wasn't tattooed on her body like Delph's, it would have been affixed to her bumper if Vee knew how to drive and owned a car.

Shit happens.

That's what she believed and has tried to persuade Delph to believe as well. "Life isn't a soap opera," Vee would say. "It's far more nonsensical. Things that seem to mean something mean nothing. Jefferson and Adams died on the same day, and that day was the fourth of July. Teddy Roosevelt's wife and mother died on the same day, and that day was Valentine's Day. Nothing has any significance."

Some people collect stamps, coins, sterling silver fish knives. Vee collects coincidences. Her favorites are the double tragedies, the triple tragedies. She's the *Ripley's Believe It or Not* of misery compounded. Did you hear the one about the old Japanese man, how during the war, covered with burns, he was rushed from Hiroshima to a hospital in—where else?—Nagasaki? Or what about the one where a woman in Delaware learns her husband and son both died the same day, each one hundreds of miles from the other, each one in a different bizarro accident? That last coincidence came with an in-your-face punch line: "God never gives us more than we can handle," the woman had sobbed gamely to a klatch of admiring reporters. A few months later there was one of those "Whatever happened to . . . ?" stories. The woman had died in a car crash. Boom! Rimshot!

And if you don't believe that so many terrible things could befall a single person in a mere twenty-four-hour period, if you think Vee is inventing or exaggerating, then just wait here. Vee will go into her room, come back with the article. Dateline: Dover, Delaware. Vee clips and saves all the articles. She stuffs them in a shoe box that she keeps in her closet. She's a curator of coincidences, the queen of quinky-dinks.

Which is only to say that she didn't think it meant a damned thing that this particular man, seventyish, perhaps even older, was sitting next to her again

That said, she found herself glancing at him. She had no idea why. She wasn't much of a people watcher. Certainly it wasn't sexual. She didn't find him attractive in any sense of the word. The bags under his eyes were substantial. His face was furrowed and specked. He was lean but too lean, a worn-out soul. Chapter 1: I Am Born. Chapter 6: I Turn Into that Guy from that Hopper Painting. (Museums! She could go to museums!) But she couldn't stop darting her eyes in his direction, noting how his hair, thin and silver, stood up in places as if he'd been running his fingers through it with worry, or how the concavity of his sunken cheeks seemed almost blue with stubble.

He, on the other hand, didn't look at Vee. His own gaze was fixed on his hands, large and ringless, which he'd placed on his knees, the fingers splayed. It was as if he was wondering if they really were his hands, as if he was concerned he'd accidentally taken the wrong pair when he left wherever he'd come from, the way people sometimes grab the wrong suitcase at baggage claim. Be careful. Many hands look alike.

A murderer would look at his hands that way, Vee thought. Not that she believed the man sitting next to her was a murderer, other than to the extent we all are—the small murders we commit through negligence or giving in to a moment's bad temper. The murders we commit when we fail to do things— fail to send money to flood victims, fail to get up early to march for issues we claim to care about, fail to catch a wasp inside the apartment and release it back into the world instead of flattening it with a newspaper. And the murders we commit simply by existing, simply by our inhabiting and exploiting this beleaguered planet.

But not a murderer like, for example, our great-grandfather, the murderer who bequeathed us our genetic code and our faces.

Vee tried to shake these thoughts from her head. They made for an inauspicious start to what were supposed to be her final six months. She tried to look on the bright side instead. Now that she knew the exact day on which she was going to die, she could be bold and brave. She could talk to her seatmate. She could say, "Nice weather," or "Trafficky today, isn't it?" or "Well, here we are again, the two of us on the good old M4." And he might say, "I know; we're always coming from roughly the same place and going to roughly the same place, though neither of us knows a thing about the other's actual starting point or destination." And Vee could say, "It feels meaningful, but it's just a coincidence." And he could say, "That's a fact, you're one hundred percent correct. But still, it's a nice coincidence, if you don't mind my saying."

Or they could have a completely different conversation. Vee could say, "Well, here we are again," and he could say, "Excuse me, what are you talking about? I've never seen you before in my life." Or he could reply in Spanish or Ukrainian. Or he could say nothing at all, just give Vee the kind of look that people on buses tend to give conversationally inclined ex-institutionalized patients of indeterminate gender. And if he did say that, or it turned out they spoke different languages, or he gave her that look, it wouldn't matter; Vee wouldn't let it bother her the way she would have, say, yesterday. She wouldn't waste any time replaying it, experiencing the humiliation again and again and again, because she'd have other things on her mind, such as the fact that she was going to fucking die on New Year's Eve.

She said nothing, though. Even as the bus began slowing for her stop and she stepped over him and into the aisle, she didn't let on that she'd been thinking about him. She stood by his seat now, holding onto the metal handle directly behind his shoulder, swaying slightly, expertly, to maintain her balance. The bus stopped, and she began making her way down the aisle, and as she did she let the scarf in her fist fall. It landed by the socked toes emerging from her seatmate's Tevas.

He didn't notice. This wasn't the belle epoque, after all, when men retrieved the handkerchiefs women dropped at their feet. It was the aisle of a city bus in 1999. He'd never look down and see it. He'd more likely step on it unaware when he disembarked. Then, for the rest of the day, other passengers would step on the scarf, until, in the early hours of the morning, a maintenance worker would sweep it up and throw it away.

Did it make her sad, the fate of this square of discarded silk? Yes, it did. It made her so sad that she allowed herself to stop at the Hungarian Pastry Shop and buy four Sacher tortes. Three for our desserts later in the evening. One for her to eat as she walked the few blocks home. The undergrad drinking coffee at one of the tables, she noted, was, if not as bald as she, then half-as-bald, with one side of her head shaved and the other side long and dyed indigo blue. She imagined this girl standing in her dorm bathroom, humming as she wielded the electric razor, as she mixed up the Manic Panic. She imagined the girl looking up now, greeting Vee, mistaking Vee for a kindred spirit. Bald women of Manhattan unite! But—New York City—neither the undergrad nor anyone else in the shop, including the man behind the counter, made eye contact with her.

Home finally, Vee stood in the foyer, waiting until Lady, who was in the kitchen futzing with dinner, and Delph, who was in the living room watching the local news, sensed her waiting there and looked up. It meant nothing to them that she was scarfless; she always whisked off her scarf as soon as she walked in. They just assumed they'd failed to witness the evening's whisking

Vee continued to wait until she had their full attention, until Lady had turned down the burner threatening to overboil the spaghetti, until Delph looked away from tomorrow's weather.

"So," she said at last. "Guess what reared its ugly head today?" and Lady and Delph, who had allowed themselves not to think about cancer for a good solid decade, knew the answer at once.

We convened around the dinette table. It was still covered with the same shit as always, or pretty much the same shit. No more issues of *Rolling Stones*; those had been replaced by the slippery mountain that was the unavoidable byproduct of a subscription to the *New Yorker*. No more weed, but at least a half dozen wine-glasses we hadn't yet carried to the sink, the purple residue of some cheap zin staining the bottom well of their bowls.

Lady and Delph said the things one says. They asked the questions one asks, although after Lady asked, "What kind of treatment plan are they talking about?" and Vee smiled and said, "None," the need for further questioning seemed minimal.

Some of the things we didn't do that evening included crying, hugging, pacing, or panicking. We are Alters, but we are also Emanuels, also Gläsers: stoics, Spartans, fatalists—quitters, if you like. We let nature take its course. We don't fight city hall. We accept the things that come our way. This is not to say we've always liked those things, or that we've made peace with them or gotten through them without a drink or two or five. It's not to say we wouldn't have preferred actually having a father or a normal mother or—let's go crazy—both. It's not that we wouldn't have preferred it if Eddie Glod hadn't died in a cheap chain restaurant, or if the shadow on Vee's latest film had turned out to be the radiologist's thumb.

It's just that we keep our reactions to ourselves. We tamp them down. We ignore them or feed them or drown them. You're thinking this is a bad thing, but no, it's a wonderful thing. It's truly a talent. Thanks to nature and nurture both, we've been blessed with the gift of repression.

We sat at the table quietly. Vee looked down, the way a child who brought home a bad report card might, regretful primarily for causing others distress. Finally Lady sighed and got up and went to our sideboard, a wall-length golden pine buffet Karin had taken from Germany to France to Haiti to here, a piece of furniture that was completely incongruous next to the cheap dinette set she'd bought when reduced to relative poverty in America. Of course, all the pieces in the dinette have sentimental value for us; we grew up with them. The vinyl and chrome chairs we were sitting on had been our chairs for five decades. Our entire apartment is like this: a mishmash of styles and eras, including a smattering of possessions acquired by the Alters when they were still well-to-do Germans, borderline Christians, and retained by them after they were reviled and exiled and Caribbean.

Lady returned to the table with a new bottle of the same old cheap zin. She twisted off the cap and refilled three of the stained glasses. We each took the nearest one, made the faintest gesture of a toast, then drank the wine down in big, crude gulps. We were after inebriation.

Lady put her glass down first. "So, Veezie," she said. "What are you going to do?"

Vee smiled again. "You of all people should know the answer to that."

Lady refilled our glasses to the brim. We had to lean down to sip before we could lift them.

"You're being very rational . . . ," Lady said.

"I'm waiting for the *but*," said Vee.

The window in the living room was open. We let ourselves hear the city sounds we normally filtered out. The sounds were all made by vehicles—squealing brakes, backfiring exhausts, car alarms, ambulance sirens, and the very specific sound of a bus coming to a stop, opening, then closing its doors and pulling away.

"I'm not sure I have a *but*," Lady said. She started to make the obvious and self-deprecating pun, but stopped herself.

"I won't have to deal with ambulances," Vee said.

"I would never wish you a life dependent on ambulances and emergency rooms," Lady said.

"We all gotta go sometime," Vee said.

"And really," Lady said, "it makes so much more sense to determine when that sometime is rather than just putting ourselves at the mercy of fate. Or time. Or the US medical establishment."

"This *is* Vee's fate," Delph said.

Vee kept smiling. "The fact that I have terminal cancer has more to do with the chemicals in the environment and the plastic in our food and, frankly, this glass of wine in my hand than with any kind of curse," she said.

Delph said nothing, but she said it loudly.

"Look," Vee said. "It's my death, and I get to say why it's happening."

We fell back into silence. We sat like that for a very long time.

Later, the three of us lying across Vee's mattress, Vee said, "I see my decision as emerging from a confluence between inclination and circumstance."

Later still: "I'm completely at peace. Really, I'm so remarkably fine."

The room had darkened. Only the lights of the city kept it from going black. The sky was the color of ocean froth.

"I could spend a week at the beach," Vee said. "Not Rockaway. A real beach. The kind where the water is actually blue."

Another stretch of human silence, another squalling of horns, brakes, sirens, hydraulics.

"I could go on a silent retreat," Vee said. "I could sit crosslegged in silence from now until then."

An hour or so later, the sun coming up, Delph said, "Here's what I think. Midnight. New Year's Eve. It's a good idea. We skip out before this whole Y2K thing. Meanwhile we have about six months to write that book we've always wanted to write. About the three generations."

That's how it began. We thought we'd write about Lenz and Richard and our mother. Those deaths. Not ours.

"We would have to work steadily and faithfully," Vee said.

"Evenings," Delph said.

"Weekends," said Lady.

"And full-time, after we quit our jobs," said Delph.

Lady nodded. "And if during that time you happen to change your mind, Vee, or—who knows?—maybe they come up with some kind of viable treatment . . ."

"Vee-able treatment," Delph said, soft little-girl voice.

Vee smiled, but shook her head

"I said *if*," said Lady. "*If* they do . . . then we reassess."

"All right," Vee said. "New Year's Eve. Six months, four hours, twenty-six minutes from now. All right. That's my deadline. And I do mean deadline."

"And mine," Lady said. "Have you not been hearing me?"

"We're not letting you go alone," Delph said.

There was the faintest note of resentment in their declarations. It was as if Vee were about to go on the Grand Tour of Europe without them. Delph could hear our mother's petulant reproval: *But your sisters? You don't even invite your sisters?*

That's how easy it was. Sure, Vee exerted some effort trying to talk the other two out of it. It seemed like—it *was*—the polite thing to do. "What's your justification?" she said.

"My sister's prognosis," Delph said.

"No," Vee said. "That's my justification, not yours."

"Don't tell us what makes our lives no longer worth living," Lady said.

Vee stopped arguing. She couldn't say she exactly hated the idea. A companion, a coconspirator, a hand to hold.

We raised our glasses. We searched for an appropriate toast.

"What's the opposite of *l'chaim*?" Lady said.

"L'pffft," Vee suggested, which sounded, if not Hebrew, then certainly Yiddish. We liked it. We clinked. "L'pffft!" we said. *L'pffft*—spitting all over each other and laughing, which was as close to crying as we ever get.

And when we looked out the window, we all saw the light shift, vertical to horizontal, gold to silver; we all saw it change at the very same time.

CHAPTER 10

But, hey, are you feeling confused by all this info that's just come at you? Would a timeline at this point come in handy? We think it might. So here—have a timeline:

TIMELINE

1972	1973	1974	1975	1976	1977	1978	1979	1980
			Lady: divorce Vee: cancer (1) Mom: Hudson		Chock Full 'O Nuts		Vee: cancer	
Lady marries Joe		Vee marries Eddie		Lady: rope		Lady: razor blade		Lady: valium and vodka

Just don't give us any shit about it. Don't call our lives a melodrama. Don't bring up the term *soap opera*. Don't tell us how hard it is to believe that so many terrible things can befall a single family in such a short time. They can. They did. Shut up.

And don't respond by telling us your own heartaches and

tragedies. Don't say, Oh, I know just how you feel because once I . . . We're generally not competitive women, but when it comes to this period of our lives, we know we have you beat six ways from Sunday.

Or . . . do we? Because isn't it true that here in this vale of tears, there's always someone who can out-tragic you? This world, after all, is nothing but a misery bazaar, and each of us just another merchant behind a booth, showing off her wares.

We have a riddle.

Q: Where can you run into all the suffering souls of this sorrowful world?
A: At a Job's fair

And those Job's fairs are everywhere; you never know when you'll stumble into one. All you know is, you'll never have to wait very long. Shortly before Christmas, 1979, the bare trees along the nicer streets of Manhattan decorated with blinking white bulbs—there was still an energy crisis, but how long could people refrain from bright lights and cheer?—Vee, who was still doing chemo, said to the oncology nurse hooking her up, "So how's things?" And the nurse, an older woman with rucked cheeks and sunken eyes and Tweety Birds all over her smock, said that things weren't so good, that she'd had to put her father into a home a couple of weeks before because of the dementia, and the next day her sister, heartbroken about his decline, and, well, there was some prescription abuse going on too, had killed herself, and the day after that, the sister's estranged husband, who'd been summoned to identify the sister's body, the sister having failed to update her contact information when the marriage fell apart, gave the okay for organ donation, which the sister had definitely not wanted, her being a Catholic who'd need her body parts in heaven, not that she'd wind up there now, not after the suicide, but the nearly ex-husband goes oh, yeah, go ahead, sure, no problem, and so they take not only the sister's eyes and liver and kidneys and heart and everything else, but also her skin, *her skin*, which, yes, of course, is an organ, but who thinks skin when they think organ donation, and besides she wouldn't have wanted want them to take anything at all, much less her skin. Only then, after all this, did they deliver what was left of the sister to a funeral home. Only then was the nurse informed her sister had died. The funeral director confided to the nurse that he'd never before in his life seen such butchery. That was the word the man used. Butchery. And you had to figure a New York funeral director had seen it all, from murder victims to people flattened by subways.

"So how bad is something when a funeral director who's seen it all says he hasn't seen anything like it?" The nurse stopped to collect herself. "I don't think it's all sunk in yet," she said after a moment. "But you know what? At least I still have my nephews and nieces," she said. "And my friends. Thank God for friends."

While the nurse was saying all this, she'd inserted a needle into a vein in the back of Vee's left hand, gently and perfectly, not even a pinch. She taped a square of cotton over the needle to hold it in place. She checked to make sure the cherry red fluid was seeping into Vee's body. Vee would be there for hours. She was what they called a long-dripper.

"But here I am, going on about myself," the nurse said, "when you're the one fighting for your life." She patted Vee's shoulder. "It helps me cope with my own troubles, when I see my brave patients like you."

"Jesus, Jan," Vee said. She didn't say, Is that your life or *The*

Guiding Light? She didn't say, It's awfully hard for me to believe all this happened to you in just the last week. She didn't say, One suicide? One measly suicide? She didn't say, Hey, you think you got troubles? Remember that massacre at the Chock full o'Nuts last year? She didn't say, I'll see you your butchery and raise you my carnage.

She said, "I'm not brave. What am I doing that's so brave? I'm just going to lie here for a few hours and watch TV. I don't have to lift a finger."

"C'mon, you're sick as a dog," Jan said generously. "And all the nausea and the throwing up."

"That's true," Vee said. "But even then I'm just lying there. Facedown instead of faceup. But still, just lying there."

"You see?" Jan said. "You're being brave right now."

As they argued, the Alphonse and Gaston of life's vicissitudes and shit storms, Vee was facing a pain-scale poster taped to the wall. Indicate your pain level on a scale of one to ten, the directions said. She wondered if there were scales like this for emotional pain. On a scale of one to ten, one being life's a bowl of cherries and ten being you're Jan this week, where do you see yourself?

Even now Vee doesn't give herself a ten. Maybe an eight. Because she isn't saying that she hasn't had some lousy days, what with the father's desertion and the first round of cancer and the mother's suicide and the husband's murder and the sister's attempted suicide and the cancer again and the sister's second and third suicide attempts, and the death of the love of the poor baby sister's life from AIDS, which happened in the early-1980s, just when we thought things had calmed down.

So, fine, Vee says. So, she's suffered. But has she suffered any more than Jan? Or any more than Joshua Gottlieb, who in the end lost his job and his health insurance and so had no choice but to move back to his parents' home in Winnetka, where his mother catered to him, but his father refused to put through the phone calls of his distraught New York friends? The price for staying in his childhood bed, for being tended to by family, for the luxury of round-the-clock nurses and the best of everything, was his admission that he wasn't gay, that he'd never been gay, that he'd only said it and gone so far as living the life and contracting this vile disease because he wanted to piss off his parents. Teenage rebellion gone amok. We'd have written more about Joshua in the era of the plague, but Delph forbade it. She still can't bear it. So perhaps, in a way, even Delph has suffered more than Vee. At least Vee was loved in return.

In fact, Vee will tell you, even Nim Chimpsky has suffered more than she has. That innocent taken from mother after mother. That sentient being raised in homes with children, showered with affection and attention and conversation, who could say play and tickle and hug, was abruptly taken from everything he knew and turned over to a primate farm in Oklahoma. The funding for the linguistic study had not been renewed. His caretakers wanted to get on with their own lives. How he'd screamed and clung to the last of his caretakers that day. She had to pry him from her, finger by finger. She left Oklahoma as fast as she could, before she had to see him locked into his cage.

At least Vee has sisters who will never leave her. At least she's the one making the choices. At least she—at least we—know how to open locked doors.

PART TWO

The Reunion

CHAPTER 11

In July, John F. Kennedy Jr.'s plane went down, and we had our usual arguments. Vee insisted the crash was not the result of any curse. Nor, she said, did it have any meaning. The only lesson to take from it was that new pilots shouldn't fly over water at night. Delph, meanwhile, argued that the disaster was the universe's way of affirming our decision to kick the bucket. If we didn't do it ourselves, the gods were telling us, they would. They'd exhale their mighty breaths, and a storm would come and literally turn us upside down.

"Really," Vee said. "You think God killed John-John as a way of sending a message to us? Whatever happened to the days when he just wrote messages on walls?"

"You want writing on the wall?" Delph indicated her calf. "Here's the writing on the wall." She sometimes talked about her tattoo that way, as if it had mysteriously appeared on her leg one day through none of her own doing, as if she hadn't gone out and requested it and paid for it with a personal check.

Vee told her as much, called her ridiculous, a wee tad narcissistic. And yet, days after the Coast Guard retrieved the wrecked fuselage with the beautiful bodies still strapped inside, it was Vee who began reading Jung.

She'd been wandering through the library, she said, looking for things to read during these, her final six months, when she'd noticed a thick book on one of the return carts. The call numbers on its spine were more discernible than its black-on-black title, but she picked it up anyway and opened it to the title page. Only then could she see that it was called *Synchronicity*.

Was it a meaningless coincidence that she'd been drawn to a book on meaningful coincidences? Yes, she thought at first, but later, halfway through the tome, she thought maybe not. She began lecturing Lady and Delph on the subject. Jung's theory of synchronicity, she said, didn't hang on the whims of meddlesome gods nor on the efficacy of generation-spanning curses. Jung was a man of science, and he was confident science would eventually explain the reason for coincidences. Answers might be unknown at the moment. That didn't mean they were supernatural. It didn't mean we had to think like primitives, invent gods and curses.

"He used to meet with Einstein, and they'd talk about it," Vee said. "Next thing you know, Einstein came up with relativity and Jung came up with the collective unconscious."

"Neither of which anyone understands," Lady said. "Probably not even Einstein and Jung."

We imagined the two men in a coffeehouse, leaning toward each other, talking excitedly, cake crumbs in their mustaches, each pretending he got what the other was saying.

"Jung had this client," Vee said. "She dreamed someone had given her a brooch in the shape of a scarab beetle. As she's telling Jung the dream, he hears something tapping on the window behind him. He turns, and it's a large insect trying to get into the room. It's attracted to the light. So he opens the window and the bug flies in and he snatches it up in his hand and it's a freaking scarab beetle! A scarab beetle! A species that doesn't even live in Europe!"

She was perspiring a little. It was a hot July day, but she was also agitated. Also: menopause. She wiped her bare forehead with her hand.

"He says the two things—the dream and the bug showing up—were linked by meaning. Not by cause and effect, but meaning. He says it's a different type of time." She looked at Lady and Delph intently. "Have I been wrong about everything?" she asked.

"Looks like it," Delph said, but Lady said, "Oh, who knows? To him the patient's talking about beetles, and then a non-native beetle shows up, and he thinks it's such a crazy coincidence, it has to have meaning. But maybe the reason the patient had the dream about the brooch in the first place was because she'd seen a non-native beetle in her bathtub the day before. Maybe there was an odd infestation of non-native beetles in western Europe that year. So he's running around saying there was no discernible cause and effect between the dream and the beetle at his window, but it turns out there was plenty of cause and effect between the beetle in the tub and the dream."

"Yes," Delph said. "Or, alternatively, Vee has been wrong all these years, and I've been right. Occam's razor. The simplest answer is always the correct answer. Ergo, coincidences have meaning. I rest my case."

"I suspect everyone contemplating their own death has at least one moment of wondering if they've been wrong about everything," Lady said.

"Acausal time," Vee said. "That's what he and Einstein called it. Time linked by meaning, not by this past, present, and future thing we cling to."

We looked at each other helplessly. We'd reached the limit of our understanding.

"He was into the I Ching too," Vee added. We all sighed nostalgically.

Not long after that Vee—yes, Vee!—went out and had a small iris tattooed at her ankle. "Why didn't you tell me it hurt like hell?" she said to Delph when she came home.

But there was more than that little tattoo. The tattoo artist Vee had visited, a young woman in a white sundress and bare feet, her toenails painted black, her arms sleeved with a rain forest motif—red bougainvillea and dark green grasses and the eyes of jungle cats—had taken a shine to Vee. "I love how you wear your hair," she'd said.

"Or rather how I don't wear my hair," said Vee.

"It's very bold. Very strong."

"It's chemo," Vee said.

"I have an idea for you," the woman said. She offered no condolences. This was just a fashion opportunity as far as she was concerned. Vee had to admit she was well put together. Her own hair was thick and curly and profuse, much like Delph's, though off her face and blacker and glistening from product. She had a hoop through an eyebrow and a large diamond by her nostril.

"No piercings," Vee said.

"No more pain," the woman agreed. "Just my powders and brush."

She'd hennaed the blank canvas that was Vee's bald head. Glossy brown diamonds now emanated from the crown of Vee's head and made their way down to her forehead and ears and nape.

Enlightenment, Vee told us, was the meaning of the pattern. She had other designs that were prettier, one that she said brought good health and one that guaranteed long life, but Vee said she figured she'd go with something she still had a shot at."

"It looks good," Lady said.

Vee lifted her hand to run it over her scalp, but stopped herself. She was still afraid to touch it, afraid it would smear or stain. But she was pleased. "I should have done this fifteen years ago," she said.

Lady laughed. "And thus has the enlightenment begun."

Another non-momentous but atypical thing we did this summer—this in late August—was leave the house on a Saturday for no other reason than to be outdoors. We don't love nature, we don't particularly enjoy experiencing it without a damned good reason. But it was a nice day, and we thought we'd try, just as an experiment, to be normal. We knew how one did this Saturday-in-the-park business: you placed a bottle of wine and several red plastic cups into a satchel and then, along with every other Upper West Sider who had not left the city for the shore or the mountains, you took the subway to Zabar's and fought your way in, and ten minutes later you fought your way back out with a cantankerous loaf of French bread, a few offensive wedges of cheese, and an early edition of the *Times* so you could do the Sunday puzzle and, if it was the right week, the acrostic.

We handled all of this splendidly, expertly. We walked down through the park to Zabar's, then up through the park to our neighborhood. We sat on as isolated a bench as we could find, and we ate and drank and fed squirrels. We could hear the tennis matches a few blocks down. We have no interest in tennis, but we liked the heartbeat sound of volleys, the steady *thwock thwock*.

As we listened and ate and got tipsy, we studied the ebony

arteries and rounds in the tree bark and the burnt-orange caps of acorns. We studied the grass, the sharp and stubby blades, green until the pale brown tip, like a dye job gone bad.

We had the kind of conversations we used to have back in college. Topic: is the beauty of nature a learned construct or are trees, flowers, and grass just intrinsically the most goddamn beautiful things not only on Earth, but in the universe? That is, if a Martian landed his craft in Riverside Park, would he be struck to near tears by the bark and the grass and the chevrons of geese leaving town, even by the pigeons, the sheen of their feathers the same silver-purple as rainbows in puddles? Or would he cry because what we find beautiful is ugly to him, especially when compared to the rough red gravel of Mars?

We talked about less ethereal matters as well. How would things turn out in Kosovo and East Timor? Who would the next president be? What would they do about Columbine? We'd never know.

"My one hope is that before we go, they reveal who Deep Throat was," Delph said. "I've been dying to know since nineteen seventy-four."

And what about the destruction of all humankind? That was something else we wondered about as caterpillars the color of limeade scrunched and stretched their way from here to there. By which method would mankind lay waste to itself? Because it seemed inevitable that it would, and soon.

But how? Poison gas in the subway like in Tokyo? Fertilizer bombs in the hands of the angry or insane or obnoxious like in Oklahoma City? Or would life end as a result of the already discernible environmental calamity?

It's impressive—don't you think?—that our controversial ancestor had a hand in or actually led the way with respect to each

of these potential means of annihilation. Even nitrogen fertilizer, once considered the savior of mankind, has turned out to be
lethal, a prime cause of air pollution, water pollution, soil acidifi-
cation, dead zones, acid rain, holes in the ozone layer, smog, and
accelerated global warming. "Among other things," the literature
always adds, lest that list isn't sufficiently horrifying.

It was late afternoon. We packed our things. Delph quietly
sang as we walked home. She'd begun singing more often, and
frequently in front of Lady and Vee. The song she sang most
often was "Waltzing Matilda." It was no accident that the song
was about a guy who kills himself.

"He's a sheep rustler who's about to be busted by the cops,"
Vee said after Delph had gotten through all three verses, all the
billabongs and tucker-bags and jumbucks. "Not exactly our situation."

"We all have our reasons," Delph said.

Sometimes Lady and Vee sang along with Delph. We all
liked the tune. It was like having a theme song.

The day we went on that picnic was lovely. Still, we haven't
done it again. Our goal is withdrawal from the world, not par-
ticipation in it. A single picnic did not change our minds about
anything.

Otherwise, it was an ordinary summer. None of us got around to
quitting her job, though Vee began missing days here and there.
None of us slept until noon, at least not regularly. We didn't
leave the city or go to the beach, not once. As it turned out, so
long as our corporeal bodies walked this earth, we had no interest in seeing what they looked like in swimsuits.

We did attend the big Francis Bacon exhibition at MoMA,
but we regretted it and left halfway through. "I always get him

mixed up with Sam Francis," Lady said apologetically, after we extricated ourselves from the crawl of people in headphones. After that, no other museum shows called to us.

We tried to read novels. We bought a hardcover about a woman who gets bitten by a rabid bat, but we couldn't get into it. We were too distracted to lose ourselves in words on the page. We tried to watch movies, but we had the same problem. We couldn't focus on the story. We saw only the actors, their faces in close-up, the flaws, the scars, the degree to which they'd aged since the last movie they'd been in.

With little else to occupy us, we got in the habit of showering and changing into our nightclothes immediately after dinner. Nothing elegant, just oversize tees and sweatpants and fuzzy socks. These, we decided, would be the outfits we died in.

As soon as we were dressed for bed, that's where we'd go: Vee's mattress, still on the floor. If we weren't at work, then we were virtually bedridden, as if we were invalids. In-*valids*, our predictable joke. We sat up beneath the blankets, the three of us in a row, and always in the same order: Lady nearest the east wall, Delph in the middle, Vee to the west, the white plastic blinds pulled closed over the window above our heads. There we indulged in cocktails and conversation. There we wrote our story. There we finished writing our story. We printed it out and held it together with a big black plastic binder clip. We put it on our grandmother Karin's sideboard.

Sometimes we spent entire weekends on that mattress. We were content in that small country, six feet three inches one way, six feet six inches the other. Sometimes Delph hooked her feet around Lady's left foot and Vee's right foot. This is how she wanted us to go out, all hooked together so we'd wind up in the same place. "Like those skeletons they sometimes find embracing in ancient graves," she said.

It wasn't until the middle of August that Vee began complaining about her back. She was beginning to find all this lying in bed physically uncomfortable. She was having muscle spasms so sudden and painful they took her breath away.

"Posture," Lady said, and we bought three wedge pillows and tried to sit up straighter, but it didn't help Vee.

"You need to do crunches," Delph said. "Your core isn't supporting you."

Vee laughed. "I've avoided exercise my entire life. I'm not starting now."

"What you need is a new mattress," Lady said. "Something firm. And maybe one of those capitalist pig box springs."

Vee dismissed this suggestion as well. It was crazy, she said, to spend a lot of money on a new bed that she'd use for only another few months.

"Yes, that makes perfect sense," said Lady. "Better to live the last months of your life in discomfort than die with a few hundred dollars less in the bank. Your nonexistent heirs will thank you."

There was no point in pursuing it, though; Vee didn't want to get rid of the mattress where she'd once slept with Eddie. Instead, when Vee fidgeted and complained, Lady told her to roll over, and she'd rub Vee's back, never quite finding the source of the pain, never able to soothe the knotted muscles, but rubbing anyway, stopping only when her fingers were stiff and her wrists ached, or when Vee said, "Okay, we've now passed pleasurable and have moved on to irritating."

The pain would eventually subside on its own, but sooner or later it would come back, always a little bit worse. One evening, on our way from the kitchen to Vee's room, glasses of wine in hand, Vee gasped and shuddered so dramatically that the zin sloshed onto the carpet.

"Come," Lady said. "Let's get you in bed. I'll give you a back rub."

Delph was about to make a joke along the lines of Vee being literally unable to hold her liquor when it hit her. With more compassion than it will seem, she said, "Oh, for God's sake, how stupid can we be? It's not your muscles that hurt. It's your bones. It's spread to your bones."

"Oh," Vee said. "Of course."

We began to laugh. All this time we'd managed to know but not know, to believe but not believe. All this time, while we were diligently preparing for the end—making sure we had enough pills; reading up on the best liquids in which to dissolve them (fruit juice yea, milkshakes nay); writing nightly about our lives and our ancestors' lives; honing and/or abandoning our various and varying philosophies; practicing meditation (we did it flat on our backs on the mattress, so naturally we called it beditation, though sometimes we had to be honest and call it napping); and affirming our pact on a near-daily basis—during all this we'd had our heads buried in the sand or wedged up our butts. We'd been unable to see the obvious.

Never mind opposable thumbs. Never mind his cognizance of his own mortality. It's this willful amnesia that really separates man from beast.

But we were amnesiacs no more. There would be no unlearning what we'd just learned. Vee's pain wouldn't allow it. Now we saw what we'd been managing to overlook: the weight loss, the yellowing skin.

Sometimes Vee would run a fever. Sometimes she'd hallucinate an eerie visitation from our mother. She'd thrash in bed. "I'm lying on Eddie's skeleton," she'd whisper. His bones were poking her. What did it mean? she said in a whisper to prevent who knows who from hearing her.

And yet, despite all this—despite the advance of Vee's illness and our unwavering determination to do what we intended to do; despite our relinquishing the last remnants of the hope we hadn't known we'd been clinging to, even as we understood we were careening toward the end of our existences, at least on this earthly plane—we were never depressed. We didn't sit around feeling sorry for ourselves. We'd written about the past, we were living in the present, there was no such thing as the future. We put one foot in front of the other. Day turned into day. All was well.

And then everything changed.

CHAPTER 12

Mid-September, two weeks after Vee finally called in and quit her job, Hurricane Floyd arrived. It was a weekday, a Thursday, when the heralding rain and wind began Businesses shut their doors early. Lady's boss closed the bookstore. Delph was sent home from the basement file room, though it was probably a safer place to be than the apartment.

The three of us sat in the dark living room. We were too tired to do anything at all. It was the weather, which was both threatening and enervating. Finally, Vee left her chair and lay on the floor.

"Do you want to go to bed?" Lady said.

Vee said nothing.

"Do you want me to put a blanket over you? Or a pillow under your head?"

Vee said nothing again. There was a bang at the window. We jumped. It was just the rain, but the rain hitting so hard it was as if every drop had coalesced and flung itself at our panes.

"What if we did it tonight?" Vee whispered.

You'd think that would have generated discussion. Instead we were silent. After a while Lady said, "Are you really that sick?" and Vee said no, she wasn't, but that was the point. She didn't want to wait until she was really that sick. Getting any sicker than she was now did not appeal to her.

We did nothing, said nothing. We weren't even drinking. We just stared at whatever—the ceiling, the wall, the street below, where an inside-out umbrella skitched along the sidewalk like a black flower with a silver stem.

"It's your call," Lady finally said. "It's always been your call."

Vee was whispering again. "I don't want to die, and I don't want to live. I just want to get out of this body." It was hard to hear her, what with the clamor at the windows.

"Why are you whispering, honey?" Lady said, also whispering.

"Maybe if we just take it one step at a time." Delph whispered too. "Maybe if we see where we're at later tonight."

That's what we did. While Vee lay on the living room rug, Lady and Delph forced themselves into action. They stripped the sheets off the bed in the Dead and Dying Room and put on fresh linens. We believe in traditions. If Vee didn't change her mind, this was the room where we would come to lie down.

We prepared what we understood might or might not turn out to be our last meal: macaroni and cheese from a box. There wasn't much else in the house, but that was partially because macaroni and cheese from a box was the only thing Vee ate now, the taste of the powdered cheese-food so strong that it overcame the metallic taste perpetually and inexplicably coating her tongue. She didn't eat a lot of it, though. Her stomach ached when she ate even the smallest meals, and everything, even ice cream, seemed to give her heartburn. These were the kinds of pains, she often said, that people who weren't dying noted but soldiered through. She imagined the spokespeople from commercials for Pepto-Bismol, Bayer aspirin, Doan's back pills, surrounding her, hawking their wares, telling her she was experiencing nothing that a little over-the-counter medicine couldn't cure. She'd thought that when the pain came, it would be a special pain that couldn't be named or described, an elegant pain known only to the dying. She'd expected shivers of agony that would come and go like cold waves in winter. Instead she had heartburn. She had cramps. She had diarrhea. Her back hurt.

Drinking, too, caused her pain, zigzags of lightning in her belly and, oddly, a fist pressed between her shoulder blades. She stopped drinking wine and hard liquor, but she refused to stop drinking entirely. Pain be damned, she drank Baileys instead, creamy and caloric, figuring both were good for her.

While Vee ate her minuscule portion of macaroni and cheese, Lady and Delph divided the rest between them. They gorged on it—the white flour, the powdered chemicals. They left not a single orange elbow behind. They killed off two bottles of wine.

There was no dinner conversation. Vee left the table early, repaired to her room. The rain was now loud as artillery. Lady and Delph washed the dishes, put them away, something they would not have ordinarily done.

In Vee's room, Vee lay on her back, while Lady and Delph knelt on the mattress, facing the window, their bare callused heels on either side of Vee's face. They watched the storm without comment. They took in the roiling Hudson, whitecaps and spray. They rubbernecked the besieged park. The older trees swayed with the wind, practiced and confident as subway commuters. It was the young, slender trees that bowed and scraped and lost their limbs. They were the vulnerable ones, their root systems not yet deep enough to allow them to stand their ground, their trunks not acclimated to gales.

"If we were writing a story and it was taught in school," Delph said, her arms on the windowsill, her chin on her arms, "the students would cite those trees in an essay: 'Nature Imagery in the Work of the Alter Sisters.' " She came up with a thesis sentence: "In this paper I intend to show how the young trees buffeted by the winds of Hurricane Floyd represent the main characters of this story, women who were too immature to withstand the blows life rained down on them.'

"It's a hurricane," Vee said. She was still whispering. It was dark, but she had her arm crooked over her eyes as if there were a ceiling light glaring down on her. "Trees fall down," she said. "All any of it means is that a tropical cyclone met a ridge of high pressure at a time in our geologic era when ocean temperatures are abnormally elevated."

Delph caught Lady's eye. The two of them smiled at each other. The weather report delivered so matter-of-factly in a hoarse whisper. It was so strange and funny. This was something no one ever told you. Decompensating could be humorous.

"Of course, when you think about it, the reason those ocean temperatures are elevated is because of us," Lady whispered. "Because of our family."

"Because of *him*," Delph said. Whispering made the word *him* sound like a sigh.

"Still," Lady said, "it's weird, isn't it, to think that the trees may have no significance to us, but our family has significance to the trees."

"Acausal time," Delph said. "Arbor version."

We might have continued like this, the three of us whispering about ocean temperatures and symbolism and the signs of global warming, if at that moment someone outside the apartment hadn't begun rattling the doorknob, shaking the door in its frame, trying to get inside.

We stopped speaking at once. We were glad we'd been whispering. Easier that way to pretend no one was home. Lady and Delph clambered to their feet, stepped into the hallway, continued as far as the foyer. They must have looked comical, the two of them tiptoeing close together as if performing a pantomime, but they didn't find what was transpiring amusing. Only Vee, still in bed, registered the humor: just our luck to be murdered in a home invasion just a few hours before our lovingly planned suicides.

Lady and Delph had stopped a few feet from the door. They watched as the brass doorknob twisted to the left, then the right, then left again, right again, faster, angrier.

"We should push a heavy piece of furniture against it, then call the police," Delph whispered. At last—a bona fide reason to whisper.

But gathering courage, Lady called, "Who is it?" There wasn't any answer, though, just the continued rattling of the door, the throttling of the knob. She and Delph looked hopefully to the array of chains and auxiliary locks on our side of the jamb, but, like the two of them, they were all completely undone.

Like turkey vultures, those pale-faced, big-beaked, squint-eyed creatures that communicate largely through hisses, Lady and Delph began to whisper again, issuing orders to each other. You should look through the peephole. You should get a carving knife. You should call 911. But they didn't move.

Their inaction was, at first, rewarded. The rattling, the throttling, abruptly stopped. It was the most welcome and yet uneasy of silences. We all listened intently, Lady and Delph in the foyer, Vee in her bed, all of us hoping to hear the rush of retreating footsteps, the ring of a summoned elevator, the sounds of someone fleeing.

We heard none of that. Instead what we heard was the distinct sound of a key inserted into a lock. Tumblers fell into place. Delph took a step back, and Lady, directly behind her, put an arm around her, pulled her closer.

The front door opened. An old woman stepped into the foyer.

She wore a blue vinyl raincoat and red Keds turned maroon from puddles. She held a plaid plastic tote. She had no rain cap or umbrella, and her hair, a salt-and-pepper bob, was a wiry mess of short springy curls. She was as drenched as if she'd just stepped out of the shower or been dragged from the river. Her eyes were small and black, her nose as beaked as ours, but even larger, such an enormous nose, irrefutable evidence of the sad truth that cartilaginous body parts continue to grow through the entirety of our lives and even for a while thereafter.

Lady and Delph knew this nose was bigger now than it had been in the old woman's youth or even at the end of the old woman's life, because they knew who the old woman was. They recognized her at once.

It's impossible to describe what they felt in that moment. They, who never cry, cried. They, who never giggle, giggled. They were deliriously happy, they were just plain delirious.

Delph was the one who dared say it out loud, sounding both sheepish and awed and afraid. Her voice caught. But she managed.

"Mommy?" she said.

Well, of course it was ridiculous. It's one thing to have faith in the unknown and unseeable, one thing to have dorm room debates or grapple with theories such as quantum or God or synchronicity or nihilism. It's one thing to decide you believe in time travel or guardian angels or curses or nothing. But to believe for even a moment that your dead mother has just walked through the door, first having checked the weather report and donning a raincoat, also having packed a small bag and remembering to grab her old house keys—well, let's face it, that's neither faith nor science, it's just psychosis, and Lady and Delph snapped out of it even before their tears and giddiness abated.

If it wasn't our mother, though, who was it? Because what remained true was that the woman in our foyer could have been our mother's identical twin. She was clearly related to us. A cousin, Lady and Delph guessed. A descendant of some Alter who'd managed to escape the death camps and, fifty-five years later, had traveled to New York and looked us up. That's what they each were thinking, that was the next ridiculous thought that came to them. Ridiculous, because how would a tourist come to possess the keys to our apartment?

What's more, this woman was not glad to see them. In fact she didn't seem to see Lady and Delph at all. Nor did she seem able to hear them. She seemed, in fact, to inhabit a different dimension from theirs. When they asked rudimentary questions— Excuse me, but who are you? Excuse me, but where did you come from? Excuse me, but what the hell's going on?—the old woman didn't give a flicker of acknowledgment. When they offered towels, it was like talking to air.

As they watched, the old woman slung her wet tote bag over the spindle of the hall chair. Rain dripped from the tip of her nose. She looked to her left: the dinette and kitchen. She looked to her right: the living room. Her face lit with joy. Leaving squishy wet sneaker prints, she toddled past Lady and Delph and headed directly to Vee's room. She flung open the door. Lady and Delph could hear Vee whispering some question, a version, no doubt, of the ones they'd been asking. Who are you? What do you want?

She hadn't seemed able to register Lady or Delph, but she clearly saw Vee. Her expression changed completely. The light in her eyes turned to fear, and she wheeled back from the doorway, bumping into the wall behind her. She looked around, suddenly confused. Her confusion turned to agitation. She fluttered like a bird trapped in an airshaft, she flapped her hands like a child gearing up for a tantrum.

Now she was the one calling for her mother. Her voice was disconcerting, a child's voice, lisping and cloying. "Mama," she called, and she sounded like the old Chatty Cathy doll our mother once brought us from Woolworths: pull the string at the back of its neck and it talks, but mechanically, robotically, not like any person you've ever known.

We didn't have the first idea how to help her. Lady tried words of comfort, but the stranger didn't hear her. Vee, emerging from her bedroom, took a few steps toward her, but the stranger's cries for her mother increased in rapidity and volume until Vee backed away.

Delph lowered her head, let her hair fall forward, hung back. The angel of death, she was thinking. The devil hath power to assume a pleasing—or, if not exactly pleasing, then a familiar—shape.

We continued like this a while longer, the three of us useless and baffled, the old woman yelling for her mother. But when her mother didn't come and she realized she was on her own, the old woman did what any little girl, soaked through and fright-ened and lost, would do. She slid to the hallway floor, held her knees against her chest, pressed her forehead to her kneecaps, and sobbed.

Delph was the first of us to realize who she was. "Violet?" she asked, and as if a spell had been broken, the stranger on the floor, suddenly able to hear us, looked up to see who had spoken her name.

Our apartment is rent-controlled. Not rent-stabilized. Rent-controlled. Rent control began after World War II and is just about a thing of the past, but so long as a lineal member of our family lives here, our place remains subject to it. It's a good thing, a source of envy, a security blanket. On the other hand, it sometimes feels oppressive, especially when you run into the landlord who has stopped being polite about your continued existence. Then rent control is like the brother in the eighteenth-century British novel who inherits the entire family estate but allows his unmarried sisters to reside in one of the property's cottages until they finally do the right thing and die.

Rent control is what made it possible for our mother to live here on her own after her parents died. She was sixteen. As children, we could never envision it. How was it that no one found it unacceptable, a girl that age, a recently orphaned young girl, living by herself? How was it that no one intervened?

"Who cared about me?" our mother would say. "Rose killed herself six months later, that's how helpful Rose was. And Violet . . . well, Violet always looked out for Violet."

But what about teachers? we'd ask. What about the landlord? What about Arthur Kram, who lived across the hall (and still does)?

"Young people were older then," she'd say. "It was a different time."

It was a different time. Go argue with that. But different how? Our questions were endless. How had she supported herself? Had there been a nest egg? Proceeds from an insurance policy? A stash of cash under the mattress? Did she work odd jobs after school? Did she shoplift?

And what about the apartment itself? Did she keep it tidy or, a teenager, did she let dishes pile up, dust bunnies roam free? Did she invite girlfriends over for unsupervised pajama parties, playing records all night, smoking cigarettes, getting sick from cheap wine until their mothers forbade them to have anything more to do with her?

And if so, was this when she began to drink? And did she perhaps start inviting boys home instead of girls? Or did she prefer grown men, soldiers recently back from Europe, obvious father figures to everyone but herself? And did she cry herself to sleep after they'd gone back home, some perhaps to wives? And had she met our father then, had he been one of those much older men?

Or did none of this happen? Were these actually happy years, maybe even the best years? No crazy parents, no selfish sisters, no lousy husband, no pesky daughters. Just a girl playing house, preening before mirrors in her older sisters' forgotten clothes, Suzie-Q'ing through the hallway in her dungarees and socks, staying up late every night and and skipping school when she felt like it, and eating nothing but cake and cookies and smoking her Luckys and drinking her Cuba Librés?

She never said, and we'll never know. The mother we knew was morose, melancholy, almost always self-medicated, and no doubt certifiable, though she sought no medical help, so no certificate was ever issued, no name ever attached to what ailed her. The one thing we have to give her, though, is that she never seemed daunted by the history of this apartment. When she and our father married, they blithely inhabited the master bedroom; that is, she slept in the bed where her mother had died and next to the window from which her father had leaped. Perhaps she couldn't afford superstition or sentiment, given the postwar housing shortage, or perhaps this was just how it was done in those different times when, more frequently than they do now, people died at home. Or more likely she knew and he knew they'd never find such a bargain anywhere else in the city. Rent control.

Many of the questions we asked her back then had to do with the sister she rarely mentioned. Not Rose, the one they found facedown in a men's bathroom in Chicago's Washington Park, her head between two mint-choked urinals. But the other one, Violet. Where had Violet been during all this?

"I told you," our mother said. "College. Chicago."

"What about summers? Why didn't she come visit you then?"

"She had a boyfriend. A very rich boyfriend. She preferred to stay with him."

"Why didn't you move to Chicago?"

"Because I lived here. Because we weren't Siamese triplets like the three of you."

We knew only a few more facts about Violet. The chemistry degree. The childless marriage to one Jack Smoke. The death by dry-cleaning bag.

How many of these facts were actually lies? Because that last one—the suffocation—that was clearly bullshit. For here was Violet, sitting on our floor live and in person, seventy-three years old if our math was correct, but apparently six or seven in her own mind. Violet Smoke in the hallway, calling for her mama, crying her eyes out.

How did Delph know the woman was Violet? "Thought bubbles," she said, but that wasn't really true. She knew from the way
Violet reacted to Vee's room, which had once been Violet's room,
which was still Violet's room as far as Violet was concerned. Instead of opening the door to the comforting familiarity she'd
expected, she'd been shocked and scared by a room emptied of
her things, emptied of furnishings of any kind except for a big,
saggy mattress on the floor on which sat a gaunt, jaundiced, bald
woman who resembled her own young self. We felt bad about
this. If we'd known she was coming, we'd have at least straightened the blankets, picked up the glassware and dirty T-shirts.

At least she'd now stopped crying. For the first time she
seemed able to see us. She wiped her cheeks with the backs of
her veiny hands. She looked at Vee, and we could see the wheels
spinning in her head, could see her trying to make sense of it all,
trying to figure out what to do, what to say. It turned out to be
this: "I want my bath," she said.

She removed her Keds and her socks. She struggled to her
feet, ignoring Lady's proffered arm. She took off her raincoat
and housedress, took off her old-lady bra and underpants. She
dropped every garment onto the floor. Naked now, she strode
to the bathroom. We heard the bathtub's taps groan as they
opened. We heard the water rush. Violet had left the door open,
and after exchanging glances meant to convey a blend of panic
and resignation, we followed her in.

If our encounters with naked people over the course of our
lives have been minimal, our encounters with naked old people
have been nonexistent, unless you counted the elderly penises
flapped at us in subway stations and movie theaters. But, aged
penises aside, none of us had ever seen an entirely naked old
person before, and while we'd always declared that older women

such as, oh, say, Louise Nevelson or Katharine Hepburn were as beautiful as any young starlet, now that we stood in the well-lit presence of an actual older woman, we realized we'd been full of shit. The old lady standing before us, with her wrinkles and brown blotches and raised hairy moles, with her warts and wattles and love handles and shrunken pendulous breasts and equally pendulous belly and varicose veins and thickened toe-nails the color of corn chips—there was no denying it, this was not beauty. This was disability. This was decay. The name of this painting was *The Angel of Death before Her Bath.*

We'd seen photographs of a much younger Violet—Violet in high school, Violet at her wedding to Jack Smoke, our mother pregnant and sullen among the background crowd—and while, like the rest of us, Violet was not what you'd call pretty, she'd had an energy about her that we could detect even in black-and-white stills. She looked right into the camera, her smile close-mouthed and cockeyed, sardonic and smart-alecky. In almost every pose she gave you the feeling that she was pissed off at the photographer and didn't care if he knew it. We'd always read that expression as the selfishness, the meanness, our mother spoke of. Now we suspected she'd just been young and itching to keep moving. Posing had put a crimp in her style.

She took a seat on the toilet lid, directly beneath the portrait of Otto von Bismarck. "Nurse," she said to Delph, "test the water for me."

Delph felt mildly hysterical. If she didn't count the old days in the clubs and the discos, it was the first time in her life she'd been singled out, had been chosen despite the presence of others. She looked at Lady the way one might look to a lifeguard. But Lady only nodded to her, and Delph sighed and knelt by the tub, dipped a hand in, fooled with the faucets, made the necessary adjustments, at which point, as if she'd mistaken Delph for a footstool, Violet pressed her wet hand on Delph's back and climbed in. One leg in the water, then a moment of precarious balancing that afforded a view of her sparse white pubic hair, her goose-pimpled labia. Then the second leg in the water. She sat slowly, tested the temperature with her buttocks, sighed without pleasure, and sank down. She closed her eyes, waited. What could Delph do but soap a washcloth and get to scrubbing?

After the bath, Violet wrapped in a towel, sitting on the toilet lid again, Delph combed Violet's wet hair. "That feels good," Violet said of the comb raking her scalp. It was the first normal thing she'd said.

She still didn't know who we were. She continued to call Delph "nurse." She hadn't acknowledged Lady or Vee at all. We'd introduced and explained ourselves several times, but she hadn't reacted. We'd offered her food, something to drink, but she hadn't heard.

Now she asked Delph for warm milk, a beverage request we'd never before heard from any other Alter, whether in person or in anecdotes. Delph warmed the milk, brought a mugful back to the bathroom. By then Lady and Vee had helped Violet change into a powder blue velour tracksuit that Vee had purchased eons ago and a pair of thick Kelly-green chenille socks that none of us remembered buying, though one of us clearly had. Now Delph, beginning to feel more at ease in the role, helped Violet take her seat atop the toilet and supervised as Violet sipped her milk. Bismarck, glossy and somber, stared at the opposite wall as if to avoid looking at any of us. Then Delph was taking Violet to our mother's bedroom—or, no, to Violet's mother's bedroom, because Violet was again a young girl.

"Someone took my bed away," she told Delph sadly, and it was true; someone had, a quarter of a century ago.

We fear it all sounds syrupy and precious. It was anything

but. It was humiliating and obscene. Delph, especially, was shaken. She'd gotten past her fears that this was the angel of death, the devil in a housedress, but she felt that there was more to Violet than mere flesh and blood. Like the Kennedy plane crash, like the trees whipsawed in the park, Violet's very existence seemed fraught with meaning. Delph sat on the edge of our mother's bed—our mother's and our grandmother's bed—watching Violet drink her second glass of hot milk, and tried to tease out the message our aunt had been sent to deliver.

Acausal time, Delph thought. Events linked not by the sequence of passing hours, but by their meaning. The gods had directed Vee's hand to a library book on the subject. Now they were showering us with illustrations. The logical conclusion was that we were meant to suss out the meaning. First a tempest. Next a visit by a ghost. Drama and disruptions.

Our lives were being disrupted. Someone, something, wanted to complicate our path.

Of course Delph was additionally concerned about Violet, the person. It occurred to her that the reversion to baby talk and bewilderment was nature's way of protecting the elderly, of evoking sympathy in younger people who would otherwise be repulsed by the visibly rotting body. An old person naked: we turn away. A helpless baby: we open our arms. We scrub them clean. We put them to bed, smooth the blankets. We lock the latch to the window. Literally—we locked the latch to the window Richard Alter had jumped from, pushing it so hard to the right that it will take a pair of pliers to get it back to the unlocked position.

Violet handed Delph her empty glass. She closed her eyes. "Sweet dreams," Delph said, and tiptoed out at last, flooded with a kind of tenderness adults rarely feel for other adults.

When Delph, in a fresh, dry T-shirt, joined Lady and Vee, who were damply stretched out on Vee's mattress, she groaned dramatically to sum up the evening and said she was in the mood for cognac. The good cognac, she said, and it occurred to Lady and even to Vee that they were in the mood for the good cognac too. Neither of them moved, though.

"Don't get up," Delph said. "Please. Let me serve you. Let me serve everybody."

Lady and Vee did; they let her. It wasn't often that Delph relinquished the position of the shy, frightened baby who needed to be indulged. If Delph was going to actually pour the cognac, Lady and Vee were going to let her.

She didn't exactly pour it. When she returned, she was holding the entire bottle in one hand, and, with the fingers of the other, three of the gold-leafed snifters Karin had brought from Berlin. She also had Violet's tote bag over one shoulder. "I have composed a verse," she said, and without apology to Clement Clarke Moore, recited:

> . . . *and I in my jammies and Vee with her henna*
> *Were all just about to buy the farm when a*
> *Stranger arrived without chauffeur or pilot*
> *'Twas our not quite as dead as we thought Auntie Violet*

Not a heroic couplet, but Lady and Vee took it. From the first to the fourth generations, silly rhymes have amused our family of murderers and self-murderers, and on this night we were grateful that we, too, could be so easily distracted. We were grateful, we realized, for so many things. We were grateful for the cognac Delph was pouring. We were grateful for the hammering rain that was also distracting and, in its own way, soothing, especially compared to the emotional storm that had just gone to sleep. We were grateful that Violet was sleeping.

We drank the cognac too quickly. No matter. There was more. We were grateful for that. Even Vee, despite the burning, was grateful.

Delph, thinking of her poem, said, "Is anyone quite as dead as we think? Maybe there are degrees of dead."

"No," Vee whispered. "There's dead and there's not dead, and that's it."

Delph frowned. "Are you honestly saying the fact that Violet showed up just as we're getting ready to check out has no meaning? You don't think her appearing here is meant to tell us something?"

"Maybe it's meant to remind us there's nothing like a good, hot soak in a tub," Vee said. "That actually might be life's one true message. Nothing more, but nothing less."

"What happened to your Jungian conversion?" Delph said.

"I don't feel Jung tonight," Vee said.

"I'm being serious," Delph said.

"Me too," said Vee.

"Let's think about this rationally," Lady said. "You've got an old lady with dementia. She sometimes reverts to her childhood. A hurricane comes along. It scares her, and so she gets it in her head to go home to her mother. There's nothing remarkable about that."

"It's true," Vee said. "It's called wandering. I see it with the law firm's older clients sometimes. It's what old people with dementia do."

"I'm sorry," Delph said. "I find it very remarkable. I refuse to believe it has no meaning."

"It does have meaning," Vee said. "It means that Mom lied to us about Violet being dead."

"It means," Lady said as she dumped out the contents of Violet's tote bag onto the mattress, "that Delph is going to have to revise her beautiful chart."

Contents of said tote bag: one pair old-lady cotton underpants; one pair well-worn socks; one package Poise Ultra-Thin Panty Liners; one well-worn toothbrush; one tube half-squeezed Colgate for tartar control; many vials of pills; and one red-checkered housedress that could double as a tablecloth at a cheap trattoria.

Also, one beaten-up Pepto-Bismol pink paperback of *The Valley of the Dolls*, and tucked inside said paperback, acting as a bookmark, a creased photograph of a fortyish Aunt Violet in a coral gown, a glittering tiara wedged into her black beehive. At her side stands a short, burly man in black tie who we assumed to be Jack Smoke. Flanking our aunt and uncle are a pair of twins: teenage girls, unattractive and with dark curly hair and bad posture, wearing identical pink gowns. These four surround one somber boy, all nose and eyebrows, who, in addition to a tuxedo and coral bow tie, wears a tallith and a velvet yarmulke.

We passed the picture around. We were like a group of adolescent boys seeing their first centerfold, except instead of whispering, "Tits!" with awe, we were whispering, "Cousins!"

The final item in the bag was a cloth pencil pouch shaped like a banana. When you unzipped it, it looked as if it were being unpeeled. Inside were several pennies, some loose Tums, and a business card for the Walt Whitman Assisted Living and Long-Term Care Facility in Huntington, Long Island. On the back of the card someone had printed "Violet: Helene W. has your tickets for Penzance. You owe her $9.99."

We'd long known of Long Island's Walt Whitman shopping mall in Huntington, one of the first enclosed malls in America, but it was a revelation that when the shoppers of Long Island grew infirm, they moved on to Walt's nursing home. Our first impulse was to make jokes—*I sing the body decrepit*—but our second and abiding impulse was to feel appreciative of whoever bestowed the name on such a place. Walt Whitman was a nurse himself during the Civil War; we knew that; we rather loved that. We were fairly certain he'd have preferred his name to be associated with a nursing facility than with a shopping mall, especially an enclosed shopping mall.

We allowed ourselves to picture the Walt Whitman Assisted Living and Long-Term Care Facility as a modern institution, but one incongruously staffed by Civil War nurses, not only men like Whitman but plain women like ourselves, women wearing white aprons over their long brown dresses, their hair parted in the middle and pulled straight back. We imagined these nurses—we imagined ourselves—proceeding from bed to bed, stopping for a while beside each one, reciting the poet's verse:

Old age, calm, da da da da da
Old age flowing free with the delicious near-by freedom of death.

We were a bit ashamed we couldn't summon all the words. All summer we'd understood the calm that can precede death if only you let it. All summer we'd contemplated the freedom of delicious death.

But old age? That we didn't know from. We would never get old, and now, after spending a single evening with Violet, we added never growing old to the things-for-which-we-are-grateful column.

Because what was there about Violet's condition that was enviable? Why would we aspire to her stage of life, why would we desire to stand in her soggy shoes?

At the same time, if we were feeling a knot of guilt about our decision re: dying, it might have been because we regretted our failure to achieve a certain kind of wisdom born from certain kinds of life experiences. Our squeamishness in bathing Violet. Our skittishness when it came to dealing with her showing up on our doorstep. Our skittishness when it came to any crisis, the preference we had for deflecting important conversations with jokes, rather than facing them head-on. It was fine, we agreed, not to want to grow old. Fine, too, to take steps to ensure we didn't grow old. But we'd also avoided growing up. We'd lived our lives like perpetual children, hiding in corners, never knowing what to say, never knowing what to do. If our plan to die was problematic, it was problematic in that it eliminated the possibility of our ever becoming serious, capable women.

We were sorry about that. Sorry that we'd spent our lives so selfishly, so narrowly. Sorry we'd never done anything useful or selfless. We were embarrassed we'd laughed at Delph's silly little rhyme. We rued all the time we spent as shy fearful homebodies.

We wished we'd never watched a minute of TV. We were distressed we hadn't risked more, that we hadn't figured out a way to love more. We admitted that our greatest sin might have been failing to fall in love again after losing our first loves, whether those loves were worthy or whether they were callow dentists or loud bike messengers who were never romantically interested in us in the first place.

We refilled our glasses. We regretted doing that, we regretted the sips we took. There was so much to regret. In fact, there was only one thing we could think of that we did not regret—that it was too damned late for us to change in any meaningful way.

Thank God for that! we said. Thank God we'd never have to change! Thank God there was no time left for us to become better people, to become grown-ups.

The truth is, we're shy. The truth is that for at least two decades now, we've been truly at ease only in this apartment with each other. The truth is that we live at the low end of the introversion scale. We are not people persons.

"You know who was a people person?" Lady said. "Lenz Alter. He loved parties, he loved being front and center, he loved performing for others. He had tons of friends and loads of lovers. He was such a people person that he couldn't abide the way soldiers got killed, bullet by bullet, one by one. He had to make dying for one's country a group sport."

Also this: a person can only fall in love with the person she falls in love with.

We all agreed: our wish to be better people was superseded only by our wish never to have to change.

"I hate a cognac buzz," Vee said. "It's so headachy and maudlin. Where's the singing? Where are the jokes?" But she was talking full voice and hadn't yet complained about a fist grinding into her spine.

We returned Violet's belongings to her bag, everything but the business card. "Someone should call the nursing home," Lady said.

"I'll do it," Delph said. She hated the phone almost as much as Lady did, but making Vee get up, totter to the dinette, was too cruel, so she rose and she did it. The ghastly beeping and squawking when she finished dialing was so loud that Lady and Vee could hear it back in the bedroom. The hurricane, it turned out, had focused its energy not on the city but on Long Island. The phone lines there were down. If anyone at the Whitman nursing home was worrying about Violet, they would have to continue worrying until the next day.

As for us, what with the weather, the unexpected guest, the hot bath by proxy and the cognac, what with the bout of self-loathing, what with one of us riddled with cancer and the other two grieving for her, we were each of us exhausted. On her way from the phone back to Vee's room, Delph had the presence of mind to take our enormous suicide note from the top of the sideboard and hide it in a drawer, but when she returned to Lady and Vee, and Lady suggested a few minutes of meditation, Delph shook her head. She was too tired to do anything but crawl on her hands and knees to the head of the mattress and wriggle between her sisters and sleep.

We all slept, soundly and dreamlessly. By the time we opened our eyes the next morning, Hurricane Floyd had gone out to sea, our building was enveloped in a preternaturally bright white fog, and our aunt was bringing us coffee in bed.

Sundowning. It was another condition that Vee recognized from her work with elderly clients. The sun begins to descend, the light changes, the shadows grow, and the vulnerable client goes mad. Later, the sun comes up, and a semblance of sanity returns.

"Dementia," Vee said, "but on a part-time basis."

When she brought us the coffee, our aunt, for the first time, introduced herself. "My name is Violet Smoke," she said. "Today is Friday, September 17, 1999. The president is William Jefferson Clinton."

This, it turned out, was the information she was required to give her caretakers every morning to prove she had regained her grip on reality. Now she looked around, shrugged with a single shoulder. It was very Jewish, this one-shouldered shrug, more dismissive, more resigned than if she'd shrugged with both.

"I'm not sure whether I'm where I think I am or if I'm having hallucinations today," she said. She sounded nonchalant about it, as if she'd accept whatever answer she received, but we could tell she was faking. Her pinched face betrayed worry. She needed us to reassure her. She was dependent on us, we three possibly illusory women beneath the blankets of a mattress on the floor of her old bedroom.

"You're not hallucinating," Lady said. "You came here last night. In the middle of a hurricane. You let yourself in with your key. How is it you have that key after all these years?"

"I gave you a bath," Delph said.

"I let myself in with my key?" Violet considered this. "I guess I'm lucky you didn't shoot me."

"Do you know who we are?" Lady asked.

"Dahlie's girls?" She pronounced Dahlie the German way. Her own German accent was faint, but still stronger than our mother's had been. "Aren't you? Who else could you be?"

We helped her sort out which of us was which. She knew our names and nicknames. She leaned against the door frame, arms folded across her chest, and addressed each of us in turn, like a teacher going down the row on the first day of class, getting to know her charges. "Do you remember me?" she asked Lady. "You were so little when I last saw you. You and your parents had come out to visit. First time in years, and what happens? You almost drown in our pool. Do you remember? Your mother was having words with your father for a change, and she took her eyes off you, which who does that? A toddler near a pool and the mother looks away? The next thing anyone knows, you've marched right into the water and gone under. All we see is your hair floating on the surface. Your father jumped in and hauled you out. She just stood there."

"I don't remember any of this," Lady said.

"You probably do," Vee said. "In some faraway recess of your mind. It's probably affected your entire life. It probably explains everything."

Violet turned to Vee. "You," she said, "you, with the painting on your head. You don't look well at all," and when Vee didn't deny it, when Vee told Violet the short version of the cancer saga, finishing up with the magic word *inoperable*—a word that led most people to mumble something, then make themselves scarce—Violet had plenty to say. "I knew it," she declared. "First, the no hair. Second, I've seen that look before. You can tell by the cheekbones, how the skin clings and hangs, all at the same time. How old are you? Forty-something, no? Well, that just stinks. It does, it stinks. But you know what? I've stopped with the bromides. After a while you sound like a fool, with the oh-you'll-be-fines and the oh-you'll-outlive-us-alls. And who does it comfort? No one. Not the person saying it, not the person hearing it. You're sick, not an idiot, am I right? You know what I say now when I see those cheekbones? I say I hope you feel better, and if you don't, I hope you go easy."

She was done with Vee. "And you?" she said. "They still call you Delph? I never liked that name. No offense, but what kind of name is that? It was a mistake, you know. I said to your father, You give your baby a mistake for a name, you fix it."

"It ruined my whole life, my name," Delph said.

"All right, but on the other hand, it's just a name," said Violet. "Don't make a mountain out of a molehill. Meanwhile, get up and get dressed like a person and come to breakfast. All of you. Yes, even you with the cheekbones. Although brunch is more like it by now. It's what—11:00 a.m. by now. I'll make eggs. Is the coffee good? You don't have the Mister Coffee. That makes it the best. I assumed milk and sugar. You keep everything in the same places in the cupboards like my mother. I open the cupboard and there's the coffee, right where she'd have left it. I only hope it's not the same package from then. Ha. Although—no. It's one of those new brands, one of those Fatty Starbuckles.

Don't look so concerned; I'm joking; I know what the name is. Come to breakfast. You can explain to me why you spend so much money when it's the same coffee as A&P. Also, why you all sleep in the same bed."

"We're just sometimes too lazy to move," Delph said.

"Lazy? Lazy is not accepted in my world."

"Well, welcome to our world," Vee muttered.

Violet put her hand on her hip. She looked straight at Vee. Her smile was closemouthed and cockeyed. She had less than an hour of lucidity left for the day, but we didn't know that yet. "I looked in those other rooms," she said. "The one in the back, that's where Rosie slept. The one in the middle was your mother's. I looked around. Don't worry, I didn't go through your drawers. I'm not interested in your underpants. Half the furniture, though, I recognized. My parents' furniture, but somehow Dahlie got to keep it all. You know what I didn't recognize? You know what wasn't there when I lived here? That chart on the back of Dahlie's door."

"Oh, God," Lady said. "If we knew you were coming, we'd have taken it down."

"Mostly it's got everything right," Violet said begrudgingly. "And I was sorry to see what it said about your mother. What a way for me to find out, by the way. I could have used some of whatever that is in those glasses you got all over the place. Not that I drink. It's why I'm still walking around, the no drinking. But—did I already tell you I stopped with the bromides? When it turns out someone's dead, you know what I say these days? I say, May she rest in peace, and I call it a day. What else can I do? Tear out my hair?" She heard what she'd just said and glanced at Vee, at the decorated canvas that was Vee's skull. She shrugged a single shoulder. "But as for me? Me, on the chart? Reports of my death have been greatly exaggerated." The smug little smile again. "Mark Twain said that," she informed us. "Or maybe Will Rogers. Who can keep those two straight? I've got enough on my mind these days. You think you have problems? Wait till we talk. We'll see who has problems."

She left the room. "Jesus," Vee said. She wasn't hungry. She didn't feel well. But at least she wasn't whispering. "I'm not going anywhere," she said.

But Lady and Delph were obedient. They got dressed in clean clothes. They carried their coffee into the dinette. Violet had been up for hours, it seemed. The table had been cleared. All the papers and publications and bills were in piles on the sideboard. If Lady and Delph hadn't already been on the verge of killing themselves, this would have been reason enough. They were certain they'd never find anything they needed ever again.

"Sit," Violet said.

Lady and Delph sat and drank their coffee. Violet scrambled eggs in the kitchen, the bluish skin hanging from her upper arms flailing as she whipped the batter. Lady and Delph didn't mind this either—her cooking for them, they meant. Violet was old, they should have been waiting on her, not the other way around. But anyone could see that the cooking gave Violet pleasure.

Violet sat in the chair our mother used to sit in. She didn't eat anything herself. "I already had," she said. Every now and then she got up, dialed the phone. Beeping and squawking filled the room. Violet sighed and hung up.

"Floyd," Lady explained. She looked across the hall and through the living room's windows. The fog was nearly blinding in its brilliance. It was the wrong consistency for fog. It was thin, like a runny sauce.

But Violet wasn't interested in Floyd. "So," she said, "tell me how you got the apartment back after giving it up."

"What do you mean?" Delph said. "We've always lived here."

"Except for me," Lady said. "I was married for a couple of years."

"Vee was married too," Delph said. "But basically, we've lived here all our lives." She smiled as if she were about to brag. "I've never once slept anywhere else."

Violet looked hard at Delph. She didn't say anything. She scowled. Then she seemed to make a decision that let her plunge ahead. "But what about the years you lived in Germany?" she asked, "which, by the way, is where I still thought you were."

"Germany?" Lady and Delph, two-part harmony.

So this was the first story Violet told us: When Lady was seven, Vee four, and Delph learning to crawl, Violet received a call from Dahlie, who said she was returning to Germany and taking us with her. She would not say where in Germany she was going. She would not give any address. She said only that she didn't want Violet to try to find her. She didn't want to hear from Violet ever again.

Oh, and Natan was gone. "But you know all about that," Dahlie said.

"Your mother," Violet said. "She thought Natan and I were having an affair. Why I'd get involved with an old man who sold buttons when I had Jack Smoke, she could never explain." She smirked, the sister who'd nabbed the superior man. "So I figured that was that," she said. "You were all gone. The apartment was gone. I called the old number just to see, but it was disconnected. So I went on with my life. We weren't close anyway. We were always fighting. We had a big fight after my wedding, right before the reception—she was out to here pregnant with that one"—pointing to Lady—"but she thought she should be my matron of honor anyway. I said, one, we never liked each other. Two, can you imagine the photographs, you with that belly?

She didn't care. Everything always had to be about her, even my wedding. And then a couple of years later, after no talking, we tried to make up, but that was the time Lady almost drowned, so we had a big fight that day too. Somehow it was the pool's fault, not hers. It all came down to she didn't like that I had money. She was a very superficial person."

"She wasn't, really," Lady said. "She had a hard time of it. She saw her father's body after he—"

"Jumped," Violet said. "You can say it. He was my father too, the last time I looked. I know what he did. I know what they all did. Even without a chart I know it."

"She lived before they had medication for people with her problems."

"They have medication to prevent liars from lying? She told you I was dead. There weren't enough tragedies in the family? She had to suffocate me? What kind of sister imagines such a thing, much less says it out loud and to children? And she told me she was taking you away. You think I wouldn't have liked to have known my nieces?"

To let us know she didn't require an answer, didn't want to hear excuses and justifications, she rose and dialed the phone again. Beeping, squawking. She hung up, sat down, glared.

"The nursing home's lines are down," Delph said. She was finding the sane version of Violet harder to take than the sundowning version.

"I'm not calling the nursing home," Violet snapped. "What good would that do me? I'm calling my son. I need someone to come get me, unless you want me to stay here forever." She looked right at Delph. "You don't, do you?"

We heard the bitterness, the sarcasm, but also the wish that she might be wrong, that we might want nothing more than to take her in, poor stray cat, and keep her and care for her and allow her to care for us.

By now the peculiar fog had lifted and the world looked familiar again, though a dreary kind of familiar. Lady and Delph had told Violet all she needed to know about the three of us. Marital status, dates of cancer diagnoses, occupations. They omitted our tentative plans for the night before. They omitted a few other things. To tell our entire life stories except for ropes, razors, pills, and massacres: it took no time at all.

Even so our lives struck her as nothing to shout about. "Well, you're certainly Alters," she'd said when they were done. She'd crossed her legs, reached over, appropriated Delph's cup of half-finished, very cold coffee. "This is a very bad-luck family. Always has been. Although if you want to know the truth, until recently my own luck was pretty good, knock wood. I'm the exception that proves the rule. I had a perfect marriage. Nothing but fun and games, I kid you not, until the morning Jack died. And how does he go? In his sleep. The cake death, that lucky SOB. Too young, but wonderful for him anyway. If you can have the cake death, you take the cake death whenever it comes. But it was hard on me. Not that I'm complaining. The only thing better would be if I'd gone first. But to be honest, I wasn't ready to go. I was perfectly healthy. Meanwhile he was already starting with the chest pains and the dizzy spells and the me-me-me-me's. You know what I say? I say may he rest in peace, my darling Jack, and then I go on and live my life. I've got a boyfriend at Whitman, you know."

Her kids, she said, were perfect. Ivy League colleges. Prestigious grad schools. The twins, both married with kids and also running businesses, Sharon in San Francisco, Margo in London. Everyone—daughters, sons-in-law, grandchildren—perfectly happy and happily perfect.

Her youngest, her boy, her Danny—he was in the arts. A very accomplished musician. After Jack died, he moved back into the house on Long Island to be with her. So devoted. They were like friends. Like best friends. And he was very handy when things went wrong with the plumbing, that sort of thing. And when her health became a problem, he did extensive research, day and night, never resting until he found the perfect home for her, which, amazingly, turned out to be in the same town they lived in.

"So now he lives in the house alone," she said, "but so close to me. It couldn't be more perfect. I go to him. He comes to me. Unless he's on the road doing his gigs. Otherwise, he visits so often, I have to say, Danny, go out, have some fun. For a boy to be so devoted to his mother, it's very unusual."

"He must be worried to death about you right now," Lady said.

Violet shrugged. "He probably thinks I'm safe and sound and playing cards with the old ladies in the day room. He probably knows the phones are down, and he figures I'll call when I can." She looked at the clock. She was cheerful and reasonable. "Lunchtime," she declared.

"We just finished breakfast," said Lady.

"It's noon," she informed us. "Where I come from, that's lunchtime. I'm going to make us tuna fish salad."

"We don't have any tuna," Lady said.

Violet smiled. She had transformed somehow, was suddenly more carefree, a younger woman on a lark, having an adventure. "Look," she said, indicating the clock. "It's already after noon. Time for lunch. I think I'll make us a nice tuna fish salad."

"We just ate," Lady said.

Violet got up and went into the kitchen. She began opening cabinets. She frowned disapprovingly. She opened another cabinet. She took out all the cans in it, decades-old cans of pinto beans, succotash, cranberry sauce, cans of food we disliked but had bought for some reason. She looked at the can in her hand. S&W green beans, so old the company no longer existed. She frowned. She sighed. She smiled broadly. "You must be starving," she said. She put the can down. "We'll eat," she said, "and then you can tell me all about yourselves."

After lunch, Delph dialed Danny Smoke's number, and for the first time the call went through. Contrary to Violet's optimistic conjecture, he'd been out of his mind with worry, and it took more than a little effort for Delph to get him to stop asking questions so she could answer them, could explain where Violet was and who we were.

Yesterday, Danny said, he called the nursing home to find out what precautions were being taken in light of the impending storm. "We're on top of it," the person who answered his call said. The residents were being taken to a nearby hotel. Beds were being set up in the ballrooms. There was food, blankets, a generator. "Games, books, everything they could want," the voice said. "It'll be like a pajama party."

Danny thought about offering to come by Walt Whitman. He thought about picking Violet up and taking her home with him. He even mentioned it to the voice. "Maybe I should swing by—," he said, but the voice detected his reluctance and placated him. "You know going home does a number on your mother's equilibrium," the voice said.

Now, on the phone, he sighed. "That was my big mistake," he said. "I should have gone there and picked her up and brought her home." Still, he said, he suspected nothing until the nursing home manager called him earlier this afternoon.

"I have some news that will cause concern," the manager said, "so I'm requesting that you listen to me as calmly as possible."

"As calmly as possible," Danny told Delph. "Can you believe that?"

At some point on Thursday, an hour or so after all the nursing home residents were settled in the hotel, someone mentioned that they hadn't seen Violet Smoke in a while. Perhaps the reason they thought Danny could remain calm upon hearing such news was that they themselves had remained calm.

Has anyone seen Violet Smoke? they called out. No one had, but still they didn't worry. They knew she'd arrived at the hotel. How far could she have gone? The storm was working in their favor, they assured each other. No one would actually leave the safety of the hotel in such weather. Even if she'd tried, the winds would have blown her back the moment she opened the door.

They kept an eye out for her, of course. Then again, they only had so many eyes, and those eyes were focused on dozens of old folks in a vast and strange room with quavering chandeliers and a garish carpet that disoriented everyone. They were a skeleton staff trying to organize medications and keep everyone busy, all the while yelling, "Don't look at the rug! Don't look at the rug!" Danny had to understand it wasn't easy to attend to every last thing. They had tried, though. They'd done their best. Every now and again someone called out, "Any sign of Violet Smoke?" and after a while when the answer was still no, they deputized two of the staffers to find her.

"And really," the manager said, "we couldn't spare one much less two of our people. We had other residents to care for besides your mother. But we did it anyway."

Danny was sputtering as he told the story. His voice scaled octaves. "I said, 'Do me a favor and stop previewing your defense for when I sue your asses off and just cut the chase.' "

The chase consisted of the deputized nurses, along with a hotel staffer, knocking on the door of every guest room in the merely three-storied hotel. They checked the kitchen and indoor pool. They peered inside the walk-in refrigerators.

By now they supposed she might have left the premises after all. But if she had, what could they do about it? There was a hurricane out there. The hotel had a generator, but the rest of Melville was as dark as a forest at midnight. The phones were dead, meaning they couldn't call the police or local hospitals.

"And it's not like we could go drive around the block," the manager said. "For one thing, we had no vehicle; the bus we rented to drop us all off was long gone. And even if we had a car, what were we supposed to do? Drive down streets at random, hollering her name? Even if we did, she wouldn't have been able to hear us over the rain and the winds."

"So *that* cheered me up," Danny said.

This morning the hotel van driver, a teenage kid who'd been sitting in the lobby reading *The Old Man and the Sea* while the winds battered the atria glass above him, noticed the commotion.

"Hey," he said, "this lady you're looking for? You don't think she's the one I drove to the train station yesterday, do you?"

Danny called the Long Island Railroad. "I don't know what I thought they'd tell me," he told Delph. " 'Oh, yes, sir, now that you mention it, we did have a deranged little old lady on the four thirty-five to New York.' "

"What we've noticed is, she's got her good hours and bad," Delph said.

"Yeah," said Danny. "Emphasis on the bad."

He wanted to drive into the city, he said. He wanted to get

Violet and bring her home. He wouldn't mind seeing our fabled apartment, either. "I never knew which pissed Mom off more," he said, "the idea that your mother moved back to Germany and told my mother basically to fuck off, or the horror of losing the family's rent-controlled apartment."

He would also like to meet us, he added. The fabled cousins. Delph especially. "Because of our brief shared history," he said.

"What brief shared history?" Delph asked.

"What?" he said. "No—I just meant, we're both the youngest."

Trouble was, though, while he wanted to get in the car this very instant, he couldn't. Not today. Maybe not until Monday. There was a tree trunk—not quite a sequoia, but damn, from where he was standing it was close—at the bottom of his driveway. A half dozen other trees were strewn across his street.

"I've got a gig in Hicksville tomorrow night," he said, not without pride. "I don't know how I'm going to get there, much less into the city."

"We'll find a way to get your mother to you," Delph heard herself say. So much for our weekend plans, she thought. So much for the literal Sturm, followed by our collective Drang. We'd have to live until at least tomorrow.

Delph also thought this as she hung up the phone: *a gig in Hicksville.* She was fairly certain this was the most pitiful thing she'd ever heard in her life—and she was a woman who knew from pitiful.

Even Vee agreed: we would postpone our weekend plans until Violet was back on Long Island. "So not tonight and probably not tomorrow," she said. She sat up in bed, pulled the blanket to her chin. She looked like an old-timey photograph, her face tinted yellow, the chapped lips milky white, the hollows beneath her eyes so dark they seemed smudged with soot. "But Sunday. We'll aim for Sunday." And when Delph said, "Does anyone maybe think we should go back to the original plan—New Year's Eve?" Vee looked at her with drowning eyes and said, "Delph, I don't think I can wait that long."

"All right," Delph said. "Of course."

"Delph, you know you can back out anytime," Lady said, but Delph waved her words away. "It's just," Delph said, "I was wondering if now that she knows us, Violet might be upset if we—when we—"

Vee was literally rolling out of bed, onto the small wedge of floor between the mattress and wall. "Violet," Vee said, "may be upset in the mornings, but by the afternoons she'll have forgotten our names and she'll be playing cards and watching TV and ordering random strangers to give her a bath."

"Hold on," Lady said. "Where do you think you're going."

"Long Island," Vee said, even as she reached around to rub her back.

"Are you crazy? You're staying here. You're not going anywhere."

"I'm okay," Vee said. "Violet had some Percocet with her. I'll take a few. I'm not staying here by myself."

"I'll stay with you, then," Lady said.

"Ha," Vee said. "Delph's going to do this alone?"

And so we all went, the entire sisterhood, the triumvirate, the team. We wanted to get rid of Violet asap. It wasn't only that with her around we felt sheepish about and began questioning the way we lived: our slovenly eating patterns, our embarrassing alcohol consumption, our predilection for dozing off in the same bed, our impending deaths that could not be accomplished with a houseguest occupying the Dead and Dying Room. It was also the sundowning. We couldn't cope with it. Violet's dementia had returned almost as soon as the fog lifted and the gray-green skies grew just the slightest bit grayer than green. Even as Delph was speaking to Danny, Violet had been ranting in the background. "Hang up, hang up," she kept yelling. "Don't you know who it is? You're giving away our location."

"Ah," Danny had said wearily. "I can hear my mom. I know this song. 'The brown shirts are coming, the brown shirts are coming.' "

"It's so sad," Delph said. "She must have been seven or eight when they had to leave Berlin. Of course she's traumatized. How can that sort of terror ever go away?"

"Yeah," Danny said. "It's all very sad. At least for the first couple of months. After that, when you hear it night after night and nothing you do or say helps, then, yeah, it's still sad, but you also want to throw yourself out a window."

"Like Grandpa," Delph said.

"What do you mean?" Danny said. "What's throwing myself out a window have to do with . . . you call him Grandpa? I mean, none of us were around when he was. He passed away so young. That's sweet, you call him that anyway."

For a moment Delph wondered if it had all been lies. Everything our mother had ever told us, every sad story, everything that still haunted us—nothing but lies and more lies. That would be ironic, she thought. You spend your life thinking you're cursed, and then it turns out it's all based on the genetics and sins of some other family.

But she knew this wasn't the case. Violet had seen the chart, and the only death she'd questioned was her own. And there were the biographies on the bookshelf corroborating most of what our mother had told us. And not only that. We possessed some of the primary source materials. Iris's letters to Lehrer, the ones she wrote him before he died. Karin's diaries. Newspaper articles and obits.

"I don't know why I called him Grandpa just now," Delph said to Danny. "I've never called him that before in my life."

Early the next morning, a warm, sunny Saturday, the sky the same gentle blue as that tracksuit we'd forced poor Violet to wear the night before—she was in her red-checkered housedress now—the three of us were on the train, returning Aunt Violet to our cousin. "Delph," Lady said, "you sit with Vee, and I'll sit with Violet," but Aunt Violet said no. "I want that one to sit with me," she said. That one was Delph, and there was no rescuing her. She and Violet sat together as Lady and Vee made their way up the aisle in search of another seat. Delph watched them go as if carried off by an unfeeling wave. She wasn't quite ready to give them up, although she was grateful not to have to support Vee. Physically support Vee, she meant. A balmy September morning, but Vee, leaning heavily against Lady, wore her wool winter coat and a turban made from a jewel-colored scarf that she'd folded and twisted around her head like origami. "For warmth," Vee said. "And for vanity," Lady whispered to Delph. "We're this close to shuffling off the mortal coil, and she still cares what *le cousin* thinks of her."

"Oh, come on," Delph said. "You don't know that's why she's wearing it," although the truth was that Delph had made an effort, too—a little mascara, a little blush.

According to the LIRR's timetable, the trip from Penn to Pine Lawn Station took sixty-six minutes. If we'd given it any thought, we'd have realized that for the first five of those minutes, the train would shudder through the East River tunnel. But even if we'd focused on the tunnel, we wouldn't have guessed that the lights in the car would flicker off and remain extinguished for those long five minutes, that the passengers would be enveloped in such darkness they'd be unable to see their own hands.

Violet had been lucid—we had a sense of her rhythms by now and chose the early departure intentionally—but her disembodied voice became tremulous. "This much darkness is not so good for me," she whispered. She took hold of Delph's arm.

"I'll get Lady," Delph said, but Violet didn't let go.

"My nurse," Violet said. She may have been referring to the bath last night. She may have been bestowing a nickname. She may have already begun sundowning. "Don't leave me, my nurse."

All her life, whenever Delph has been forced to talk at length, she's grown self-conscious. She doesn't recognize the timbre of her voice. It's not her usual speaking voice, certainly not her singing voice. It's a strangled voice, and she imagines her vocal cords twisted and tangled, unable to thrum the way they're meant to. Whenever she hears herself speaking like that, she reddens and then she clams up.

But she didn't have the option of clamming up that morning. She channeled Lady instead. "Okay, close your eyes," she said. "Focus on your breath." Those were the words Lady intoned when we did our beditation. Delph knew the script by heart. "Feel the breath and follow the breath, but don't think about breath," she said in a tight, stringy voice.

As she recited the words, replicated Lady's gentle tone, she felt, not to put too fine a point on it, like an idiot. She was certain the strangers in the seats in front of hers and behind hers were listening and rolling their eyes. She lowered her voice. She wondered if Violet could even hear what she was saying, this summon to do what Violet was already doing: to exhale, to inhale, to exhale again. Violet's breath came loud and exaggerated. She inhaled and exhaled not like a meditator, but like someone getting a chest exam.

But when the train emerged into the light of industrial Queens, and Delph told Violet to open her eyes—"Slowly. Only when you're ready"—Violet was ready immediately. She blinked and gazed around the car as if she'd emerged into a strange new world. Delph couldn't tell if she was ridiculing the experience or if she was unfazed or if she had achieved nirvana.

She smirked at Delph. She said, "Feel the breath, but don't think about the breath? This to you makes sense?" but she seemed calm. She seemed rescued.

"It helped, didn't it?" Delph said.

"All right, my nurse, so it helped." This was as much gratitude as Violet planned to express. "Could you do me a favor?" she said. "Could you please get all that hair out of your face? God gave you two ears for a reason. Stick your hair behind them."

"You sound like my mother," Delph said, although our mother never took such a harsh tone.

Aunt Violet snickered. "God forbid," she said. Then she did something no one had ever done to Delph, nor to Lady or Vee for that matter. She reached over, pinched Delph's cheek, and gave it a wiggle.

We'd never been to Long Island. On the train Delph was a tourist fascinated by everything she saw. There were factories huffing black smoke as if a bishop had just lost the election for pope. There were enormous billboards featuring larger-than-life men wearing nothing but colorful briefs and newsboy hats. There was Cavalry Cemetery, where the monuments tended toward black and gray granite for the same reason people sometimes wear black or gray clothing: to hide the dirt.

Because she was awkward and intimidated by Violet and because she was a terrible conversationalist and because she wanted to talk about the curse, was dying to get Violet's take on the curse, Delph introduced the subject of Lenz Alter. "So," she said nonchalantly, "did you know the manna process is responsible for all this pollution?"

It didn't work exactly the way Delph intended. She meant to generate a discussion, to encourage Violet to tell some family stories. Instead Violet took offense. "Not all the pollution," she sniffed. "Only some of it."

Delph nodded, retreated. "That's true," she said, although she wasn't sure it was.

"My grandfather was a great man," Violet said. "You judge people by the times they live in, not by the now they never got to see. In the times he lived in they had starvation. They didn't have pollution."

Right, Delph thought. They didn't have it because he hadn't caused it yet. But she said nothing, just spent the next minute or so excoriating herself. Why did she ever open her mouth? Why did she try to engage? She was so bad at it. Lady would not have made this mistake. Lady would have realized that Violet had known Lenz Alter—not from family stories or books, but from playing under his feet and sitting on his lap and calling him whatever German Jewish children called their grandfathers. Not Zayde. Our mother had made it clear that her family did not do Yiddish. Maybe, like Shirley Temple in *Heidi*, Violet had called Lenz the Grandfather.

Violet was the one who tried to rescue the conversation, steer it in a less personal direction. "Did you know this is the biggest cemetery in the country?" she asked. "Miles and miles of plant food."

"Maybe you should close your eyes again until we pass it," Delph said. She was trying to be caring, nurturing. She was trying to be the nurse.

Violet waved the effort away. "I don't do so well with the dark, that's true, but death doesn't bother me. It's getting to death, that's the problem. Believe me, I know. I grew up in a family full of people busy dying. That was how they lived their lives. *Should I die today? No? Okay, how's about tomorrow?* I spent my whole life trying to escape that craziness. And I did. I made it. And what's my reward? I get old. My mind goes—and I once was so smart, quick as a whip, you ask anyone. Not that there's anyone left to ask. Also, I get shoved into a warehouse full of nothing but people busy dying." She rolled her eyes, made a face. "Life," she snorted.

Delph proceeded with caution, but she proceeded: "I thought you said it was the best nursing home in the area."

"Sure, and the dilapidated shack is the best home in the tent village." She was done talking about herself now. "Tell me about Vee," she said, abruptly maternal. "Is there really nothing they can do for her?"

Delph turned her head, looked out the window at the thousands of begrimed tombstones. "That's what she says."

"But you got a second opinion."

"She didn't want one."

"Who cares what she didn't want? You don't let a depressed person make decisions like that."

"She's not depressed." It was our party line. Admit to depression, and your philosophies turn into pathologies. "And we would never drag her around to other doctors against her will. We wouldn't want to fill her with false hopes. It would be too much like spouting bromides—don't you think?"

Violet didn't think. "You have the best hospital for cancer in the city where you live, and you don't go once?"

"As far as Vee was concerned," Delph said, "Sloan Kettering's just another tent in the tent city."

When she looked out the window again, the cemetery was gone. Now there were rows of mom-and-pop stores, now strips of attached houses, each with a small lawn covered with lawn ornaments. The Virgin Mary looking much like the Blue Fairy from Disney's version of *Pinocchio*. Gnomes. Large reflective blue orbs on pedestals.

At the Forest Hills station, the homes a little larger, many of them mock Tudor, Violet said, "I'm going to die soon too. I've got a bad heart, and I'm losing interest in all that hullabaloo out there. That's the kiss of death. The no interest."

Delph couldn't resist going for the bromide. "Oh, come now," she said. "What about your boyfriend at the nursing home?"

"Oh, him," Violet said. And without a change in facial expression or inflection, but her glance suddenly dropping to her fingers, which were interlacing into this pattern, then that pattern, she said, "So, I want you to know the truth before I die. I think that must have been why I came to see you yesterday. I don't think it was just my"—she made a fist, knocked on her head—"I think there had to be a reason."

Delph nodded. A reason. She leaned in to hear it. It wasn't a terribly long story. Violet had finished it by the time the train reached the Floral Park station. It didn't begin with once upon a time, but it might as well have. It began: One fine day in spring.

One fine day in spring, about forty-two years ago, Aunt Violet received a call from our father. This, she said, was not entirely unusual. Though our mother and Violet hadn't spoken in years, our father called from time to time to let her know what's going on with us girls and to borrow money. Violet and Jack Smoke had a rule. If the money was for us, they gave it to him. If the money was for our mother, they didn't.

Although her well-being affected ours, Delph is too cowardly to say.

On this day our father wasn't calling for money. Instead he said, in a sadder tone than the one most people use when uttering the phrase: "It's a girl."

"Another girl," Violet said. "And how does my sister feel about that?"

"Good. Everyone's healthy. Ten fingers. Ten toes."

"Good is good, but that's not what I'm asking. How about is she happy?"

"We're talking about Dahlie," said our father.

A pause before Violet continued. "Did she give it a name yet?"

A pause before he confessed. "Delphine."

She made him spell it. She said, "What is that? Is that French? I don't know a single person in the world named that."

"She says it's another flower. I think she meant delphinium. I'd have corrected her, but—Delphinium Frankl?—I didn't think I'd be doing anyone a favor."

"Delphine Frankl's no poem either."

Our father didn't respond.

"Nat?" Violet said. "Are you there?"

"Listen," he said. "I want to come out and talk to you."

"Really? She's willing to visit the persona non grata?"

"Just me. Are you kidding? She ordered me not to call you.

She said, 'And just in case you're thinking of calling my sister, do me a favor and don't.' "

"Fine," said Violet. "Come alone. And bring me a picture of that baby."

Our father took the same train line we're on now. His seat faced Manhattan; he could see only what he was leaving, not where he was going. It made him nauseous. That was the first thing he told Violet when he got into her station wagon. "I rode backward the whole way. I feel like I'm going to throw up."

"Hello to you too," she said.

It was a weekday. Sharon and Margo were at school. Danny, four, was down for his nap. Jack Smoke was at work. The New York branch of his brokerage house was in the financial district, not far from Vee's office, as it turns out. For all we know they spent years eating at the same luncheonette counter, the two of them side by side, staring straight ahead. For all we know they boarded the same subway car at the end of the day. Maybe, after Jack Smoke got off at Thirty Fourth Street, Vee rushed to take his vacated seat, felt the uncomfortable warmth left by the departing stranger. If she'd known who he actually was, it would have changed everything. The lunches would have been convivial, the warmth of the seat familial. In fact, had they known each other, he'd never have let her stand in the first place. He'd have given the seat to her right from the start. His little niece, after all.

Natan Frankl and Violet Smoke sat on vinyl lawn chairs by the aqua-walled pool in the Smokes' backyard. They drank iced tea from sweaty highball glasses.

"Iced tea," Violet said to Delph. "No alcohol in my house ever. Not even cooking wine."

"I know that Richard and Karin . . ."

"Drank. They were drunks. You can say it. Why don't you girls just say things when you have things to say? They drank and they fought. When they got tired of that, they fought first and drank later. They fought over money, they fought over his lousy job, they fought over his family, how if my father had any foresight at all he'd have slipped poison into his father's schnapps. That was at the end, when they found out about the gas. The Zyklon—see? I'm not afraid to say things out loud. She called me at college to make sure I heard the news, my mother. First she called Rosie and then she called me. I said to her, 'What does it have to do with Pop or you or any of us?' But my mother, who according to herself was never wrong a day in her life, she says, 'If they'd used the Zyklon to cure cancer, believe me, the Alters would be taking the credit.' "

Violet interrupted the story to think about this for a moment. After all those years she was still trying to formulate a withering comeback. When she couldn't, she said, "She also threw things at him. Dinnerware mostly like in the movies. Though never the good china from Germany. But here's the difference." Her voice was prideful. "She never threw things at us girls."

"Our mother never threw things at us girls either," Delph said.

"Sure," Violet said. "That would have required her to look at you for five minutes. Please—don't think I don't know what went on."

"Nothing went on," said Delph.

By the pool, Natan Frankl sipped his iced tea. The water's surface was strewn with pink filaments—the decaying strands of mimosa blossoms—and half-inflated rafts and plastic swimming tubes with the heads of laughing turtles. Our father made his usual joke: "So, how are things here at the Smoke House?" Delph immediately heard the double meaning—Smoke House—but she wasn't thinking hams, she was thinking people, the naked bodies lined up, heading to the small, stark building—how did their legs not buckle?—soon to fill with the smoke of our great-grandfather's invention.

Violet, however, seemed never to have made that connection. "Things are fine," Violet told Natan. "Wonderful. Perfect as ever. And how are things at the Loony Bin?"

He grimaced. "She's right when she says she can't handle three of them." He fished for and lit a cigarette. "She can't even handle one of them. I swear Vee thinks Lady's her mother. Only Lady can feed her, only Lady can dress her. She cries her head off when Lady has to leave for school. And I'm no help, I admit that. I don't know what the hell to do with them. We've been to the Central Park Zoo I don't know how many times. I can't look at those goddamn apes anymore. I'm pretty sure they can't stand looking at me anymore either. They turn their backs when I show up. And there's this ice bear there. Its cage is too small. Its pool is filthy. People throw cigarettes into the water. The poor thing just stands there swinging its head back and forth, back and forth. It's been driven insane. It hits a little too close to home. It makes me think about the war, all of us behind the barbed wire. I'm afraid someday I'm going to go to the zoo and tear down the bars."

"I wouldn't worry. You're not exactly Hercules."

"I thought, maybe if it was a boy this time, I could do some-thing with him. But even if it had been a boy . . . I mean, look at me. I'm too old. I'm too"—he searched for the word, first in En-glish, then in French, then in German; nothing came to him—"shell-shocked," he finally said, the old word from the Great

War, but that's not what he meant. They hadn't come up with the word he was searching for then. They'd only just recently come up with the word *genocide*.

He took out his wallet, removed the picture he'd brought along. Violet laughed. Never had she seen so much hair on a baby.

"I begged her to get rid of it," Natan said, and at first Violet thought he was talking about the hair. "But she wouldn't do it, and now here it is."

This was when he made his proposition.

"Well," Violet said after a few minutes passed, "I've never known Dahlie to give away something that belongs to her, even if she doesn't want it. Especially not to me."

"If we can figure out how to handle it. Maybe if we make her think it will make you miserable."

"Have you felt her out on it yet? The sooner the better with this kind of thing. I have a friend who adopted. They didn't let the real mother hold the baby, not even once. Whisked it away, and that was that. Better for everyone."

"I wanted to feel you out first. If you say no, I wouldn't go any farther. I wouldn't give it away to a stranger."

"Not it," Violet said. "Her."

"We'd keep it if you said no. So I wanted to see what you said. You and Jack, I mean. You'd have to check with Jack."

"Well, yes. No kidding. It's expensive enough raising our three."

"That's why I didn't say anything to her yet. There's a lot for the two of you to talk about. You and Jack, I mean."

"So she doesn't suspect anything?"

"All I said to her was the truth. It's the same thing I said after the other two were born. The lesson from the camp. I tell it to

Lady and Vee, too. When they're asleep. 'Never love anyone too much. You never know when they might be taken away.' I whisper it in their ears. Every night, I whisper it."

"You didn't have to be in the camps to learn that lesson," Violet said. "My mother. My father. Rosie. One right after the other. Gone, gone, gone. Boom, boom, boom."

"True. Although your father . . . It was because of what he found out about the camps, right? The gas. And maybe that's why Rosie, too. So in those cases, we're back to square one: it all comes back to Hitler."

"Boom, boom, boom," Violet said, "and you tell yourself, that's it. I'm done. No one's going to get to me ever again. Then Jack comes along. Then the girls. The first time I held them— the very first second—all my wisdom flew out the window. The brick wall I built around my heart, gone forever. Boom."

"Dahlie is wiser than you are, then. No one's going to knock down her brick wall. When I told her not to love the baby too much, she told me it was way too soon for her to love it. She said, 'You don't love them at first. It takes time. A few years.' "

"Well, that's my sister. With me, I'm telling you, the very first second I held my girls, that was it. I'd have ripped out Jack's throat with my teeth if he'd tried to take one of them from me. If he even suggested it. Not that he would. But Dahlie. Yes. I can see how it would take Dahlie years to love her own kid. If then."

If then, Delph thought. Like *but then* and *and then*, it was a phrase Vee might like.

"That's when the idea came to me," Natan said to Violet. "When she said that she doesn't love them at first. I said to myself, Natan, you've got a window of opportunity here. It would be better for the baby. It would be better for Dahlie. It would be better for the other two. And let's be honest, it's probably better for me too. And, who knows? She could surprise us. Maybe she'd be relieved."

"Maybe. You never know with her."

"Of course it wouldn't be so easy on you. Danny's only what? Four?"

"It would be a handful. But that's not what I'm worried about."

Violet finished her tea. She was thinking she'd like to get up, skim the pool's surface. After that she would go inside, clean up the kitchen. She was feeling a need to get her home in order, clean out some closets, put scattered toys onto the shelves where they belonged. Another little baby, and Danny not yet in school. If the house wasn't picked up to begin with, she'd have no fighting chance.

"I'll have to talk to Jack," she said. "And the girls. Margo would have to move into Sharon's room. I'm not sure how they'd feel about that. Although they both love babies. And look at this one." She showed him the photograph of Delph as if she were the one who'd taken it, as if he'd never seen it before. "Is that a real-life doll or what? Also," she said, "there would be a condition. My condition would be none of you—you, Dahlie, the girls—none of you can see her. Not for a few years at least. Not until I say when. She has to know who her family is. She has to know her mother."

The train whistled past Hollis Station. The people waiting there were teenage girls mostly, their shirts cropped, their pierced belly buttons glinting, their hair straightened and slicked back into high ponytails. They wore hoop earrings as big as salad plates. They didn't look at the train rushing by them. They could tell by its speed that it wasn't going to stop for them. Only a scrawny boy wearing a pink seersucker suit with an oversize purple bow tie watched the cars tear past. His hair, bleached white and shaved on the sides, popped up thick and curly on top. He seemed young, and Delph wondered if he'd put this look together with bold, idiosyncratic care—a fashion statement, a queer boy's flair—or if it was the doing of his mother. Whatever the pink suit's provenance, the boy seemed at ease with himself. He beamed at the train. He seemed to be beaming at Delph. He waved. Then the train had whizzed by and he was gone. Or was she the one who was gone?

She turned back to Violet. "My mother said no, I take it. She wanted to keep me."

"She said yes. She was angry and hysterical and paranoid, accusing your father of every crime under the sun, but she said yes. But then after seven months, that's when she says no. Your father calls. She wants you back. Immediately. She's hysterical. She's talking about calling the police. Jack and I talked too, believe me. We talked about going to court. We even talked about moving away in the dead of night, packing everyone up and starting over someplace else. But it wasn't practical. Jack's business was in the city. And legally, what could we do? We had a deal, but we didn't have any papers. We should have, but we said to ourselves, Who has their sister sign papers? It seemed cruel. Salt in the wound. But it turned out to be our big mistake."

Delph imagined our mother coming for her, and Violet saying no. Violet saying, You can't have her. She's staying with us. Delph had never thought about the King Solomon story from the baby's point of view before—the baby all grown up, with a phantom pain in her side where the sword was going to slice her in two. "Is that when our father left her?" she asked.

"First he came and took you home. Next thing I heard was from your mother. Nate's gone and she'd going to Germany. What happened to him, who knows? He wasn't a happy man, that's for sure. All I know is, after he left, no one ever heard from him again. I sure didn't. But you know how your mother picked the river? When I saw that on that crazy chart of yours, the first thing I thought was it would not surprise me one bit if she was looking for him there . . . if you get my drift."

"Drift," Delph murmured. "He'd have thought that was a good one."

Violet looked confused. She didn't get it. She just went on. "My kids all remember you. They talk about you sometimes. Even Danny remembers. He liked to hold you. You were such a little fatso. It's nice in a baby. A little bundle. It was very hard on him when they took you away. He used to cry. My baby, my baby. You'd just started to creep."

This was too much; Delph had to turn the subject away from a tearful four-year-old longing for her own little hairy fat baby self. "You said you'd have changed my name," she said. "Did you?"

Violet smiled, a full smile, a warm smile, the smile of a woman who fell fiercely in love the very first second she held her child in her arms. "Of course," she said. "The minute you arrived. Julie, we called you. Not after anyone special. Just a name I liked."

"Julie Smoke," Delph said, and thought: Julie. Dahlie. Not sound-alikes. But look-alikes.

The story was finished. The train pulled into Floral Park. It waited a brief moment. People got on. People got off.

There are times, Delph believes, when the gods are so afraid you'll miss the point that they stop being subtle. They just shove the meaning of it all in your face. So: Good-bye, Floral Park. Good-bye, all things floral. Delph was off to visit Julie Smoke's brother and Julie Smoke's house and Julie Smoke's swimming pool. "Built in," Violet assured her. "Gorgeous." And it was a warm day, nearing seventy-five degrees, and, Violet said, there were swimsuits that once belonged to her daughters. Any one of them would fit Delph fine.

But seventy-five degrees in September isn't as warm as seventy-five degrees in July, and while Violet and Danny talked inside the house, the three of us only rolled up our jeans and sat at the edge of the pool, the water lapping at our calves. Delph pushed her hair behind her ears. She tilted her head back, let the sun do its damage. It never ceased to amaze her how everything bad for you feels so goddamn good. And vice versa. (Exercise. Vegetables.) It's as if life is constantly issuing a warning: Don't trust anything, especially yourself.

"This is the life," Lady said.

Vee had her head on Lady's shoulder. Her woolen coat was draped over her shoulders. Her turban had slid back. In the bright light Lady and Delph could see how haggard and gaunt her face had become, in a way they never could inside our apartment.

"It's someone's life," Vee said.

Danny Smoke, that awkward bar mitzvah boy, had turned into a handsome man. Alter has always looked better on men than women, and Danny wore it especially well. He'd tidied his eyebrows. His hair was blue-black: either he had not yet gone gray or he'd resorted to dye. He had the Emanuel eyes, pale blue, to counter all the dark. And his nose appeared to have been broken multiple times. There was a divot, then a slight twist to the right. You had to absorb it in sections. It was better, less overwhelming, that way. It was less coming at you.

He was beautifully dressed, too, unlike us, each in jeans and tees. He was wearing a blue polo shirt tucked in to belted khaki shorts, which he'd told us, when he'd picked us up at the station, he'd bought in the boys' department.

He was short. Very short. Taller than we are, yes, but that's never been much of an accomplishment. At the station he'd greeted us with warm hugs plus a self-deprecating and obviously much-practiced joke: "Danny Smoke at your service," he'd said, "unless you need something off a high shelf. Then you're on your own."

"Like Great-Great-Uncle Rudi," Delph said.

"Who?" Danny said.

"On Lenz's side. He was a dwarf."

"Heigh ho," Danny said mirthlessly.

"Danny is hardly a dwarf," Violet muttered. She was in the passenger seat next to him. The sun was bright. She pulled down the visor, recoiled at the sight of her face in the vanity mirror. She pushed the visor up again.

"True," Danny said. "I believe the technical term is 'shrimp.' " No one said anything. "Five foot four," he finally said. "And one-half. Taller than James Madison. Shorter than Tom Cruise."

"More handsome than both," Violet said.

"Well," Vee said, "if we're answering questions people are too polite to ask, then my answer is, 'After chemo it never grew back.' " She patted the turban.

We saw Danny's eyes in the rear view mirror. "Wow," he said. "Man. Sorry to hear that. I'd just figured you were incredibly stylish. I thought you were rocking a look. Are you okay?"

"I'm fine now," Vee said quickly and with finality. Even Violet said nothing.

"Phew," Danny said.

We'd driven on in guilty silence. Later Lady would say that Danny's Toyota had been like a hearse, not in appearance or color, but in that he'd been ferrying four bodies that might as well have been corpses—that *would* be corpses soon enough. "I have a joke," Lady would say then. "What do you call a hearse transporting bodies that aren't dead yet, but soon will be?" and Vee would guess the answer—a rehearsal—but none of us would laugh. Our hearts were no longer in it.

It had been hard not to think in terms of hearses. Not only because Vee was so sick and Violet so frail. But in the car, even as Vee uttered her lie about her health, we were driving along a boulevard of cemeteries. Long Island National Cemetery, Beth Moses Cemetery, Pinelawn Memorial Cemetery, New Montfiore Cemetery, Saint Charles, Wellwood. One right after another. Delph and Vee exchanged glances. Coincidence, this route we were traveling? Or a pointed message from the gods?

We should say that, unlike Cavalry, these cemeteries were suburban cemeteries, middle-class cemeteries. Each one was grassier, better groomed, less crowded, than the cemetery in Queens. The monuments tended to be white marble. There was a brightness, a prettiness, to these cemeteries.

"When I was in high school," Danny said, slowing down as if we were passing a well-known tourist attraction, "we'd hang out here. We'd drink beer or get stoned or, you know, do whatever. We didn't think it was disrespectful. We were convinced the dead people would enjoy a bunch of kids doing kid things behind their graves. We had this theory the dead would be very pro make-hay-while-the-sun-shines." He was slowing down, pulling over. "You know what they call a bunch of ghosts hanging out in a group?"

We thought he was going for a joke, asking us to be straight men. "No, what?" we said.

But he was just passing along some interesting information.

"A reunion of ghosts," he said. "You know, like a litter of puppies or a herd of buffalo or a gaggle of geese."

"Or a murder of crows," Vee said.

He'd stopped the car by the Jewish cemetery. You could tell by the Stars of David in the iron gates' scrollwork. He wanted to get out of the car, show us his father's grave, but thick chains and locks were making sure that no one defiled the Sabbath by visiting a loved one. "Well, my dad's over to the side there," Danny said, pointing. We turned to look, as if we expected to see someone waving.

"We have no idea where our dad's buried," Vee said, "or how he died, or where he was during most of our childhoods."

"God," Danny said cheerfully. He pulled away from the grassy strip by the roadside, continued home. "You are so competitive, Vee. I'm getting a shellacking here."

We'd been expecting a manor, but the Smoke House was just a split-level on a quarter acre lot. Violet went immediately upstairs, leaning heavily on the banister. "I want to get out of this rag," she said of her housedress. Danny commenced another tour, this time of the house. In a corner of the living room, the furnishings done in hunter-green velvet, the walls papered with hunter-green flocking, there was a life-size porcelain pony midprance, all gleaming white, its body pierced with a brass pole that touched the floor and reached the ceiling. Across the fireplace mantel were at least a dozen porcelain shepherdesses, some with white porcelain lambs by their porcelain blue or pink gowns. A white porcelain fawn the size of a fawn slept underneath the glass coffee table.

Once, in preparation for a painful procedure to determine the exact location of her second constellation of tumors, the hospital had doped Vee up and slapped some earphones on her. They'd promised soothing music, but what she'd gotten as she woozed in and out of consciousness was a series of love songs from Disney cartoons. She hadn't objected entirely. A rerelease of *Snow White* had been the first movie she ever saw, and she retained a soft spot for "Someday my Prince will Come." But she came home joking that she'd had a revelation: she was certain that the heaven everyone seemed to aspire to would be just like her procedure—antiseptic, populated by the overly solicitous, and with Disney music piped directly into everyone's ears. "That's what people are hoping for," she said. "That's everyone's idea of paradise." Now, in Aunt Violet's living room, she added a new element to the concept. Heaven would also share this decor. Everywhere you went, there'd be velvet and knickknacks. There'd be shining white creatures and demure maidens in pastel gowns, all without mobility, bodily functions, and eyeballs—but pretty. Pretty and sweet. And everyone would be happy about all this sweetness, all this pretty. Everyone would be happy but Vee.

Lady, on the other hand, was most fascinated by the gallery of family portraiture on the wall along the staircase to the second floor. Along with countless framed photographs of varying sizes hung in no discernible order, there were three exceptionally large, glossy oil paintings, one of each of the Smoke children. The paintings were in the style of Vermeer, the children's faces aglow with light, the backgrounds dark and moody. None of the extended family was included in the gallery, certainly none of the old European family. Just this family, the ordinary Smoke family, celebrated and memorialized as if they were royalty, as if their visages needed to be preserved for generations and perhaps biographers to come.

Thus, while Vee was thinking warily of heaven, Lady was

reassessing domesticity. This was how it was done in regular families, she realized. She hadn't been fond of the white porcelain animals either, but she was struck by the fact that they were relatively new. Aunt Violet had gone to some store and purchased that pony, that fawn. They were tacky, but they'd spoken to Violet, they'd touched her. There was no antique furniture, dark and heavy, passed down and then passed down again. There were no old chairs and sideboards glowering like refugees. No ghosts on the walls from the late eighteen hundreds reminding you daily of who they were and what they did and, therefore, who you were. Nary a Prussian chancellor in the bathroom. In the bathroom were pastel cartoons of cherubic little boys peeing, each framed in ornate gold leaf.

No daily reminders of what you could never escape. Here, Lady realized, you could escape. You did escape. You weren't the suicide's daughter. You were a shepherdess, you were a lamb, you were Cinderella in a pair of pretty shoes that fit you perfectly.

Her attraction to the house frightened her. She was filled with a longing she couldn't name or abide. She felt hot tears in her eyes. "Well," she said when the tour was over, "I guess we ought to get going. We can just take a taxi back to the station. We know you have a lot to discuss with your mother. We don't want to be in the way."

Danny gave her a look: you are being ridiculous. "Have something to drink," he said. He gestured toward the kitchen. "Help yourself to whatever you find. I'll be down in a minute."

He went up to see Violet, we poked into the fridge. We weren't pleased, but we knew we had no choice other than to stay. We could not have felt more trapped if we'd been in our coffins—which, ironically, perhaps even amusingly, had been our original weekend destination. Still, when we opened the refrigerator expecting pitchers of iced tea and lemonade, gallons of milk, there was only beer and half-drunk bottles of white wine and jars of half-eaten salsa, inside each jar a mélange of tomatoes and peppers and mold. A refrigerator, in other words, not unlike our own, not in the precise nature of the contents—we do not drink beer; we do not buy salsa—but in the ethos, the culture, the way of life, and it did make us feel at home, so much so that Lady, hopeful and emboldened, opened the small freezer compartment and found a frosted bottle of orange-flavored vodka among the crystallized cardboard cartons of sorbet and piles of Hungry Man frozen dinners. She poured a few fingers of the vodka into plastic coffee mugs—she couldn't find any stemware—and filled the mugs to the top with flat tonic water. One for herself, one for Delph, who sipped the liquid down until she could transport her mug to the pool without spilling, and one for Vee. Vee, her pain diminished from the Percocet, was drinking again.

A swimming pool and cocktails. It was the closest thing to a Hawaiian vacation we'd ever experience. Vee, determined and stalwart, drank in quick, wincing gulps. We all got mildly drunk in near record time. Is it shameful to say that we were happy, there in that suburban backyard? Everything was bland but easy. The afternoon began to feel like a send-off, like the going-away party we hadn't expected anyone to throw us.

We shared the jokes and observations that had come to us on the train, in the car, on the tour. We caught up with each other. "Lady," Delph said. "I've got a question for you. Was there a seven-month interval between Mom giving birth to me and me coming home that you've maybe forgotten to mention to me?"

Lady wrinkled her brow and dredged her memory as if it were a swamp full of old tires and lost shoes and discarded weapons. "So much of my childhood is in shadows," she finally said.

"You always say Dad left when I was swaddled," Delph said.

"Mom used to say that. Why? Did Violet know something I don't? Were you too small to come home for a few months?"

"Here comes Danny," said Vee.

"I'll tell you later," Delph said.

Danny carried a baby monitor and a bag of chips and a beer. He dropped the monitor onto the grass. He joined us at the pool's edge. He opened the beer, then the chips, each with his teeth. He smiled, aware that we were aware he was showing off for us. He passed the chips around. "You should have seen it yesterday," he said. "Trees in the road everywhere. But now, it's like Floyd never happened."

He told us that Violet was sleeping. "She's finally down," was what he actually said, the way you would of your cranky child or, in different circumstances, your old dog. "She says she wants to go back to the nursing home. I told her to sleep first. Hence, the monitor." He sighed. "She's in and out," he said.

We tried to bring him up to speed on our lives, which, since, as with Violet, we omitted most of the sad stuff, again did not take long. Next we filled him in on his own family history. Delph, especially, was grateful that she felt so at ease with him. He was one of those men: her old teacher, her old therapist, her cowboy-boots-wearing boss, her Joshua. Also, the blend of vodka lazing through her bloodstream and the warm chlorinated water licking at her calves didn't hurt. There was such pleasure, she thought, in slowly lifting one's submerged feet until they broke through the blue surface, then dunking them under again. We were all doing this, Danny included, as we talked. Drown the toes. Save the toes. Drown the toes. Save the toes.

"This is mind-blowing," Danny said of our family stories. "Mom told me our grandfather got hit by a car."

"Maybe he did," Lady said. "He landed in the street. A car could have been coming. Who knows? What about Rose? Do you know about what happened to her? Or our mother?"

"I know your mother moved to Germany when you guys were kids. But who's Rose?"

We laughed. We said, "Have we got a chart for you."

But after we'd finished the narrative and he'd finished saying wow and expressing his sympathy and carping a little because he bet both of his sisters knew all of this, and it drove him crazy sometimes, how his family still thought of him as the baby who needed to be coddled and protected from bad or even interesting news, so no one ever told him anything—and after he said, "Too bad Lenz Alter didn't invent Prozac instead of chlorine gas; that probably would have saved them all," reducing our family's moral drama and compromised souls to an easily remedied chemical imbalance—and, who knew, he was probably right—after all that, he hadn't much else to say on the subject.

"Are you hungry?" he asked. "You're staying for dinner, right?"

During dinner—pizza, delivered to the door—we were persuaded to stay overnight. We would wear Sharon and Margo's old nightgowns. In the morning we'd avail ourselves of their old underwear, socks, whatever we needed. We had to say yes, Danny told us. He had that gig in Hicksville in a few hours. If we didn't stay with Violet, he didn't know what he was going to do.

More than once that day we'd whispered to one another the same jokey complaint: staying in the city and preparing for our suicides would have been more fun than being with Violet. "I want to go home this instant," she repeated throughout the day. She was saying it now as her pizza grew cold and congealed. "I want to go home." None of us—not even Violet—could say

which home she had in mind. Danny tried to get her into the
car, to head to the nursing home. She wouldn't go. Danny tried
to call the nursing home, say she would be spending the night
here. She started the chanting: No, no, I don't want to stay here.
I want to go home. "Do you mean our home?" Lady asked and
Violet pounded the table. "Just take me home," she said, spitting
each word.

After a while you just had to make a decision for her. "All
right," Lady said. "We'll stay with her tonight," and Danny ran
to her, hugged her

It was 7:00 pmwhen he began loading amps into the rusty old
VW bus he used for his shows. Vee had already gone to sleep in
Margo's old bed, Margo's old nightgown. "I don't suppose one
of you wants to come hear me?" Danny asked Lady and Delph.

"Yes," Lady said. "Delph wants to."

"No, I don't," Delph said.

"Take Delph with you," Lady said. "Contrary to popular
belief, she's a terrible nurse."

In Hicksville, Danny Smoke performed on a rough-hewn platform that passed for a stage, his act a frenetic three-hour set of
folk songs and oldies, songs that seemed to have no relationship
to one another except for the nostalgia they provoked. Seated on
a high stool, leaning into a standing gooseneck mike, he played
and sang without break, as sweat riveted down his face and the
middle-aged audience, fat-bellied men and deliberately with-
ered women, all of them dressed in *Married to the Mob* couture,
danced and sang along.

The name of the place was Freddie's. It was a dive bar that
called itself a pub. Long wooden tables and uncomfortable bench
seats. Red and green Christmas lights from last winter swagged

along the walls, dusty plastic plants hanging from a dropped ceiling. Delph hid at the corner of the bar, one of those fake plants directly over her head. She was the only person in the entire place who wasn't dancing, the only customer who wasn't swilling cheap beer from the bottle.

She was pretty sure she was the only person in the place listening to the words of the songs Danny was singing. Danny sang a song about a broken heart. He sang a song about the Mississippi River. He sang a song about evading the law. It didn't matter what he sang. He played every song with the same upbeat tempo, the very same beat. The dancers gyrated and they shouted along with him, a happy, drunken braying. They knew all the lyrics. They just didn't seem to know what any of the lyrics meant. Danny sang a song about the YMCA, and the pop tune lost all its innuendo, became a song about actually taking a room at the Y. The middle-aged dancers threw their arms in the air, turned their bodies into hip-swiveling Ys, as perhaps they had done thirty years ago in their parents' refinished basements when the song first came out. Or maybe as they did in discos. Although, Delph is certain, not in the same kind of discos where she and her friends were also dancing to this song, also throwing their arms up in the air.

There had been elation and energy in those clubs too, the gay bars in New York in the 1970s, but now, looking back, she had a clearer perspective; she knew—everyone knew—that the elation had been one click away from despair and disaster. Step outside the club, say good night, walk away from the line—even at three in the morning, there'd be a long line—and there was danger. Even for her, though not as much for her. As she walked, head down, to a street where there might be a cab, she'd feared muggers, rapists, but she'd never had to fear simply bumping into someone she knew. And yes, of course, she feared the plague, used to run her eyes and, when he'd let her, her fingers over Joshua's body looking for lesions, touching them, wishing some sort of magic would emanate from her fingertips, erase them, cure him—but her fear had not been anything like Joshua's fear. Delph knew the plague would not be the cause of her own death.

Now in Freddie's, it dawns on her that begging Joshua to stay with her, to sleep with her just once—maybe that had been her first attempt at suicide. If Joshua were going to die, she would die with him. Cause of death: love. She would die from what Joshua was dying from. She would be Romeo chugging the poison. Of course, Joshua hadn't seen it the same way. He wouldn't sleep with her when he was healthy; he certainly wasn't going to sleep with her sick. Thinking back, she can almost understand why he'd preferred to spend his last months with his thickheaded, bigoted, withholding parents than with her and her tears and her mewling and pleading and clinging. The frosty air in that midwestern home of his must have been refreshing.

Here, at Freddie's, no one's in danger. These are white, middle-class suburbanites. Maybe they're in danger of heart disease. Maybe diabetes, or living the unexamined life. But plague? No, not plague. By having your life ruined by someone seeing you here? By fucking someone you love or like or who you just feel like fucking? Death by fucking? No, none of that for this crowd.

Danny sang the last song of the night—"Goodnight, Irene," predictably enough—and the sticky dancers looped their arms around each other's shoulders, held each other close, and swayed, shouting the chorus as if it were their college fight song rather than a bluesy lament. The bigger men, the drunkest women, swayed so aggressively that the row of singers, like a row of dominoes, nearly toppled to the ground.

And then it was done. Danny stood, bowed, held his guitar aloft. The crowd cheered as if they'd witnessed a performance by Caruso, Pavarotti, a Beatles reunion with John showing up.

Delph ordered a fresh drink as the crowd shambled out the door. The couples—and they were almost all couples—would drive home to their own split-levels, to their sleeping kids, sleeping babysitters. They would drive drunk, convinced that nothing bad would happen to any of them, not for many, many years, and, Delph suspected, for the most part they'd be proven correct.

"That last song you sang," Delph said to Danny, when he joined her at the bar,

"Goodnight, Irene." He sang the title.

"Do you think they understand what it's about?" she asked.

"It's about lost love," Danny said.

"It's about a gambler who wants to kill himself. The last song of the night is about despair and suicide."

"Yeah, but no one cares what it's about," the guy behind the bar said. This was Freddie, the owner. He'd brought three shot glasses and a bottle of Jack Daniels. "None of them want to kill themselves any more than any of them want to shimmy like their sister Kate."

Freddie was older than Danny and Delph, maybe in his fifties, maybe his sixties. His hair was silver and disheveled, standing up as if he'd just run his fingers through it. His face was shadowed in the dim light, his cheekbones prominent, his jaw aggressive and dimpled. Once, perhaps thirty years ago, he'd been handsome.

He poured each of them a shot.

"My cousin Delph," Danny said. "From the city."

"Cousin? Too bad. I thought maybe you'd finally gotten over what's-her-face."

"I am over what's-her-face. It's just, how am I supposed to meet anyone new when I spend my weekends in this dump? I need to move to New York. No decent single people live on the Island."

"Thanks a lot."

"You're divorced. You've got kids. You're an *alte cocker*. It's different for you." Danny slapped the bar with his palms. "I'm going to change and load the van."

Delph had assumed Freddie would wander off, wash some glasses, pick up the wet bills left behind on the bartop. But he stayed by her. "I'm thinking it's just as lonely in New York as anywhere else," he said to her. "Am I right?"

She nodded.

"What the hell," he said. "We're all doomed no matter what songs we sing."

He seemed to want her to say something. "That's depressing," she said.

"Alcohol's a depressant," said Freddie. "My business is giving depressed people something guaranteed to make them more depressed." He reached under the bar, handed her a card. On one side the name of the bar, his own name, a phone number. On the other side, the number of a suicide hotline.

"Wow," Delph said.

He turned the card to his own info. "Call me next time you're in town," he said.

"I'm going back to the city tomorrow."

"Hold onto it, then, for next time." When she took out her wallet to pay for her drinks, he scoffed. "When you're in my place," he said, "I take care of you."

For a moment she'd forgotten who she was, that there would not be a next time. She put the card in her wallet. She said, "Well, in that case, I guess I'll have one for the road."

It was two in the morning when Danny and Delph drove off in the van. Delph could see the surface of the road through the holes in the floor by her feet.

Danny tried to drive slowly to compensate for how drunk he was.

"You drink like an Alter," Delph said.

"You guys are obsessed with the Alters," said Danny. "I think I have more Smoke DNA than Alter DNA. I think I drink like a Smoke."

"It's a weird name, Smoke."

"It's the Ellis Island version of the German name Schmuck. I shit you not." He grinned. "Think about it," he said. "You came this close to being adopted by a bunch of Schmucks."

"God bless the bureaucrats at Ellis Island," she said.

The van moseyed along Old Country Road, a main thoroughfare, four lanes. Car dealers and burger joints. A gas station on every corner, and, look—it's the Parkway Diner from that old Billy Joel song.

Old Country Road. Once, she supposed, it was a single lane, all packed dirt and tufts of wayward grass. Long before Billy Joel began singing about Long Island, Walt Whitman's father must have driven a cart filled with raw lumber along this road.

"Did Freddie ask you out?" Danny said.

"He did, I think. Why? Does he ask every woman out?"

"No. Not at all. You must be his type."

"Poor Freddie," she said. "Me as his type."

"Stop fishing," Danny said.

"What do you mean?"

"Oh, come on. Men must ask you out all the time."

She was tempted to pull down the visor, peer at herself in the vanity mirror. She'd been completely at ease with Danny, fairly at ease with Freddie. Why? Was Julie Smoke more outgoing than Delph Alter? Was Julie Smoke prettier? Maybe Sharon and Margo had passed along some beauty tips to Julie that Lady and Vee never mentioned to Delph.

She decided to nudge the subject away from herself. "Was your school life hell?" she asked. A shrimp named Schmuck, she thought. Jesus.

He laughed. "No. Was yours?"

"Of course. I was a very strange kid. I was withdrawn and gnomish."

"I wasn't. I was on the small side, yeah, but I was a normal kid. I always had a gang of friends. I always had a girlfriend. I always had music."

He made and repaired stringed instruments. His studio was in the basement of his house. That was his real job, the one that supported him. Not that he was getting rich off it, either. But after dinner, before he and Delph headed out to the pub, he'd showed her a mandolin he was working on. "Mandolins and ukuleles," he'd said. "They're the big sellers these days. Old rich guys like them for some reason."

Now he said, "The trick for me was not letting the world tell me who I was. It's how I got into my business. The world wanted me to buy a short man's guitar. That meant a kid's guitar. I was, fuck that. I wanted a badass guitar. I wanted a one hundred percent guitar, not a three-quarters guitar. So my dad commissioned a custom job. I hung out with the guy while he made it. Then I just kept hanging out there. He taught me the craft. I still have that guitar. I'll show it to you when we get home. I still play it from time to time. It's got tall frets to compensate for the reduced scale length. It's got a narrow neck so I could reach around to do thumb cords, but it's not neck-heavy because, the guy said, 'Sometimes you'll want to throw it around some, and you don't want to leave broken peg heads all over the stage.'" He laughed. "I was fifteen. Already as tall as I was going to get. Or as short as I was going to stay. But a badass guitar adds a good six or seven inches to a kid in high school."

She didn't know what to say to all the peg heads this and pedal boards that. She was fairly sure that if she'd walked through the halls of junior high school with a guitar, badass or otherwise, someone would have taken it from her and bashed it against a wall.

"It must have been expensive," she said. "A custom-made guitar."

"He did okay, my dad. He was a Wall Street guy. But a good Wall Street guy. I wish you could've known him."

He used to pick me up when I cried, she thought. She tried to imagine herself rocked in the arms of burly Jack Smoke, she, the size of a ukulele, a mandolin.

They'd just left Hicksville, a sign said. She thought: Hicks' Ville. As in, you won't meet a single sophisticated person within our borders. Now they were still on Old Country Road, but in a town called Plainview. Plain View, as in, nothing to look at here.

She, who almost always had a drink in her hand but who never got more than a mild buzz, was drunk now. Those last few shots of Jack had pushed her over. What if, she thought, but then she couldn't remember what she wanted to think about. The phrase just repeated in her head. *What if, what if, what if. . .*

Now they were in Huntington, almost home, and traveling down a different street, a narrow street, an actual old country road. The houses looked like nineteenth-century farmhouses. The trees were thick, both in the girth of their trunks and their proximity to one another.

"Nice moon," Danny said, and it was, low and smudged, as

if someone had reached up and rubbed it with the pad of her thumb, the way a mother might rub a spot of her lipstick off her child's cheek.

"Are we going straight home?"

"We don't have to. We could do something. If you want to know the truth, I never go straight home after a gig."

"Let's do whatever you usually do."

The dark road ended at a six-lane state highway, a retail strip called Walt Whitman Road. "It makes you want to cry, doesn't it?" she said of the name. But Danny made a sharp turn right just before the highway, and they were on Old Walt Whitman Road instead, and this road was much better, more what you'd want a road named after a poet to look like.

Danny parked by a broken-down house. The paint was peeling, the roof staved in near the disintegrated chimney. The railings by the front doorstep were rotted through.

"Speaking of wanting to cry," Danny said exuberantly, "here's Old Walt's birthplace." He reached across her, popped open the glove box, removed a silver flask. "I love the quiet after all the noise of Freddie's," he said.

Delph wasn't sure how he could call this quiet. It seemed to her there was a racket out there: screeching owls and the babylike screams of what Danny promised her was only a fox, and, one road over, semis speeding past the malls and all-night diners. Still, she nodded; why not agree? She was equally agreeable about accepting the flask when he passed it to her. More bourbon. Danny reclined his seat all the way back, and she did that too. "And the stars," Danny said. "I love the stars." She looked up through the windshield. The grimy veil that falls over the city sky at night didn't extend to this part of the world. She located the Big Dipper. It was the only constellation she could identify under any circumstances, but here she couldn't possibly miss it.

"There aren't any stars in the city," she said.

"There probably are."

"No," she said. "They've left. Light flight."

"You see that big shrub by the front door?" Danny said. "That lilac? You know who pruned it back this year? And every year before that?"

"Whitman's ghost?"

"Only if I'm Walt reincarnated. I'm out here every fall, three in the morning with my clippers. How can you not? I know that nobody gives a fuck about this place, but I don't understand how you can let the goddamn lilac bush by Walt Whitman's front door go to hell."

"By his dooryard," she said to let him know she knew the poem, that she got it. "Do you read a lot of poetry?" she asked.

"I don't read any poetry. Who reads poetry? Although," he said, "sometimes I write it. It's just that Walt is the hometown hero. Whitman and the guy who played the Karate Kid. That's pretty much it for the Huntington hall of fame."

"There's you. Pub singer and mandolin maker."

"Yeah," he said. "I used to write my own songs. I had a band. We did some recordings, some touring. Now I go from dive to dive, and I sing shit like 'YMCA.' I tell myself there are worse ways to live one's life than to make guitars by day and play music by night. I tell myself that anything that leads to more strumming and singing and dancing in this godforsaken world can't be all bad. Then I wonder if putting 'YMCA' into the environment night after night doesn't constitute some virulent form of air pollution."

" 'YMCA' is a great song," she said. "It's catchy. Not exactly a crime against humanity." She couldn't help it. She had to sing a few lines. It was that kind of song. And maybe she was showing off a little, the way he had with the beer and the bottle cap.

"Hey," he said. "You can sing."

"Maybe if I were still Julie Smoke, we'd have a brother-sister act."

"Maybe we would," he said. "Go ahead. Sing something."

She hesitated. But why? She realized she was hesitating to appear shy and modest. What she really wanted to do was accommodate him. Maybe impress him. She launched into "Matilda." She billabonged, she tucker-bagged, she jumbucked.

He hugged her when she was done. He pulled her toward him, kissed the top of her head. "That's going into the act," he said when he released her.

They fell into silence. "What's your position on fate?" she said after a while.

"Whoa," he said.

"No, really. Do you believe in it? Do you believe in God? Or when strange things happen, do you just chalk them up to happenstance?"

He had his mother's smirk. He was not nearly as much a Smoke as he thought. "I'm just curious," he said. "How did we get from 'Waltzing Matilda' to do I believe in God?"

"The three of us—my sisters and me—we were just living our lives," Delph said. "We had certain plans, right? A certain game plan all mapped out. And just as we were coming close to putting our plans into action, your mother shows up. In the middle of a hurricane. And now I, at least, am reconsidering those plans."

"What plans?"

"Nothing. Moving. We were thinking about moving."

"Where?"

"I don't know. Somewhere else. It's complicated. It's not important. The point is that we were making these plans, and then, before we could carry them out, there's your mother in our front hall making us—well, at least making me—rethink everything."

"They couldn't have been very firm plans if that's all it took to change your mind."

"The point is that there's something so predetermined about the way she popped up. More than predetermined. It's overdetermined, I think. Coincidental but beyond coincidental. Like the hand of God at work. If you believe in God."

"If you believe God has hands."

"I'm serious. Do you think the timing of these things are sheer coincidence? Or do you think God or the gods or whatever you want to call it manipulated events, sent your mother to us, made sure we knew we had family here before we packed up and left?"

He laughed. "I'm just picturing God trying to convince my mother to do something she doesn't want to do. It wouldn't turn out well for God, I'm betting." He took a swig from the flask. He grew serious. "I don't know," he said. "Does it matter why it happened?"

"The *why* always matters," she said. "Look at me. I have all my life believed that our family was cursed. All those terrible lives. All those suicides. Now we find out that Violet escaped the curse. And you escaped. And your sisters escaped. What does it mean?"

"You believed the family was cursed? Seriously believed it?"

"People think it's absurd to believe in curses, and then they tell you they believe in karma. Or God. Or angels."

"Well, I don't believe in God or angels."

"But karma?"

"Well, karma is real."

She laughed. "Look at this," she said. It wasn't easy, showing him her tattoo. She rolled up the leg of her jeans, contorted so he could see her calf in the smudge of moon. He couldn't make the words out; she had to tell him what they said. "From the Bible," she said.

"Right," he said. "Except all those words mean is try not to be a complete asshole or the next few generations of your family are going to die of embarrassment every time your name is mentioned. It doesn't mean the generations will literally be punished."

"Hunh," she said. "Tell that to John-John Kennedy."

"I'm not sure I understand what you're saying," he said. "I'm not sure I've understood what you're getting at for a good five minutes now."

She wasn't sure what she was saying either—they had that in common. But she knew what she was thinking about, and what she was thinking about was living, and that she was thinking about living shocked her in a way that thinking about dying never had. It was as if all this time her attachment to life had been lurking beneath her willingness to die, like an impervious base metal beneath cheap gold plating.

"Hey," Danny said, "let's not just sit here and talk. Let's do something. Let's go inside."

"You mean break in?"

"You wanted to know what I do after gigs. That's what I do. I break into the Walt Whitman Birthplace and serenade his ghost."

"There," she said. "I knew that ghost was going to show up."

He took a guitar and a blanket from the back of the van. He used the side of a credit card to open the front door to the house. The Smokes, Delph thought. So good at barging into homes that aren't their own.

He led her into the birthing room. They sat on the blanket, which did nothing to cushion them from the hard, wide, warped slats of the pine floor. The walls were bowed horsehair, mildewed.

He tuned the guitar, strummed, his head close to the strings.

"How do you know this is the birthing room?" she said.

"Everyone knows it's the birthing room."

He began to play. She watched the strings vibrate, noted the optical illusion, the way there appeared to be many more strings than just the six. He sang a verse from "Goodnight Irene," this time with more heart, more pain. He changed the name of the girl in the song. "Goodnight, Delphine."

"You think of me as Delphine?" she asked.

"I didn't," he admitted, "but now I do. It's like, Julie's dead; long live Delphine."

It upset her, the death of poor Julie. She didn't want to let Julie go. She said, "If I'd never stopped being Julie Smoke, what would my life be like now?"

"You're the one who said we'd have a brother-sister act. So I guess you'd have been onstage with me tonight."

He was strumming the guitar again, but for the first time she didn't recognize the tune. One of his own compositions, she supposed. Or maybe something he was making up on the spot. Sweet, she thought, but forgettable. Later, though, she'd remember, if not the tune, then the chorus:

> Now her man's dead at sea, and her son's dead from war,
> And her fire's died out 'long with mem'ries of yore,
> So she raises her glass and she sings her last toasts:
> Here's to heavenly death and reunions of ghosts.

When he finished, he stopped the vibrating strings with the flat of his palm. He put down the guitar and picked up what he'd been saying. "Then we'd have hung out at the bar for a while with Freddie," he said. "Like we did. Then we'd have stopped here to decompress with a little nature and a little booze. Like we did. Then I'd have said, 'Hey, let's break in.' Like we did. So, I guess if you'd lived this other life, you'd be sitting right here, where you're sitting now."

"Both roads would have led to this very place at this very time?"

"They'd converge at this very moment," he agreed. He took a beat: very theatrical, very effective. "And then," he said, "now, in this moment, they'd diverge again."

He came closer. He was doing that movie thing where a face moves toward another face, then back away, then forward again, a way of asking a question and, at the same time, making a declaration, but each approach less questioning than the last, and now the two faces tilting this way, then that way, until the noses finally bump. The bumping of noses: the first touching, so silly and clumsy.

Everything she knew about sex came from the movies, and from tame movies at that, where kissing led to sex under sheets and fade out till morning.

"God," he said as he tried to maneuver them into a position that would avoid elbows and knees banging against the unyielding floor, "when was the last time you did this someplace other than a bed?"

"I've never done it—" She took her own beat, far less effective than his. She was aching, not only with longing but from the press of the flooring through the blanket. The dominant emotion she felt was embarrassment. She longed to confess: I've never done it, and accordingly I will be inadequate, I will be inexpert, I will be horrifyingly bad at this. She wanted to ask for a second chance even before the first chance had been taken. She wanted to ask if he believed in second chances—if, literally, he believed there were such things as second chances, that there were times when people could start all over again, different parents, different childhood, different fate. Is that ever possible? she wanted to ask him. And she wanted to apologize: Forgive me, Danny, for I have never sinned. Nor have I shaved my legs anytime recently.

Most of all she wanted to ask him about his motivations, about what it was that made him decide he wanted to do this with her, of all people, the only acceptable response to that question being, "Because I'm shitfaced and you're shitfaced and I'm here and you're here." That, after all, was the only reason she was not saying no. Also because at that point in her life—how much of it was left, a day? maybe two?—why wouldn't she?

But she had enough sense and had read enough advice to the lovelorn columns—she liked thinking of herself that way, as lovelorn—to know that you did not ask a guy why, exactly, he was trying to remove your clothes. Nor was this the time to call his attention to the fact that you were first cousins, and that once, briefly, you were more than cousins, although not officially, not on paper. All you could do at a time like this was make sure the beat you'd taken after the words you'd just spoken was a short one. All you could do was finish your sentence:

"I've never done it—on a floor this hard."

Afterward, rising to dress, she felt sad. Also sticky, sore, wet. She tugged her jeans on. Semen continued to leak from her. She was annoyed that no one had ever mentioned this unpleasant seeping when speaking of afterglow, and she was struck by the hypocrisy: gay men got all kinds of grief about body parts ill-suited to receive other body parts; but how was the female body designed any better? The imperfect vessel that was her body turned out to contain a second and even more imperfect vessel.

Danny was dressed again too. He lay back down on the blanket, hands behind his head. "Come here," he said, and she lay down, using one of his flanged arms as a pillow. She warmed her nose in his armpit. They lay in that position without speaking. At times she thought she was sleeping. She was only certain she wasn't when he broke the silence.

"Jerry Lee Lewis," he said.

She knew right away why he'd said it. "Albert Einstein, too," she said, "although I think Elsa may have been his second cousin, not his first. And of course, our great-great-grandparents."

"Our great-great-grandparents were cousins?" he said, at first aghast, then abashed, finally amused. "Wow," he said. "So I guess we come by incest honestly."

Outside the sky buzzed gray like a 1950s TV screen after the networks signed off. "Who's what's-her-face?" she asked.

"What's-her-face? She's no one. Or the only one. Or the one that got away. Really, I'm past her now. You must have a string of no ones you've left in your wake."

"I do," she said. "A long string of no ones."

"We've both been unlucky in love," Danny said.

She said, "I don't know that I believe in love."

"You believe in curses, but not love?"

The answer was yes, but she didn't want to say so. She wanted him to like her for at least a little bit longer. They lay quietly until the air horn of a semi wailed as if to assert its dominance over the owls and foxes and the two of them, as if to demonstrate the rightful order of things in this modern world.

She said, "I think I want to tell you something."

"Shoot," he said, and she told him about the horizontal light.

This was what she liked about him: he tried to understand. "Like weft as opposed to warp?" he asked.

She weighed that, envisioning the small plastic loom we had as children, the woven potholders we made for our mother. What had happened to those potholders? When had our mother thrown them away? "Maybe. But more like the empty spaces between the warp threads that the weft passes through. And when those empty spaces open up, it's all I can do to resist passing into them."

"But you have resisted. Right? You're here."

Now was the time for full confession, but full confession brought the possibility of rescue or, at least, intervention or a call to a suicide hotline. She even had the phone number on a card in her pocket.

"Yes," she said. "I'm here." She was trying to sound as though her interest were mostly clinical. "But the impulse has run through the family. They called it political dissent or shame or loneliness. And those things were real, and maybe they made the light even brighter for them, but for me, that's all there is, just this change in the light. For me, there's just this moment every day when I'm invited to leave and I want to leave and I have to make myself stay." She could hear her voice shake. So much, she thought, for clinical.

"Do you see that light now?" he asked.

"Right now? No. I can't imagine I'd ever see it when I'm with you."

She didn't mean it to sound romantic. She just meant she was typically alone when the light came upon her. But he seemed flattered and touched and pleased. He held her now, tightly. It made her want to sleep with him—just sleep. If she still didn't understand the pleasure in physical coupling, she did understand the pleasure of sleeping with a warm male body. Eddie. Joshua.

He yawned. He wondered how late it was. Getting to his feet, he offered her a hand, tugged her upright. They folded the blanket together. He took his guitar.

"You have an interesting approach to pillow talk," he said as they left the house.

She laughed, cuffing him on the shoulder. "Next time bring me an actual pillow and I'll do better." She could feel the semen continuing to drip down the inside of her thigh. How quickly human fluids, once expelled, turned cold. "Anyway, who are you to criticize? You're the one who brought up incest. Talk about turnoffs."

He grinned. "Are we having our first fight?" he said, hugging her close, knocking her off balance. "Are we breaking up?" It was a joke. It was teasing banter. She blamed the tears on the hour and the bourbon and the screaming trucks.

The next morning, Violet slumped like a bag of laundry in the passenger seat of the Toyota, Danny dropped us off at Pinelawn Station. There were hugs and kisses. "I'll be in touch," he said. He left to return Violet to the best shack in tent city.

We waved until we could no longer see the car. We were the only ones at the station. The small waiting room was padlocked as the cemetery had been the day before. It was slightly cooler than it had been yesterday. Vee, too tired to stand, sat on the cold-blooded concrete, leaning against a wooden post. She shivered. Above her, Lady and Delph were talking.

"I would hate to be in Violet's shoes," Lady said. "No real home in the world."

"If we moved out here, she could stay in her real home," Delph said. "We could take turns caring for her."

From the vicinity of their ankles, Vee said, "No."

"Vee's right," Lady said. "We don't even know these people. They're total strangers when you get right down to it. And honestly, Delph, if I had to stay up one more night with Violet, I swear it would have killed me."

"Death by Aunt Violet," Delph said.

When the train arrived, Vee struggled to her feet, using Lady as a steadying device. We boarded through the rear door of the last car and took the first seat we came to, a bench seat, room enough for all three of us. There was another bench seat facing it. Room enough for us to rest our feet on. Or for Vee to lie down on, which, after a moment, before the train was even in motion, she did.

From her new vantage point Vee could see a metal-framed poster on the wall above Lady and Delph. The poster, black letters, white background, said:

Treat every day that dawns for you as the last.
The unhoped-for hour's ever welcome when it comes.
—HORACE

She pointed the sign out, and Lady and Delph swiveled in their seats to read it. We couldn't help ourselves: we went through the familiar debate. Was it merely a coincidence that we'd situated ourselves beneath a message trumpeting the joy of living just one more day, or had the gods directed us to these seats? Had some poetically inclined member of the Long Island Railroad's marketing team hung the sign there, or was it God's way of suggesting we reevaluate our plans?

"I wish those cockamamie gods of yours would make up their minds," Lady said to Delph, and Vee groaned. "We've made up our minds," she said. "Can we please stop seeking the universe's opinion every five minutes?"

She'd had trouble sleeping the night before. She'd drifted off early, only to wake to a strange house dark and silent. She didn't recognize any of the shadows. Gradually it came back to her— we'd left the apartment, were spending the night at Violet's.

It had seemed the right thing to do that morning. But now it seemed she'd been left alone.

She got up and wobbled through the hall until she found the bathroom. She knelt before the toilet and got sick. She sat on the toilet and got sicker. Everything she'd eaten the day before. So desperately humiliating, to be at someone else's home when the body decided to be at its most repulsive. She wanted to cry. She held her face in her hands.

When she felt emptied—she could barely abide being in the small room now—and had cleaned herself, she opened the medicine cabinet and drank from a bottle of Pepto. She read the labels of all the prescription vials. They all seemed to be for Violet; they all seemed quite old. One, its label pruney and faded, contained diazepam. She poured four pills into her palm and swallowed them with another swig of the Pepto.

The pills had done what they were supposed to do, knocked her out for the rest of the night, but it hadn't been what she'd call sleep. It was more a kind of dozy paralysis. And now she couldn't shake the pills off. She twisted and turned on her narrow seat, fidgety and fetal. "I can't stand it," she said. "I can't keep my eyes open, but I can't fall asleep either. This is a nightmare."

"Switch seats with Delph," Lady said. "You can rest your head on my lap."

But, no, Vee also couldn't bear to be touched or to touch. She hid her face in the seat cushions, tried to pretend she was already dead and thus could feel nothing.

The train chugged along. We let ourselves be silent. The handful of other passengers were silent as well, their backs to us.

Vee raised her head. She looked confused, a trace of spittle at the corner of her mouth.

"Did you fall asleep?" Lady asked.

"I don't think so," Vee said. She lay down again, and Lady and Delph could see that the drugs hadn't let her go yet, that she'd succumbed to a deep if unnatural slumber, her mouth open, her lips wet with saliva.

"When you were little," Lady said to Delph, as if they'd been in the middle of a conversation, "you'd insist on doing whatever Vee and I did. I'd say, 'But, Delph, you hate scary movies,' and still you'd carry on until Mom said, 'Just take her with you already.'"

Delph knew which movie Lady was talking about. She saw herself seated between her big sisters in a dark theater, watching as a man discovers his beloved bride is a vampire, watching him murder her to save himself. For weeks after seeing this movie Delph had lain awake in her bed, unable to calm herself. People could be something other than what they pretended to be, what you thought they were. A sister could be a monster. A mother could want to kill you.

"My point is," Lady said, "you're not a baby anymore. You don't have to do everything we do."

"I don't disagree with you," Delph said. "I'm not doing anything because you two are. I'm doing what I want."

"You were singing last night when you came in. You and Danny."

It was true. "We were working on our harmonies."

"Am I wrong? Did you have a good time yesterday?"

"I don't know." She said it automatically. But she did know. No, she did not have a good time. That wasn't how she'd describe it. What she'd had was a confounding time. A problematic time. And possibly an illegal time, depending on New York's statutes regarding sexual relations between first cousins.

"All right," Delph said. "Here's the thing. Well, here are two things. Thing number one: it turns out that Aunt Violet raised me for the first few months of my life."

Lady's eyes widened, then narrowed in rapid succession.

"So said Violet, anyway. And Danny remembers, so I assume it's true. Mom and our quote unquote father gave me away. Then Mom decided she wanted me back. It sounds like for Danny it was like losing a puppy."

"I am gobsmacked," Lady said.

"Thing number two," Delph said. "Last night? Or rather early this morning? Danny and I had soup."

"Uh-huh. And?"

"No, no. Not soup. Soup."

The same facial expression in reverse order: first the confused narrowed squint, then the wide-open goggle of comprehension.

"I wish I'd saved gobsmacked for this," Lady said.

"We were both pretty drunk. It wasn't spectacular. At least I didn't think so. Although by now my expectations may be so out of whack that nothing would live up to them. But I think for a person like me the only reason you have the soup is for the grilled cheese sandwich afterward. You know, the holding and talking."

"Nothing wrong with grilled cheese," Lady said. She reached out, pushed Delph's hair away from her eyes. "Delph," she said. "This is exciting. Look what happens the minute you leave the house and do something on your own without us."

"Yes. I have sex with my brother." She paused. "The bartender asked me out too."

"Really. Wow. Life begins at forty."

"Not in our family, it doesn't. Or never has before."

"Delph," said Lady. "Listen to me. You've always thought the family curse was what caused all of us to take our own lives. But now we've learned that only two members of the third generation killed themselves. Why wouldn't that apply to our generation as well? Not all of us have to give in."

Vee raised her head. "Violet's not alive," she said. "I wish you'd stop talking as if she were. I have the obituary in a shoe box." She turned over again, burrowed back into her deep, unnatural sleep.

But a friable sleep. It cracked and shattered at the least little interference. "Oh, God," Delph whispered, "do you think it's spread to her brain?" and Vee popped up, said, "Oh, we're on a train all right," then lay back down and returned to her chemical dreams.

"Everyone's crazy," Delph said, "except you and me, and I'm not so sure about you."

Lady brushed the joke aside. "If we're going to rethink the pact," she whispered, "we need to rethink it fast."

"Here's what I'm thinking," Delph said, whispering too. "I think you may be right, I do. I think the curse may never have had its eye on me. Looking back, I see now that it's been going after Vee this entire time. She's had such a star-crossed life, hasn't she? I think I just couldn't bear to admit it, that she alone would bear the brunt of the first generation's sins, and I would get off scot-free."

Her emotions had gotten the best of her: she was speaking in full voice. Heads turned to catch a glimpse of her. She recalibrated the volume of her voice, was once again whispering. "But I think if you and I decide we're not going through with it, we should try to talk her out of it too." Lady began to speak, but Delph held up a hand. "I know. I know we can't save her life. I understand that. But she doesn't have to die simply because she's uncomfortable. She can go on a while longer. There are options.

There are second opinions. There's Sloan Kettering. There are experimental trials. And if we exhaust those, there's comfort care. It was one thing for her to reject palliative chemo or hospice when she was asymptomatic. But now that she's suffering, she may have an entirely different outlook. She may be hoping and praying that we talk her into changing her mind."

"Delph," Lady said. "Vee isn't going to change her mind. And I'm not going to change my mind. That's not what I meant when I said we should rethink the pact. I meant you. You're the one who wants to be talked out of it."

She felt tricked and trapped, and she denied it.

Lady wrapped her fingers around Delph's arm, squeezed. There was an urgency to the gesture, but also, Delph thought, a hint of anger. "Yes," she said. "I think you do. I can see it in your eyes."

"I've never believed anyone could really see anything in anyone's eyes except for their own reflections."

"What if Eddie is still twenty-six?" Vee muttered. "That's the part that concerns me."

"Listen," Lady said. "This is a situation that requires no more thinking. We just have to act. You get off at the next station. You buy a one-way ticket right back to Pine Lawn. When you get there, you phone Danny and have him pick you up. You go home with him, and you never look back."

"But the two of you—"

"After a few days you'll be so wiped out from caring for Violet, plus all the soup you'll be having, you won't have the energy to think about us."

"I would never not think about you."

"You would, though. You'd move on."

"I wouldn't be able to live with myself."

"You would. I think you know that you would."

"Even if I did, how would I support myself?"

Lady laughed. "Now that's a question only someone who isn't ready to die would ask. I don't know, Delph. You'd work with Danny. You'd learn how to paint mandolins and ukuleles. And you'd still have two sisters. You'd chat on the phone with Sharon and Margo."

"Do you know what I think is funny?" Delph said. "Aunt Violet was so determined not to name her daughters for flowers, and then she names the first one Sharon. As in rose of Sharon. And Margo sounds a lot like marigold."

"Think about it," Lady said. "Maybe it's not too late for you to have a child."

"A child? You want me to have a child with my elderly eggs and first cousin?"

"Have it with the bartender, then. Go to a sperm bank. Adopt. Kidnap. Just stop splitting hairs. You know what I'm saying."

Delph looked past her and out the window across the aisle. The train had already carried us from Long Island to Queens. It stopped at Floral Park.

"Delph," Lady said. "Go. Get off the train."

She doesn't get off at Floral Park. Nor does she get off at the next station or the next, though she can feel Lady tensing, hoping, each time the train stops. She looks past Lady again, out the window across the aisle. Old cars. A man in a trench coat and fedora. Clothes hanging on a line stretched diagonally from one window to another across an alley. It makes her think of photos from the turn of the century. She would let herself pretend the train has jumped backward through time if most of the items on the line weren't jeans and vibrantly colored bikini bottoms.

"Cemetery," Vee says, as if they're playing a game: I spy with my little eye Cavalry.

Delph has a joke:

Q: Why has every part of this trip begun and ended with a cemetery?
A: To get to the other side.

She doesn't share the joke, though. Instead she says, "I told him about the horizontal light. He didn't know what I meant. Intellectually he did, I think. But not in the way we understand it."

"Lucky him."

"He just listened. He was sympathetic and nonjudgmental."

"That's good."

"Is it? If someone you care about tells you they are constantly thinking about ending it all, shouldn't you be unsympathetic and very judgmental?"

"What are you saying?" Lady asks. "Do you want me to be unsympathetic to you? Do you want me to throw you off the train at the next station? Do you want me to say, no, nuh-uh, this time you're not coming to the movies with Vee and me?"

Vee rolls to her side, raises herself. Her face is yellow. The iron gates and black graves are gone. We've been plunged into the East River tunnel. "This trip was a terrible mistake," she says, "but there's no getting off the train now." She's right, of course. The next station is home.

Vee is right: there's no more time, not on this leg of the journey. But Vee is wrong, too. Because there's always more time. Isn't that what Einstein's been trying to tell us? You just have to accept that you can't always keep going forward. You have to accept that you don't always end up where you believed you were going.

We get off at Penn Station, climb the dark sooty stairs to the terminal. Lady takes Vee's arm. "Let's cab home," Lady says. "You'll be more comfortable"

"No." Vee's teeth are clenched. "Subway's faster. Let's do faster."

"Or," Lady says, "we could go to an emergency room and get you some serious pain meds."

"Home," Vee says. "Now. Please."

Lady and Delph meet each other's eyes, but only for the swiftest moment. Lady turns, leads Vee toward the uptown IRT. She doesn't turn back.

Delph, for once, is the more sentimental. She watches Lady and Vee hurry off, passing the wall where there once was a line of pay phones and a kiosk that sold giant lollipops with faces made of hard candy.

Lady and Vee turn a corner and are gone.

At the information booth Delph inquires about the next train to Pine Lawn.

"Are you all right?" the woman behind the window asks.

"Yes," Delph says. She's aware that tears are falling down her cheeks so hard and fast, there's no blinking them away. Even wiping them away with her hands is useless. She laughs. "Well, no," she says. "Obviously not." She's embarrassed, of course. "I'm sorry," she says. "My sister died today." She holds on to the small lip by the window, lowers her head.

The woman's hand seems to rise of its own volition. It presses against her throat. "My God," she says. "I'm so sorry." She looks over Delph's head, at the impatient travelers on line behind her.

"You stand there as long as you need to," she says loudly. "No one's going to rush you away."

The woman is middle-aged. She is beautiful. You can tell that she cares about beauty. Her hair has been straightened by some modern technique, her eyebrows threaded into perfect chevrons. She is of a Middle Eastern culture. She is of America. Delph feels a piercing envy, the wish to be someone else.

"Pine Lawn," the woman repeats, and then: "Your sister must be looking out for you, dear. The last train going there's just arrived." She hands over a wad of tissues along with a schedule on which she's written the track number. "Head there directly, and you'll get yourself a seat facing the right direction."

CHAPTER 13

How do three sisters write a single suicide note?

By sublimating the egos of the individuals to the needs of the group. By forbidding arias and requiring the entire opera be performed by the chorus. By walking in lockstep, as regimented as an army. By turning off spotlights, even if that means sitting in the dark.

When they do this, when three women spend months presenting themselves as one, they can quickly get used to it. After you say "we" long enough, it becomes uncomfortable to switch back to "I." Saying "I" feels and sounds strange. It feels alien and alienating, egoism run amok, a betrayal. There is no I in team, as they say.

But the truth is, I should have been saying "I" for some time now. We—the three of us together—wrote our life stories and the stories of our ancestors with emphasis on Lenz and Iris Alter. But only I wrote of this summer. Only I wrote of the blustery weekend when Violet Smoke blew into our lives. Only I— Delph, Julie, whoever I am—have been writing today. I should

have been more honest about that. But I'm confessing now: I am
on my own

After I bought my train ticket back to Long Island, I rushed
to the platform fully intending to board and return to the Smoke
House. But as I neared the open entrance and caught sight of the
stairs leading to the underground tracks, I became aware of the
horizontal light. It had seeped into the windowless depot from
no discernible source. It was perhaps more distinct than usual.
It wasn't harsh like electric light or aglare like sunshine. It gave
off no heat. It was the color of the underside of the last cumulus
cloud in the sky just before storm clouds blow in, and for the
first time it was right upon me, close enough so I could step into
it, which I did. It was like being inside the white fog we'd seen
from our apartment window after the hurricane. I stood there,
enveloped. I held up my hand. It was silver now too.

Then I stepped back out of it. I turned my back to it and
changed my course. I tossed the tissues and schedule that I still
held in my hand into the first trash bin I came to. As I passed
the information booth, I kept my head down lest the beautiful
woman notice me and call out, "You're going the wrong way!"

I went upstairs to the Amtrak waiting room, much newer,
much nicer. Here there were not only windows but huge windows, and through them, at its peculiar angle, the horizontal
light seeped into the hall. I sat a short distance away from it,
on a polished wooden bench. I watched other people pass into
and out of the silver. I resented them, the ease with which they
passed through.

I considered what awaited me on Long Island—that ready-
made family with everyone playing multiple roles: brother and
cousin and lover, aunt and mother and mother-in-law—and I
knew it was not what I wanted. As for what awaited me at the

apartment: I didn't want that either. It occurred to me that I was homeless.

After a while the requirements of the body took over: I was hungry, and my eyes burned with the need to sleep. I left Penn Station. I walked downtown. On a Sunday in the summer this part of New York feels like a no-man's-land. It isn't Chelsea, isn't Gramercy, isn't quite Murray Hill. It's just the tail end of Herald Square, the stores and businesses dark. The only people I saw were silhouettes inside cabs. I stopped at a corner store, bought a premade sandwich and a bottle of wine. Because I'd acquired the habit of writing, I bought a composition notebook and a Bic pen.

I found a hotel. It wasn't quite a fleabag, but it was dreary and cheap in every way but for the nightly rate. I didn't care about the price, though. I offered my credit card and, at my request, they gave me their best room. It had a king-size bed and a small kitchenette along one wall. I washed my face in the small bathroom with liquid soap from a wall dispenser. I tried not to look at myself in the mirror. I sat on the bed and ate the sandwich, using one of the scratchy white hand towels as a napkin. I used the plastic cup in the bathroom for the wine. This is how I will live from now on, I thought, alone in a single room, paying only haphazard attention to my well-being. I lay down and fell asleep in my clothes.

When I woke up, I was lying diagonally across the mattress. The red blare of the bedside clock said 8:00 p.m. Only eight. I picked up the phone. I put down the phone. I began to write. I wrote: "In July, John F. Kennedy Jr.'s plane went down, and we had our usual arguments." We. That's what I wrote.

I wrote through the night. I didn't turn on the TV. I didn't open the window. I finished the wine. I was hungry again. I would have liked more to drink. I thought about going down-stairs to the bodega. Instead I plowed on.

Check-out time was 11:00 a.m., and that's when I left, as ex-hausted as when I arrived. It was raining hard; there was no light at all, not even from the calcite crystals that usually sparkle in city sidewalks. And yet, even without the light, I knew I'd made a decision. I'd changed my mind again. I could not live this way. I took the IRT home.

As soon as I opened the front door, I could tell my sisters weren't in the apartment. I closed the door, fastened the locks, the chain, and I stopped to listen and heard no human sounds. Even when I found Lady and Vee, not in Vee's bed, but in our mother's, I didn't revise my initial impression. My sisters weren't here.

I retrieved the long note we'd written together from the drawer where I'd stashed it when Violet showed up. I added the pages I'd scribbled at the hotel. Soon I'll add these last few pages, the ones I'm writing now. And then I'll bind the entire thing to-gether with the black plastic clip. I'll seal the whole thing inside a FedEx envelope and address the envelope to Danny Smoke. I'll go downstairs and lay the envelope against the super's door. "Pls Mail ASAP," I'll write on a Post-it.

And then I'll go back upstairs. I'll make myself a drink.

And then . . . and then . . . and then

PART THREE

Last Words

DECEMBER 2010

How do three sisters write a single suicide note that is also intended to be a memoir of sorts? With the knowledge that someone else will write the ending, that someone else will have the last word. That someone turns out to be me, Dan Smoke.

On Tuesday, September 21, 1999, after Lady Alter had failed to show up at work for the fourth day in a row, the owner of the bookstore where she worked did something she'd never done before: she stopped by the building on Riverside Drive and rang the bell. When she got no answer, she buzzed the super. He used his passkey to enter the apartment. He found the sisters in their mother's old bed. Lady and Vee were holding hands. Delph lay at the foot, holding onto Lady's left and Vee's right ankles.

The super became hysterical; it was the bookstore owner who plugged the disconnected phone into the jack and called the police. The police came and called my friend Freddie; his home number was on a card in Delph's pocket. Freddie called me. The

FedEx package containing the tome that Delph and her sisters referred to as a note arrived an hour or so later. I stayed up all night reading. The next day, full circle, I called the bookstore owner to ask who should be notified, who should come to the memorial I'd decided to hold. I don't know why. I just felt there should be a memorial.

The note, I have to say, confused me. Parts of it filled in a lot of blanks when it came to my own family history. Parts of it made me laugh. But all of it made me sad. I'd known my cousins for only a few hours, when you got right down to it, but in some ways, it seemed, I'd known them better than they'd known themselves. They were not unattractive, not at all. Nor had they seemed awkward or unable to fill silences. They'd actually seemed delightful, even Vee, who I now realize should never have left her own bed that weekend.

And I'd really dug Delph's hair.

It was, of course, disconcerting to read about myself and disheartening to read Delph's version of our encounter. Just as she hadn't told me she was a virgin, so she failed to tell the full truth of that night in her (incredibly difficult to decipher) last pages. What she omitted was this: before I drove them to the train station on that Sunday morning, I'd taken Delph aside. I said that I regretted giving in to my impulses the night before. I'd been fuzzed up from booze—my mother was right; none of us should drink, and I'm trying to stay sober or at least more sober these days, though that's another story. But, I told Delph, the night before, the night together—that had been a mistake.

"I love you," I said, and that was the truth. I'd loved her immediately, the way you might a new niece. She has your blood. She's part of you. You recognize her. "But I don't see me loving you in that way."

"Oh, thank God," she'd said, entirely convincingly. "I feel the exact same way."

She must have known, then, that I wouldn't have been thrilled if she'd come boomeranging back to me the very same day she'd left. Still, you can imagine how I feel now. If only I'd kept my mouth shut. Because certainly I'd have preferred her to come back to me by train than the way that she ultimately returned. "I can ship them to you," the guy at the funeral home said of what he called my cousins' cremains, but I told him I'd drive into the city, pick up the three cardboard boxes myself. When I arrived, the package wasn't quite ready. I had to wait in a hallway by a coffee cart with an urn and a large brown jar of—I swear to God—Cremora. I have to admit I let myself wonder if my cousins' comical spirits had placed the jar there. Cremains. Cremora. The jab of a ghostly elbow in the ribs. One final pun for the road.

Now the cremains are comingled in a single urn that stands on the mantel in my living room. For a while the urn shared the space with my mother's porcelain shepherdesses, but when my mother died shortly after the turn of the century—peacefully, in her sleep, the only Alter of her generation and the two before hers to achieve what she called the cake death; the only Alter of those generations to be buried in a cemetery (alongside my father, alongside another plot where someday I'll be)—I wrapped up the maidens and their lambs and their delicate crooks and stuck them in a box and mailed them to Margo who has a fondness for them that I don't share at all.

So now the urn is the only thing up there. Each afternoon the setting sun comes through the picture window and spotlights it.

I scheduled the memorial on a weekend several weeks after their deaths. It was held in a public room off the lobby of their building. They'd made it sound as if they hadn't any friends in the world, but the gathering was not ill attended. I met neighbors who'd liked them, even one who remembered Dahlie. I met the super, who could not stop weeping. "I knew them since they were born," he said, rocking an imaginary baby in his arms. "They were like my own little girls."

I met two men Lady had dated at different times, long after the affair with the dentist. These men were similar in appearance, somewhat scrawny and pale, both balding and bland. Each said he'd wanted a serious relationship with Lady. Each had been rejected. Now they were meeting each other for the first time, and they agreed that, despite the many years that had passed, they still remained wounded. For each of them, she was, and would always be, the one who got away.

"She told me there was no chemistry," one of them said.

The other nodded. "No chemistry," he repeated. "Exactly. That was her line."

I met a coterie of paralegals, four middle-aged women who considered Vee an integral part of their gang. "We used to go out all the time," one said. "Well, not all the time. We all have kids; it's hard. But sometimes we'd go out. We'd do brunch—light on the eggs, heavy on the bloody marys. We'd go to readings and galleries. We'd talk about the three *m*'s: men, makeup, and menses."

"We didn't really talk about that," another one said. "It's a joke."

"She'd taken off her scarf. We thought it was a good sign. It seemed healthy, you know? It seemed strong. We didn't realize it meant it was over. And then she calls in and quits just like that. She never came to work again, not even to clean out her cubicle."

"We called and called. No one answered. We thought she'd moved."

"We read the obits every day just in case."

We ate greasy croissants and drank increasingly lukewarm coffee. Delph's boss, sans cowboy hat and sporting a valiant comb-over, called for quiet. He wanted to give a eulogy, he said. He got up and spoke at length about Delph, which irritated the paralegals who wanted equal time for their friend. They flapped at him when he was finished, telling him all their Vee stories. Meanwhile the two men whose hearts Lady had broken bonded over sports. I'd called Vee's oncologist to let him know what had happened, and he wound up stopping by too. He was ripshit. "She wouldn't let us even try to help her," he said. I asked if there had been options available, interventions that might have saved her. "We'll never know, will we?" he said. "There are always experimental therapies out there. She didn't give us the chance to try any of them out." He was shaking with anger. The crumbs from his croissant fell to the floor as he gestured with it. "I could kill her," he said. "I really could kill her."

Later, while I was cleaning up, throwing paper plates and paper cups into a trash bag, a PhD dissertator from Columbia who'd seen the announcement in the *Times* came by. She asked if the sisters possessed any primary materials regarding the life of Iris Emanuel Alter. "It would be such an important breakthrough if I could get my hands on Iris's suicide note," she said.

"No one in the family left suicide notes," I said. I knew this from reading the sisters' suicide note, though I didn't tell that to the scholar. If I were going to tell anyone about the sisters' note, I sometimes joked to myself, it would be the people at the *Guinness Book of World Records*.

Lady, I knew, had once had a will, but there was no sign of it now, and I didn't say anything about it. For the state's purposes, then, they died intestate. "Imagine that," the paralegals said, and Delph's boss, who now knew everything there was to know about Vee, said, "The cobbler's children go barefoot." The court appointed me to administer their estates, which were larger than one would have guessed. Although their respective group insurance policies did not pay out, they'd socked away quite a bit in savings and the market and their 401(k) plans. I paid their last bills and the expenses of cremation, and after the probate process, I distributed their combined assets as I thought might please them: 75 percent divided among several international charities dedicated to ending chemical warfare and 25 percent to the Center for Great Apes.

This is what I kept for myself: The boxes under the bed in the Dead and Dying Room. The shoe box Vee had filled with newspaper articles about real-life coincidences that would have strained credulity had they not been published in the *New York Times*. The rubbery blue Philip's head screwdriver. The painting of Otto von Bismarck. I had the latter appraised, and it wasn't worth much. I hung it in my own bathroom. It seemed the right thing to do.

Although they died without wills, Lady, Vee, and Delph did leave me a legacy: I inherited their obsession with Lenz and Iris Alter. I'd never heard of Lenz Alter before I met my cousins, not from my mother, not from my sisters, not even in my tenth-grade chemistry class. After the memorial, though, I began asking about my great-grandparents. When my mother was lucid, she was able to answer some of my questions. She spoke about her grandparents with equal amounts of pride and shame, emotions that you'd think would be diametrically opposed and therefore confusing to the listener—that is, to me—but which actually helped me understand. It was like experiencing an exotic cuisine where sweet and bitter coexist in every spoonful. It made sense in a discomfiting way.

The scholar from Columbia called me a few times. On Mondays, when I came into the city to empty the apartment or deal with my cousins' estates, she'd join me. She'd sit cross-legged on the floor while I packed up the sisters' belongings, scheduled Goodwill pickups, shipped the antiques to my sisters, and had the rest hauled away by a guy with a battered truck on which he'd painted "The Junk Punk." The only piece of furniture I hung on to, if just for a while, was the bed in the Dead and Dying Room. The scholar liked to have sex in it. Sometimes, after, she would sigh contentedly and say, "Can you believe we're lying in the very same bed where Richard once slept?"

For this woman, it seemed, my ancestors were celebrities. She used their first names as if they were Oprah or Beyoncé. I wondered if, as we hooked up, she fantasized that I was Richard. No, that's not true—I didn't wonder. I assumed that she did; I was certain she did. I wondered what Richard would have made of this: an attractive and bright young woman driven sexually ravenous by the thought that at one time his atoms had bounced about this room.

Eventually, though, I got rid of the bed. I returned the keys and stopped seeing the scholar. I don't know who eventually took the apartment. A very wealthy family, no doubt. Who else could afford such a place at market rent? Or, who knows, maybe it's gone condo or co-op. I don't know how those things work. All I know is that whoever they are, the new occupants must be immune to superstition. I sometimes amuse myself by imagining the ad the landlord placed: Pre-war, riv vu, 7 rms, 6 dths.

Maybe it was because my antennae were up, but in 2000 I began hearing more about Lenz Alter. Articles began appearing in both academic journals and popular magazines. In 2001, one of the biographies on my cousins' bookshelf, *Lenz Alter: Deutsch, Jude, Hielige, Sünder*, was updated and translated by an American publisher as *Lenz Alter: German, Jew, Saint, Sinner*. Five years after that a new biography was written by an American journalist. This bio contained much more information about Lenz's personal life. It also addressed the link between his work and climate change. Let's just say that the manna process will probably wind up being responsible for more deaths than either chlorine gas or Zyklon. It may be what finally does in all of us.

Grete Rosenthal's slim memoir, *Mein Leben mit Lenz Alter*, was also reissued in 2005, although not in translation. After discovering how much professional translators charge, I spent weeks typing paragraphs into BabelFish and came up with a mangled version of the chapter that dealt with Iris. As best as I can tell, if you believe Grete, Iris was a shrill bitch, Lenz a screaming lunatic, Richard an unbearable brat, and Grete a put-upon martyr, not to mention a rare beauty who came this close to having a career as a Hollywood film star.

There was also a documentary on PBS. There was even an off-Broadway play about Lenz's relationship with Einstein. The *Times* said it was *The Odd Couple*, but without the laughs. I didn't bother going into the city to see it.

But though I missed the play, I read all the bios. I saw the documentary. I pored through the boxes from the Dead and Dying Room. I also began searching the Net. In early 2000 I was still asking Jeeves about Lenz, but then Google took off and then came Google Alerts, and quickly I was receiving all sorts of news about the Alters. Lenz first showed up on Wikipedia in 2003, Iris in 2005. A long, carefully researched piece about the murder of Rudi Alter popped up in 2007. I also came across a tourist brochure from the city where Rudi died that urges a visit to his memorial. There's a photo of it—*unser* misspelled as *unserer*—and beneath it the caption says, "Many romantic couple come to enjoy picnic lunch and see cherry blossom."

Also, as of this writing there are 10,800,000 results if you search for "Chock full o'Nuts massacre victims," though significantly fewer if you want to know anything about their surviving spouses.

In other news, the Walt Whitman Birthplace was gorgeously restored in 2000. Someone else prunes the lilac bush now. Deep Throat's identity was revealed in 2005. He turned out to be some guy no one had ever heard of, and it was all very anticlimactic. Also in 2005 *Miami Ink*, a TV reality show about tattooing, debuted. It's hard now to remember a time when a discreet little adage encircling one's calf would be found shocking. I have several tattoos myself, including an iris like Vee's, though mine is bolder and larger. Mine trellises down my entire right arm.

Last month I took a vacation to Chicago. Early November is not a great time for visiting a famously frigid city, but I'd recently made a discovery that compelled me to go right away.

Over the years I'd been regularly but futilely searching for information about Rose. Suddenly, in October, I got a few hits. Someone had uploaded the archives of the long defunct *Chicago Daily Tribune*, and on my screen was this headline: "Coed Commits Suicide in Men's Washroom: Girl Was Descendant of Inventor of Death Camp Poison."

This is when I learned that my cousins had been wrong when they'd written that none of the family suicides left a note. Rose had. Reproduced in the article, her note was pithy and frank and concise enough to fit inside a Hallmark card. It said, "You don't want me and nobody else gives a damn either. It's better to die than to live without love." She'd mailed it to her chemistry professor.

The professor's name was also in the article. It was such a ridiculous name that I thought it must be a pseudonym or some sort of obnoxious joke. Even if it were his real name, I thought, the man had to be dead by now. But I searched for him anyway, and there he was, still listed as emeritus faculty at the University of Chicago: Professor Abbott P. Costello. I wrote to him in care of the school, and he agreed to see me, but suggested I come soon. He was not a young man

Chicago took pity on me: it was sunny and in the mid-fifties when the elderly professor and I met at the university's bookstore. He was in his early nineties, but he strode in under his own steam, stooped yet still managing to thrust out his bony chest. If a popinjay and an old stringy rooster had procreated, their offspring would have carried themselves the way this man did.

His face was the color of a bad sunburn. The veins in his neck were prominent, the flesh there pimpled and hollowed. The only fleshy parts of him were his earlobes. And yet, despite the indignities of time, not only could you easily tell how handsome he'd once been, he remained handsome even now.

He was carrying a bouquet of limp yellow roses that, I was certain, had come from a supermarket. He extended his free hand.

"Abbott Costello?" I said. I wasn't questioning his name. I was questioning whether he was the man I was meeting. But he assumed the former.

"I was named in nineteen eighteen," he said. "My parents had no idea what I was in for."

"If you had a nickel for every time you've said that, right?" I said.

"If I had a nickel for every time someone said if you had a nickel for every time you've said that," he countered. He spoke with a slight British accent to which I knew he had no claim, although he'd also let me know right away that he was of the Irish, not the Italian, Costellos.

He told me to call him Ab. I said I would, but it turned out I couldn't. I called him nothing at all.

He told me he not only remembered Rose, he also remembered my mother. Rose, he said, had been high-strung and skittish, but not so Violet. "Your mother wasn't as bright as Rose," he said. "She wasn't as sensitive. She slept in class with her eyes wide open. That was memorable. I once asked her how Lorenz Otto Alter's granddaughter—not to mention Rose Alter's sister—could be so bad at chemistry. She laughed. She didn't care. She was one of those girls who took up valuable space in the classroom to pursue the MRS degree." If he hadn't been so old, I might have socked him in the nose. There was a purple spot, probably a small cancer, on the tip that I could have aimed at.

He seemed aware of my anger. "I'm sure she was an excellent mother," he offered.

"Well, she didn't name me Abbott Costello," I said. "She gets points for that."

We exited the bookstore. To our left, across the street, was the campus. To our right was Washington Park. It was almost sixty degrees now, aberrant weather that was frightening if you believed what climate scientists were saying, but delightful if you didn't. I opened my jacket. Students in shorts and flip-flops padded by, kicking through leaves the color of Bosc pears. The leaves became caught between their toes, slipped under their soles with each step they took.

"That was the old chemistry building." Professor Costello pointed. "And over there, across the park, is where I used to live. I'd leave Chemistry and cut through the park at night. It was safer then, although it had already started to turn."

We entered the park, taking the first path we came to. I'd been picturing something vast like Central or Prospect Park, places where people could hide or get lost, thousand-acre expanses filled with woods and duck ponds and swan boats. This park was small enough and the trees sparse enough that I could see across it from where I stood. There was a museum to the north. There was a ghastly concrete sculpture and a fountain to the south. Mostly, though, there were lawns and paths. I didn't see any people at all.

We walked for a few yards. At a fork in the path the professor pointed to a small cottage a few feet away. We headed toward it, and I saw that it wasn't a cottage but a public washroom. Chains and padlocks had been threaded through the door handles to both the women and men's sides of the building. I rattled the handle to the men's room anyway. Of course the door failed to open. I was disappointed, and not a little angry. I'd come all this way but couldn't get in. I'd wanted to see the very spot where Rose had lain. I was like all those dissertators, including the one I'd slept with. I wanted to stand right where Rose had stood. Right where she'd collapsed.

"Why did it have to be a men's room?" my mother had cried when I finally got her to speak about Rose. My mother had been the one called to identify the body. All these years later, she had grown reconciled to the grim sight of her sister's corpse—the skin decidedly pink, she said, the puncture wound on Rose's arm encircled with bright purple blood—but she was still pained by what she saw as Rose's perverse choice of location.

"A ladies' room, no one would have said boo," my mother bemoaned.

The location was still on Professor Costello's mind too. "I don't know how it is she stumbled into the men's side," he said.

And yet, standing there, it seemed so obvious. I longed to tell my mother. I longed to tell Delph. Instead I told the old man at my side. He, the object of Rose's youthful passion, had lived in an apartment building directly across the park. When he left his office in the chemistry building at the end of the day and headed home, he'd take the path we'd just taken. If he'd needed to use a bathroom on the way, he'd have veered off as we had done. He'd have come here, found her, saved her.

She hadn't meant to die. She'd been banking on Abbott Costello's need to take a piss.

I was certain of this. She'd wanted him to find her, to stop her before she could stab the needle into a vein. She'd imagined him embracing her and sobbing with relief and from the realization that his foolishness, his head's refusal to acknowledge what his heart had always known, had nearly cost him what his entire being now understood: that she was the woman he loved, the woman he'd marry.

And if he'd arrived at the washroom too late? Or if he'd taken a piss in the chem building and had no need for the washroom?

Better to die than live alone, Rose's note had said.

But that had been her plan B. Her plan A, I was convinced, was rescue.

"The family always speculated it had to do with her guilt over

Lenz Alter's involvement with the concentration camp gas," I said. "But now I'm wondering."

"I never heard her say a word about the gas," Costello said. "I didn't even know he'd worked on it until the articles came out. It would have been absurd, anyway. Why would she feel bad about Alter's work? She was training to be a scientist. Scientists have a duty to perform their best work, to go where their explorations take them. We understand that; she understood. What politicians do with that work is when the crimes occur."

"I suppose," I said.

"No," Professor Costello said, sighing grandly. "You're right. She did it because of me. I've always known that. I never figured out the men's room connection, but there'd been the note. And I never told the papers, but she'd come to my apartment the day before, throwing herself at me, crying and embarrassing herself. Embarrassing me."

"What did she see in you?" I meant it to be blunt and insulting, though I mitigated the insult by adding, "Obviously you didn't like her. You weren't even kind to her. She'd just lost both her parents, and you weren't even kind to her."

He glowered. The hoods of his eyes descended. "I was perfectly kind," he said. "I was never anything but kind. That was my downfall. My kindness was the very thing that exacerbated the situation. I had to finally forget about being kind and become firm instead. You can't have them ringing your doorbell at all hours of the night. This sort of thing happens often, students with crushes on their professors, and I must say I had more than my fair share. I was right out of Harvard. I was a good-looking young man. I was already regarded as a great scientist. I had to learn how to keep them at bay. But Rose Alter—there was no dissuading her. She was obsessive. She was not of sound mind.

After all, none of the other women who fell in love with me took their own lives." A thought came to him, and he brightened. "It's just like blaming your great-grandfather for what happened in the camps. He was just doing a job. Synthesizing nitrogen. I was just doing a job. Teaching chemistry. What other people did—it had nothing to do with us."

I thought about Delph, her death. I imagined myself some time in the future telling an inquisitive stranger, "It had nothing to do with me."

I thought, *Better to die than live alone.*

Costello handed me the roses. "Crouching is no problem," he said, laughing sadly, "but getting back up is nearly impossible." I knelt down, placed the bouquet at the bottom of the padlocked door. While down there, I recited a blessing I'd not thought of since my Hebrew school days, when I'd studied for my bar mitzvah, the one rite Jewish boys from even secular households must endure. It was the blessing one says at the moment one learns about a death, which means I was reciting it almost sixty-five years too late. What the hell, I thought. I recited it anyway. Translated, the Hebrew words mean nothing more than "Blessed is God, Power of the Universe, the True Judge." And the prayer itself meant nothing more or, I guess, less profound than: This is it. This is the way it works. We live, we die, and hopefully you know why, God, because it makes no fucking sense to us.

"Rest in peace, Rose Alter," said Abbott Costello.

I walked him back to the garage where he'd parked his car. He suggested we have coffee. I recognized that this was the cost of doing business with a lonely old man. I recognized that this is the way it works.

I got in the passenger side. He drove to a Starbucks, adhering to a harrowing speed limit of roughly five miles per hour. At the coffee shop he ordered tea and a cookie. We sat by a window, looked out at a used car lot, and he asked if I'd heard the news about indigo.

I thought I'd misheard him, but I hadn't. Rose, it seems, had told him some of the family history, and he knew that her great-grandfather—my great-great-grandfather—had perfected the hue in his dye factory.

"Whenever I hear mention of that particular color," the professor said, "I find myself thinking of Rose." Then he told me that scientific consensus now holds that Newton was wrong. Indigo wasn't—it never had been—a distinct color unto its own. It should never have been considered part of the spectrum. It no longer was.

In the cab back to the hotel I found myself stewing over the ouster of indigo. Who the hell had that seventh arc been annoying, anyhow? And what were they trying to tell us, these self-appointed arbiters of refracted and reflected light? That we'd all been hallucinating whenever the sun shone through a crystal chandelier and we counted seven colors in the prismatic stack on the wall?

My reaction amused me, yet somehow that didn't allay my anger. I was really pissed off. Indigo sheared from the rainbow! Indigo disappeared like an Armenian, a Chilean, a Jew! When will Roy G. Biv get political? How long until yellow says, "First they came for indigo, and I said nothing"?

In my room, I succumbed to the scotch in the minibar. I told myself to stop being so absurd, so emotional. I told myself to be a Smoke, not an Alter. I reminded myself I hadn't even known these people, these Alters, for most of my life. And yet it still felt like a personal loss, the erasure of indigo. It felt like something of mine stolen while I slept. It felt like the adding of insult to injury, a disinheritance, a metaphorical reenactment of the slicing and dicing of my great-great-uncle Rudi. It made me think about what my great-great-grandfather Heinrich Alter must have felt when he gave in to the inevitable, and chemicals finally replaced *ai* leaves and sake in his factory, and, I'll bet, not a single customer noticed the difference.

It's funny, I thought, what causes you to grieve and what doesn't.

If Lenz Alter were living today, I thought, would he feel this loss as sharply as I did? Or would he not have cared one way or the other?

Who knows? Maybe *he* was the eager beaver scientist; maybe it was Lenz Alter's ghost come back to earth in the form of a contemporary naysayer for the sole purpose of arranging the coup and expelling indigo from the fellowship of colors. Lenz Alter grew up to be a chemist, after all. So perhaps that explains it. The ghost of Lenz Alter come back to oust his rival for his father's devotion. A chemist's and a son's revenge.

It wasn't until the flight home that the rest of it came to me. I had my head against the window and was dozing on and off. My dreams were filled with images from Auschwitz and Treblinka, those photos of naked women and their children lined up, waiting for the showers. Dreams for Beginners, I call such dreams. You don't need Freud to tell you why you're having them or what they mean.

I was awake, though, my seat upright for landing, when it hit me. The showers in the death camps. The women filing into those seemingly innocuous buildings ostensibly meant for cleansing, ablution. Their fear as they walk in, cognizant now of what is to come. Their deaths, quick but not quick enough, from

Zyklon, that cyanide-based poison.

The plane descended. It landed, and everyone around me pulled out their phones, called the loved ones or friends who were poised to come pick them up. *We just got in. Meet me in baggage. Love you.* I remained in my seat. I imagined Rose entering the men's room in the park. I didn't envision stalls and urinals, not at first, but rather, just the sinks. Cleansing. Ablution. I imagined her fear, her knowledge of what was to come. I imagined the injection, the cyanide.

Then I let myself see the stalls and the urinals too. The humiliation of dying amid the stench of others. She'd re-created that too.

And I saw mirrors, reflective surfaces everywhere. I imagined the final confrontation with one's own reflection, one's self.

I still believe she was waiting for Professor Costello, hoping for rescue and love. But I saw now that the family had also been right. Even she may not have known it, but it seems undeniable— she'd also been trying to expiate Lenz's sins by dying the same way his final victims had died. She'd looked at herself, seen echoes of the face that was responsible for the gas. She knew she was cursed. She believed the curse was justified.

Or maybe she'd been trying to divert the course of that curse. Maybe she'd hoped that if she died this way, the curse would be sated and would not set its sights on Violet and Dahlie and the nephews and nieces she'd never meet. Maybe she'd made herself the sacrificial lamb. (And, Jesus, God, only now as I write do I see the shepherdesses lined up, pure white, on the mantel. A frivolous hobby, I used to think of those saccharine figurines. "For pretty," my mother said of them. But now I'm thinking of that mantel and seeing it anew, my mother's unwitting altar, her subconscious shrine to the sister who'd died for our sins. Jesus,

God—I take it back; Freud would have had a field day with my family.)

It was a good try on Rose's part, I guess. A valiant effort. But the sins of the father are visited on the children to the third and fourth generations, and she couldn't stop it from knocking on everyone's doors.

Although . . . not my door. Not my mother's door, not my sisters' doors. This is not to say we've never known sorrow or grief. But we've known far less sorrow and grief than most people experience. Why were we spared?

Who knows?

This is all I know: Life no longer feels like an imperative. Every day I live, it's a choice I'm making. We're all surrounded by people who see the horizontal light and the welcoming loom. Sometimes we are those people. When I think I can see that light or when I think of my cousins, I try to force myself to look around, to derive strength and pleasure from whatever it is I see: the ebony arteries and rounds in the tree bark, the burnt orange caps of acorns, the grass. Or if I'm in a dive bar in Hicksville or Plainview, I'll buck myself up by singing one or two of my own songs. Sweet but forgettable, Delph wrote of my music. Probably so, but there are worse reviews of one's work than sweet but forgettable. There are worse things for a person to be. Blessed is the Power of the Universe. Which means: Go ahead, sing your forgettable songs. My small band of followers, those aging dancing suburbanites, don't seem to mind when I do. In fact, they've come to know all the words.

AUTHOR'S NOTE

The characters in *A Reunion of Ghosts* are fictional and not intended to resemble real persons. Certainly the three main characters, Lady, Vee, and Delph, and all the people they encounter throughout their lives, are products of my imagination. Any resemblance between these characters and actual persons are coincidental and unintended.

That said, some of the characters and events in the historical portions of the book were inspired by real people and events. Lenz, Iris, Richard, and Rose Alter were based, respectively, on the German-Jewish scientist Fritz Haber, his first wife, Clara Immerwahr Haber, their son Hermann, and Hermann's eldest daughter Claire. The Einstein family was based on the Einstein family. John Updike once said: "Nothing in fiction rings quite as true as the truth, slightly arranged." The truth (to the extent we can ever know the truth about people who lived long ago) regarding my historical characters has been arranged, sometimes slightly as Updike recommended, but more often significantly.

In the end, this is a novel, and it's about an imaginary family.

Yes, I did a lot of research to help me understand my characters and to establish a realistic chronological framework, but when I sat down to write, I wrote about Alters, not Habers.

To give just one example, while the aforementioned Claire Haber did commit suicide, her two sisters did not. The lives of Dahlie and Violet Alter are in no way based on the lives of any of Fritz Haber's granddaughters. I purposefully did not research on his other granddaughters' lives so I could make those characters completely my own.

Which is not to deny that the novel occasionally quotes from or paraphrases historical material. The excerpts from Heinrich von Treitschke's "A Word about Our Jews" and Theodor Mommsen's "Another Word about Our Jews" have been edited for length and to conform better to my story, but most of the words are theirs, and I have not changed the original sentiments or arguments. The description of the appropriate dress for dancing the New Knickerbocker was adapted from an article by turn-of-the-twentieth-century dance master Alan Dodsworth that was quoted on Sonny Watson's Streetswing.com, http://www.streetswing.com/histmain/z3knick.htm. (I admit I tried to inject some humor into Mr. Dodsworth's original prose.)

Einstein's conditions to Mileva can be read in full in the Walter Isaacson biography cited below. The excerpt from Lenz Alter's letter of resignation is taken verbatim from the letter Fritz Haber wrote when he left the Kaiser Wilhelm Institute rather than fire his Jewish employees and associates, as required by new law. The excerpt from Max Planck's "My Audience with Adolf Hitler" has been elided as indicated but otherwise has not been changed from the original. The testamentary stipulations regarding the burial of Lenz Alter and the relocation of Iris's ashes from Germany to a more hospitable burial site are from

Fritz Haber's will, as is the suggested epitaph: "He served his country in war and peace as long as was granted him." Hermann Haber carried out his father's wishes, and Fritz and Clara Haber are now buried side by side in Hörnli Cemetery in Basel.

Some (though certainly not all) of Iris Alter's letters incorporate or paraphrase sentiments Clara Haber expressed in correspondence with her doctoral adviser and confidant, the chemist Richard Abegg. Abegg is very much fictionalized here as Richard Lehrer.

Also, in the novel I allude to Clara Haber's very real letter to the Supreme War Staff, which she mailed very shortly before her suicide. In it she decried her husband's work as a "perversion of the ideals of science" and "a sign of barbarity, corrupting the very discipline which ought to bring new insights into life."

The speech Kaiser Wilhelm delivers at the opening of the fictional Dahlem Institute for Physical Chemistry is a paraphrasing of information provided on the website of the Fritz Haber Institute (formerly the Kaiser Wilhelm Institute) at https://www.fhi-berlin.mpg.de/history/h1.epl. And a review by Andrea Stevens published in the *New York Times* on October 8, 2005, did indeed compare (though not in a good way) the Fritz Haber/Albert Einstein relationship, as portrayed in Vern Thiessen's play *Einstein's Gifts*, to Felix and Oscar's relationship in *The Odd Couple*.

The content of Rose Alter's suicide note, and the manner in which she died, is the same as Claire Haber's.

There are also deliberate (and no doubt inadvertent) deviations from fact in the book. Was Fritz Haber really the first person to synthesize Ecstasy? Some of the biographies say yes, others say no. I don't know, then, if Haber had anything to do with Ecstasy. All I know is that in my fictional universe, Lenz Alter did.

Another deliberate departure from what I know to be true: *Mamm: The Magazine for Breast Cancer Patients and Survivors*, which I placed on the Alter sisters' dinette table in 1976, did not actually begin publishing until 1997. But once I came across this magazine in my own doctor's office, I knew I had to add it to the junk on that table, anachronism be damned. I mean—a cancer journal with a pun for a title. Talk about audacity! Talk about chutzpah! Talk about the beautiful human instinct to make jokes in the face of what is painful and terrifying! What can I say? Slam, bam, and thank you, Mamm.

BIBLIOGRAPHY

For readers interested in the lives of Fritz and Clara Haber, here are some of the resources I found helpful and fascinating while working on this book:

Charles, Daniel. *Master-Mind: The Rise and Fall of Fritz Haber, the Nobel Laureate Who Launched the Age of Chemical Warfare.* New York: CCC Press, 2005.

Dick, Jutta. "Clara Immerwahr." *Jewish Women: A Comprehensive Historical Encyclopedia*, March 1, 2009. http://jwa.org/encyclopedia/article/immerwahr-clara.

Dunikowska, Magda, and Ludwik Turko. "Fritz Haber: The Damned Scientist." http://arxiv.org/ftp/ arxiv/papers/1112/1112.0949.pdf.

Fraenkel, Peter. "Ludwig Haber—The Counsel and the Samurai: The Murder of Ludwig Haber in Hakodate, 1874." www.ludwighaber.blogspot.com.

Goran, Morris. *The Story of Fritz Haber.* Norman: University of Oklahoma Press, 1967.

Haber, Charlotte. *Mein Leben Mit Fritz Haber.* Düsseldorf: Spiegelungen der Vergangenheit, 1970.

Isaacson, Walter. *Einstein: His Life and Universe.* New York: Simon & Schuster, 2007.

Mazón, Patricia M. *Gender and the Modern Research University: The Admission of Women to German Higher Education, 1865–1914.* Stanford, CA: Stanford University Press, 2003.

Morreall, John. "Humor in the Holocaust: Its Critical, Cohesive, and Coping Functions." In *Hearing the Voices: Teaching the Holocaust to Future Generations; Proceedings of the 27th Annual Scholars' Conference on the Holocaust and the Churches, March 2–4, 1997, Tampa, Florida.* New York: Merion Westfield, 1999. Also available at Holocaust Teacher Research Center website, November 22, 2001. http://www.holocaust-trc.org/humor-in-the-holocaust.

Stern, Fritz. "Fritz Haber: Flawed Greatness of Person and Country." *Angewante Chemie International Edition* 51, no. 1 (2012): 50–56. doi:10.1002/anie.201107900.

Stolzenberg, Dietrich. *Fritz Haber: Chemist, Nobel Laureate, German, Jew.* The Philadelphia: Chemical Heritage Foundation, 2004.

ACKNOWLEDGMENTS

I'm grateful for the fellowships I received in support of my work on this book including, from the University of Wisconsin–Madison, the College of Letters & Science's John Jartz Faculty Fellowship, the Vilas Associates Award, the Art Institute's Creative Arts Award, and several Graduate School research grants; and from the Wisconsin Arts Board, an Artist Fellowship Grant. I am also grateful to John Jartz, Karen Reno, and Lynne McCreight for their generous support; to Susanna Daniel, Melissa Falcon Fields, Jesse Lee Kercheval, Ron Kuka, Jean Reynolds Page, and Michelle Wildgen for their friendship and insights; to Anja Wanner for help with the German (though any remaining mistakes are completely my own); to Seth Abramson for research assistance (but see preceeding parenthetical re: remaining mistakes); and to Henry Clark, Elizabeth Hilts, and Eric Miller for the Cremora, the light, and Danny's guitar.

Finally and always, I thank Don Friedlich for his love, his humor, and his remarkable patience.

ABOUT THE AUTHOR

TO COME